A LAND DIVIDED

ALSO BY K. M. ASHMAN

K. M. ASHMAN

THE BLOOD OF KINGS: BOOK ONE
A LAND
DIVIDED

THOMAS & MERCER

Published by Thomas & Mercer, Seattle

www.apub.com

Amazon, the Amazon logo, and Thomas & Mercer are trademarks of Amazon.com, Inc., or its affiliates.

ISBN-13: 9781503945241
ISBN-10: 1503945243

Cover Illustration by Alan Lynch
Cover Design by Lisa Horton

Printed in the United States of America

MEDIEVAL MAP OF WALES

Though the borders and boundaries of early Wales were constantly changing, for the sake of our story, the map below shows an approximation of where the relevant areas were at the time.

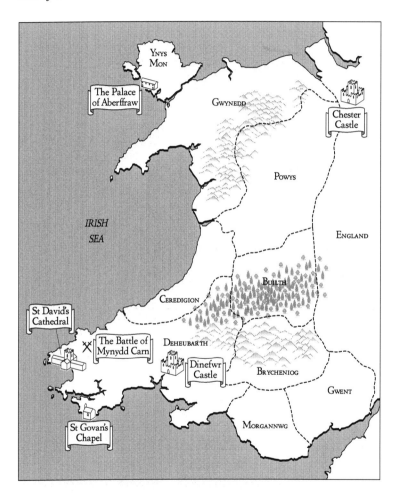

Pronunciation Guide

Although correct pronounciation is not really necessary to enjoy the story, for those who would rather experience the authentic way of saying the names, explanations are provided in italics.

THE HOUSE OF ABERFFRAW

GRUFFYDD AP CYNAN: Would-be King of Gwynedd – *Gruff-ith ap Cun-nan*

ANGHARAD FERCH OWAIN: Married to Gruffydd – *Ang (as in hang) Harad*

ADELE: Angharad's maid – *Ad-Ell*

LORD DARCY: Gruffydd's cavalry officer from Ireland – *Dar-sea*

IESTYN OF YNYS MON: Gruffydd's right-hand man – *Yes-Tin of Un-iss Mon*

NIAL OF LIMERICK: Moneylender – *N-eye-al*

THE HOUSE OF TEWDWR

RHYS AP TEWDWR: Newly crowned King of Deheubarth (known as Tewdwr) – *Rees ap Tewd-oo-rr (the letter 'R' is rolled at the end of the name)*

GWLADUS FERCH RHIWALLON: Married to Rhys ap Tewdwr – *Goo–lad–iss*

HYWEL AP RHYS: Oldest son – *How-well*

GRUFFYDD AP RHYS: Youngest son (known as Tarw) – *Tarr-oo (roll the letter 'R')*

NEST FERCH RHYS: Daughter (known as Nesta) – *Nessa or Nest–A*

MARCUS FREEMAN: Warrior and close comrade of Tewdwr

WALTERS: Castle cook

ANNIE APPLES: Peasant woman

DYLAN: Farmer – *Dill-an*

THE THREE KINGS ALLIANCE
THE HOUSE OF GWENT

CARADOG AP GRUFFYDD: King of Gwent and enemy of Tewdwr – *Car-rad-og*

PETERSON: Caradog's right hand man

BOWEN: Cavalry officer in Caradog's army

THE HOUSE OF POWYS

MEILYR AP RHIWALLON: King of Powys – *My-l-irr (roll the letter 'R')*

EDWARD AXE HAND: Warrior

THE HOUSE OF GWYNEDD

TRAHERN AP CARADOG: Self-proclaimed King of Gwynedd – *Tra-Her-n*

MEIRION GOCH: Advisor to the king – My-ree-on

The beginning of the second name is simply 'Go' but the second half is more difficult to pronounce. In Welsh, the letters 'ch' form a guttural sound at the back of the throat by drawing the tongue fully back while allowing air to escape over the top of the tongue. Non-Welsh speakers struggle with this – audible representations are available online.

PLACE NAMES

DEHEUBARTH: *Du-hi-barrth (roll the 'R')*

GWYNEDD: *Gwin-eth*

DINEFWR: *Din-e-foorr (roll the 'R')*

MORGANNWG: *Morr-gan-oog (roll the 'R')*

MYNYDD CARN: *Mun-ith Ca-rr-n (roll the 'R')*

POWYS: *Pow-iss*

YNYS MON: *Un-iss Mon*

Prologue

When the Roman occupation finally came to an end in approximately AD 410, Britannia became a land of many kingdoms, each ruled by its own minor king. These times became known as the Dark Ages and over the years countless internal battles or conflicts arose resulting in many different dynasties, culminating in the reign of Harold II and the famous battle in 1066. William the Conqueror, or William the Bastard as he was often known, led his invading army to a great victory on Senlac Hill near Hastings and within two months was crowned king of all England.

William set about consolidating his rule across the country but in the west lay the last stronghold of the native Welsh, a proud and fierce race, known for their prowess in battle and fanatical loyalty to their culture. The people, and the harsh landscape, proved a problem for William and over the next few years, his armies endeavoured to make inroads into Wales, but with limited success. Subsequently, William, having more important things to deal with across England, left the Welsh mainly to their own devices.

Despite this, William was nothing if not thorough, and realising the Welsh could pose a significant risk in the future, he put in place a simple but effective strategy to manage the border between the two countries. To combat any risk of attack, he gifted parcels of land to those nobles who were the most loyal to him, along the entire border with Wales, with only the easternmost boundaries defined.

This area came to be known as the Marches and each noble made their own laws as they saw fit, not beholden to Welsh or indeed, English law. Subsequently, the threat was contained, and though conflict was always possible, the nobles soon identified a far more effective strategy for controlling the Welsh: encouraging their tendency for infighting, and nurturing division between the landowners, all the time ready to step into any subsequent political vacuum.

Thus is the background of our story, the tale of a struggle for freedom that stretched down the ages from the times of the Norman Conquest until the death of Owain Glyndwr, centuries later. During this time, many heroes were born, lived and died in the name of freedom, but the events leading to their glorious struggle started on a typical spring day in eleventh-century Ireland.

What followed next is the making of legends.

Ireland

March 1st, AD 1081

Gruffydd ap Cynan walked through the grounds of the manor house, graciously loaned to him and his family by his grandfather, King Olaf of Dublin. Beside him walked his wife, Angharad ferch Owain, her arm threaded through his as they took the morning air. Angharad's fair hair fell loosely down her back, glowing in the warm sunshine and the smell of bluebells wafted gently from the carpet of blue about their feet. Her demeanour was elegant and considered, as was expected of a woman born of a long line of Irish kings, yet here, on one of the few times she was alone with her husband, her face was relaxed and they chatted freely. Her hand seemed tiny in comparison to her husband's, enclosed as it was within his giant clasp, yet despite the difference in size and the calloused skin across his palm, his touch was gentle and caring.

Angharad was a tall woman amongst her peers but Gruffydd stood at least a head taller than her again and his muscular build, born of countless hours in the practice fields, made him stand out in any company, a characteristic welcomed by any man who called himself a king. His dark brown hair was kept short, as was his neatly trimmed beard, for though he was more at home on a battlefield, he was painfully aware that while he was a guest of King Olaf, he must endure the niceties of court life, especially if he was to gain any new allies in his long struggle against his usurper back in Wales.

Gruffydd was the son of Cynan ap Iago, a Welsh prince of the House of Aberffraw who had inherited the kingdom of Gwynedd from his father. Cynan ruled for a few years but died when Gruffydd was still very young and the family had to flee to Ireland for their own safety. As he grew up, Gruffydd's mother told him of his heritage and as a young man he had sworn a bloody oath to eventually rule Gwynedd and return the House of Aberffraw to its rightful place amongst the royal families of Wales. At first his endeavours had proved fruitful and he had staked his claim when, after the death of the incumbent king, Bleddyn ap Cynfyn, several conflicts broke out resulting in Gruffydd's defeat of another claimant called Trahern ap Caradog. However, Trahern had survived the battle and after rebuilding his forces had defeated Gruffydd at the battle of Llyn, slaughtering Gruffydd's army in a cunningly prepared ambush, and claiming the throne of Gwynedd for himself. Gruffydd narrowly escaped death and had retreated back across the Irish Sea while he considered his next actions. Several years had passed, and though he had since married, he thought of his homeland every day and was impatient once more to reclaim the land he believed was rightfully his, the kingdom of Gwynedd in Wales.

Gruffydd breathed deeply, his gaze resting on the faraway hills, knowing that far beyond them and across the Irish Sea lay the lands of his birth and the place where his heart longed to be.

'Your thoughts seem far away, dear husband,' said Angharad, 'is there anything on your mind?'

Gruffydd squeezed her hand reassuringly.

'I am fine, my love, though I suffered a sleepless night.'

'I heard you pacing the room,' replied his wife, 'as I have on many nights of late. Perhaps I should have come to your chambers.'

Gruffydd smiled.

'Your attendance would not have helped for my mind is a storm of thoughts with little chance of settlement.'

'Anything I can help with?'

'Alas no, for the pain is over battles past and opportunities missed.'

Angharad sighed inwardly as he said the words, frustrated by her husband. Their life together was good, their status as family to King Olaf of Dublin ensured a privileged life and they loved each other deeply. But as long as her husband had this shadow etched on his soul, she knew they could never be entirely happy.

'Surely this is not about your losses in Llyn?' she asked, knowing deep inside she would not like the answer.

'A defeat is not easily forgotten to any man,' said Gruffydd, quietly.

'But that was so many years ago. I thought your heart was at peace with the outcome and you had moved on.'

'As did I,' said Gruffydd, 'but recently I have found it in my thoughts every waking moment, and at night my dreams are filled with the screams of those who died at my side.'

'Gruffydd,' said Angharad, 'you cannot hold yourself responsible for their fate; it was not your blade that cut them down. After all this time, surely you must realise it is time to lay their memory to rest.'

'How can I,' replied Gruffydd, 'when their blood is on my hands?'

'I have oft heard you say that the death of any man in the servitude of a just cause is an honourable way to die.'

'It is, but when that death is brought about by treachery and falsehoods then they are wasted lives. I would go up against any man on the field of battle, as would my men, but to be tricked by the likes of Trahern in such a cowardly manner leaves the taste of poison within my throat.'

'The Lord will settle his account in a suitable manner when his time has come.'

'Perhaps so, but if God presents me with an opportunity, then I swear there will be a reckoning before that day comes.'

Angharad stopped and stared at the back of her husband. Gruffydd turned to look at the distraught face of his wife.

'What ails you?' he asked. 'Surely you knew I would not sit back and settle for this defeat like a spanked child?'

Angharad shook her head in disbelief.

'I hope you are not saying what I think you are.'

'It has been on my mind for many months, my love,' said Gruffydd. 'Yes, the years have passed us by but each one that passes reinforces the unjust outcome of that day.'

Angharad turned away and walked over to a bench beneath a tree. She sat down and stared towards the distant mountains, fear striking her heart at the implications of her husband's words.

Gruffydd waited, gathering his thoughts. Many men imposed their will on their wives, irrespective of standing. But Gruffydd was different. He loved his wife dearly, and though his pain burned like a fire within his heart, he also knew he could not pursue his destiny without Angharad's full support. Eventually he walked over and sat beside her, looking over at the same hills as he considered how to win her over.

'Angharad,' he said eventually. 'I know it's not what you wanted to hear but to carry this burden to the grave will see me dragged down to the depths of hell, such is its weight. I cannot simply sit back in comfort and accept the fate that now lays before me while a false king wears a crown that is mine by right.'

'*Why not?*' shouted Angharad, jumping to her feet and turning to face her husband, tears flowing down her face. 'You lost upon the field of battle, Gruffydd; you were defeated by a better man. There is no shame in such a thing and it is only by the grace of God that your life was spared. Why can't you be thankful and settle down here to live the life of a lord? We have a fine estate, a princely allowance from your grandfather and a place amongst the nobility of Dublin. Surely the blessings we have here far outweigh the benefits of a minor kingship in a place such as Gwynedd?'

Gruffydd stood and walked over to his wife, resting his hands on her shoulders as he tried to ease her worries.

'My love,' he said quietly, 'it breaks my heart to hurt you so and what King Olaf has done for us is generous beyond compare, but I too am a king and as long as I am beholden to his charity then I am no more than a mere serf. The kingship of Gwynedd is mine by right, and though I know it is an impoverished place at the moment, that is only from the misrule of Trahern. If I can drive that traitor from the north, then I have no doubt that we can restore the House of Aberffraw to its rightful place as a family of note as it was in the time of Rhodri Mawr.'

'But times have changed since the Normans came; the enemy strength can be multiplied a hundredfold. No longer is there just Trahern to worry about but also the Marcher lords. You would be facing enemies on many fronts.'

'And that is even more reason for me to return,' said Gruffydd, pushing a stray wisp of hair back from her tearful face. 'We need a strong nation with all her kingdoms united against the Normans. Don't you see, my love, this is not a quest of revenge or a wish to right a minor wrong – it is a battle for Wales itself.'

'Perhaps so,' replied Angharad, wiping her eyes with a handkerchief. 'But why does the task fall at your feet? Surely there are others who have a greater reason to set out upon such a crusade?'

'Like who?'

'Well, I would start with any king native to that country; they have the most to lose and indeed the most to gain. Why risk your life for those who did not come to your aid six years ago?'

'Someone has to pick up the banner, Angharad, and if every man waits for his comrade to take up the burden on his behalf then it lays unclaimed. Gwynedd was once a proud kingdom and can be again, but to do that it must rid itself of the rot at its centre. Once Trahern has been deposed then we can start to rebuild.'

'But why you, my love? Why not petition others to take up the mantle?'

'It has to be me, Angharad. I am a direct descendant of Rhodri Mawr and the crown is mine by right of lineage. I was born for this task and will not be found wanting.'

'But it does *not* have to be you, Gruffydd, you make this choice of your own free will.'

'Sometimes we do not choose our fate, Angharad, it is decided by a higher office.'

'Is this your justification?' she replied, staring at him intensely. 'Do you really believe that God saved you, only to put you in harm's way a few years later?'

'Perhaps he did,' said Gruffydd quietly, 'perhaps he granted me life so I could return and put right a dreadful wrong.'

Angharad's head dropped, realising that despite the strength of her argument, there was no moving him from his stance.

'Angharad,' said Gruffydd, taking her hands in his once more, 'look at me.'

She lifted her head and stared up into the eyes of the man she loved more than life itself.

'My sweet,' he said, 'the last thing I want to do is hurt you, but please believe me: if I thought there was any other way then I would take it.'

'And is your mind fixed in this matter?'

'It is, my love. I cannot deny myself this quest, even if I fall upon the path.'

'Let me ask you one last thing,' said Angharad. 'Do you truly believe you are the rightful king of Gwynedd in the eyes of our Lord?'

'With all my heart.'

'Then this conversation is ended,' she said with a deep sigh. 'Your mind is made up and there is nothing more to be said.'

'Then do you give me your support in this matter?'

'I wish to God with every fibre of my being that you would turn away from this path but deep down inside I know that even if I was able to change your mind your heart would be heavy for the rest of your life. I love you, Gruffydd, and will not bestow that burden upon you. So, despite my opposition, you are still my husband and I will support you in anything you do.'

Gruffydd took her in his arms and held her tightly before kissing her gently on the lips.

'Thank you, my love,' he said, 'I will make you proud of me, I swear.'

'I am already proud of you, Gruffydd,' said Angharad with a tearful smile. 'I just pray you do not make me a widow any time soon.'

'So,' said Angharad, as they walked back towards the manor house, 'now your mind is set, when do you intend to return?'

'It has to be soon,' replied Gruffydd. 'I already receive dispatches from those still loyal to the house of Aberffraw. It seems the Marcher lords foster disputes between the kingdoms and stand ready to cross the border should the opportunity arise. Welshmen spill the blood of Welshmen while the English laugh at our folly. If I don't act soon, I fear it will be too late.'

'But you don't have an army . . .'

'There are still some loyal to my banner in Gwynedd, as well as those who came to Ireland on the same ships as us. I will send a message requesting they muster in my name, and in the meantime try to assemble a force of Irish willing to fight in return for coin.'

Angharad stopped again and stared at her husband in surprise. 'Mercenaries?' she said.

'Aye, an unfortunate yet necessary step to ensure success.'

'But we have little money to pay such men.'

'I will hire them on promise of repayment when we are settled. Once we are back on Ynys Mon, the taxes upon the people of Gwynedd will quickly accrue to meet any price agreed.'

'Surely those taxes will be payable to the English Crown?'

'I will pay not a single Welsh penny to the English coffers until our lands once again flourish under our home rule. After that, well, we will see what treaties can be negotiated, but by then, all my debts will be paid off.'

'Granted, but will you not need capital to arm such a force?'

'I will seek sponsorship from King Olaf. He has always been supportive and a grandson on the throne of Gwynedd will be a significant alliance for Dublin.' He stopped and looked at Angharad. 'My love, I have a favour to ask.'

'You want me to represent you at your grandfather's court,' she replied, a statement rather than a question.

'All I want you to do is to deliver a letter to him asking for men at arms and enough coin to sustain them in the field for two months.'

'Why me?'

'I can entrust it to no other. These preparations must remain secret at the moment lest my ambitions fall upon the ears of those I call enemy.'

'Would not such a petition be better delivered in person?'

'Perhaps so, but my time is better served here, fostering allegiances with those familiar with the ways of war.'

'Then I will leave in the morning,' she said and tiptoed up to kiss him once more.

'It is a dangerous path before you, my love,' she said, 'but despite my concerns, henceforth we will share it together.'

Wales
Dinefwr Castle

March 1st, AD 1081

Across the Irish Sea, another king stood alongside his queen, enjoying the early morning sun, though this time from the battlements of an imposing castle perched on an escarpment high above a valley in Deheubarth in South Wales. Rhys ap Tewdwr had claimed the throne three years earlier when the previous king, Rhys ap Owain, had been killed at the Battle of Goodwick by the Prince of Gwent, Caradog ap Gruffydd. Caradog had wanted to extend his own kingdom, but the dead king's second cousin Rhys ap Tewdwr had moved quickly and claimed the throne before Caradog could seek the support needed for such an audacious move. Caradog was incensed, but needing the support of others to justify his claim, he waited, knowing the time wasn't right.

At forty years old, Rhys ap Tewdwr was well respected throughout the courts of Wales, and though he had several children by various mistresses, his only legitimate children were by Gwladus, his wife. He had an eight-year-old daughter called Nesta and a ten-year-old son called Hywel. In addition, his wife was pregnant with another child.

Tewdwr was slight and lacked the strength and skill of his men-at-arms, but over the years he had gathered a loyal and trustworthy corps about him. He was a first-class horseman and an excellent hunter but he had never drawn a weapon in anger and his skill in battle was unproved. Politically he was a very clever man and throughout his life had managed to achieve his aims through discourse and agreement rather than by sword and spear.

'It seems we have seen the last of the winter snow,' said Gwladus, pulling her shawl tighter around her shoulders, 'and I will not be sad to see it go. For too many months we have been holed up within these walls.'

'It has been a long winter,' said Tewdwr, 'but we have been warm and our kitchens have not been found wanting.'

'Perhaps so, but a warm castle does not a kingdom make. I want to get out and see more of the land, take Nesta to the local church and perhaps speak to the people.'

Tewdwr agreed, knowing that the support of the people was vital if he was to be a successful monarch.

'We have been incarcerated within this palisade for far too long,' continued Gwladus, 'and need to get out more. The girl is eight years old and already she yearns to see the world. Her search for knowledge is relentless and I swear I will hurl myself from that tower if she asks me one more question about the village.'

'I don't think it will come to that.' Tewdwr laughed. 'But I see your point. Don't forget, I have had to keep Hywel occupied these last few months and he is only two years older than Nesta. So I share your burden.'

Gwladus smiled and snuggled closer into her husband's side, comfortable in his company after many years of marriage.

'Hywel has the attention of your men-at-arms,' she continued, 'and spends countless hours weapon training. Nesta only has the gossip of the courtiers and tapestry to keep her occupied. No, the quicker we can go down to the valley the better.'

'Another week or so, my love,' said Tewdwr, 'and we will step out together to meet our people.'

For a while there was silence as king and queen gazed over the valley before them. A winding river snaked its way through the treeless valley before heading westward towards the sea about thirty leagues away. The natural barrier acted as an extra defence against any enemy coming in that direction and, except for high summer when the water levels were lower, could only be crossed by a solitary bridge directly below the castle.

Further upstream lay the village of Dinefwr at the base of the hill upon which the castle stood. The village was fairly large and protected by a palisade against anyone coming from the east, and though it was not very formidable, it was designed to hold off any attackers long enough for the populace to reach the safety of the castle and its imposing timber walls.

'Tewdwr,' said Gwladus quietly, 'do you think we have done the right thing?'

'In what way?'

'You know, moving so quickly to claim the throne.'

Tewdwr continued staring out over the valley as he considered his answer. His claim was not a spurious one for he was directly descended from Rhodri Mawr, the last king of the Britons a hundred years earlier, and as such the people of Deheubarth welcomed his assertion as just and honourable.

He turned to face Gwladus.

'A strange question,' he said. 'Are you not happy?'

'I just worry that Caradog will end the truce and set his army against us.'

'I understand your concern,' said Tewdwr, 'and I cannot guarantee he will not, for he is not known for his honour. But this was an opportunity I could not ignore. My ancestors ruled Deheubarth and this crown is mine by right. Of course there is a risk but it is one that I had to take.'

'I don't know much about the ways of war, Tewdwr, but I am no fool. Our army cannot face the might of Caradog and hope to emerge victorious.'

'Perhaps not, but that is something we cannot control. With Gwent and Morgannwg already under his control Caradog has a much larger population to draw upon when he needs to recruit men-at-arms. Our lands are far larger but more sparsely populated. We could never match him with strength of numbers.'

'And what if it comes to war?'

'We will have to deal with that when it comes. Hopefully these walls will be strong enough to repel him while I seek allies to our cause.'

'But what of our children, do you not fret that they are at risk?'

'As soon as the weather breaks I will send petitions to Caradog himself and seek stronger ties between us. If I can make it profitable for him, he could even become an ally.'

'Do you really think Caradog will agree to such an alliance?'

'I know not, but I can try.'

Gwladus nestled in against her husband's side once more.

'I love you dearly, Tewdwr,' she said, 'and trust in everything you say. In this, however, I worry that we might have taken on more than we can manage.'

'Fret not, my love,' said Tewdwr, squeezing her in against his side, 'I would never put you or the children at risk. As long as I have breath in my body, I swear you will remain safe.'

As the sun's rays started to sweep along the valley floor, the king and queen of Deheubarth gazed out over their new kingdom, blissfully unaware that high in the nearby forests Caradog's spies were already watching the castle, gathering information for the iron-clad storm that would soon fall upon it.

Ireland

April 2nd, AD 1081

'My lord,' said the servant, 'I have been tasked with informing you that the lady Angharad has returned and is currently seeking refreshments in the minor hall.'

'Thank you, Adele,' said Gruffydd, 'I will be along shortly.'

The girl bowed and turned to run back to the manor.

'So,' said Gruffydd, continuing the conversation he was engaged in, 'that is the size of the task, my friend, and depending on the response from King Olaf, I intend to return to Gwynedd at the earliest opportunity and seek out Trahern. Once I have him on the field of battle, this argument over lineage will be decided once and for all.'

'A noble quest, my lord,' said the Irish nobleman sat upon the log before him, 'but what has this to do with me?'

'I will be honest with you, Lord Darcy; I have heard good things about the mettle of the men in your cavalry. It is said they are peerless warriors with destriers second in quality to none this side of France.'

'They are indeed good men and their mounts are familiar with the screams of war. But why do you display such an interest? Surely you don't expect me to ride at your side during this campaign?'

'Why not? The spoils could be great and surely it is always prudent for men such as yourselves to be forging alliances with one eye on the future.'

'Perhaps so, but this is a fight in a different land. With respect, my lord, you have already been defeated in one battle with this man; how do I know you have the beating of him this time?'

'Because I will not make the same mistakes again.'

'And what mistakes were those, may I ask?'

'I trusted him,' spat Gruffydd. 'I expected him to engage me upon a level field as agreed in despatches between us days earlier, only to find he had deployed a secondary force to my rear, cutting us off from favourable terrain. By the time I had realised the danger, a force of Belgian mercenaries fell upon our flank and left our strength unbalanced.'

'Can I suggest that far from being trickery, such tactics in times of war are admirable, for only the victors remember the methods employed.'

'Call it what you will, Lord Darcy, my blood still boils at the remembering.'

The noble got to his feet and whistled to recall his hunting dogs laying in a patch of sunlight, their tongues lolling from their jaws after a hard morning's work. Darcy picked up the brace of hares and threw them over his shoulder.

'If you give them to my manservant, I will have the cook prepare them and send them over to your kitchens,' said Gruffydd, looking at the results of the morning's hunt.

'No need, my lord, I will convey them myself.' Darcy looked up at the exiled Welsh king. 'I will consider your offer,' he said, 'and respond before the month is out. I imagine you will not sail prior to then.'

'It is unlikely,' said Gruffydd, 'for even if my wife carries good news, there is still a fleet to organise.'

'Then I have time to consider, but I will say this. My thoughts are not favourable upon the matter; however, if there are gains to be made then each man will be allowed to decide for himself.'

'And the cost to me?'

'Let them decide first, and if there are any takers, then I will convey my estimate in due course.'

'That's all I can reasonably ask,' said Gruffydd. 'You have my gratitude.'

'If you will excuse me, my lord, I will take my leave. But as promised, I will respond before the moon is next full.'

'I will look forward to it,' said Gruffydd, and he watched the Irish nobleman set out across the fields to return to his estate.

***

'Angharad, my love,' Gruffydd said, entering the minor hall and seeing his wife sat at the table, 'your return is most welcome.' He leaned down and kissed her forehead.

Angharad placed the piece of cheese back onto the trencher and swallowed the food already in her mouth before wiping her hands with a cloth.

'Dear husband,' she said, 'I considered waiting to share my fayre but was grievously hungry from my travel. I hope you don't mind.'

'Not at all,' said Gruffydd, taking a seat on the other side of the table. 'I will eat presently but first you must tell me – how went your trip?'

'It went well,' said Angharad, 'your grandfather is in good health.'

'And was he sympathetic to my plea?'

'Surprisingly yes, though he has insisted on some financial agreement being committed to parchment first.'

'Is the amount excessive?'

'Such judgements are not for me to make but he has sent a document for your agreement. Would you have me retrieve it for you?'

'No,' said Gruffydd with a smile, 'the document will wait. I would share time with you and hear of your journey.' He turned to the serving girl. 'Adele, can you bring me a trencher of meat and a hand of bread?'

'Of course, my lord,' said the girl.

'And bring a flask of mead,' he added as she scurried away, 'it looks as if our lady needs colour in her cheeks.'

'As you wish, my lord,' said the servant and disappeared through the doorway towards the kitchens.

'So,' said Angharad when Adele was gone, 'how was it while I was away?'

'Quiet as usual,' said Gruffydd, 'but I have managed to speak to some useful contacts.'

'Really?' asked Angharad, placing a small piece of cheese into her mouth. 'And who may that be?'

'Lord Darcy,' said Gruffydd, 'and a Dublin merchant who has access to a fleet of ships.'

'And have you agreed terms?'

'Not yet but once I know what force of arms I have at my disposal, I will open negotiations.'

'Do you have any firm numbers yet?'

'I have received despatches from a kinsman back in Gwynedd. He was wounded at the battle of Llyn, and though I had thought him long dead, apparently he was saved by a shepherd and nursed back to health in the local village. He has now recovered and holds a mighty grudge against Trahern. He has assured me he can muster at least two hundred men to my banner when the time comes.'

'It is a good start,' said Angharad, 'but many more are needed.'

'Agreed, but I have many irons in the fire and I only need a few to come to fruition.'

The door opened and the servant brought in the meal for Gruffydd.

'Thank you, Adele,' said Angharad. 'Could you have the fire made up in my room and arrange some hot water? I am weary and dusty from my journey and would take the opportunity to sleep as soon as possible.'

'Of course, my lady,' said Adele and left the hall again.

Angharad looked across at Gruffydd who had a knowing smile upon his face.

'Does something amuse you, my love?'

'On the contrary,' said Gruffydd, 'my smile is one of love, not merriment.'

'And I suppose you think your kind words will get you an invite to my bedchamber this very day?' She raised an eyebrow.

'Well, if offered it would certainly not be turned down.'

Angharad wiped her hands and stood up, walking towards the door.

'Well,' called Gruffydd from his seat, 'am I to follow or sit here like a wretched pauper, unwed and unloved?'

Angharad paused and looked over her shoulder with a playful smile.

'But what about the letter, my love? Surely your forthcoming campaign is far more interesting than the affections of a mere woman?'

'On occasion,' said Gruffydd, 'but today is not one of them.'

Angharad laughed.

'You men are so transparent. Yes, my love, your affection will be warmly received within my bedchamber, but finish your meal first.'

'To hell with the food,' said Gruffydd, and pushed the platter away from him. He strode across the room and kissed his wife upon the neck.

Angharad placed her hand on his chest and gently pushed him back.

'Eat your meal,' she whispered, 'for I need time to bathe, and anyway, I suspect you will need the extra strength before this day is out.'

'You toy with me, woman,' growled the king hoarsely.

'All good things come to those that wait.' She laughed and opened the door to leave.

'But . . .' started Gruffydd.

'Later,' said Angharad and left the hall, closing the door firmly behind her.

Frustrated, Gruffydd stared at the closed door before wandering back to the table. He knew many other men, nobles and kings who kept mistresses or even slept with the household servants to fulfil their needs, but he was not such a man. Angharad was more than enough woman for him, and though her fiery personality was often the cause of upset between them, it also fuelled the passion that kept him true to their vows. With a deep breath he sat back down to his meal, knowing that though she frustrated him with her arrangements, if he knew his wife then the wait would be worth it.

The following morning saw no frost upon the ground for the weather was getting warmer by the day. Adele opened the shutters in the bedchamber and allowed the spring air to flood the room. The lady Angharad groaned and turned in her bed, pulling the covers over her head.

'Adele, do you have to?' she asked.

'My lady, if you recall, last night you told me to wake you soon after dawn and not to take any retraction upon pain of punishment.'

'Oh yes,' groaned Angharad, 'but never mind that, close the windows and let me sleep a little longer.'

'My lady,' said Adele, 'you also said I was to disregard all pleas for extra time and to ignore anything you said until you had set foot upon the carpeting.'

Angharad leaned over the bed and peered down at the rug, wondering if by placing just one foot upon the sheepskin would free her of the monstrous demands of this horrid girl.

'I know what you are thinking, my lady.' Adele laughed, pouring water from a jug into a bowl. 'But alas, you made my responsibilities clear and unfortunately I am bound by your instructions.'

'You are a horrid servant, Adele,' said Angharad, 'and I should have you thrown to the dogs.'

'And then who would run around clearing up your mess,' asked the servant, 'for surely there is not another girl in the land who would put up with such treatment.'

Angharad smiled, and forced herself to sit up in the bed. Despite the girl's lowly position in the household, Adele had grown into a personal friend and they often enjoyed such banter in private. When the king was present, however, she was the model of servitude as befitted her station and nobody knew of the close bond between her and the queen.

'I see my dear husband has arisen early,' said Angharad. 'Has he retired to his own room?'

'No, my lady, he is breaking his fast with some of the soldiers from the estate. They talk of men's things and conquests of old.'

'Again,' yawned Angharad, 'what is it about battle that men find so interesting? Surely they must sicken of so much talk of death and destruction.'

'Alas, their minds are too small to consider anything outside the realms of warfare,' said Adele handing over a wetted cloth.

'Apart from the action that takes place between the bed sheets of course,' said the queen.

'My lady,' gasped Adele in mock horror, 'I'm sure I don't know what you are talking about.'

'Stop your nonsense.' Angharad laughed. 'I have heard the rumours about you and the stable hand amongst the hay.'

This time Adele's embarrassment was real and she blushed furiously, much to the amusement of the queen.

'My lady,' stuttered Adele, 'I never, I mean, I wouldn't . . .'

'Oh, don't be so silly,' said Angharad, 'there is nothing more natural than a young couple sharing their passion. In fact, it is rather lovely.'

'Pray don't say anything to my family,' said Adele, 'for I am yet unmarried and my father would be aghast. He has already identified some local boys as prospects for they each have trades, but though I know my future would be better served with such a man, they each fade in comparison to the stable boy.'

'My lips are sealed,' said Angharad, 'but can I give you some advice?'

'Of course.'

Angharad leaned forward and whispered into the girl's ear.

'If it is a husband you seek, try a few out before you settle. That way you will know who has the best prowess between the sheets.'

'*My lady*,' squealed the servant and stepped back in shock, 'you are outrageous.'

'Yet tell the truth.' Angharad laughed. 'Anyway, bring that bowl over so I can get dressed. We have guests this evening and there is much to prepare.'

Outside, Gruffydd finished talking to the estate men and made his way back to the hall, calling his dogs to attend him. He consulted his squire about the state of the swords hanging upon the wall, and after selecting several for sharpening, took a seat at the hall table to consider his accounts with the manor steward.

'So we are not yet destitute,' said the king eventually, sitting back in his chair.

'Not by a long way, my lord, though I am bound to say that your finances are in decline. Without a sponsor or a source of taxes, the costs of running this manor eat into your treasury on a daily basis.'

'I would worry not,' said Gruffydd, 'for if my plans come to fruition, then soon we will be once more enjoying an income as befits the house of Aberffraw.'

'I have heard tell there are plans to return to Gwynedd,' said the steward, 'is there truth in such rumours?'

'Idle talk can make live men dead very quickly,' said Gruffydd, 'so be careful who you heed.'

'I never believe anything unless it is direct from the horse's mouth,' said the steward, 'and only ask as it will have a bearing on how I manage your estate.'

'In what way?'

'You will undoubtedly need money, my lord, for no campaign can be run by goodwill alone.'

'Granted, but I expect to have many allies before we set out.'

'Maybe so, but even if your armies are paid by their sponsors, your household will still need funding, both here and in Gwynedd.'

'My treasury is not about to get fuller any time soon, Master Steward, so we must manage on what we have.'

'Have you thought about using a moneylender?'

'It had crossed my mind but I balk at the thought.'

'I know of such a man,' said the steward, 'one with access to wealth untold but be warned: the fact that you are a king will bear no weight for all he is interested in is his money and many have disappeared after failing to meet his terms.'

'What would be the cost of such a venture?'

'I know not but all you have to do is say the word and I will ride myself to seek terms.'

'I don't know, Master Steward.' Gruffydd sighed. 'To take on another debt when I am already short on funds seems like a dangerous move. What surety could I offer?'

'Let me find out, my lord, for if it is too high then it is easy to say no.'

Gruffydd considered for a few moments and was about to speak when the door opened and Angharad entered, closely followed by Adele.

'We will talk of this later,' said Gruffydd and stood up to greet his wife. 'My love,' he said, 'you look as radiant as the morning sun itself.'

'And a good morning to you, my lord,' said Angharad. 'I see you have been industrious while I have been dressing.'

'Just some bookkeeping,' said Gruffydd.

'And are we yet paupers?'

'Not quite,' said Gruffydd with a smile, 'but even if that was the case, I would still stay at your side unto the grave.'

'You say the sweetest things,' said Angharad. 'Anyway, in the heat of last night's, shall we say, liaison,' she glanced at Adele who turned away to hide a smile, 'I neglected to give you this.'

'Is that the document from King Olaf?'

'It is, and as you obviously had other things on your mind, I thought it prudent to wait until this morning.'

Gruffydd took the parchment and sat back down at the table before breaking the seal and unfurling the scroll.

'It is indeed his reply,' he said eventually. 'He starts by voicing concerns yet goes on to grant me access to his army, though at a cost.'

'Is it prohibitive?'

'I will read out the list,' said Gruffydd. 'Each foot soldier will cost twenty pieces of silver for the duration of the campaign, up to a maximum of one year from the date of sailing. An archer is double the cost and a lancer complete with horse, one hundred pieces. Olaf will arm them but I will have to find the provisions to sustain them. Any man who dies on campaign will command double the price so his family will be cared for.'

'And the wages for the soldiers?'

'They will settle for any bounty found on the battlefield or in any villages sacked.'

'It sounds a steep tally.'

'Perhaps, but it is cleverly done for he enables me to build an army according to my purse.'

'Ha.' Angharad laughed scornfully. 'Then the army will be the smallest in Christendom, for we have no purse to speak of.'

'Not yet,' said Gruffydd and looked towards the steward still standing near the hall doors.

'My lord,' said the steward, catching his glance, 'do you want me to seek out the agreement under discussion earlier?'

'Aye, that I do,' said Gruffydd.

The steward left the room and Angharad turned to her husband.

'This agreement which he seeks in your name,' she said, 'is it something that may concern me?'

'No, my love, just the business of men. Now, take a seat and I will have the kitchens send something up, for surely this past night has set an appetite upon you.'

Chester Castle

April 3rd, AD 1081

Huw D'Avranches, Earl of Chester, sat upon his horse and stared over the river at the improvements being made to his castle. Since it had been built ten years earlier at the orders of King William, it had suffered many attacks from the Welsh but had always managed to withstand any assault, mainly due to the thickness of the stout wooden palisade surrounding the bailey and the battle-hardened men-at-arms defending the walls from the inner ledge.

Inside the defending walls and across the muddy courtyard that made up the bailey, several wooden huts were home to the castle garrison, a mixture of Norman and Flemish soldiers who had stayed in England after the battle of Senlac Hill. In addition, the garrison boasted of many English infantrymen who, in order to avoid execution, had joined the forces of William after the battle. Since then, the dividing lines had become blurred between the three nationalities. They were joined in a mutual hatred of the Welsh people, just a few leagues westward. Despite this, the Welsh were a constant thorn in his side, and whenever they posed a threat, Huw responded with a savagery unmatched in many a county. Often the bodies of the enemy were hung in rows along the road to Rhuddlan as a reminder to all those who challenged his authority that this was a man not to be trifled with.

Outside the palisade, a deep ditch ran the full circumference of the castle, filled with sharpened spikes of fired elm and awash with human waste, a necessary evil constantly added to from the latrines of the castle. In places, rotting corpses hung upon the spikes like macabre flowers, evidence of earlier failed assaults, and though the sweet smell of death hung in the air like the heaviest blanket, the stench was a small price to pay for the difficult obstacle the defences brought to the beleaguered castle.

Usually the keep would be constructed of timber but several months earlier, Huw had learned of a similar castle in the north falling to one of the few rebel forces still resisting the rule of William, when it was simply burned to the ground along with all its inhabitants. Any who had been lucky enough to escape found naught but death waiting for them in the bailey, and the tales of good Norman knights being skinned alive and hung in the sun like deer carcasses left him cold with anger.

Subsequently, he had commissioned improvements to the keep and now, after almost a year's work, he looked on in satisfaction as the craftsmen went about their work like an army of ants.

Huw looked around the valley as he waited. He had been a guest of a fellow noble at Worcester while the works had been carried out and was glad to be back at his own castle after nine long months. Chester was now the seat of his undisputed earldom, having seized the vacant title when the previous incumbent, Gerbod the Fleming, had been captured at the Battle of Cassell seven years earlier. Since then, Huw had cemented his position with cunning, treachery and a brutality that had earned him a fierce reputation; despite this, his love of food and subsequent enormous girth had gained him the nickname, Huw the Fat. Eventually, one of his knights approached and reined in his horse alongside the earl.

'My lord,' said Alan Beauchamp, 'the mason is here. I believe you wished to speak to him.'

Huw turned and looked down from his horse. The mason was familiar, for he had talked to him on many occasions over the last few months.

'Edward,' said Huw, 'it is good to see you again.'

'And you, my lord,' replied the mason, 'I was not expecting you for another few days, a timespan that would have seen your keep finished.'

'It matters not, a few days I can manage,' replied Huw. He looked across the river. 'It looks impressive, is it true to our plans?'

'It is,' said the mason, 'and truth be told, outside of London I have never seen a keep built in such a manner. The stones themselves were carted over twenty leagues from the nearest quarry.'

'I know, for the expense is considerable. Nevertheless, it will be worth it. No longer will we run the risk of flames burning the keep from beneath our very feet.'

'You truly show the way for other nobles, my lord, for once they see the strength of your fortifications then I suggest men of my trade will be in great demand.'

All three men fell silent as they stared at the grey stone walls of the new building. In contrast to the oaken timbers that had made up the previous structure, the tower had a look of might and permanence about it. Any man, friend or foe, could not fail to be impressed at the message it sent to all who gazed upon it: 'Attack us at your peril, for we are mighty.'

Huw dismissed the mason and turned back to the knight at his side.

'Alan, I have a task for you. I want you to take a patrol into Wales and seek out King Trahern of Gwynedd. Once there, seek a truce between our nations. Give him my word that no man, whether he be English, Norman or Flemish, will cross into Wales with ill intent on condition that he meets me to discuss certain matters.'

'What matters?'

'They must remain unrevealed at the moment but you may say it will be in his interest to attend.'

'You would seek parley with a Welsh king?' asked Alan, disbelief etched on his face. 'I thought there was more chance of the seas freezing over before I would see such a thing.'

'You must trust me in this matter, Alan. Whilst in Worcester I was in receipt of communications from William himself and met with him in secret to discuss the ongoing problem of the Welsh. I can tell you, he has set me upon a task to . . . *pacify* the Welsh nation. The details will remain with me for now but to set upon this course of action, I need to talk to the strongest king in Wales.'

'I fear he will not talk,' said Alan. 'For too long we have been at each other's throats like wildcats. I see no reason why he would withdraw his claws now.'

'That is a risk,' said Huw, 'but there is no other way. To appease him in the first instance I will send him a gift to dampen his fire, but the money will be secondary to my main aim.'

'Which is?'

'To engage him in an alliance.'

'Forgive me, my lord, but an alliance demands trust amongst all participants. Since when have Welshmen ever honoured anything except their love for power and land?'

'You may be right but don't forget, Trahern is a new king and desperate to be recognised as one.'

'What about the man he deposed?'

'Gruffydd hides away amongst the Irish, no more than a beggar at Olaf's table. Despite his drunken threats from across the sea, I believe we have seen the last of him. This Trahern, on the other hand, is hungry and ambitious and with the right incentives could be made to dance to a tune of our choosing.'

'What would you have me do?'

'Seek him out and tell him I have a proposal that will make him a very rich and powerful man, but in order to hear it, he must be here before midsummer. In the meantime, I will prove to him I am a man of my word.'

'And how will you do that?'

'By not attacking any of his interests with immediate effect. Ensure you tell him of this, and when he sees I have indeed carried out my promise, he will be more inclined to attend.'

'So be it,' said Alan, 'when should I set out?'

'Dine at my table tomorrow night and set out as soon as your head is clear the following day.'

'As you wish, my lord.'

'Good,' replied Huw, 'now, let's go and see what sort of fortress this mason has prepared for us.'

Two short months later, the building of the keep was complete and King Trahern was expected that very day.

In the kitchens, an army of servants ran everywhere, responding to the barked commands of Karl, the castle cook. Karl was a favourite of Huw the Fat, and though his skills with meat and spices were legendary, his temper often got the better of him and many kitchen hands suffered as a result. Today his mood was particularly foul, for though he took pride in his work, the idea that he had been ordered to create his best dishes for an expected group of Welsh nobles disgusted him to the core. For the second time that morning, his temper got the better of him. The boy, Mathew, never saw the blow coming and he flew across the floor to land in a crumpled heap against the far wall, the leg of roast chicken flying from his hands and skidding across the cold stone slabs, much to the delight of the kitchen dog.

For a few seconds Mathew lay still, wondering what had happened but as the pain kicked in, his mind cleared and the approaching sound of the bellowing cook signalled a severe beating was imminent. Desperately he crawled under the table, seeking refuge from the boots of the giant man now screaming his name across the kitchen.

'*Greengrass!* Get out here, you thieving rat, and get what's coming to ya.'

The servant crawled even further, curling himself into a ball, hoping that the cook couldn't reach him in the dark recesses beneath the giant table.

'I know you're under there, boy,' shouted the cook, 'and when I reach you I'm going to cut off your hands. Now get yourself out here before I break these boards apart.'

Though the cook was a very fat man, Mathew fully believed he was capable of such a feat and looked hopelessly up at his temporary shelter, expecting the boards to splinter at any moment.

'Out of the way, Karl,' said a woman's voice calmly. 'Let me deal with this and stop your shouting, you'll scare the poor lad to death.'

'*Scare him?*' roared the cook. 'I'll surely kill him when I get my hands on him. How dare he steal from my kitchen?'

'No, you won't kill him,' said the voice in a kindly tone, 'for he is yet a child and probably hungry. He is new here and does not know the rules. How would it be if we killed every person who made a mistake in their first few days? Why, we would be preparing all these meals on our own and that would never do.'

'He still needs to be punished,' said the cook.

'And he will be, but leave it to me. Now, get out of the way and let the boy come out for there is work to do and I can't do it all alone.'

For a few seconds there was silence. Everyone knew the cook had a soft spot for Alice and if anyone could save Mathew from a severe beating, she could.

'Just this time,' said the cook eventually, 'but if he steals from me again, I promise he'll see what real punishment is.'

'I'll make sure he understands,' said Alice, 'now get back to that pot while I sort him out.'

Mathew watched the swollen ankles of the cook waddle away. A pretty face appeared below the table edge and Alice gave him a smile.

'Are you all right, Mathew?'

'I think so,' said Mathew with a nod.

'Good, then why don't you come out here so we can sort this out properly?'

'Am I going to get a beating?'

'Well, Karl is busy mumbling threats into his soup, so if you are quick, perhaps we can get you out of here until he calms down.' Alice held out her hand and smiled again. 'Come on, we don't want to make it any worse than it is, do we?'

Mathew hesitated but finally shuffled forward on his knees before taking the girl's hand and standing up to hide behind her skirts.

'Don't think you have got away with this, boy!' shouted the cook, looking over his shoulder. 'You're lucky there is much for me to do. But there may yet be a price to pay.'

Mathew swallowed hard as Alice whispered into his ear. 'Take no notice, he will have forgotten all about it in an hour or so, now come, let me look at that injury.'

'*Alice!*' roared a voice, interrupting her.

'Yes, Karl?' she replied.

'Start plucking the swan and quick about it, I want it in the oven as soon as you can.'

'Yes, Karl.' She sighed, and walked to the cold store to retrieve the bird. It was going to be a long day.

Later that day, Mathew was busy carrying buckets when he heard Alice calling his name. He looked over and saw her by the kitchen door, gesturing for him to follow.

'Quickly,' she said, 'before Karl returns.'

'Where is he?'

'He has been summoned to the hall by the earl to discuss tonight's feast. He won't be long, but if we are quick, there is something you may like to see.'

Mathew followed her out of the kitchen and towards the keep doors. Other servants were already there and Mathew had to push his way through to see what they were staring at.

The elevation of the motte meant he could see far beyond the castle palisade and across the river towards the lands of Wales. At first, he wasn't sure what he was looking at but then saw a procession of horsemen riding slowly towards the castle.

'Who are they?' he asked.

'That, my little chicken thief, is the column of a king.'

'The one you were talking about earlier?'

'Yes, his name is Trahern.'

'Which one is he?'

'I'm not sure from this distance but I would expect him to be somewhere in the middle.'

'Should not a king be at the front?'

'In his own lands, yes, but the riders to the fore are Englishmen, as are the ones to the rear, sent by the earl to ensure his visitors' safety.'

As the column approached, those watching from the palisade and the keep could see more detail. The visitors were easily distinguished from the escort for the sunlight glistened off the English riders' hauberks, the chainmail shirts that hung down to their thighs, while the Welshmen behind were all clad in long black woollen cloaks. Unlike their escorts they wore no helmets upon their heads, and their dark hair either hung down loose about their shoulders or was tied back out of the way. They wore beards hanging down to their chests.

'They look nasty,' said Mathew, 'and I believe they *do* eat babies.'

'Cut your nonsense, Mathew,' said Alice, 'and come on, I think I can hear Karl shouting at some poor soul, we had better get back to work.'

They returned to the kitchen and set about their tasks alongside the other servants, each burdened with a heavy workload to ensure the success of the feast.

Huw was also watching the approaching column albeit from the castellations atop the keep. Beside him stood Alan Beauchamp.

'Well,' said the earl, 'it seems like your trip in the spring was not in vain, Alan.'

'It would seem so,' said Alan, 'always assuming of course that Trahern is actually present and hasn't sent a vassal in his place.'

'Oh, he is here,' confirmed Huw, 'I see his standard towards the centre.'

'Well, whatever business lays between you, all I can say is that it must be worth a fortune for him to risk his life coming here and not even request a hostage.'

'Yes, that was surprising but it just means you can now be party to the negotiations.'

'My lord?'

Huw turned to Alan.

'Tonight we will feast with him as our honoured guest but our mead will be watered to keep a clear mind. Once the festivities are done, we will retire to my chambers and enter negotiations with Trahern and his seconds. I want you alongside me as a friend and to offer counsel where needed.'

'An honour indeed,' said Alan, 'but to what end? I have no knowledge of the endgame and would respectfully request I am fully briefed so I can consider carefully.'

'A fair point,' said Huw, 'and perhaps I have been too secretive but this is an important alliance and if Trahern had decided to ignore my invitation then it was best that as few people as possible knew of the proposal. Come, I will share what I know before they arrive so you are fully armed. After that, we must play the dutiful host.'

Alan looked again at the approaching column. 'I never thought I would see the day I would share mead with a Welshman,' he said quietly.

'Nor me,' said Huw, 'but these are strange times. Come, there is much to discuss.'

The Welsh column entered through the giant gates of the palisade and while the escort dispersed to stable their horses the Welsh riders stayed astride their mounts, looking nervously around the interior of the castle. All around them, men armed with crossbows stared down from the parapets, equally uneasy about the proximity of their traditional enemy. Slowly the noise from the column fell away and an unnatural silence settled upon every man in the fortress.

Trahern stayed motionless, his face a picture of calm as he stared resolutely forward, seemingly unimpressed at the impressive defences and strength of the enemy forces upon the walls. Despite his calm exterior, inside his heart raced, a condition fed with a heady mixture of fear and excitement. One false move would mean he and his men would lie dead in the mud within seconds, but his fear was tempered with anticipation, for despite the undoubted danger, he was no coward and he knew that there was an opportunity here too good to be missed. He glanced over to the rider alongside him, a shifty-looking man with a shock of red hair that gave him his name, Meirion Goch.

Meirion was spiteful looking with gaunt features complimented by a hooked nose and deep-set eyes. He had risen from a serf background to his present position as king's advisor through a mixture of cunning, brutality and an uncanny knack for striking deals to further his position, at times murdering the very people who had helped him upon his meteoric rise. He was universally disliked yet had a strange hold over Trahern, fuelled by his keen mind and ability to protect the king from the many intrigues that plagued any monarch's court.

For several minutes nobody moved and the tension increased as many hands crept to the hilts of their swords.

'Who is the master of this place?' shouted Meirion Goch eventually.

'The Earl of Chester,' came the reply from the entrance gate tower, 'Huw D'Avranches, as well you know, Welshman.'

'Is this hospitality typical of the English,' shouted Meirion, 'to leave a visitor unwelcomed in his saddle after a long ride?'

'The earl is a busy man, he will greet you when he is ready, not a moment sooner.'

'I suggest you tell him to make haste else we return whence we came before a single word has been exchanged.'

Trahern turned in his saddle and gazed around the castle, taking in the enemy strength along the parapets. Men gazed back with undisguised hate in their eyes and nervous fingers played on the stocks of their crossbows. For a few seconds, Trahern's steely manner weakened and he swallowed hard, realising that potentially he had led his men into a situation entirely out of his control and, if this was indeed a trap, there was no way any of the Welsh could escape the rain of death that would fall amongst them in a moment.

Another minute passed until eventually Meirion leaned towards Trahern, talking quietly so as not to be overheard.

'My lord, I have an uneasy feeling about this. Can I suggest we retreat outside the castle walls, for I fear they have us at a disadvantage.'

'No,' replied Trahern, 'we will wait. The situation is indeed unsavoury but even the English are bound by the traditions of hospitality. It may be that he is just not ready. Besides, if their intentions are indeed foul, how far do you think we would get with all those crossbows trained upon us?'

'My lord,' said another voice behind them, 'there is movement at the keep.'

Trahern looked up and saw the doors to the keep open before a squad of armour-clad men filed out and lined the steps leading up to the motte. Each soldier held a flag and formed a guard of honour before another party of soldiers marched down the steps, closely followed by the Earl of Chester.

'That's better,' said Meirion, 'a reception fit for a king.'

Huw descended the steps and walked towards the mounted party, stopping a few paces away as a herald unfurled a scroll.

'Honoured guests,' he announced, 'his lordship Huw D'Avranches, Earl of Chester, heir to the Avranches titles and councillor to William, Duke of Normandy, King of England, welcomes you to his estate. Let this meeting of two great men be a beginning that will be talked about for many generations.

'Here ye also, all those that witness this day, the earl decrees that all ill feeling be shelved between parties for the duration of the attendance. Be it known to all that His Majesty King Trahern of Gwynedd enjoys the hospitality of the Earl of Chester, and any man who raises voice against him while he enjoys the hospitality of this house will be hung as a traitor.'

The herald lowered his parchment and as the words sunk in the armed men around the parapets slowly lowered their crossbows.

Welsh hands returned to their bridles and tensions eased as Huw stepped forward to stand before the Trahern's horse.

'My lord Trahern,' he said, 'now all the ceremony is over, perhaps I can interest you and your seconds in some quality wine up at the keep?'

'Thank you, Earl D'Avranches,' said Trahern, 'the chance to wash away the dust of the road would be most welcome.' He dismounted and after handing the reins to a waiting squire, grasped the earl's wrist in friendship.

'Welcome to my home,' said Huw, 'my courtiers will look after your men. Please, come this way. Alas, the steps are many but the waiting refreshment is of good quality.'

The two men led the way up the steps followed by their respective courtiers while back in the bailey, the earl's bailiff started allocating accommodation to the Welsh soldiers.

'I have to say, your stone keep lives up to the rumours,' said Trahern as they climbed, 'for it is surely the most impressive I have ever seen in these parts.'

The earl followed his gaze up towards the stone tower looming high above them.

'A necessary evil in these dangerous times,' he said, 'but should these next few days go as I hope, there is a chance there may not be a need for such structures in the future.'

'We will see,' said Trahern and followed Huw through the doors into the keep.

Several hours later, the main hall in the keep resounded with the celebrations of hard men enjoying the hospitality of a generous host. All suspicions had been put to one side and hardened warriors now drank alongside those they had once sworn to kill.

Tables previously piled with meats and pastries were now awash with ale and the stripped carcass of the roasted swan dominated the top table like a miniature haunted shipwreck.

'*More mead,*' came a shout and the demand was repeated by a dozen voices around the room.

Huw turned to speak to Trahern.

'I'll say this for your men,' he said, raising his voice to be heard above the din, 'they certainly know how to drink.'

'Such indulgence is rarely experienced in Gwynedd,' said Trahern, lifting his own tankard of strong mead, 'and I suspect the sight of your groaning tables was too much for men more used to the pangs of hunger.'

'But surely, as members of the king's household, they are used to such abundance?'

'Since my victory at Llyn over Gruffydd ap Cynan, my forces have had to be kept strong against those still loyal to Gruffydd, and maintaining such an army is a costly matter.'

'I thought he was exiled in Ireland?'

Trahern drained his goblet and placed it back on the table before him, letting out a satisfied belch as he watched a serving girl refill it from an ornate silver jug.

'Indeed he is,' he continued as he waited, 'but the Irish Sea is no barrier to a man such as Gruffydd. He sees Gwynedd as his birth right and I suspect he will stop at nothing until he has once more faced me upon the field of battle.'

'Welshmen killing Welshmen,' said Huw, 'forgive me for seeing the humour in such a situation.'

'An unfortunate national trait we could well do without,' replied Trahern.

Huw took a sip of his own drink, not mead as was served to his guests, but well-watered wine, a precaution against drunkenness before any talks of note began.

'Of course,' he said eventually, 'there is another way.'

Trahern slowly placed his own goblet on the table and turned to stare at the earl.

'And this other way, is it the reason we were invited here this evening?'

'It is,' said Huw, returning the stare. 'What if I was to say there is a way for you to enjoy a peaceful reign, unhindered by the English Crown and indeed be recognised by William himself as a fellow monarch, equal in stature and free to rule Wales how you see fit. Not only this, but you would benefit from his men-at-arms fighting under your banner should you face any challenger.'

'Even Gruffydd ap Cynan?'

'Especially Gruffydd,' said Huw, 'for William has a particular dislike for that man. He caused us a lot of trouble in the Marches when he held the crown.'

'He has never held the crown,' answered Trahern coldly, 'he stepped into a void and called himself king without the agreement of his peers.'

'Forgive me, but as an outsider, I would have thought the house of Aberffraw would have a genuine claim to the kingdom?'

'You confuse Ynys Mon with Gwynedd itself,' said Trahern. 'The island is but a minor kingdom and if Gruffydd's claim lay there only, then I would gladly gift him the land in return for allegiance to my colours, but alas, his ambition stretches far beyond the estuary, a situation I cannot allow.'

'Why not?' asked Huw, nonchalantly picking on the remnants of a chicken carcass. 'I am led to believe you are from Powys. Why fret over a kingdom that was never yours in the first place?'

'My family hail from a place called Arwystli on the border of both Gwynedd and Powys,' replied Trahern, 'and in the past, ruled over both nations. I seek only a return to the natural order of things.'

'My apologies, I did not know. Still, when Gruffydd held claim to *your* throne, it seems his interference along the border left a sour taste in William's mouth and my promise of the king's support remains unaltered.'

'Of course I am interested, but I suspect to achieve that sort of backing I would have to sell my very soul.'

'Nothing so drastic,' said Huw, 'but I agree it is potentially a huge undertaking for one man. Now, if there were certain *allies* that you could call on, perhaps there is a bigger deal to be had.'

Trahern took another drink and stared into the eyes of Huw the Fat.

'What exactly are you getting at?' he asked. 'Surely you are not asking me to betray my nation?'

'Not at all,' said Huw, 'I am simply suggesting that diplomacy is better than the sword and there is an opportunity here for peace between our nations. William has his hands full in the north and doesn't need war with the Welsh. All I am saying is this. If you could form an alliance able to control the whole of Wales, then perhaps we could agree a peace deal and all this killing could stop. Do you know of any such-minded men?'

'Perhaps,' said Trahern. 'Meilyr of Powys is a close ally and I have had favourable dealings with the king of Gwent, a man called Caradog.'

'And can you trust them?'

'I can, but to what end?'

'Let me put it like this,' said Huw, leaning closer. 'William is distracted by the constant fighting along the Welsh borders. A strong Welsh alliance could ensure the fighting stops and he can concentrate on other things. Our soldiers would stop being killed and your young men could return to their farms. William, of course, would support such an alliance with coin and armies should you need them.'

'At what cost?'

'Nothing more than a pledge of allegiance. There are some other minor details but we can discuss those later.'

'And who would rule Wales?'

'The Welsh, of course,' said Huw, 'though there would have to be one ruler, for the sake of diplomacy.'

'And who would that be?'

Huw didn't answer but simply lifted his goblet again before draining it dry.

'We'll leave that to you, as it is Welsh business,' he said eventually, 'but King Trahern of Wales has a certain ring to it, don't you think?'

Trahern stared in astonishment. He had come here hoping for an alliance to secure Gwynedd but what Huw was offering was beyond his wildest dreams.

'Come,' said Huw, 'I can see you find my proposal interesting and such things should be discussed in less rowdy circumstances, don't you think?'

Trahern nodded in silence, still struggling to comprehend the opportunity laid before him.

'Good, then rescue a flask of mead and we will withdraw to discuss the finer detail. You can bring your second with you but he is to be sworn to secrecy.'

Trahern turned and glanced at the man who had been at his side since arrival in the castle. Meirion Goch nodded, indicating he accepted the burden.

'Agreed,' said Trahern, 'lead the way, D'Avranches, for I have to admit, I am intrigued by the proposition.'

The two nobles left the room accompanied by Alan Beauchamp and Meirion Goch and what they discussed over the next few hours would eventually alter the course of Welsh history.

Caerleon Castle

May 9th, AD 1081

Caradog ap Gruffydd stood within the bailey of Caerleon Castle, gasping for breath in the late evening air. The matted hair on his barrelled chest glistened with sweat from the afternoon's exertions and trickles of blood ran down his weather-worn face from a cut above his brow. At his feet lay one of his comrades, groaning after receiving a crushing blow from one of the king's giant fists, and all the men cheered as the latest victim struggled to his feet and staggered from the arena. Caradog's stature was squat but his build was impressive with not an ounce of fat visible anywhere on his torso. His muscular arms seemed too long for his body whilst the livid white scar running from brow to temple paid testament to how close he had come to death in a fight many years earlier.

The men surrounding him were in no better state, as each was battle hardened and well known for their prowess in combat. Each and every one looked forward to these monthly training sessions as it gave them the opportunity to test themselves against their peers without the risk of too much blood being spilled.

Squires formed an outer circle around the warriors, each holding various training weapons ranging from wooden swords to lances with points wrapped in sackcloth to avoid mortal injury.

'*Who's next?*' roared Caradog, wiping a trickle of blood from the side of his mouth.

'That would be me,' said a voice behind him and Caradog turned to face the largest of them all, Lord Morgan of Gwent, showing the black pebble drawn from a pouch.

'What?' Caradog grinned as the other men laughed. 'Surely there is witchcraft involved here, for I swear we meet more regularly than the cock crows.'

'No witchcraft, sire,' said Morgan, tossing the pebble over to a squire. 'The draw was made fairly before witnesses but you hurt me with your words; surely you enjoy our monthly exercise as much as I?'

Caradog bent down and picked up a wooden training sword from the ground, his bald head glistening as it reflected the light from the setting sun.

'I wouldn't say I enjoy it,' he said taking his place at one edge of the circle marked in the sand, 'but nevertheless, I suppose every blow from you is one less I need take from an enemy's steel.'

'A good way to look at it,' said Morgan, taking an offered sword from a squire, 'now stop your whining, good king, and take your guard.'

Up on the battlements, many foot soldiers cheered with excitement, some taking bets on the outcomes of the bouts as they watched their officers beat lumps out of each other.

Caradog knew the monthly spectacle gained the soldiers' respect and he had instigated the ritual over a year earlier, not only to increase the standing of his officers but also to establish whose mettle was the stronger amongst those he called comrade.

Since he had conquered Morgannwg, Caradog had declared himself king of Gwent, and though the title was not formally recognised by any other monarch, he revelled in its majesty, taking every opportunity to have it declared across South Wales. His court consisted of a dozen loyal nobles from Gwent and an impressive standing army of over five hundred men-at-arms, a number easily increased in times of conflict if needed.

Already he had taken Gwent and Morgannwg and after defeating Rhys ap Owain of Deheubarth the previous year would have claimed those lands as well had not Rhys ap Tewdwr secured the throne while Caradog was away on campaign, a move that made Caradog seethe with resentment.

Ordinarily he would have ridden to challenge Tewdwr and simply wipe him from the field of conflict but Tewdwr was a popular man amongst the other kings of Wales and Caradog had decided that now wasn't the right time to be making fresh enemies.

'Come on then,' he called, crouching down into a defensive stance, 'do your worst, big man.'

Both men crouched low, circling each other, while the other five nobles cheered them on, anticipating the contest. With a roar, Morgan of Gwent charged across the circle, raining blow after blow down on the king's upraised sword. Men cheered from the battlements as Caradog was forced onto his knees, desperately defending himself from the unrelenting attack. Within moments he knew that, as had happened so often before, Morgan would soon land a blow upon his torso, possibly resulting in a cracked rib or two, and thus win the contest outright. In desperation Caradog sought an opening and, seeing no other way to better the stronger opponent, resorted to trickery.

'Wait!' he shouted as Morgan lifted his sword to strike again and as the attacker paused in confusion Caradog took the opportunity to smash his cudgel onto Morgan's kneecap, causing him to collapse screaming to the floor. Immediately Caradog pounced upon his adversary and rammed his forehead into Morgan's nose, forcing him backwards onto the sand, following up the vicious attack with his wooden sword across the wounded man's throat.

Morgan's eyes bulged as his breath was cut off and he struggled to push the sword up, but to no avail. Slowly he weakened but there was no sign of Caradog's attack relenting as the king's face grimaced with increased effort.

Slowly the cheering subsided as the watchers realised the fight was over but still Caradog pressed upon his sword.

'Sire,' shouted one of the nobles, 'the fight is done, give quarter.'

Caradog ignored the shout and leaned forward, effectively choking his comrade.

'Sire,' shouted the noble again, 'the contest is over, set him free.' More voices joined the call and soon every man was shouting their opposition to the impending death of Morgan.

For a few more seconds Caradog continued the pressure but as Morgan fell towards unconsciousness the king's rage finally abated and he released his grip, standing up as his opponent gasped in pain, straining to fill his empty lungs.

For a few moments the castle fell quiet and everyone stared at the king in shock. Caradog's rage was legendary but this time he had almost killed a valued ally. As Morgan's breathing returned to a semblance of normality, Caradog walked back over to stand beside the fallen man, his training sword still in his hand.

'Do you yield?' he asked, waving the wooden cudgel menacingly.

Morgan looked up from the floor, his face covered with blood from his broken nose.

'Never,' he growled.

For a few seconds, Caradog stared down at the fallen man and every man held his breath, waiting to see the king's next move.

'Right answer,' replied the king with a grin and throwing away the cudgel, held out an arm to help his comrade to his feet.

Immediately the garrison burst into cheering as both men grasped wrists in friendship.

'Well done,' shouted Morgan over the noise, 'you have done what no other has managed to do, though it has to be said you lowered my guard with a falsehood.'

'I would suggest a falsehood can be just as lethal as the sharpest of blades,' replied Caradog.

'As you have just proved,' said Morgan, 'and therein lays the lesson. Now can I assume this day is over? For I have a great thirst about me.'

'Lead the way, my friend and perhaps you can even the contest with amounts of ale drunk.'

'Challenge accepted,' said Morgan and, with the cheers of the men ringing in their ears, the nobles walked towards the keep for a well-earned drink.

Hours later, the king's guests were sharing oft-told tales of glory spoken between tankards of ale and mouths full of roasted chicken. Most of those present boasted blackened eyes or swollen lips, and at least one man had an arm strapped close to his chest – the results of the day's activities. The aroma of roasted meat filled the air, fighting a battle for supremacy against the scent of unwashed bodies and ale-laden breath; the flagstone floor was awash with spilled wine and remnants of discarded food.

Caradog himself was relatively quiet; though he was of royal lineage, many of those present had acquired their titles by force of arms and, while that itself was no problem for the king, it meant that their knowledge of courtly manners was often limited.

An arm-wrestle erupted into a fistfight and as the men eagerly gathered around to witness the spectacle, Caradog's eye was caught by a servant standing near a doorway, desperately seeking his attention yet wary of entering the den of iniquity.

'Excuse me, gentlemen,' Caradog said to those nearest him, 'it seems my presence is required elsewhere.'

'A buxom wench, no doubt,' said Morgan with a laugh.

'Alas, simply matters of kingship.'

'Then indeed I am correct, for you surely have your eye on a comely wench yet are reluctant to share with your brothers.'

The men's laughs echoed behind him as Caradog left the hall and followed the servant out into the corridor.

'Sebastian, you beckoned me?'

'Indeed, my lord, for the scouts have returned and their commander requests immediate audience.'

'Where is he?' asked Caradog.

'In the lesser hall, my lord.'

'Thank you, Sebastian, you are dismissed.'

Caradog walked briskly out of the keep and down into the bailey before entering a separate building constructed near the palisade. A man stood near the fire, enjoying the brief comfort the flames offered.

'Are you the scout?' asked Caradog as he entered, not recognising the soldier before him.

'I am, my lord, Bowen Boarswold of Gwent.'

'You are back sooner than expected. I trust you have good news?'

'I do,' said the leather-clad traveller. 'As ordered, we approached Dinefwr under the cover of darkness. For seven nights we watched from the trees and learned the ways of their defences.'

'Can they be bettered?'

'The castle is indeed formidable but with subterfuge and bravery I believe the walls can be breached.'

'You have a plan in mind?'

'We have, my lord.'

'Excellent. Get your men rested and fed while I entertain my guests. Tomorrow you will give me a full report and we will make our plans accordingly.'

'Yes, my lord.'

The minor noble left the hall while Caradog sat at a table to consider the news. If the report was as good as he hoped, then he would soon be sending word to his men across Gwent to muster once more. The time for practice was over; the real thing would soon be upon them.

Deheubarth

May 15th, AD 1081

Nesta ran through the lush new growth in the vale below the castle, laughing joyfully as the butterflies escaped her outstretched arms for the umpteenth time that morning. The sun was warm upon her back and the plaid woollen cape lay discarded by the side of her mother just a stone's throw away.

'Nesta, stay away from the river bank,' called Gwladus, 'the waters are still swollen and you would be washed away as surely as if you were a leaf.'

'I will, Mother,' answered Nesta, frustrated she was not allowed to explore the fishing lines so carefully tended by the village children.

She looked up at the escaping butterfly now seeking the safety of the vertical bank stretching high up to the fortress perched atop the escarpment. For a moment, she let her gaze rest on the imposing castle, her home for the past two and a half years.

When she was small, her mother would regale her with tales of the noble knights of King Arthur's table and the beautiful princesses that were always part of the stories – but now she was a princess in her own right, the reality seemed so much more mundane.

Her days were taken up with matters of etiquette and courtly routines while her evenings were busy with sewing, flower arranging and listening to the boring chatter of the court ladies as they shared the latest gossip from the noble houses of Deheubarth. Despite the boring life enforced upon her, she still managed to find time to play with Hywel, her older brother, yet though the day was perfect for play fighting with wooden swords, Hywel was absent from the riverbank. Still suffering the lingering effects of a winter ague, Hywel lay in his sickbed back in the keep, tended by the queen's loyal servants.

This wasn't how it was supposed to be, thought Nesta. *Where are the princes, the dragons and the wizards? Surely it is time they made an appearance?*

Her mind returned to the matters at hand and she looked around, seeking any other winged victim worthy of the attentions of a princess.

For the past few months it had seemed like the incarceration would never end for Nesta. Throughout the winter months the snows had lain heavy on the ground, and though the castle courtyard was pure white on the mornings after any fresh snowfall, the constant foot traffic and exercising of long-stabled horses meant it soon turned into a dirty mush and she had to seek the pristine freshness of newly fallen snow high upon the battlements. Once there she would stare over the stunningly beautiful landscape of Deheubarth, which stretched as far as she could see into the distance. The distant hazy hills were almost blue in hue while the river glistened like frost jewels in the winter air and snow-laden trees hunched their shoulders against the biting cold. On occasion she would see her father's huntsmen ride through the crisp fields, seeking deer or boar to supplement the dried fish and fruit that was the mainstay of their diet. But despite the beauty of such scenery, many were the days when she longed for the kiss of the springtime sun.

At last those days had arrived and to Nesta's delight, after a very long winter, her mother had suggested a walk down to the river that very morning. Nesta could hardly contain herself, such was her excitement.

One of the servants packed a bag with a rug and some sweet cakes, and after checking that Hywel was as well as could be expected Nesta and her mother walked down the stone-lined track into the valley.

The banks of the river were a hive of activity. Inhabitants of the local village went about their business along the well-trodden paths, taking their wares up to the castle to sell or reporting for work in the kitchens. Others set up fishing poles along the banks of the river, hoping the warm summer sun would stir the fish to hunger, while the braver men took their small boats out into the deeper flow where larger fish were known to lurk.

'Mother,' said Nesta, returning to the blanket where Gwladus sat, 'can we walk to the village?'

'Not today, Nesta,' replied Gwladus, 'I need to rest. Perhaps in a few days I will be a little stronger.'

Nesta glanced at her mother's belly, now large enough to advertise the fact she was again with child.

'Do you think it will be a girl?' she asked.

'Only the Lord knows,' came the reply, 'but as long as the child is healthy then we will be happy.'

'I want another brother,' decided Nesta eventually, 'someone who I can fight with and share adventures.'

Gwladus laughed but winced as the action resulted in a piercing twinge.

'Mother, are you well? Is the baby coming?'

'I am fine, child,' said Gwladus, 'and no the baby is not coming. At least I hope not; it's not due for another three months. Come, sit alongside me while I brush your hair.'

Nesta sat on the blanket and waited patiently as her beautiful locks were teased back into place by the careful attention of the hairbrush in the queen's hands.

'Mother,' she said, eventually, 'am I pretty?'

'Of course you are,' said Gwladus gently, 'the prettiest girl in all the world.'

'Am I as pretty as her?' asked Nesta, pointing to a peasant girl walking along the path.

'She is indeed fair of face,' said Gwladus, 'and every child is beautiful in the eyes of the Lord. But you, my sweet, are surely the prettiest girl I have ever seen.'

'Yes, but you have to say that. I would wager that girl's mother says the same thing to her.'

'No doubt she does and in her eyes she would be telling the truth. Anyway, why would you ask such a thing?'

'Because I don't think I want to be pretty anymore.'

Gwladus stopped brushing for a moment but soon re-gathered her composure.

'And why would that be?'

'Because I heard some of the court ladies talking last night and they said that the prettiest girls always get married first and I don't want to get married.'

'Why not?'

'Because when you get married you have to do embroidery and have babies. I want to climb trees and do archery and fight the squires, like Hywel.'

Gwladus struggled not to laugh and concentrated on Nesta's hair.

'Well, there is still enough time to do that,' Gwladus said eventually, 'but one day, would you not like to be a queen of your own kingdom?'

'I don't think so, the poor children seem to have so much more fun.'

Gwladus followed her gaze over to where some children were playing a game of chase. She stopped brushing and whispered in Nesta's ear.

'I have an idea,' she said, 'why don't you go over there and ask if you can join in their game.'

Nesta's head spun to face her mother.

'Really? Do you think they will allow me to?'

'I don't see why not; go and ask but be polite.'

Nesta jumped to her feet and ran over to the children. Within moments her squeals of delight echoed across the grass and Gwladus smiled as her daughter joined in the innocent games, the difference in station of no importance to children. For a while she watched her daughter, filled with contentment, but soon her mood dipped as her thoughts returned to the reality of their situation. Despite the warm weather, the mood in the castle was still tense, for though her husband had sent despatches to Caradog, seeking terms for a lasting truce, no answer had been forthcoming. Throughout the spring she had beseeched Tewdwr to increase the strength of the garrison as a precaution but to no avail. The king was convinced he could negotiate a peace and so there was no need for the extra expense raising an army would bring. Soon the warmer weather tempted the king into once more following his first passion and he took to the forests of Deheubarth to hunt, the threat of invasion long forgotten as he spent days away from the castle with his fellows.

For the next hour or so, Gwladus watched as Nesta joined in the fun along the riverbank, playing various games and throwing sticks into the water, much to the chagrin of the fishermen.

Gwladus looked lovingly at her daughter. Even at the tender age of eight years old, Nesta was a beauty. Her jet-black hair tinged with hints of raven blue fell down to her lower back. Her father had already received expressions of interest from neighbouring kingdoms about her availability for marriage when she came of age but had steadfastly rejected all advances, determined to allow her to enjoy her childhood until she had reached the age of at least thirteen years. Nesta, of course, knew nothing of such things and just lived her young life as a child, albeit within the protection of those mighty castle walls.

Gwladus smiled inwardly. Another winter had been bettered and, despite the harshness of the weather, they had reached spring relatively unscathed. There was still food in the cold rooms, plenty of wood for the fires of the castle, and though her son was unwell, the apothecary said he would soon make a full recovery.

The morning moved gracefully to noon and the queen relaxed, enjoying the warmth upon her skin. Many women came over to speak to her and she engaged each one in polite conversation, keen to make a good impression on those she deemed to rule. Soon it was time to return to the castle for the midday meal but as she was about to call Nesta the queen was approached by a middle-aged woman selling her wares.

'My lady,' said the woman, 'may I approach?'

'Of course,' said Gwladus with a smile.

The woman came closer and sat upon the grass.

'Oh, don't sit there,' said Gwladus, 'this rug is big enough for both of us. Please join me.'

'My lady,' said the woman nervously, 'I am surely not worthy to share the blanket of a queen.'

'Nonsense,' answered Gwladus, 'please sit.'

The woman lowered herself onto the blanket, albeit as far as she could away from the queen.

'So,' said Gwladus, 'what wares do you have for me to see?'

'Alas, nothing fit for a queen, my lady, though I have sprigs of lucky heather to ensure the good health of your unborn child.'

'How wonderful,' said Gwladus, 'may I see?'

The woman withdrew a small bunch of freshly picked plants from her basket and offered them shyly to Gwladus.

'They're lovely,' said Gwladus, 'and how much are you selling them for?'

'I was heading to the castle and hoping to exchange the whole basket for a loaf of bread.'

'Are you hungry?'

'Hunger is always a bedfellow, my lady.'

Gwladus paused and stared at the woman.

'What is your name?' she asked.

'They call me Annie Apples,' said the woman, 'in the autumn I carry baskets of freshly picked fruit between villages.'

'I think I have seen you in the castle.'

'Indeed, for when the juiciest are ready upon the trees, I harvest them and bring them for your table. When you arrived at the castle in the autumn, I presented you with a basket of fruit as a welcome gift.'

'I remember,' said Gwladus with a smile, 'a very kind gesture. I'll tell you what, Annie Apples,' she said reaching beneath her cape, 'I will buy a lucky sprig from you, but will pay with coin. Does that suit?'

'My lady, a penny will buy the whole basket.'

'I have no need of the whole basket but will take a sprig.' She held her hand out and the woman's eyes widened in astonishment for in her hands she held a silver penny.

'My lady, I don't understand.'

'Take the coin, Annie,' said Gwladus, 'and ensure your family are well fed.'

'Alas, I have no family but there are many old and infirm within the village who will bless your name this night. I could also buy some chickens, perchance?'

'Whatever you wish,' said Gwladus with a smile. 'The coin is yours. Now, where is my heather?'

The old woman retrieved the prettiest of the sprigs and offered it to the queen.

'May the blessings of the Mother be upon you,' she said as she handed it over.

'Are you not a Christian soul?' asked Gwladus.

'My needs are best served by the old gods, my lady, I hope you are not offended.'

'Not at all,' said Gwladus, but before she could continue, Nesta's voice came from the riverbank.

'Mother, look.'

Gwladus looked up and saw her daughter running towards her with a bucket.

'What do you have there?' she asked.

'Fish,' replied Nesta excitedly, 'one of the boys caught them on a night line and he said I could have them in return for a kiss.'

'And did you kiss him?' asked Gwladus, her smile dropping for a second.

'No, but he gave them to me anyway. What shall we do with them?'

'What do you want to do?'

'I'm not sure. I like eating fish but they look so sad, I think they would be happier if I set them free.'

'No doubt they would,' said Annie, 'but a gift of food is a wonderful thing from someone so poor and it would be an insult to release them after the boy gave them to you.'

Nesta looked towards her mother for guidance but Gwladus stayed silent, interested in which path her daughter would choose.

'I think we should kill one and release one,' said Nesta eventually, 'that way the gift is not wasted but we have also shown compassion.'

Both women smiled at the decision.

'A good choice,' said Annie. 'If you place one back in the river, I will show you how to kill and gut the other.' She turned to the queen. 'That is if you allow me to?'

'Of course,' said Gwladus and watched as her daughter ran to the riverbank with the bucket. Within moments she returned and watched with fascination as Annie Apples produced a knife from within the folds of her dress.

'What are you going to do?' asked Nesta.

'It is important to kill any beast as quickly as possible,' said Annie Apples, 'for it is cruel to make any creature suffer needlessly.'

'Why?' asked Nesta. 'Did not God make the fish for us to eat?'

'They are indeed intended for our consumption,' said Annie, careful not to enter into a conversation about a god she did not believe in, 'but there is no reason to let them die a painful death.'

'But Peter said he just bashes them over the head.'

'We can do that but this is quicker and doesn't let the animal suffer.' Annie reached in the bucket and pulled out the trout, placing it on a nearby flat rock. Within seconds she had cut off the head and tail before slicing open the belly and removing the innards. Finally she washed the body in the bucket and gave the fish to Nesta.

'Here,' she said, 'give this to your kitchen cook and tell him to remove the bones. It will make a hearty meal for you and your brother.'

Nesta surprised her mother by clapping her hands in delight and was about to take the prize when her attention was drawn to something in the distance.

'Mother, who are they?'

Gwladus followed her daughter's gaze, noticing that many of the villagers had also stopped what they were doing and were looking downriver.

'Who is it?' she said getting slowly to her feet. 'Can you see, Annie?'

'Alas, my eyes are hazy,' said the woman, peering downstream.

'It looks like horsemen,' said Nesta, 'hundreds of them.'

Gwladus gasped and for a few moments, stared at the approaching line of horses spread out across the valley.

'Who are they?' asked Nesta again.

'I have no idea. Come, we should return to the castle.' She bent to pick up the blanket but cried out in agony as a searing pain shot through her stomach.

'Mother!' shouted Nesta. 'Are you all right?'

'I don't know,' gasped Gwladus, 'the pains are bad. Come, we must go.' She leaned on her daughter and aided by Annie Apples, started to make her way towards the path leading up to the castle. But before they had gone a dozen paces, a frightened cry echoed around the valley.

'They bear the colours of Caradog,' shouted a man, 'and they advance with swords drawn.'

'Heaven help us!' cried a woman. Within seconds, everyone on the riverbank turned to run towards the castle, seeking shelter within its imposing walls.

The women quickened their pace but again the queen cried out, this time falling to the ground.

'It's no good,' she cried, 'I can't walk. Nesta, get to the castle as quick as you can and take refuge.'

'*No!*' shouted Nesta. 'My place is with you.'

'You will be killed, now do as I say.'

'No,' cried Nesta again, 'I will not leave you.'

Gwladus turned to Annie with desperation in her eyes.

'Annie,' she said, 'please, take my daughter to a place of safety, I beseech thee.'

The strange woman stared at the queen and then at the horsemen who were now only minutes away.

'My lady,' she said, 'it is too late to get you to safety but there may be one thing we can do.'

'Anything,' said Gwladus.

The old woman turned to Nesta. 'Child, we may have a chance to save you both but you must do as I say.'

Nesta nodded.

'Good. Run quickly to the gorse bushes at the base of the hill. Once you are out of sight of the horsemen, hide yourself amongst the thorns. Take no heed of cuts or scratches, for your life is more valuable, do you understand?'

Nesta nodded again.

'Take yourself deep as do the hares and once there stay as still as death until darkness falls. No matter what you see or hear, you must stay hidden. In the midst of night you are to crawl back out and make your way downriver to the first bridge you find. I will await you there. Do you think you can do that?'

'What about my mother?'

'I will do what I can but if you are with us I fear all will be lost.'

'Then I will do as you say.'

'No,' gasped Gwladus, 'she is still a child and cannot do this alone.'

'This is the only way,' said Annie, 'and if the gods are with us then we may all yet survive.'

'It's all right, Mother,' said Nesta, 'I will be fine.'

'Then run,' said Annie, looking at the encroaching riders, 'before it is too late.'

Nesta paused a moment more before kissing her mother on the cheek and turning to run towards the castle. Villagers jostled in panic as they ran, causing some to fall in the rush and it was all Nesta could do to avoid a similar fate.

Despite her status in life, nobody gave her a second glance, for there were few who knew who she was and the thought of an army descending upon their backs meant their focus was on self-preservation.

Nesta pushed herself through the crowd and headed over towards the banks of the escarpment.

'Child,' called a voice, 'where are you going? Come with me to the castle, it is not safe out here.'

Nesta stared at the unknown woman and for a moment considered joining the throng but eventually shook her head and backed away from the stranger.

'Thank you, but I must go elsewhere.'

'You will surely be slain if you stay out here, a pretty thing like you. Come quickly before it is too late.'

'No,' said Nesta, 'I have to go.' With that she turned and ran as fast as she could towards the bank while the friendly woman was engulfed in the crowd running up the path to the castle gates.

Once she was out of sight of the riders, Nesta turned off the path and headed for the bushes as instructed, the thorns tearing at her skin as she forced herself through the matted undergrowth. Eventually she was deep within the gorse and pushed herself back against a rock, her hands and face covered with bleeding scratches.

Back on the bank, Annie removed her dirty cloak and placed it over Gwladus's fine gown.

'Now listen,' she said quickly, 'in a few moments they will be upon us. I have no knowledge of this man or the strength of his honour but hopefully he will not lower himself to kill a beggar.'

'A beggar?'

'Yes, you must sit alongside me and hold out your hands thus, asking for food. Pull the hood low about your face for your beauty will give you away but, with luck, they may ride straight past.'

'What of my son?'

'Where is he?'

'Still in the castle.'

'Then he is in the safest place. All we can do now is try to keep you alive and hope the men of the garrison protect him well. Now try to act like a peasant and pray your god is looking over you this day.'

Gwladus did as she was told and soon both women sat at the side of the road, hands outstretched begging for alms.

'May the Lord have mercy,' whispered Gwladus as the horses thundered nearer.

A few leagues away, Gwladus's husband trod carefully through the undergrowth, blissfully unaware of the attack on his family home. He and his comrades had tracked a large boar to a cave in a hill, and though there was no way out, every one of the hunting party knew the trapped animal was more than capable of killing a man.

'My lord, let us light a fire,' said Marcus Freeman, one of Tewdwr's best men, 'the smoke will force him out and he will soon fall to our spears.'

'Where's the fun in that?' asked Tewdwr. 'It is a long time since I challenged Sir Hog to a duel and the winter months have put fat about my belly. Let's see if he has the better of me.'

'So be it,' said Marcus and watched as his king approached the cave.

Without warning the boar burst from the cave entrance and charged straight towards the safety of the nearby undergrowth. Tewdwr cursed, hoping for a head-on attack, but knowing he only had seconds, changed the grip on his spear and launched it at the side of the disappearing animal.

The flight of the weapon was at completely the wrong angle. The point hit the haunches, but the spear glanced off and the boar disappeared into the bushes relatively unharmed.

Marcus retrieved Tewdwr's spear and handed it back to the king. 'Come, this valley ends in an escarpment. Perchance you will get another opportunity.'

Tewdwr took the weapon and walked back to his horse but before he could mount a shout echoed through the trees.

'My lord, are you there?'

Tewdwr glanced towards Marcus before mounting his horse and all six members of the hunting party waited as the sounds came closer.

'My Lord Rhys,' came the shout again, 'where are you?'

'Over here,' shouted Marcus on the king's behalf. 'Who comes seeking audience?'

Seconds later, a horse burst through the undergrowth and a rider galloped up to the hunters. Marcus's hand immediately went to his sword.

'Hold,' said Tewdwr, 'I know this man, his name is Walters, a cook from the castle kitchens.'

'What cook rides a destrier?' asked Marcus suspiciously.

'A question already in my mind,' replied Tewdwr, 'but we will see what causes him such angst.'

The cook reined in his horse beside the king. His face was bloody and his left arm hung limp at his side.

'Walters,' said Tewdwr, 'why are you abroad from your duties and what has caused you such injury?'

'My lord,' gasped the cook, 'I bring terrible news: the castle has been attacked and already they have breached the outer gate.'

'*What?*' gasped Tewdwr. 'How can this be? The guards were under strict instructions to keep alert.'

'Most of the men were struck down with illness two days ago. We think the water had been poisoned, for the garrison were still abed, a great illness upon them. When the attack came we were poorly manned and the gate guards were set upon by soldiers disguised as peasants bartering their wares. They had no chance.'

'What about my family?' asked Tewdwr quietly. 'Are they safe within the keep?'

The cook glanced nervously at the king.

'Your son was in your quarters when the attack came but the whereabouts of the queen is unknown.'

'*Unknown?*' shouted Marcus. 'You have obviously escaped the danger astride the horse of a better man, so unless you have a good reason I may well cut you down as the coward you seem to be.'

'My lord,' cried Walters, 'I did not flee the castle for my own life but to help the lady Gwladus for she was without the safety of the castle walls.'

'She was *outside?*' gasped Tewdwr.

'Aye, as was your daughter. They had left the castle to enjoy the springtime sun, as had many others, but were caught out when the enemy attacked. Alas, there was not much time for them to get within before the attackers reached the castle. Many were cut down where they stood though some escaped into the trees.'

'But you did not find them?'

'Alas no. The lady Gwladus and others from the castle were down on the plain when the enemy came amongst us. Some were struck down as the riders passed but others ran to safety. During the confusion I took the opportunity to escape down the slopes. I searched for the queen but she was nowhere to be found nor did I hear of her fate from others who had escaped. I even checked amongst the dead, but there is no sign of either the lady Gwladus or the lady Nesta.'

Tewdwr swallowed hard. The fall of his ancestral home was devastating, yet the fate of his wife and daughter tore at his heart. He turned to see the worried looks on the faces of the hunting party.

'My lord,' said one of the riders, 'what would you have us do?'

'If the castle has fallen, there is little to be gained in riding back that way.'

'Our families may yet live, my lord.'

'Aye, they might but will be no more than prisoners at the whim of Caradog. In time, he will ransom them back to us but the aftermath of the battle is not a time to be broaching the subject to the victor. The blood will still be high and they may take great joy in executing our loved ones as a message to all. No, we should wait before sending representation to the castle.'

'I agree,' said Marcus, 'but in the meantime, the lady Gwladus may be in need of our aid and we should seek out her fate.'

'A burden upon my shoulders alone, Marcus,' replied Tewdwr. 'The fate of my family is my concern, not yours. You men are free to do what you can to help those kinsmen who escaped or seek your own families. But I will not ask you to return with me.'

'My lord,' said Marcus quietly after a few moments, 'you may be my king but for once you will heed my words. Long ago I pledged my life to your lineage and nothing has changed. I would die for you, for Gwladus and for Nesta. For many years we have enjoyed the bounty of your patronage and have been honoured to serve at your side. Now the tide has turned, do you really think we would abandon you at the first time of asking?'

'You know I do not think that, Marcus,' replied Tewdwr, 'but if my family are dead then so am I, for there will be naught to live for.'

'If they have been slain, we will continue this discussion then, but until we know for certain there is everything to live for.' He turned to face the other men, each still upon their steeds. 'I speak for myself only,' said Marcus, 'but think I know your minds. Let all speak who think the same way. Do we run or do we stay alongside our king?'

'I will stay with my lord,' said Frederick.

'As will I,' shouted William.

'What of you, Gerald?' asked Marcus.

'I am my king's sword,' came the reply.

'As am I,' said the last man, Carwyn.

'There you have it,' said Marcus turning back to the king. 'We are all your men, my lord, and will ride alongside you even unto death.'

Tewdwr stared at each man in turn. The rewards of kingship were many and often counted in wealth or power but one of the most valued was loyalty. Many men swore oaths to their masters but it was only in times of adversity that the strength of those oaths were tested. Each of the men before him had been at his side for many years and now the time had come to prove their mettle, they had not fallen short.

'You have my gratitude,' he said, 'and I promise you this. If, by the grace of God, this should end well, then every man here will receive their just rewards.' He turned to face the cook. 'What of you, Walters?'

'The castle was my home, my lord, and the servants my family. I have nothing else. If you will have me, I will ride alongside you.'

'Well, a cook is always a useful asset,' said Tewdwr, 'and as you already have such a magnificent horse, how can I refuse?' He turned back to his men. 'The days have just taken a darker turn, my friends, and I'm not sure whether we have the besting of them, but there is one way to find out.'

'To the castle, my lord?' asked Marcus.

'Aye, Marcus, to the castle.'

Dinefwr

May 18th, AD 1081

Window shutters slammed as Caradog's cavalry thundered into the village of Dinefwr. Frightened parents hid their children beneath their cots, terrified their houses would become a target for the thugs of Caradog's men. The sounds of dogs screaming in pain echoed through the empty streets as arrows thudded into their scrawny bodies, their angry barks silenced forever. In the church, dozens of people knelt before the cross, each praying for protection against the marauding army.

Husbands nervously fingered whatever weapons or tools near to hand, knowing that any resistance would be futile, yet determined to sell their lives dearly in defence of their loved ones.

It had been three days since the forces of Caradog had taken the castle and each day since, his men had enjoyed the spoils of war, an act condoned by Caradog himself, keen to keep his Belgian mercenaries amused. Women had been dragged from their homes in front of their children and taken away as mere playthings for the soldiers, while any men who fought back were beaten remorselessly or killed outright in retaliation.

Terrified villagers held their breath behind pointlessly barred doors as an officer reined in his horse and dismounted before walking slowly down the main street. His face cracked into an ironic smile, amused at the lack of life. Midday should see the village a hive of activity but it would seem the attentions of his men were not as eagerly welcomed as they might have been.

'I have seen more life in a graveyard.' A man astride a destrier laughed. 'Perchance they have all run away like the frightened vermin they are.'

'On the contrary, Bowen,' replied Peterson, 'I feel their eyes piercing my soul as we speak. Their gaze goes deeper than the sharpest arrow.'

'A frightened gaze has been the death of no man in my experience.' Bowen laughed once more. 'At least, not the man upon which it rests.'

'Perhaps not, but be about your guard lest looks of hate are replaced with willow and steel.'

'If any of my men are as much as bruised this day,' growled Bowen, 'I swear this village will be burned to the ground before nightfall and their children fed to the pigs.'

Peterson nodded silently. Both he and Bowen knew the banter was for the benefit of those hiding amongst the houses, for although terror abounded within their walls fear often made men do stupid things, and that they could not risk.

He walked slowly down the street and climbed up onto the platform where, only weeks ago, the village had celebrated bringing in the May with ale and dancing. Now it echoed no such music, just the creaking of the ropes about the necks of the three men they had hanged the day before.

He pushed one away, setting the macabre pendulum in motion before making his way to the far edge and facing the village centre.

'People of Dinefwr,' he called, 'heed my words well, for they may be the last you ever hear. My master, Caradog ap Gruffydd, lord of Gwent and Morgannwg and soon to be true king of Deheubarth, sends his regards and a promise of peace into your miserable lives. He has decreed that for a period of two days and two nights, no man under his command will come unto Dinefwr with ill intentions. Indeed, with me I have a cart of foodstuffs from the castle kitchens for you to share as you see fit, such is his generosity.

'He has ordered me to tell you that the time for killing and raping is over and peace should be the bedfellow of all in his name.' He held up his arms and turned slowly so all the hidden villagers could see his face. 'Do you hear what I am saying? You are free to go about your business for two days without fear of attack or ridicule. Bury your dead and see to your wounds. Feast in his name or make love to your partners, the time is yours to do what you will.' He fell silent and looked around the silent village.

'And after the two days are done,' called a hidden voice, 'what then?'

'Ah, indeed,' said Peterson. 'After that the choice is yours, for you can go on enjoying a fruitful life and the freedoms it brings but there is a small price to be paid. Somewhere within this village hides the wife and daughter of Rhys ap Tewdwr. They are kinsmen of the false king and should be in the protective custody of Caradog. Worry not for their safety, for they will be treated well. Indeed, Tewdwr's son already enjoys Caradog's hospitality up in the castle, but my master is concerned for the safety of the queen and her daughter. Deliver them unto our hands within two days and your freedoms will be secured under the laws of the land. There will be no more killing and you can go about your lives without fear in your souls. However, keep them hidden and you will all pay the price, every man, woman and child. We will destroy this town and everything around it. The castle will be pulled down to its foundations and the rubble dispersed across the cantrefs, never to be spoken of again. Every home will be burned and every citizen of Dinefwr, whether tradesman or wastrel, hanged from the roadside trees from here to Kidwelly.'

He looked around again, seeing nothing but shadows from between the slats of ill-fitting shutters.

'Do you hear me, people of Dinefwr? Ensure you heed my words, for you are but two days away from death. Those who think they can seek shelter from Caradog's wrath elsewhere, let me tell you this. My men encircle this village as we speak and any who try to escape this decree will be executed without question.'

'My message is done,' Peterson added eventually. 'Enjoy your two days of freedom but think well upon what lays upon the other side. Deliver the pretenders to me – or say goodbye to your miserable lives forever.'

Without another word he climbed from the platform, returned to his horse and galloped out of the village with Bowen. Those who ventured from their hiding places watched them go, and though the sight of the leaving soldiers was a great relief, the sight of many more riders spreading out along the base of the hills in the distance added credence to his words. They were surrounded.

***

Caradog stared out over the lands of Dinefwr from the highest room in the tower. Behind him, Peterson had entered to give his report.

'Well,' asked Caradog, without turning.

'I have issued your decree as instructed, my lord,' said Peterson, staring at the back of the warlord.

Caradog's chainmail was tight about his torso and a belted sword hung low to the floor. His gauntlets and helmet lay on a side table and in his fist he held a silver goblet of wine taken from the castle cellars.

'And was the nature of the reception favourable?'

'Alas, they hid away like frightened mice but they are under no illusion as to what to expect if they fail to meet your demands.'

Caradog turned and stared at his messenger.

'So you did not discuss these terms with the elders nor the priesthood?'

'They were nowhere to be seen, my lord, and I suspect many have already fled.'

'If that is the case, who is to say that Tewdwr's bitch has not also fled?'

'We can't be certain but the servants say she was heavy with child and suffered an ill pregnancy. She would be in no fit state to travel far.'

Caradog scratched at his well-cropped beard, deep in thought.

'Let us hope it is so,' he said eventually, 'it was ill fortune that the queen managed to escape our initial assault but at least we have her son. How is he – I hear he suffers from the cough?'

'He is a sickly child,' said Peterson, 'and if he represents the strength of the house of Tewdwr then I would suggest you will have no problem wiping them from the path before you.'

'Don't underestimate Tewdwr,' said Caradog, 'he is a very clever adversary and will be no pushover.'

'Do you want the boy killed?'

'No, not yet. If he dies through illness, so be it, but let us not hasten his demise; he may yet have value. Send him back to Gwent and instruct my sheriff to secure him in chains until I return. I will decide his fate then. In the meantime, free Tewdwr's men from the dungeons and offer them a chance to ride with us. Provide those who accept with ale and women in return for their declaration and see them well horsed.'

'And what of those who still proclaim allegiance to Tewdwr, shall I have them hanged?'

'No, the prisoners will be given a free choice: Tewdwr or me. Those that choose the false prince will be allowed to ride out without harm. That way, those who stay will see I am a fair man with rightful claim to the throne and their loyalty will be unquestioned.'

'I don't understand, my lord, why would you free men who may turn their swords against you in the future?'

'Dead men wield no swords, Peterson. Once they are clear of these walls my vow is fulfilled. What happens after that is out of my control.' He paused and stared at his comrade. 'Do I make myself clear?'

'You do, my lord. I will make the necessary arrangements immediately.' He turned and left the tower room while Caradog returned to the window and sipped from the goblet of wine still in his fist.

'I may not know where you are, Tewdwr,' he said quietly, 'but once your bitch is in my hands, it is only a matter of time before all your heads lie amongst the filth of the pigpen.'

Since Caradog's messengers had left the village two days previously, many frightened people wandered aimlessly about, engaging in nervous conversation with any others willing to listen. Some preached the importance of defending themselves, whilst others saw sense and realised such a direction could only end in one outcome. Some took the situation into their own hands and ran from house to house, searching stables and pigpens for any sign of the fugitives but to no avail; there was no sign of them anywhere. In desperation they turned to the priest and asked for his intervention, and on the evening of the second day he called a meeting at the village tavern.

The single room was crammed with people and many stood outside, straining to hear the talk from within. The meeting had been going on for an age with voices raised on both sides of the argument but still there was no agreement.

'But she is our queen,' said the widow Weaver, 'how can we betray her?'

'Nobody asked you, old crone,' interrupted John Pigman. 'Who allowed you in to discuss the business of men?'

'I have made cloth in this village since before you or your pigs were born,' snapped the old woman, 'and my family were amongst the first to settle here, even before the castle was built.'

'So you keep saying at every opportunity,' sneered Pigman, 'but that does not make you wise in such matters.'

'Listen to you,' roared a voice, 'bickering like washer women while Caradog sharpens his blades. Don't you understand, if we don't do something we will each be dead before noon tomorrow. In the name of Christ, can we not put aside our petty squabbles and concentrate on the matter in hand?'

'And what do you suggest, Jonas?' shouted another man. 'You are quick to spout your opinion yet I hear no answers from you.'

'I have no answers, blacksmith,' replied Jonas, 'but I know this meeting is getting us nowhere. If our death is the only outcome, then I for one will fall with a blade in my hand.'

'Aye!' shouted a number of voices in support.

'Are you stupid?' shouted the blacksmith. 'These men are seasoned warriors and will come with crossbows and swords. We will stand no chance against them. I say we run while we can.'

'Then you are a coward,' shouted Jonas, 'and deserve to die as such.'

'I am no coward,' retorted the blacksmith, and he pushed through the crowd towards his accuser.

'*Enough!*' roared a voice above the furore and all eyes turned to look at the priest. Father Croft was a large man and his calloused hands belied the ways of a gentle calling. Unlike other men of a similar ilk, he helped the villagers on the land when extra labour was called for and was respected far and wide as a godly man, wise in the ways of the world and fair to all in matters of complaint. It also helped that he was an ex-soldier who had turned to the church a few years earlier and had no problem knocking heads together when people were stubborn or stupid. Subsequently, not many would face him in a fistfight should any situation deteriorate and he was often the source of agreement and common sense.

'The time for argument is done,' said Father Croft, 'and we need to make a decision. The facts are these. The lady Gwladus escaped the assault on the castle along with her daughter – that much is clear. Caradog seems to think that we hide her away amongst our homes, though to be honest, I have not seen her myself nor spoken to anyone who knows of her whereabouts. As far as I am aware, she is not in the village.'

'Then we have nothing to worry about,' said Pigman.

'On the contrary,' said Father Croft, 'I have already had such discourse with the men of Caradog but they refuse to listen, believing instead that we employ lies and trickery to keep her from his grasp.'

'They have to listen,' said Pigman, 'else we are surely doomed.'

'And therein lies the problem. I know of nobody who knows the lady's whereabouts and without that information, there is nothing we can do.'

'There is something we can do,' said Pigman, 'we can search every house in the village until she is found. Rip apart every wood pile and check every cold store until there is no place left to hide.'

'And what if you find her?' asked the old woman. 'Are you just going to hand our queen over to be killed at the hands of Caradog?'

'You heard what his messenger said, her life will be safe in Caradog's hands as will that of her daughter.'

'And you believed him?'

'We have to believe him,' said Pigman, 'else what are we to do? To withhold the location is to invite retribution. Look about you, widow, these people face certain death before this night is out. Not only that, their children will also hang although they are innocent in all this. Would you have their deaths on your hands for the sake of a woman who has been in residence less than a year?'

The widow backed down and looked around at the frightened faces.

'It is irrelevant,' intervened Father Croft, 'for we know not her whereabouts.'

'Then let us search the village,' said Pigman again, 'at least that way Caradog will see we are taking his threat seriously and perhaps he will show mercy.'

'I know where she is,' said a small voice and all heads turned to see a young girl no more than six years old standing against a wall.

'Who let a child in here?' asked one of the men. 'And a girl at that!'

'She has every right to be here,' snapped the landlord, 'she is my daughter.' He turned to face the girl. 'Bethan, you should be abed, these are matters for grown-ups.'

'But I know where Nesta is,' said the girl, 'she was stuck in the mud by the river and the pretty lady pulled her out.'

For a few seconds there was silence then the room broke out into conversation with many shouting questions towards the child. Bethan took a step back, intimidated by the noise.

'*Silence!*' roared Father Croft again. 'Give the child room.' He pushed his way through the throng and knelt down before her, taking her hands in his. 'Don't worry about all those silly men,' he said with a warm smile, 'they are just a bit noisy. You're not scared, are you?'

Bethan smiled and shook her head. 'The grown-ups are always noisy when they drink Dada's ale,' she said.

Some of those present stifled a laugh at the innocent yet accurate reply.

'So they are,' said Father Croft. 'Now, about what you just said, what did you mean?'

'I saw Nesta and her mother when the bad men attacked the castle. I was feeding the chickens when the horses came and I was afraid so I hid in the bushes by the bridge.'

'And then what happened?'

'I was there for a long time because there was lots of shouting but when Annie Apples came she said it was all right and I could come home.'

'Annie Apples?'

'Yes, she was with the lady with the pretty dress and she gave me a penny not to tell anyone.'

'A whole penny?'

'Yes, I am going to buy a piggy off Johnny Pigman when they have babies.'

The priest smiled again.

'And what makes you think it was the princess from the castle?'

'Because they were looking for Nesta but she was stuck in the mud and the lady pulled her out.'

'Do you know Nesta?'

The girl nodded.

'How?'

'I played with her when my dada took ale to the castle when it was snowy.'

Father Croft looked towards the innkeeper.

'She speaks the truth,' said her father. 'A few months ago, I took some barrels up to Tewdwr and the child came with me, but the storm blew in and we were stuck in the castle for two days. While we were there, Bethan was allowed to play with Nesta.'

Father Croft turned back to Bethan. 'So you saw them both. Do you know where they are now?'

'They are living with Annie Apples,' came the reply. 'I know because I heard her say she had a spare cot.'

Father Croft straightened up and looked around the tavern.

'This Annie Apples, she is not part of my congregation, does anyone here know of her?'

'Everyone knows Annie Apples,' said Pigman, 'and the reason she does not frequent the church is because she is a witch.'

'She is no witch,' interrupted the widow Weaver, 'she just worships the old gods and knows the ways of animals.'

'Her calling is irrelevant,' said Father Croft. 'Where can we find her?'

'She lives in the tin mine,' said Pigman.

'I thought that was abandoned?'

'Aye, it is, but Annie Apples has made her home there.'

'Then our path is clear,' said Father Croft, 'the lives of many outweigh the safety of two. The location of the lady Gwladus is the key and we should let Caradog know as soon as possible.' The priest stood up. 'If someone gets me a horse I will take the burden upon my own shoulders so if this turns out ill then the responsibility lays with me.'

He turned back to face Bethan now held within her father's arms.

'Little girl,' he said, 'you are extremely brave and have just saved many lives. Is there a gift we can give you to say thank you?'

Bethan whispered in her father's ear.

'She asked could she keep the penny.' Her father smiled.

'Of course you can,' said the priest, 'and what is more, John Pigman will give you two of the prettiest piglets from the next litter, won't you, John?'

'Will I?' responded Pigman, a look of surprise upon his face.

'Yes,' came a chorus of voices from around the tavern.

The girl beamed in delight and her father put her back down so she could run and tell her mother.

'Are you sure this is the right thing to do?' asked the landlord quietly as the rest of the room sought the ale barrels to celebrate.

'We have no choice,' said the priest, 'but there is something you can do for me.'

'Anything.'

'If I bide my time riding to Caradog, do you know of anyone who may be able to get through the perimeter guard and warn the queen she is in danger?'

The landlord thought for a moment before answering.

'If any can do it then it will be Tom One-eye.'

'The poacher?'

'Aye, he knows these hills better than any man alive.'

'Can he be trusted?'

'I would trust him with my life,' said the landlord.

'That's exactly what we will be doing,' said the priest. 'You go and charge him with his task. Tell him that Caradog will know by midnight; though I doubt he will send riders in the dark, there is no guarantee. He has to get the queen from the mine as soon as possible.'

'And if she's gone before Caradog gets there, what will become of us?'

'As long as Caradog is happy she was there, then he has no need to kill anyone. Our part of the bargain will be fulfilled.'

'But his prey will be gone. He may not believe us.'

'His trackers are not stupid men, they will know whether she has been there or not and will try to catch up with them. I can't do anything about that but at least they have a chance.'

'So be it,' said the landlord and turned to leave the tavern.

Several hours later, Tewdwr and his men made their way through the forests to the west of Dinefwr. They had left their horses way back in the trees, tasking the cook and one of the men to look after them. Carefully they walked forward, conscious that every snapped twig or heavy footfall could bring the attentions of an enemy sentry.

'How much further?' whispered Tewdwr.

'The top of the next hill overlooks Dinefwr,' replied Marcus quietly. 'From here on in we must be extra vigilant, for if Caradog is as good a warrior as they say he is, no doubt he will have patrols amongst these woods.'

Slowly, they continued forward, each step carefully considered and hands rested on sword pommels as they walked, ready for instant defence should the need arise.

As they neared the ridge they dropped to the floor to crawl the last stretch before reaching the crest and peering down into the valley. Below them they could see several fires along the lower slopes, the glow from the fires sending moving flickers of light amongst the trees. Shadows moved between them and it was obvious there were many guards deployed along the hill.

'What do you think they are doing?' whispered Marcus.

'I have no idea,' responded Tewdwr quietly, 'but it doesn't look good. Perhaps they mean to attack the village.'

'No, there is no reason to set up a perimeter to do that,' said Marcus, 'Caradog is not known for patience or leniency; if he wanted them dead, they would already be corpses. It's almost as if he did not want them to leave.'

'It doesn't make sense,' said Tewdwr, 'I fail to see what threat mere villagers could pose a warlord such as Caradog.'

'There's only one way to find out,' said Marcus, 'and that's to go down there.'

'It's too dangerous,' said Tewdwr, 'there may be other guards amongst the trees that we cannot see.'

'To go down together would indeed invite failure but alone I can get in and out before dawn.'

'Are you sure?' asked Tewdwr.

'Absolutely.'

'Then make it so,' said Tewdwr, 'but be careful, I don't want any more lives lost in my name.'

'Fret not, my lord,' said Marcus kneeling up to unfasten his sword belt. 'I grew up in these hills, remember?'

'I do,' said Tewdwr, 'but still, this is not a game of our youth.'

Marcus removed his chainmail and placed it alongside his weapon.

'Are you not taking your sword?' asked Tewdwr.

'Too heavy and too noisy for a quest such as this,' said Marcus. 'My dagger will be my only friend.'

'Is that wise?'

'If I am discovered I feel a sword will not be enough anyway; at least this way I can move quickly.'

'When you get there,' said Tewdwr, 'you need to find someone you trust and ask about the fate of Gwladus. With God's grace she and my daughter yet live and once they are safe we can turn our attention to what we are going to do about Caradog.'

Back at the castle, Peterson once more knocked on the door of Caradog's quarters.

'Come in!' roared a voice, and Peterson entered to find Caradog sitting behind a table opposite two men. Their faces were unknown to him but he could see they were still dressed in travel clothing, obviously having only recently arrived.

'Peterson,' said Caradog, 'I trust you come with good news.'

'I have, my lord, but perhaps it would be better said in private.'

Caradog glanced at the two men sipping warmed wine from silver goblets.

'No need for secrecy between allies,' said Caradog, 'these men are messengers from my old friend Meilyr ap Rhiwallon. Do you know of Meilyr?'

'I do, my lord, he is the king of Powys.'

'Indeed he is and his messengers have brought a fascinating proposition to me.' He turned to one of the men. 'Please, retell the offer your master has made.'

'My lord,' said one of the men, placing his goblet upon the table, 'my master, Meilyr ap Rhiwallon, king of all Powys, offers a treaty between himself and the kingdom of Gwent. In addition, I am empowered to tell you that King Trahern of Gwynedd entered into negotiations with one of King William's nobles many months ago agreeing a treaty giving him favourable terms. Those terms are to be extended to all three monarchs, should you join them in this agreement.'

'A treaty of three kings,' said Peterson, turning to Caradog, a question upon his face. 'An interesting proposition but, I would ask, to what end?'

'Several ends,' said Caradog. 'If this comes to fruition there would be free trade between the three kingdoms, mutual military support should either get threatened and a stability across Wales that has not been seen for many a year.'

'My lord, it sounds very good, but what about the lands of Deheubarth and Ceredigion? Surely they would have a say in such matters.'

'Deheubarth is in my hands now, Peterson, and the sooner we find Tewdwr the quicker I can free his head from his shoulders. Once that is done, his people will have no choice but to follow me, as the title will be mine by right of conquest. As far as Ceredigion goes, they are naught but farmers led by a sheep and will bow to our combined will.'

'It is important to know,' interjected the messenger, 'that if this alliance goes ahead, Wales will be divided equally between the three new Welsh kings, all of which will be recognised by the English Crown. In addition, King William has offered us favourable trading terms and freedom of rule in return for certain assurances.'

'What assurances?' asked Peterson.

'That you would supply men-at-arms to any cause in his name should they be needed, that taxes are doubled from all incumbent landowners and that the lords of the Marches are able to extend their lands threefold into Wales.'

Peterson looked at Caradog.

'A heavy price, my lord.'

'Nonsense, compared to what is to be gained, the lands are minimal and any increase in taxes will be passed on to the people. As far as soldiers are concerned, if the King of England needs men to fight a war elsewhere, it means his attention is not on me and that can only be a good thing. No, I think I like this proposal and will send a favourable response on the morrow. In the meantime, what news of Tewdwr?'

'My lord, the priest of Dinefwr has furnished us with a location where Tewdwr's wife is hiding.'

'And where is that?'

'Apparently she is sheltered by an old hag in a tin mine further west. I have taken the liberty of despatching a unit of cavalry to drag her back here.'

'And the girl?'

'She is thought to be with her.'

'Good, and what about Tewdwr himself?'

'Alas, there is still no news, but as we seem to either have recruited or executed most of his men, I can't see him being a threat.'

'You are wrong, Peterson, a deposed king can often be more of a threat than those who boast of castle walls. People rally to a lost cause and it is important we get rid of him once and for all. Double the search parties and bring his wife to me as soon as she is apprehended.'

'I will, my lord.'

'Good, keep me informed.' Without another word he turned his back on Peterson and carried on his conversation with the messengers.

Peterson could see his audience was over and quietly left the room. On his way back down the stairs of the keep he heard a commotion in a side room and, drawing his sword, barged in fully expecting to see a conflict between men.

'What goes on here?' he roared, seeing two men with swords drawn.

'My lord,' stuttered one of the men, 'the boy was caught trying to escape. We found him just in time but he has armed himself with a blade and wounded one of our men.'

Peterson looked over at the young boy in the corner. His face was covered in blood from a gash on his head and he held a knife before him as if it was the biggest sword.

'Stay away from me,' shouted the boy, 'or I'll stick you like a pig, I swear.'

Peterson looked at the two soldiers in disgust and sheathed his sword.

'Am I to believe this urchin has bettered three warriors of Caradog?' he sneered. 'For if this is indeed the case, I'll stab you myself.'

'Of course not,' spat one of the soldiers, 'but Caradog wants him unharmed and it is difficult to know what to do without hurting him.'

'Who is he?'

'He's Tewdwr's brat and worth a pretty ransom.'

'Perhaps so,' said Peterson, 'but anyone wounding one of our own, be he man or boy, deserves no special treatment. Get out of my way.'

The soldiers stepped aside as Peterson walked forward.

The boy pushed himself back against the wall, his eyes wide with fright. His clothes were torn from the fight and his curly black hair already blood-soaked from his head wound.

'What is your name, boy?' asked Peterson, coming to a halt a few paces away.

'I am Hywel ap Rhys,' snarled the boy, 'son of Rhys ap Tewdwr and prince of Deheubarth. Come one step closer and you will feel my blade.'

'Well, listen to me, Hywel of Deheubarth,' said Peterson, a menacing edge to his voice, 'I care not whether you be prince or pauper but you have wounded one of my men and there is a price to pay. Normally I would gut you myself, but our master sees value in you so, despite my urge to cut you down right now, I will be merciful. Throw away that knife and I promise you will not be hurt. Continue this farce and I will not be held responsible for my actions.'

'I would rather die right here than spend a minute more as a captive to that pig Caradog,' barked Hywel, 'so do what you have to do.'

'Brave words for the son of a coward,' said Peterson with a sneer.

'My father is no coward!' shouted Hywel.

'No? Then where was he when we attacked?'

'He was hunting,' roared Hywel, 'and I demand you retract your insult.'

'He is a coward, boy,' said Peterson, 'as I believe are you.'

With a roar Hywel lunged forward and aimed his blade at Peterson's chest but with a swing of his chainmailed fist Peterson knocked him aside and Hywel crashed into the wall, before falling to the floor, bleeding. Peterson picked up the knife and threw it over to one of the guards.

'When he comes around, place him in chains and throw him in the dungeon. He may be a boy but he is still in line for the crown of Deheubarth and we cannot risk his escape. Now, if there are no more children you want me to fight on your behalf, I will take my leave.'

The two men stepped aside but as he left the room Peterson paused and spoke over his shoulder.

'Just in case you have forgotten, we are in the middle of a war here; it would be better if you both remember that fact. You may live longer.'

With that he turned to leave the keep while behind him the son of Tewdwr lay unconscious in a pool of blood.

The Hills above Dinefwr

May 21st, AD 1081, midnight

Marcus crawled slowly down the slope, each movement carefully considered as he tried to avoid the attentions of Caradog's guards. At first the going had been relatively easy and he had run from cover to cover, but eventually he neared the enemy cordon and had no choice but to drop to the ground to pass through their lines. Voices talked quietly in the darkness as men sat around campfires but Marcus continued carefully, inching his way through the rotting leaves of the forest floor towards the feature he knew would increase his chances of success: Nant Goch, the red stream.

Eventually he slid down the slime-covered bank into the shallow water, the freezing water momentarily snatching away his breath. The stench of sodden leaves filled his nose and the mud oozed between his fingers like rotting flesh. Nervously, he looked around, wary of the spirits reputed to haunt the banks of the stream. Nant Goch got its name from a battle that once took place on the hills above when so many men were killed that the stream ran red with blood for two whole days. Subsequently it gained a reputation for being haunted by the spirits of the slain and few men ventured along its banks in darkness, no matter how great their reputation.

Slowly he continued his journey downhill, crawling like a lizard through the freezing water and mud, always keeping his body lower than the stream's banks. The going was painfully slow but it was the safest route down to the river, and once there he could reach the village within minutes. Several times he paused as soldiers passed close by, their feet crunching through the crisp undergrowth, but each time he went unseen and continued his task undiscovered.

The edge of the forest loomed ahead and he increased his pace, but just as it seemed he would reach it safely, a hand shot out from between the exposed roots of a tree and he felt the cold blade of a knife pressed hard against his flesh. His eyes widened in fear as he awaited the drag that would open his throat, but it never came, just an overpowering smell of fetid breath as a whispered voice hissed into his ear.

'If you want to live, keep very, very still.'

Marcus froze, his body as still as a corpse. He knew there was no escaping the perilous situation he was in. All he could do was wait for the hidden man to ease the pressure on his blade and perhaps he may be able to throw himself to one side before fleeing down the hill.

'Get down,' whispered the voice and a hand pushed Marcus's head into the mud as a soldier walked over and set about emptying his bladder into the stream.

Marcus closed his eyes and shut his mouth as the urine splashed about his head but he made no sound, knowing that to do so invited certain death. Within moments the guard retreated back into the darkness and Marcus raised his head to peer into the face of the man who had saved him.

'Who are you?' whispered the mud-covered man. 'And why do you hide from Caradog's men?'

'My name is Marcus,' came the reply, 'and I aim to get to the village.'

'To what purpose?'

'That is no business of yours.'

The face came closer and once again the smell of fetid breath filled the air.

'I know you,' said the man, 'you are the son of Steffan Thatcher.'

Marcus's eyes narrowed in suspicion.

'I am,' he said, 'but I am at a disadvantage. Who are you that knows my lineage so well?'

A smile appeared on the man's face, revealing a jagged line of rotten teeth as the pressure on the blade eased.

'You do indeed know me, Marcus, for when you was a mere stripling I showed you how to hide amongst the king's forests without being seen, a skill I see that you have long kept fresh in your mind.'

'Tom Rivers?' said Marcus.

'Aye, though I am now known as Tom One-eye.'

Marcus relaxed. As a boy he had spent many happy days with Tom learning the ways of the forest, and classed him as a true friend. Despite Tom being a poacher, Marcus's father had entrusted his son to the older man in order to learn the survival skills so useful in times of hunger.

'It is good to see you,' whispered Marcus, 'though I would ask how come you are laying at the bottom of a stream in the middle of the night. Surely there are more important matters afoot than poaching the king's game.'

'Just as well I was here,' said Tom, 'for that guard was almost upon you. Without my intervention you would have walked onto his blade. Did you learn nothing from me?'

Marcus grinned. Tom had lost neither his cutting humour nor matter-of-fact way of talking.

'Nobody will ever be as good as you, Tom, but alas, I have no time to relive the past. My task is before me and I need to go.'

'What is so important that you risk being killed to reach the village, or are you not at liberty to say?'

'Now I know it's you I am happy to share. I seek the lady Gwladus on behalf of Tewdwr himself. We have heard she escaped the castle but lays hidden in the village. Do you know of her whereabouts?'

'God indeed works in mysterious ways, Master Marcus, for I am also on the same quest though for different reasons and in the opposite direction.'

'She is not in the village?'

'Gwladus and her daughter are being looked after ten leagues hence but she is in great danger.'

Before Marcus could reply, One-eye grabbed Marcus's head and forced him down into the mud again, both men hardly daring to breathe as a patrol of four soldiers walked past the stream.

'Are you sure about this?' hissed Marcus as soon as they were able to get up.

'As sure as I can be. Do you have fresh horses?'

'Aye, we do, secreted on the reverse of this hill.'

'Then we should get there with all haste for it may already be too late.'

Marcus looked back up the steep slope. It had been difficult enough coming down but going up would be ten times harder.

'Is there another way?'

'No, Caradog's men are everywhere. They will be gone by morning, but by then it will be too late.'

'Why?'

'Before this night is done, Caradog will send a force to apprehend Gwladus and, no doubt, lever Tewdwr's surrender on pain of her death. If we are to get them to safety, there is no more time to lose.'

'Then what are we waiting for? Lead the way.'

The West Coast of Deheubarth

May 22nd, AD 1081

Nesta lay back on the furs of the bed. The scratches on her face still looked sore but the bleeding had stopped and the pain had long ceased.

'It's all right, Mother,' she said quietly, 'they don't hurt so much anymore.'

Gwladus smiled and dipped the linen pad back into the bowl of warm water before dabbing it gently onto her daughter's wounds.

'The scratches don't seem so angry,' said Gwladus, 'this potion seems to have done the trick. Perhaps Annie Apples knows what she is talking about after all.'

'Do you think she's a witch?'

'Be she a witch or an angel, we owe her our lives, for surely we would now be incarcerated in our own dungeon had she not taken care of us.'

'What about the baby?'

'The baby is fine. Annie Apples gave me a drink and the pain eased. She says if I take it every day then I should see out my full term. Don't you worry about me, Nesta, you just get some rest and let those scratches heal.'

'What will become of us?' Nesta asked, turning slightly to look at her mother.

Gwladus's smile faltered. 'Our future is not clear yet, Nesta, but for the moment we are safe.'

'Will we be going home soon?'

'Not yet. Caradog has taken the castle but hopefully he will soon leave and we can go back.'

'What if he never leaves?'

'Then we will find your father and set up home somewhere else, perhaps Ireland. We have family there.' As she spoke, Gwladus rested a reassuring hand on her daughter's arm.

'Do you think Father is alive?'

'Yes, I do,' she replied confidently. 'He wasn't in the castle when the attack came and your father is a very resourceful man. If I know him, he already seeks us out and will stop at nothing to see us safely by his side once more.'

'What about Hywel?'

'Your brother will be fine. As a prince of Deheubarth he is worth more to Caradog alive than dead and I'm sure he will be treated well.'

'Is Dada still the king or is Caradog the king?'

'Caradog is nothing but an invader who seeks to build his own empire by destroying those of others. Your father is a very clever man, and though we may be on the back foot at present, the situation will change soon enough and we will return to take our place in the castle at Dinefwr.'

'Promise?'

'I promise,' said Gwladus. 'Now, try and get some rest.'

'What's this?' asked a voice. 'Am I to believe you are not happy with Annie Apple's hospitality?'

'Of course not,' said Gwladus with a smile as she turned to face the old woman, 'you have truly been sent by God himself and will have our gratitude until the day we die.'

'Nonsense,' said Annie, sitting on the bed, 'I did what many would do in the same circumstances.' She turned her attention to Nesta. 'Do you think you can sit up a little?'

Nesta pushed herself backwards until she was sitting and took the offered bowl of soup from the woman's hands.

'What is it?' she asked, sniffing the steam nervously.

'Some lizards, a frog and the hair from a horse's tail,' said Annie with a lowered voice.

Nesta looked up in alarm and both women burst out laughing at the horror upon her face.

'Only mushrooms,' said Annie, wiping the tears of mirth from her eyes, 'and a bit of chicken.'

'Honestly?' asked Nesta.

'Upon my oath,' said Annie, 'it's just that I overheard your question to your mother and thought I would have a little laugh.'

'If you are sure,' said Nesta, 'it does smell rather nice.'

'Good,' said Gwladus, 'it means your appetite is coming back and that is a good thing.'

'Eat it up,' said Annie. 'There is plenty in the pot if you want some more.'

Nesta sipped some soup off the spoon and nodded in appreciation.

'As good as the soup in the castle,' she said and set upon the meal with renewed enthusiasm.

Annie glanced at Gwladus and indicated she should come away for a moment. Gwladus joined her near the fire at the entrance to the mine.

'She has grown a lot stronger, my lady,' said Annie quietly, 'and you should think about leaving here as soon as possible.'

'I know,' said Gwladus. 'You have put yourself in danger for us and for that you have our gratitude.'

'It's not my safety that concerns me, but that of you and your daughter. It is not wise for you to stay.'

'But surely nobody knows we are here?'

'Perhaps not, but when they find out you were not in the castle, it is only a matter of time before someone recalls seeing you with me. After that, the end will be upon us like a storm.'

'But we have nowhere to go.'

'I know people in other villages,' said Annie. 'We could go there and stay as long as we think we are safe. We can say you are the wife of a farmer who was killed in the attack. At least that way it gains us some time.'

'No,' said Gwladus, 'it won't work. Caradog will send messages to all the local villages warning them not to offer us succour on pain of death. He will know I am with child and a heavily pregnant woman travelling with a daughter will be too much of a coincidence. I have to think of somewhere else.'

'What about a place of worship? I have heard tell that your god offers safety to those with just cause.'

'You mean sanctuary?'

'Aye, can you not seek refuge within a church?'

Gwladus stood and walked around the man-made cavern, her mind racing.

'Annie,' she said eventually as she returned to the bed, 'I think you may have come up with the answer. A church is too small to offer refuge for Caradog's men would simply barge their way in and ignore its sanctity. We need somewhere not even he would dare desecrate, a place such as a cathedral.'

'There is a cathedral in the town of Saint David, not twenty leagues hence.'

'I know,' said Gwladus, 'for I have been privileged to pray there on two occasions. The bishop is a truly godly man and has the ear of the pope himself. He wouldn't refuse us the protection of Christ and there is no way Caradog would dare breach the sanctity its walls offer, for to do so would incur the risk of ex-communication.' She turned to look at the old lady. 'That is what we will do, Annie: make haste to the cathedral of Saint David as fast as a horse will carry us. Do you have such beasts?'

'Alas, I own nothing except that which you see around you. However, I have many friends and should be able to borrow anything we need.'

'Therein lays our path. If you can secure a cart in my name, then as soon as this situation is over, you have my word I will pay whatever it costs plus more.'

'Then that is good enough for me,' said Annie. 'Shortly I will go to the village and see what I can do.'

Silence followed for a while as Annie brought two more bowls of broth and both women ate their meal in relative silence. Finally they finished and Gwladus looked over at the woman.

'So,' said Gwladus, between mouthfuls, 'you obviously know who we are, what about you? Do you have a family?'

'Alas no, I am alone in the world.'

'But you must have had one once, where did you grow up?'

'My childhood was spent amongst the forests and valleys of Wales. I never knew my father but my mother ensured I was kept warm and fed.'

'Did she have employment?'

'Not as you know it, she lived off the land and made a few coins telling the fortune of passing travellers and supplying potions to those who still followed the old ways.'

'Then she was a witch?'

'Some would call her that but her only crime was to not follow the masses in worshipping a false god.'

Gwladus stared at the woman in shock.

'Your words stab me like a blade, Annie,' she said eventually, 'for I believe there is surely only one God and the only other option is to be a servant of Satan.'

'I do not decry the existence of your god, my lady, on the contrary, I too believe in one creator but the goddess I recognise created these lands long before any man set foot upon them. Perhaps the creators we both worship are actually one and the same but have grown different identities through the ages.'

'Is your mother alive now?'

'No, when I was still a girl, she was murdered by a man she knew as a lover. I was taken in by a washer woman and grew up in poverty.'

'That is a very sad story, Annie,' said Gwladus, reaching out and touching the woman's hand.

'No sadder than many, my lady,' replied Annie, pulling her hand away, 'but I am one of the lucky ones. I survived to live a semblance of a life. Many do not get past childhood and die with a life unfulfilled.'

'You are a special lady, Annie Apples,' said Gwladus, 'and should we come out of this alive, perhaps we can find you a position at court to see out your days in comfort.'

'A lovely gesture, my lady, but I fear it is one I would decline. My place is out here amongst the trees and under the stars. This mine gives me shelter and I feel I would wither and die should I be held behind a palisade.'

'Well, make no decisions yet,' said Gwladus, 'let's see what transpires first.'

Annie Apples smiled and got to her feet. 'Well, this is getting us nowhere; we need to secure some horses. You wait here, my lady and I will return as soon as I can. Make preparations for travel but keep it light, for we will need to move quickly.'

'That shouldn't be difficult,' replied Gwladus, 'for we have nothing to call our own but the clothes in which we stand.'

'There is fruit in the basket and some dried pork within the box upon which you sit. It's not much, but enough for the journey.

I will be back soon.' Without another word she ducked out of the entrance and replaced the willow wall behind her.

'Where is she going?' asked Nesta from her bed.

'To get the help we need,' said Gwladus, 'finish your soup, Nesta, for we will soon be leaving this place.'

———

The following morning, the sun's first light had just about lightened the sky when the dawn chorus was interrupted by the sound of galloping hooves. Deer, already about their breakfast, pricked up their ears before bouncing into the protective undergrowth, their instincts already aware that where there were horses, there were usually men.

In the distance a dog barked and within moments, six horsemen, wrapped in the warmth of their fur-lined capes, rode their mounts from the forest path and into the clearing at the base of the hill.

In the far bank they could see the mine entrance covered by a screen woven from willow, and all around the clearing were signs of recent life. A fire still smouldered outside the entrance, a necessity to keep away the wolves of the night, and piles of dead wood lay scattered everywhere along with empty baskets and some broken pots. A pig snorted in a far pen, hopeful of any titbit these strangers may bring, but its comforting grunts were replaced with squeals of pain as an arrow thudded into the animal's chest.

Bowen, the captain of the cavalry, turned to look at his archer, an unspoken question clear upon his face.

'Fresh meat will be welcome by the men,' replied the archer with a shrug.

Bowen turned back to face the clearing without answering.

'You two, guard the perimeter,' he said with a gesture, 'the rest come with me.' He dismounted and walked across the clearing towards the mine entrance. He grabbed the screen and pulled it away, hurling it halfway across the clearing before pausing to one side of the opening.

'Old woman,' he said, 'I know you are in there. You have someone we want. Send her and the brat out and you will be allowed to carry on with your strange life. Hesitate a moment too long and I swear you will be tried and found guilty of witchcraft this very morning and tortured until you beg for death. Do you hear me?'

When there was no reply he nodded towards two of his comrades and on the count of three, both men crouched low and ran into the gloom, throwing themselves sideways to avoid any arrows that may be fired their way. Quickly they regained their feet and looked around the gloomy interior.

A small fire still glowed in the hearth and a pot hung from an iron frame above the embers. Bowen walked slowly around the man-made cavern and pulled away the few furs that remained on the bed space.

'Gone,' he said simply.

'Do you think they hid down there?' asked his comrade, peering into the shaft that led to the abandoned mine workings.

'No, I think they knew we were coming and got out while they could.'

'They can't have gone far,' said the second man, 'the cawl is still warm within the pot.'

'I agree,' said Bowen, 'but the men are weary. Share out the soup and butcher that pig. We will rest here for a while and set out again when the horses are rested. An old hag, a child and a pregnant woman will not set a good pace. We will be upon them by midday.'

Three leagues away, two horses trotted down a muddy path, drawing a small cart behind them. Annie Apples encouraged them from the seat at the front; behind her, Gwladus and Nesta lay nestled amongst a pile of furs, necessary cushioning from the vibration of the road. Despite this, the movement was already making Gwladus feel sick and deep inside she feared the journey might bring on the birth of her child.

'I'm sorry, my lady,' called Annie over her shoulder, 'I know it is uncomfortable but it is the best I could do. The journey is far but these are a fine pair of horses and they will see us to the cathedral by tomorrow night.'

'Don't worry about me, Annie,' replied Gwladus, 'I pray to God my baby will be all right but my fears are for Nesta, her safety is paramount.'

'I understand,' shouted Annie and cracked the reins again, encouraging the horses to increase their speed.

Less than an hour had passed when Annie looked over her shoulder in alarm.

'What is it?' she shouted.

'You have to stop,' shouted Nesta again, 'Mother is unwell.'

'You heard what she said child, we have to keep going.'

'Annie is right,' groaned Gwladus from the cart, 'we have to keep going. Caradog's men could be right behind us. Hold your tongue, Nesta.'

'*Annie!*' screamed Nesta, disobeying her mother for the first time in her life. 'She is bleeding!'

Annie Apples glanced over her shoulder again before reining in the horses and alighting to the forest floor. The horses' breath billowed into the morning air and their hides shone with sweat. She walked to the back of the cart and climbed aboard, looking down at the queen amongst the furs.

'Does she speak true?' asked Annie. 'Do you bleed?'

'It matters not,' said Gwladus through gritted teeth, 'you have to keep going for Nesta's sake.'

'Do you bleed?' asked Annie again, and after a few moments, Gwladus nodded and pulled away the grey wolf fur. Annie looked down and saw the furs beneath the woman were sodden with blood.

'You should have said sooner,' said Annie, 'perchance I could have prevented this.'

'Annie, listen to me,' said Gwladus weakly, 'I fear it is too late and the child comes early. If this is so, you must leave me to my fate and get Nesta to the cathedral.'

'If I do that you will surely die, both you and the baby.'

'If that is the price I must pay to save my daughter then it is one I will gladly pay.'

'And your baby?'

'I will carry him in my arms to the kingdom of heaven. God will look over us.'

Annie sneered. 'Surely, only a male god would expect a woman to go through childbirth on her own.'

'Annie, take not the Lord's name in vain,' groaned Gwladus.

The old woman stifled a laugh but admonished the queen anyway.

'Childbirth is the domain of the great mother, my lady, and if I blaspheme before your god then I will pay the price soon enough but for now I have powders that will ease the pain. First, we need shelter. Can you walk?'

'I think so.'

'Good, then let me help you down but make haste, for there is little time. Nesta, bring as many of these furs as you can carry.'

The old woman led the way through the trees and down a bank towards a nearby stream, pushing her way through the tangled undergrowth until they found a small area beneath a giant leafy oak. Annie looked up and made a sign of gratitude upon her lips.

'What are you doing?' groaned Gwladus.

'It is a good omen,' said Annie, 'the oak represents the arms of the great mother. This is as safe a place as any.'

Gwladus was about to remonstrate about the old woman's pagan practices but a pain shot through her womb once more and she collapsed to the floor.

'Nesta, bring those furs,' called Annie as she tried to help the queen, 'and the flask of water from the cart. Hurry.'

Nesta turned and ran back as fast as she could. Within minutes she had returned but with a worried look upon her face.

'Annie,' she whispered as she handed over the flask, 'I saw riders upon the crest of the hill behind us.'

The woman thought furiously before pointing to the furs in the girl's hand.

'Place them over your mother,' she said.

Nesta did as she was told and as she tried to make her mother comfortable against the tree trunk, Annie poured a handful of white powder into the neck of the flask.

'Out of the way,' she said quietly and knelt beside the woman who was clearly starting her labour. 'Drink this,' she continued, holding the flask to the queen's mouth.

'What is it?' asked Gwladus.

'Powder ground from the bark of the willow, and some herbs from the forest. The flavour is bitter but it will ease the pain.'

Gwladus leaned forward and drank as much as she could before coughing at the terrible taste.

'Drink a bit more, my lady,' said Annie and waited patiently until the woman finally leaned back against the tree, the flask emptied.

'Good,' said Annie, 'now listen to me, both of you. My lady, you have given birth before so know what to expect. The powder will ease the pain but the baby will be along soon.' She turned to Nesta. 'Child, have you ever seen a birth before?'

'I watched a servant have a baby in the kitchen last winter.'

'Good, then you know it can be painful but fear not, for we women were born to such things. I want you to tend your mother and do whatever she asks, but more than anything else, she must try to keep her cries of pain to a minimum. If the baby is born before I return, clear its mouth and make sure it is breathing before wrapping it up warm and giving it to your mother.'

'Where are you going?' asked Gwladus.

'If we wait here and do nothing, Caradog's men will be upon us by noon. You are in no state to continue, my lady, and there is no way I can fight a group of men alone. That leaves us with one option.'

'And that is?'

'If I can lead them away, we may have a chance.'

'But what about us? If you leave us here, then we will be naught but meat for the wolves.'

'I know these valleys well, my lady, and if I can keep Caradog's men at bay until dark, I can circle back around to pick you up. We can make our escape in the dark, and by the time the dawn comes, be at the gates of the cathedral.'

'I don't know, Annie. It sounds like too great a risk.'

'There is no other way,' said Annie. 'I have to do something before they see where we have turned off the track. The baby will be along soon and if you can survive until dark then you have a chance.'

'Annie,' said Gwladus weakly, 'please don't go.'

'I have to,' said the woman, 'or we are all lost. You can do this, my lady, you are in good hands.' She glanced up at the oak tree before standing up and walking back the way they had come.

Nesta watched her go before turning to face her mother, the fear evident in her eyes.

'It will be fine,' said her mother with a smile.

'Are the powders working yet?' asked Nesta.

'Yes,' said Gwladus, but Nesta knew she was lying.

———————

Annie Apples climbed back aboard the cart and with a crack of the reins urged the horses forward. As soon as they were clear of the narrow forest track, she drew the whip from its sheath and sent the leather flying over the animal's heads.

'Come on, you mangy animals,' she shouted, 'there's a kingdom at stake here! Let's see what you've got.' Within seconds the horses were galloping as fast as they were able across the grassy meadow, pulling the cart behind them.

———————

'Look,' said one of the riders on the hill above. 'I think we have been seen.'

Bowen watched the cart careering across the meadow, obviously heading towards the distant wood line.

'I don't know where they think they are going,' grunted Bowen. 'There is no way they can escape horsemen.'

'They don't have to,' said one of the other soldiers. 'That way lies the cathedral of Saint David. If they reach that, then she will be protected by the laws of sanctuary.'

'Oh, you clever bitch,' said Bowen quietly, staring at the disappearing cart. 'Come,' he added eventually, 'they are still within our grasp.' With a kick to his horse's flanks, he sent the steed racing down the slopes of the hill towards the track across the valley, closely followed by his men.

The Forests of Dinefwr

May 23rd, AD 1081, mid-afternoon

Tom One-eye crouched in the mud, his experienced gaze checking for signs of recent activity. Nearby, Tewdwr and his men checked the mine entrance and the surrounding area, hoping they wouldn't find the bodies of the young king's family.

'Anything?' asked Tewdwr.

'They were definitely here, my lord,' said Marcus, 'the remains of a pig carcass lies near the entrance and there are traces of pig fat around the fire. Someone had a hearty meal of pork before they rode away.'

'Could that not have been my wife?'

'No, the carcass is stripped of meat and it seems several people enjoyed the bounty. No platters have been used despite there being some upon a ledge. That says to me that the slices of meat were cooked on the ends of knives or spears and as we know your lady is used to a privileged position and would have used a trencher.'

'Perhaps not,' said Tewdwr, 'but who knows what situation they were in?'

'He is right,' called Tom One-eye from the track, 'there is sign here that at least six men rode this way.'

'Do you think my family was with them?'

'I do not, for there are also older tracks of a wagon leading the same way. I reckon whoever was at this mine left in a cart and was followed later by the horsemen.'

'Are you sure?'

'Nothing is certain but I know this. The cart came in from the east and headed west. A few hours later, the mounted party came and left the same way. If they had found the queen here, then they would have surely returned the direction they came. It would make no sense to continue westward.'

'I agree,' said Marcus, 'and fear they are in terrible danger, for if these horsemen are Caradog's men, they will catch up with the cart in no time.'

'Then there is no time to waste,' said Tewdwr, mounting his horse, 'come on, and spare not the horses.'

The group galloped down the westward track, hoping against hope that they would be in time

———⁓———

'Keep going, you mangy mules,' shouted Annie Apples, cracking the whip, 'don't you give up on me now.'

The lathered horses strained at the bit, their galloping hooves throwing up clumps of mud to fly about the old woman's face. As the track sloped upward the pace slowed until eventually she reined them in at the top of the slope, knowing that to drive them any harder would see them collapse from exhaustion. A small spring flowed from the rocks a few paces away and, after taking a few mouthfuls herself, she led the horses over to drink their fill.

'Just a few leagues more,' she said comfortingly, patting their necks as they drank, 'and you can get all the rest you need.' She walked back to the crest of the hill and peered down into the valley. Down below, she could see a party of riders galloping in her wake, evidently the horsemen who were seeking the queen and her daughter. Fear was tempered with gratification for though it was now obvious they would soon be upon her, it was also clear that they had taken the bait and ridden straight past the queen's hiding place.

Annie turned and ran back to the horses, using them to manoeuvre the cart close to the edge of the cliff. She unhitched the harness and lifting the rails, eased the cart onto the slope, standing back in satisfaction as the momentum took the cart over the edge and into the valley below. Task done, she mounted one of the horses and, leading the other by its reins, led them through the rocks and down the northern slope, out of sight of the following men.

'Where are they?' shouted Bowen an hour later. 'They can't have disappeared.'

'There are no tracks,' said one of his men, 'and there hasn't been since we left the mountain.'

'Then they must still be up there,' said Bowen and without another word turned his horse to ride back up the slopes. Within ten minutes they reached the top and all the men spread out to search for tracks.

'Over here,' shouted a voice eventually and Bowen ran over to see one of his men peering down into the gorge.

'Where?'

'Down there,' said the soldier and Bowen followed his gaze to see the remains of a smashed cart lying on the rocks below.

'Can you see any bodies?'

'Not from here.'

'Then get down there and check it out. If they are there, bring the heads of the queen and the child back up here. Caradog will want proof that they are dead.'

'As you wish, my lord,' said the soldier and took three others to clamber down the steep slope while Bowen and the remaining soldier took the opportunity to water the horses from the spring. Ten minutes later the soldiers reappeared, panting for breath after the short but arduous climb.

'What news?' asked Bowen, getting up from his seat upon a rock.

'My lord, they are not there.'

'No bodies at all?'

'None, and what is more, there are no bodies of the horses. It seems the cart was pushed over the edge deliberately.'

'The clever witch,' growled Bowen. 'The old hag seems to have her wits about her and employs trickery to throw us off the trail.' He turned around and shouted to his men. 'Spread out and scour this ridge, I want to know which way they went.'

The men ran in all directions, their eyes glued to the ground as they sought any sign. Finally, a voice called out and all ran to see what the man had found.

'Hoof prints, my lord,' said the soldier, 'leading northward.'

'Why north?' asked his comrade. 'There is nothing for many leagues.'

'It matters not,' replied Bowen. 'They have gained valuable time and will probably circle westward again as soon as possible.'

'Perhaps it would be prudent to ride westward with all haste and set a trap.'

'No, they employ a level of deviousness to be admired and could sneak in to the cathedral via a different route while we wait upon the road. I would rather get this done as soon as possible and have had enough of the chase. Come, let us bring this farce to a close.'

Within moments they were riding northward, following the trail of Annie Apples and the horses.

Despite the destrier beneath him, Walters struggled to keep up with the rest of Tewdwr's party. The thoroughbred sensed his nervousness and struggled to comprehend what was wanted, resulting in them falling behind the men riding in pursuit of Bowen, but when the horse stumbled and hurt his leg, Walters knew he could continue no further.

'My lord,' he shouted, 'you have to continue without me, I fear my ride is lame.'

Tewdwr turned his horse and rode back.

'What's the problem?'

'The horse stumbled and I fear he is injured.'

Tewdwr glance down at the animal, clearly resting his right foreleg.

'It doesn't look broken,' said Tewdwr, 'but it's obvious you will slow us down. I suggest you wait here and we will pick you up on our return. I would suggest losing the horse. A servant with a destrier is going to draw attention and you will be labelled a thief. Now, I must be gone, for every moment we delay is a moment more my family is at risk.'

'I understand, my lord, and will await your return.'

Tewdwr turned and rode after his comrades while Walters dismounted and led the injured horse off the path, seeking a sheltered spot amongst the trees. Whatever happened next, he knew he was in for a long wait.

Caradog's men waited for the scout to report his findings, the mountain now far behind them. Eventually, after scouring the area, he came back and approached Bowen, a concerned look upon his face.

'Well,' asked Bowen, 'which way did they go?'

'I'm not sure, my lord,' said the scout.

'Not sure?' shouted Bowen, his face red with anger. 'Have you found their trail or not?'

'I have, but something is wrong.'

Bowen leaned down from his horse and spoke quietly, the tone making it clear he was growing frustrated.

'You listen to me,' he said menacingly, 'you are paid to follow our quarry, not waste my time. Now, do you know where they have gone, yes or no?'

'The trail leads in two directions,' said the scout nervously, 'one north and one west, as if they split up to make the pursuit harder.'

'In that case, we will pursue both,' said Bowen.

'No,' said the scout, 'for I believe it is yet another ploy.'

'You mean one is a false trail?'

'My lord, I believe both are false.'

Bowen looked up at the skies in exasperation.

'In the name of God,' he shouted, 'why can I not get a straight answer to a straight question?' He looked back down and drew his sword, resting the tip on the man's throat. 'I have had enough of your double-meaning words. Tell me quickly where they have gone or else I swear I will leave you dying here in the mud.'

'My lord, the signs that lead north are clearly from an unladen mount which, I believe, has been set free. I would wager that if we go that way we would soon find the animal grazing in some pasture not far from here.'

'Then our direction is west.'

'No, for although that horse is laden it is not with three people. Whoever rides westward does so alone. I think we have been tricked and two of the fugitives lay hidden far behind us.'

'Are you sure?'

'It is the only possible answer, somewhere on the pursuit, we have passed them by.'

Bowen's face screwed up in anger.

'By the Devil's teeth!' he shouted. 'These women mock me with their trickery and I swear I will have their hides stripped from their backs.' He turned to face the scout. 'Do you know which one rides west and which have hidden away?'

'Alas no, but I suspect the hag leads us away from the prize.'

'Perhaps not,' said another voice and Bowen turned to face one of the other men.

'Speak your mind, Brynley, for this man is proving to be of little use.'

'My lord, the queen knows that both she and her daughter are at risk of death. In her shoes, would you not split the group so that at least one had a chance to continue the lineage?'

'A fair view,' said Bowen, 'but which one has gone where?'

'I would imagine the girl hides away under the custody of the hag while the queen leads us away from them, knowing that even if we catch her, her daughter would be many leagues away in a place of safety.'

'I agree,' said Bowen eventually, 'so this is what we will do. Brynley, you and one other will go back and seek the child and the hag. I will continue in pursuit of Gwladus for she has raised my ire and I will have my retribution.'

'And if we find them, what fate would you have me bestow?'

'Kill the hag without hesitation, but with regard to the girl, I want her to suffer first. Do what you will to her for I care not, but when you have finished, remove her head so I can prove her death to Caradog. Lucas, you will ride with Brynley, the rest of you come with me.'

The group split into two and, as one started retracing their journey back towards Dinefwr, the other raced westward, determined to catch whomever it was leading them a merry dance.

The Forests of Dinefwr

May 23rd, AD 1081, early evening

Walters was dozing in a warm patch of sun when he heard the approaching riders. Carefully he stood up and walked to the forest edge, unsure whether they were friend or foe, but as they got closer, he could see they were not of Tewdwr's party. Luckily, the two riders were too busy looking for tracks on the path to have noticed him but they were rapidly approaching his position.

The cook realised he was in trouble, for if these were Caradog's men, his tracks would soon be seen and they would find him in no time. Desperately he looked around but seeing no route for escape ran back to the clearing where he had left his horse. Again he looked around for an escape route but seeing none looked the only other direction possible. Upward.

Out on the track, Brynley stopped his horse.

'Wait,' he said 'it looks like someone rode off the path here not long ago.'

Lucas concurred and looked into the trees.

'It could be a trap?'

'I think not, those riders we saw earlier were obviously men of Tewdwr and did not know we were riding this way.'

'If they were men of Tewdwr,' said Lucas, 'then Bowen could face a fight sooner than he thinks.'

'Fear not, for I have never seen Bowen bested in any fight and besides, our task is still before us. Caradog wants the woman and the girl, and if we can return one, then who knows what purse he may bestow?'

The two men dismounted and walked into the trees, their blades drawn. Within moments they came across the destrier and looked around nervously, seeking the owner of such a magnificent beast.

'There's nobody here,' said Brynley, 'perhaps the rider has fallen and the horse has wandered here alone.'

'I think not,' said Lucas, 'it bears the colours of Caradog and we are too far from Dinefwr for it to come this far. The owner has to be here somewhere.'

They looked around for several minutes but found nothing.

'It makes no sense,' said Brynley, 'this is a strange situation, why would a man leave his horse unattended?'

'I know not,' replied his comrade, 'but we waste time. I suggest we continue our quest and seek Tewdwr's brat. She must be somewhere in this valley.'

'And the horse?'

'It seems lame but our pace is slow. We will take it with us, for it will command a pretty price back at the castle.'

'So be it,' said Brynley, and taking the destrier's reins he led it slowly from the trees.

———

Deep in the thick foliage of a nearby holly tree, Walters held his breath, terrified he would be discovered. The dense leaves meant he was hidden from prying eyes yet he was close enough to clearly hear the conversation and, after they had left, he climbed down and sat on a nearby log, his mind spinning at the implications. If what he had heard was correct, those two men were seeking Tewdwr's daughter and that could mean only one thing: she had hidden somewhere in the valley while fleeing with her mother and these men had backtracked to find her. Yet Tewdwr and his men were leagues away, so there was no way of getting any help.

Walters pushed through the bushes and peered at the backs of the men, riding slowly back towards Dinefwr, their eyes glued to the floor. He knew that as a mere cook to even try to fight them invited certain death, but he also realised the queen and her daughter were in desperate trouble and he had to do something. With no real plan in mind, he started to follow the riders, albeit concealed just within the forest edge, hoping that something would come to him. Somehow he had to get a message to Tewdwr: the queen's life depended on it.

Ten leagues away, Peterson burst into the main hall of Dinefwr Castle, still breathless after his ride from the village. All around him heads turned to watch him enter and see the hall was already full of Caradog's best men standing in groups, each as surprised as he at the sudden summons to attend the Gwent king.

'Simon Wellman,' he said, seeing a comrade close by, 'are you aware of why we were summoned?'

'Alas no,' said Simon, 'though as every officer and sergeant-at-arms seems to be here, I would imagine it affects the whole command. It is strange that you are not aware of events, Peterson, for you have the ear of the king himself. I thought you would be involved in any decision-making of note.'

'It would seem that these days his attention is held by men from distant places.'

Both men looked towards the far end of the hall and saw the king enter, clad in a gleaming chainmail hauberk secured with a leather belt holding his sword. Accompanying him were the two messengers Peterson had seen with the king a few days earlier.

Using a chair as a step, Caradog climbed onto a table and held up his hand for silence. The noise died away and Caradog looked around the room slowly.

'Men of Gwent,' he said, 'you have always followed me loyally, even through the hard years when there was often not much meat upon the tables. Together we have conquered lean times and fat kings. As a united army, we swept all before us including the old king of Deheubarth and today we drink his successor's wine. Despite this, the riches that you would expect to see from such victories are in short supply and yet still you follow my lead. Surely no king can ask for more.'

Some of the men cheered in response but soon quietened as Caradog paced along the tabletop. The colours on his tabard were faded from age and the sleeves of his chainmail hauberk showed glimpses of rust, a testament to the use it had over the years. Caradog was not one for finery on campaign, preferring instead the armour he had worn for many years, albeit worn and bloodstained.

'As you know,' he continued, 'I have promised all those who follow my colours that the day will soon come when your loyalty is repaid and you become rich men.' He stopped walking and looked around. 'Well, that day has arrived, for I can tell you that we are about to embark upon a campaign that will see each man here retire with a heavy purse within a year.'

This time there were more cheers and Caradog waited until they died away before continuing.

'Today,' said Caradog, 'I have sent despatches northward agreeing a treaty with two other kings. In that document, I have committed to join with the forces of King Trahern and King Meilyr, not only to build an army capable of withstanding any potential aggressor against our proud nation but also to once again bring the peace to Wales that has long been absent. Together we will build a country to be proud of and bring settlement to the masses, but to do this we need to clear away the weak and the stupid. Those who hide like frightened sheep yet expect to enjoy the benefits of kingship need to be drawn from their hiding places and treated as the cowards they are. Once they are wiped from history, they will be replaced with men who have earned such rewards by battle, not by chance of birth but men like those who stand before me now.'

As voices raised in support, Caradog leaned down to accept a jug of ale, and as he waited for the noise to subside he drank deeply before wiping the suds from his mouth with the back of his hand and throwing the jug against the wall.

'Even as we speak,' he continued, 'there are so-called lords throughout this land who are no better than leeches, feeding off our people while giving nothing back except lethargy and weakness. Why is it that nobles with manors and chests of gold sleep safe in their beds, while warriors such as you fight tooth and nail to make a living? I'll tell you why: because we have allowed it to happen. For too long men such as I have looked inward to our own kingdoms, wrongly believing it is no business of ours what happens to the west or north, but we were wrong, it *is* our business, for with weakened men at our backs, how can we ever hope to face William as equals?

'Well, no more! This travesty ends today, for as soon as our business here is done, our horses will be harnessed and our swords once again honed to sharpness. Fill your water skins and look to your mounts, for soon we will set out to join with the other two kings putting Wales back where she belongs: a sovereign country equal to England and Ireland.'

The cheering started again, and Caradog reached over to retrieve a spear from a rack upon the wall. He turned around, his face red, his blood raised and everyone could see the passion in his eyes.

'*Before this year is out*,' he roared above the noise, 'our combined forces will sweep through Wales, removing the unworthy and exposing them as the cowards they are. Their lands will be forfeit to the new alliance and any bounty taken from their manors, shared out between the men standing before me now.' He held the spear out before him and over the heads of his men like a staff. 'Follow me with fire in your heart and I swear that by the time this is over every man under this roof will be rich. *What say you?*'

This time the whole room erupted into an excited frenzy and the noise went on endlessly as each man banged their fists onto tables in support. Caradog raised his hand one more time and once more the room fell silent.

'I will take that as a yes,' he said, 'so I charge you to now muster your men and prepare them for campaign. Not to capture a little castle as now lies beneath our feet but for a greater campaign for glory, riches and honour. Look to your weapons, men of Gwent, for this day we go to war.'

As the room broke into cheers for the last time, Caradog raised his spear to shoulder height and launched it across the room to thud into a painting of Tewdwr on the far wall. As the men roared their appreciation, the king climbed down and left the great hall, closely followed by the two strangers from the north.

'Well,' said Simon, his voice loud against the noise, 'that was unexpected. It would seem our path leads northward to untold wealth.'

'It may lead northward, Simon,' said Peterson, 'but I suspect the path will not be as smooth as our king believes.'

'What makes you say that?'

'I'm not sure but I hope his mind is not clouded with the promises of those men at his side.'

'But he is right: there are too many kings in Wales and it would be better ruled if there were fewer heads at the top table.'

'Perhaps so, but those men he intends to depose may have a say in such matters.'

'Like he said, they are nothing but leeches and cowards.'

'Simon, no man reaches the position of lordship through weakness. No, I think that before this thing is done, there will be more blood spilled than Caradog leads us to believe.'

'Time will tell,' said Simon.

'Aye, that it will. Come, there is much to do.'

Nesta mopped her mother's head with a damp rag, torn from the hem of her dress. The last few days had been a shock for the girl and no longer were her thoughts filled with play and the destiny of princesses. The horror of real life had descended upon her like a heavy cloak, and though her thoughts were often clouded with fear her mother's plight forced her to focus on the task in hand. Her mother was in pain and as Annie Apples had been long gone, the only person available to help was Nesta. She was afraid of the impending birth but she had to be strong, for her mother's sake.

The pains were coming quicker now and Gwladus knew her time was getting close.

'Nesta,' she said, 'find me a stick the size of a large spoon.'

'Why?' asked Nesta.

'Just in case there are any of Caradog's men near. When the baby comes I may not be able to control my cries but if I bite upon a stick, as do the soldiers when having their wounds treated, then perhaps they may not hear.'

'Annie will be back by then,' said Nesta, nervously, but despite her words doubt clouded her mind and she knew there was always a chance that Annie wouldn't return. 'When she does,' she continued, 'as soon as the baby is born we can go to the cathedral where I will take care of you until Dada returns.'

'Of course she will,' said Gwladus, a strained smile upon her lips, 'but nevertheless, we must prepare the best we can.'

Nesta found a stick and peeled away the bark.

'Nesta,' said Gwladus, 'listen to me. When the baby comes, it will need to be cleaned and wrapped up warm. If I pass out, worry not, just concentrate on the baby.'

'Yes, Mother,' replied Nesta.

'When the fear is strongest in your mind, don't forget you are of royal blood, the daughter of a king, and as such are able to take on great burdens such as these. You are young but I have often seen a hint of steeliness within you, a strength I want you to call upon now. God has seen fit to test you with a challenge, Nesta, one that I know you can meet, for soon there will be a little baby that needs your help. I will be too weak to do much, so whether it be a boy or a girl, they will need the strength of their big sister to help them survive. Whatever happens, your focus must be on the safety of the baby and nothing else, do you understand?'

Nesta nodded, overwhelmed at the burden of responsibility.

'I know it is a great thing I ask, Nesta, but you are a clever girl and today I need you to become the woman I know you can be. You must be brave and no matter how scared you may be, remember you are a princess of Deheubarth and find the strength within. The baby will need you, Nesta; *I* need you.'

'I promise I will be brave, Mother,' said Nesta, 'and do all I can.'

'Good, then there is one more thing to discuss. If I should die, take the baby and follow the road back towards Dinefwr as quickly as possible. Find someone to offer you shelter until this thing is over.'

'You are not going to die,' said Nesta, fear overwhelming her.

'Perhaps not, my love, but we must be prepared. Follow the road but stay inside the treeline. As soon as you see a farmhouse, head there with all haste and tell our tale to the lady of the house.'

'What if they are bad people?' Nesta asked, her voice tight.

'There are few allegiances to Caradog in these lands, my sweet, and any woman worth her salt will take care of a child and a baby. Ask them to give you sanctuary until times are more peaceful, and once things quieten down, ask them to send word to my brother. He will arrange to collect you both and see you safe unto adulthood.'

'What if the farm people want paying?'

'Promise them that my brother will pay whatever price they want, give them my word as a queen.'

'If all this comes to pass, what then?'

Gwladus smiled.

'Just settle down in Ireland with your uncle and live your life the best way you can. When the time is right, you will meet a wonderful man and raise a family. Do you understand?'

'I do, Mother,' said Nesta, 'but it won't be necessary; you are not going to die, I won't allow it.'

'Nesta, our fate is in God's hands, and should he decide it is my time, then we should embrace it. Worry not, for I am ready but I fear for you and the baby. As long as I know you two are safe then I will be at rest.'

Nesta was about to answer when the sound of breaking branches reached the clearing.

'What's that?' asked Nesta.

'Nesta, come here,' said Gwladus nervously pushing herself back against the trees.

'I think it's Annie,' said Nesta, 'she must have found help.'

Gwladus reached out and pulled her daughter to her side, holding her closely as she stared into the undergrowth.

'I think not,' she said, her voice filled with fear, 'the footfall is too heavy. Keep quiet and perhaps they will pass us by.'

Nesta held her mother tightly, hoping against hope that, who-ever the unseen people were, they would pass them by, but it wasn't to be. Within moments, the bushes parted and two men stepped into the clearing.

'Well, what do we have here,' said one with a sneer, 'it looks like we've found ourselves a runaway queen and her snot-nosed brat!'

Annie Apples's horse finally ran out of stamina, and though it stumbled onward, she knew it was done. She could run no further.

For a while she just sat astride the horse, realisation dawning that she would fail in her task. Without a mount, there was no way she could continue any distance and soon she would be captured by her pursuers. Her heart was heavy, for though she had known the queen and her daughter only briefly, the thought of them and the unborn baby being killed was almost too much to bear.

Her options were few, and she soon realised she could either just wait and meet her pursuers on the path or she could run and hide, not for her own safety, but to add precious moments to her pursuit, moments that could mean the difference between life and death for those she had left behind.

Decision made, she climbed down from the horse's back, and pulled away the harness, allowing the horse to walk away to a nearby stream. She looked around for a suitable hiding place, settling for a rocky slope high above. Using the last of her strength, she scrambled up the slope and hid amongst the boulders, exhausted but satisfied she had given the queen every chance to survive. She hadn't hidden long when the sound of horses reached her ears and she peered down to see four riders, circling her tired horse.

———⌣———

'This is it,' said the scout down on the path, 'as far as she has got.' He looked up and pointed towards the escarpment. 'She's up there.'

'There's no way she could have crested that ridge,' said Bowen, 'so she must be hiding amongst the rocks.' He took a deep breath and called out, his voice echoing around the valley. 'Gwladus Tewdwr,' he cried, 'I know you can hear me; you may as well come out, for your race is run. You have led us a merry chase, it has to be said, but the time for such things is over. Come out and surrender yourself to me in Caradog's name. I promise you will come to no harm but if you make me come up there to get you, then you will die amongst these rocks.'

When he received no response he called out again.

'Last chance, queen. I will count to ten then the offer will be withdrawn. One . . . two . . . three . . .'

When he reached ten, Bowen took a deep breath and dismounted. Without taking his eyes off the high ground he undid his sword belt and hung it over his saddle.

'So be it, woman,' he shouted, when he was ready, 'the die is cast.' Drawing his knife he walked over to the rocky slope and started to climb.

Annie held her breath behind the boulder where she had hidden. She knew her discovery was only moments away and that the likelihood was that she would soon lay dead amongst the rocks. Despite the shock of the realisation, her mind was at ease. Death held no great fear for Annie, for in her eyes it was just the nature of things and just brought her soul nearer to the great mother. She closed her eyes and chanted an incarnation to prepare her soul for the afterlife, but moments later jumped as a gruff voice interrupted her self-induced calm.

'Who are you?' snapped Bowen, his eyes narrowing in confusion.

'Not the one you seek,' said Annie Apples. 'By now, she is probably halfway to Ireland.'

Bowen's heart raced as he realised he had been duped and this was actually the woman who had helped the queen escape.

'You listen to me, witch,' said Bowen, pointing at her with his blade, 'I don't know what games you play but let me promise you this. I have had enough of riding across Deheubarth on this foolish quest, and whether it is the queen's blood or yours upon it, I swear my blade's shine will be dulled this day. Now, I will ask you just once and if you answer truthfully I will spare you your life. If not, you will suffer the consequences.'

'Do what you will, soldier. You will hear no more from me this day but know this: wherever lays your path, I forgive you and will see you again in the afterlife.'

With a terrifying roar, Bowen discarded his knife and launched himself forward, knocking Annie back against the rock, her skull cracking with a sickening thud. Despite the pain, she remained conscious and screamed as Bowen dug his thumbs deep into her eyes.

Bowen grimaced and pushed his thumbs deeper, his face splattered with blood, as his grip tightened.

'I told you, hag,' he gasped, as he increased the pressure, 'I have had enough of your silly games.' With an almighty effort, he forced his thumbs as far back as he could to break through the eye sockets and into her brain, laughing hysterically as the woman writhed in agony. Bowen tightened his grip on her head and brought it up towards him before slamming it back onto the rock over and over again until it exploded in a bloody mess of bone and brain. Even then his anger knew no bounds and picking up his knife, he plunged it into the dead woman's heart, taking out his frustration on her corpse.

Finally, his temper eased and he sat back against a rock, staring at the mess before him. He had little recollection of the last few moments, for at such times a haze came upon him and he lost all control. It wasn't the first time he had raised the blood of the berserker within him and he knew it wouldn't be the last. Eventually his heartbeat slowed and he came back to reality. This was the end of the road as far as he and his men were concerned but hopefully the two men that had retraced their steps had been luckier in their quest.

Slowly he got to his feet, staring down at the old woman's body. There was no pity, no regret, only anger that she had died without revealing the location of the queen or the daughter. Life was cheap in Wales and the hag had paid the price. As he turned to return to his comrades he saw his knife, still lying in a pool of the woman's rapidly congealing blood. He bent down to retrieve the blade and in the process saved his own life.

For a few seconds, Bowen stared uncomprehendingly at the steel-tipped arrow that ricocheted off the rocks around him but he hadn't lived through so many battles without being able to react instinctively to danger. He ducked between two rocks before crawling forward to find a vantage point. For a few moments he could see nothing but then a movement in the treeline above revealed the position of the archer. Bowen cursed, realising that the clear ground between them meant he could never reach his attacker without being brought down by one of the arrows.

Frantically he looked around, desperate for an escape route. His comrades were down at the base of the hill, as was his sword, but mostly he needed the strength that numbers brought.

He crawled further forward, intending to call his fellows to circle around the back of the attacker and take him by surprise, but when he finally had a clear view of the path below, his blood ran cold. The very men he was relying on to get him out of his predicament were now laying in the mud, slaughtered by the riders who had taken them by surprise. Bowen realised that in the height of his rage, he hadn't heard the noise from the battle below. He was alone against these men.

His situation was dire. He was alone amongst the rocks, in enemy territory and surrounded by men intent on his death. On top of that, he was armed only with his knife. Desperately he racked his mind for a solution, knowing there was no way he could fight his way out. His mind cleared slowly and a plan emerged. It was a long shot but just may save his life.

Taking off his helmet, he held it high and waved it back and fore, attracting the attention of the men below and the archer above.

'*Hold your fire*,' he called, 'I would have words.'

For a few seconds there was silence but then a voice echoed up the hill.

'Say your piece, Bowen, and quick about it.'

'How do you know my name?' he replied, feeling at a disadvantage.

'One of your fellows kindly obliged upon pain of death.'

'Does he still live?'

'For now, though mortally wounded. Now say what it is you have to say.'

'Am I right in saying you are men of Tewdwr?'

'You are.'

'And do you seek the whereabouts of the queen?'

'We do, and if you have harmed a single hair upon her head then your death will last a hundred days.'

Bowen thought furiously. They obviously still thought the queen was with him, but that was bad news. Unless he could prove otherwise, they would stop at nothing until she was recovered, alive or dead.

'Listen to me,' he shouted, 'the lady Gwladus is not up here.'

'*Liar*,' roared the soldier, 'we have followed you from Dinefwr and know you trailed her intent on harm.'

'You are right,' called Bowen, 'but we were tricked by the wiles of an old woman. I too thought Gwladus was up here but was wrong. If you disbelieve me, send up an unarmed man to check but I swear before God I tell the truth.'

For a few minutes there was silence but eventually the soldier shouted again.

'Even if you speak true, Bowen, I am still of a mind to prise you from your hiding place and remove your head from your neck.'

'You could do that,' shouted Bowen, 'but you would be wasting time, and while you gloat over my body, my men could be raping the queen and her daughter.'

'*Where is she?*' roared the soldier. 'What have you done with her?'

'I have done nothing but I think I know where she is.'

'Then tell me, Bowen or die here.'

'I will tell you,' replied Bowen, 'but first you must give me your word before God you will call off your men, including the archer, and let me ride away a free man.'

'Never!'

'If you don't, those you seek will be dead before the sun sets.'

'How do I know you speak the truth?'

'You don't, but my name is Bowen of Gwent and I ride with Caradog. If I speak false then you can seek me out and challenge me under the terms of chivalry. Make up your mind, stranger, for every moment you waste, my men get closer to the queen.'

Again there was silence but eventually the voice echoed up the slopes again.

'So be it,' he shouted. 'My men will withdraw and leave you a horse.'

'And the archer?' asked Bowen.

'He will come with me.'

As if to underline the promise, up above Bowen could see the bowman already making his way down a track towards the waiting men.

'So, where is she, Bowen? Where is my wife?'

Bowen gasped, realising he was negotiating with King Tewdwr himself. For a few seconds he considered withholding the information and paying the ultimate price out of loyalty to Caradog but soon realised that even if the queen died this day Tewdwr would still be at large. Placing a greater price on his own life than that of the queen, he decided to honour the agreement.

'Do I have your word?'

'You do.'

'Then I will tell you what I know. She hides away somewhere in the last valley you passed through. Don't ask where because I don't know but what I do know is that two of my men seek her as we speak.'

'If that is the case,' called the archer from the path, 'who is the woman you just killed?'

'The old hag who helped her escape the clutches of Caradog. Yes, she is dead, but waste no tears upon her, such is the way of things when kings collide.'

There was a pause. 'Bowen of Gwent,' Tewdwr said, 'I will take you at your word but know this. If I find you have lied to me, then not only will I seek you out but when this is over I will wipe your seed from this earth. Every man, child or kinsman who ever called you friend or family will die a horrible death, even if it takes me and my offspring a hundred years, do you understand?'

'Aye, I do,' shouted Bowen, 'but it worries me not, for I speak true.'

Bowen sat back against the rock in relief as the men galloped away. He was going to live. For a while he recovered his breath as his heart slowed. It was the closest he had come to death for a long while and he knew fate had been heavily on his side. Despite his joy at being still alive, he knew he had to move and move quickly. The fate of Gwladus was probably out of his hands but at the very least he needed to let Caradog know. Quickly he descended from the hill and, after checking his fallen comrades, turned to run back towards Dinefwr.

'Who are you?' gasped Gwladus, staring at the two men who had appeared in the thicket.

'Your worst nightmare,' said Brynley with a sneer.

'Listen to me,' said Gwladus, realising they were in mortal danger, 'if you are from Caradog then I beseech thee to show mercy, if not to me, at least to my daughter.'

'Ah yes,' said Lucas, 'the pretty lady Nesta.' He looked down at the girl who pushed herself in front of her mother in a brave attempt to defend her. 'You and I are going to be real close friends very soon, little girl, very . . . close . . . friends.'

'No,' moaned Gwladus, 'please, not even Caradog would condone that; do what you will to me but leave my daughter alone.'

'You?' Lucas laughed. 'You jest with me, woman. You are about as appealing as a fat cow and if I'm not mistaken you are about to be split apart by that brat you carry within you. No, me and the very pretty princess Nesta are about to have some fun and there is nothing you can do about it.' He undid his sword belt and stepped forward towards the two women.

'*No!*' cried Gwladus, holding her daughter tightly. 'In the name of God, don't do this.'

'Mother, what does he mean?' cried Nesta. 'What is he going to do?'

'You are about to find out, little girl,' sneered Lucas and grabbed Nesta's hair, before dragging her screaming into the trees.

'*Nooo!*' screamed Gwladus and tried to get up but fell back to the floor as another contraction wracked her body.

'Well, well,' said Brynley, sitting back on his haunches, 'this will be interesting. I've never seen a baby born before, though to be fair, it will be the shortest life any child has ever had.' To emphasise his point, he drew his knife and stuck it into the ground before him.

'Hurry up back there,' he called over his shoulder, 'for when you are done, I will take your place.'

Tewdwr and his men pushed their horses to the limit, the animals galloping as fast as they could along the path back into the valley.

'My lord!' shouted Marcus over the sound of the galloping horses. 'We have to stop.'

Tewdwr reined in his horse and caught his breath. He stared resolutely forward as if avoiding the gaze of his second, his barely disguised look of fear gazing through the tears and sweat upon his face. Long strands of spittle hung from his horse's mouth and the beast's flanks heaved with the strain of the gallop.

'My lord,' said Marcus again, 'we have to slow down.'

'We can waste no time, Marcus, we have no idea where they may be. We could spend days upon this track and not find them.'

'I share your fears, my lord, and if I thought we were doing good then I would push my steed until it fell from a burst heart, but I fear at this pace we will miss any sign where the riders turned off the track.'

Tewdwr glanced over at his friend, realising he talked sense. He nodded in agreement and turned to his men.

'A few moment's rest,' he said, 'see to the horses but be prepared to move.'

The soldiers retrieved their water skins and drank deeply before watering the horses. While they were doing so, Tom One-eye walked further up the path examining the tracks, but soon dropped to his knees as something caught his eye.

'My lord,' he shouted, 'come quickly.'

Tewdwr handed the reins of his horse to Marcus and ran to where Tom One-eye was crouched in the mud.

'What have you found?' asked Tewdwr.

Tom pointed down into the mud. On an undisturbed part of the track, someone had piled a small pyramid of stones next to an arrow made from twigs pointing back towards Dinefwr.

'Someone is leaving signs to be followed,' said Tom, 'and this has been done recently.'

'How do you know?'

'The sticks forming the arrow are freshly broken and still seep sap.'

'But who would leave such a sign?'

'There can be only one man,' said Tom, 'they have been left by the cook and he means us to follow them.'

'How do you know?'

'Whoever left the sign is on foot and wears the boots of a poor man.'

'Walters has a horse.'

'Yes, but it was lame, remember? Perhaps he had to leave it behind in a hurry.'

'It could be a trap,' said Marcus joining them.

'If it is, we will soon find out,' said Tewdwr. He turned to his men. 'Mount up, we ride immediately.'

The riders climbed aboard their horses and joined Tewdwr on the path.

'We can still move fast,' said Tewdwr, 'but now we have many eyes capable of recognising the signs.' He pointed down to the arrow upon the ground. 'Every one of you, look for similar marks and call out as they are found. If God is with us, we may still be in time.'

'Stop your struggling,' snarled Lucas with a grimace, and cried out as Nesta bit into his hand. 'Why you little devil,' he shouted and with the back of his hand hit her hard across the face, sending her sprawling into the mud.

Nesta was stunned, and sobbed as she lay bleeding on the ground.

'That's more like it,' sneered Lucas, 'now be still, because this is going to hurt, it's going to hurt a lot.' He knelt before her and pinned her down on the ground while unhitching his leggings.

'Please,' whimpered Nesta, as he fumbled with her dress, 'please let me go.'

'Shut your stinking mouth,' said Lucas, 'I have been anticipating this all day. Now lift up your dress before I slap you again.'

'*No!*' shouted Nesta, '*I won't!*' but cringed as she saw the anger rise on her attacker's face.

'Why, you little bitch,' shouted Lucas and raised his fist to strike her again, but before he could swing the punch his head flew forward accompanied with a sickening thud, and Nesta was splattered with blood.

The girl screamed and struggled out from beneath her attacker's motionless body before looking up to see a familiar face looking down at her. The shocked man stared at the large bloodstained rock in his hands before throwing it aside and gazing at the girl in silence.

Nesta pushed herself back until she rested against a tree.

'I know you,' she said, her voice breaking, 'I've seen you in the castle.'

'My name is Walters,' said the cook nervously. 'Where's your mother?'

'Back in the woods,' said Nesta. 'There's another man with her and I think he's going to hurt her.'

Walters looked around nervously before getting down on his knees.

'Nesta, you have to listen to me,' he said, 'I took this man by surprise but I am no warrior and there is no way I can fight that other man. Your father is close by but there is no guarantee he will be here in time. I have to get you to safety before it is too late.'

'No,' said Nesta, 'we have to help my mother.'

'*Princess*,' hissed Walters looking around again, 'if we stay here we will all die, including your mother. I'm sorry but once I have hidden you away perhaps I can return and see what I can do. We must leave immediately.'

'But . . .'

'*Princess*,' said Walters again, 'I am doing this for your family name. You must survive, for if your mother and father are killed, one day you will bear the new king of Deheubarth. Now come quickly before it is too late.'

Nesta stared at the cook in confusion. The sight of her attacker's head being smashed in had sickened her to her stomach and her heart raced with fear. Despite her mother's words, she yearned to run from this place as fast as she could, to leave the horror and the fear far behind her. She knew the cook made sense, for if they all died then there was no lineage, but her mother's reminder of the burden on her shoulders still echoed through her mind. She was a princess of Deheubarth and as such needed to act like one.

'Master Walters,' she said eventually, her voice shaking with fear, 'I know you only think of my safety but I will not leave without my mother. She is about to give birth and it is our duty do everything we can to ensure the baby's safety. Now, either you will help me or I will go back myself.'

Walters stared at the girl with exasperation. Though she was only a child, her manner was regal and he had difficulty meeting her cold, steely gaze.

'Lady Nesta,' he started, but before he could continue Brynley burst out of the bushes and smashed the cook across the face with his shield. Walters flew backwards, his nose split wide open and his mouth pouring with blood where he had lost several teeth.

'What's going on?' roared Brynley, throwing aside his shield. 'Where's Lucas?'

His eyes fell on his dead comrade, seeing his caved-in skull, and for a second he stared silently at his fallen comrade before turning with murder in his eyes.

'*You little shits!*' he shouted and drew his sword before lunging towards Nesta, swinging his weapon at her head. The girl screamed and ducked behind a tree, her attacker's blade missing her by the smallest of margins before cutting into the tree trunk.

'Walters!' screamed Nesta. 'Help me!'

The cook struggled to his feet, his smashed face a sea of blood, but as he lurched towards the attacker, Brynley turned and punched him again, sending him sprawling in the mud. This time there was no getting up but realising the injured man might still be a threat Brynley dislodged his sword from the tree trunk and strode over to stand over the semi-conscious cook.

'I don't know who you are, stranger,' he snarled, 'but you should have minded your own business.' With both hands around the handle of his sword he raised it up, ready to drive the blade down into Walters' heart. But before he could carry out the final thrust, his body lurched as his comrade's sword burst out of his chest.

Brynley staggered a few paces with the impact but slowly turned to see what attacker had taken him by surprise.

'*You?*' he gasped in disbelief. 'I should have killed you while I had the chance.' He fell to his knees into the mud and as his life ebbed away his last thought was one of shame, that he, a seasoned warrior of Caradog and bettered by no man on the field of battle, had finally been killed by a mere girl.

Nesta stared at Brynley as he died at her feet. The sword had been heavy and it had taken all her strength but the deed was done, she had killed him.

'*Nesta!*' gasped Gwladus, from behind her. 'Help me.'

The girl spun around and saw her mother leaning against a tree.

'Mother,' she cried, and ran over to help her mother to the ground.

'Nesta,' whispered Gwladus, 'are you all right?'

Nesta yearned to tell her mother the horror she had just experienced, to feel herself being pulled in to her mother's comforting embrace. More than anything she wanted to be told everything was going to be all right but she knew that wasn't to be; too much had happened and she had passed a turning point in her life. Gone was the young girl obsessed with pretty things and the trappings of royalty and in her place stood a young woman of responsibility, one with a task still to perform.

'I am fine, Mother,' she replied, 'worry not, for we are safe.'

'But the blood on your face?'

'It is not mine. Lie still, I will get the furs.'

Moments later she returned and wrapped the furs around her mother but it was obvious her time was close.

'I'll go and get help,' said Nesta. 'Father isn't far away, the man from the castle said so.'

'No,' gasped Gwladus, 'you have to stay here with me, the baby is coming!'

———

'Over here,' shouted One-eye and waited as the men caught up with him on the path. For two leagues they had found more arrows made from twigs, but this one was different. It pointed southward, off the path.

'This way,' shouted Tewdwr, and he ran through the bushes, drawing his sword. 'They can't be far.' Within moments, he and his men burst into a clearing and stopped in astonishment at the sight before them.

On the ground lay two dead men, one with a smashed skull and another with a sword sticking out of his back. A third man sat back against a tree, his face an unrecognisable mess, while Gwladus lay still upon the ground, covered with animal furs and exhausted from the trials of the past few hours.

A movement caught Tewdwr's eye and he turned to see his daughter walking slowly from her hiding place within the bushes. Tewdwr dropped to his knees as Nesta approached, a small bundle cradled in her hands.

'I knew you would come, Dada,' she said quietly, 'I knew you wouldn't leave us here alone.'

Tewdwr held out his arms and Nesta handed over the bundle. Gently he opened the wraps and stared down, gasping as he saw the sleeping face of a newborn baby.

'I did the best I could, Dada,' said Nesta, 'I did what Mother said.'

'You have done well, sweet child,' said Tewdwr and cradling the baby in one arm held out his other arm to embrace his daughter.

'No,' said Nesta taking a step backwards, 'don't touch me.'

'Nesta,' said Tewdwr, 'what's the matter?'

'I am evil, Dada,' she said as the tears started to flow, 'and am surely cursed by the Devil. You shouldn't touch me, lest you are poisoned by my spirit.'

Tewdwr stared in dismay as his daughter turned to run into the trees. Before he could move, Marcus came over and took the baby from him.

'My lord,' said Marcus quietly, 'your wife seems fine and is sleeping soundly. Go after your daughter.'

Tewdwr ran after Nesta, calling her name as he ran through the trees. Within moments he found her on the edge of a crag, staring down into the void below.

'Nesta,' he gasped, coming to a halt, 'what are you doing? Come away from the cliff.'

She ignored him and stared at the river at the base of the crag.

'Nesta,' repeated Tewdwr, 'please, look at me.'

Nesta turned and gazed at her father, the tears rolling down her face.

'My sweet child,' said Tewdwr gently, dropping to his knees, 'tell me what makes you so sad. Is it your mother, for let me tell you she still lives. Soon she will be well again and hold you as she once did.'

Nesta shook her head.

'I know she is well,' she replied, 'and Tarw will one day make you a fine son.'

'Tarw?'

'The name I gave him,' said Nesta. 'Mother was sleeping but he had to have a name so I could tell him a story.'

'And you chose Tarw?'

Nesta nodded and wiped her eyes with her sleeve.

'I know it is not a proper name, but when he was born Mother said he had the lungs of a bull so I called him Tarw.'

'Tarw is a wonderful name, Nesta,' said Tewdwr gently, 'but tell me, why did you say those things back there? Why do you think yourself evil when you helped your brother be born into this world?'

'Because I did a terrible thing,' cried Nesta, 'and when you take me back to Dinefwr, I will be hanged as a murderer.'

'Hang *you*?' gasped Tewdwr. 'I would never even consider such a thing, even in my worst nightmares.'

'But you must,' sobbed Nesta, 'for I am no better than the worst brigand.'

'How can you say such a thing?' asked Tewdwr. 'You are my little girl, my beautiful princess and your heart is as pure as the springtime rain.'

'Because I killed a man, Dada,' shouted Nesta. 'I stuck him with a blade and now he lies dead.' Once more she broke down into tears, her hands covering her face as her whole body wracked with remorse.

Tewdwr too started to cry and had she not been so near the edge of the cliff he would have run forward and scooped her into his embrace, never to let her go.

'Nesta,' he said eventually, 'Nesta, look at me.'

Nesta lifted her gaze towards her father.

'Sweet child,' he said, 'you have not done a bad thing and never could, for there is not an evil bone in your body. That man back there was the evil one and had you not done what you did, you, your mother, your brother and even Master Walters would surely lay dead amongst the bracken. You never took a life, sweet child, by stopping that monster, you saved the souls of three others.'

Nesta wiped her running nose with her sleeve once more.

'Don't you see?' added her father. 'It was not your hand that wielded the sword, but that of our Lord.'

'I stabbed him, Dada, the blow was mine and mine alone.'

'Perhaps, but it was surely Jesus that gave you the strength. How else can a girl as young and pretty as you have wielded a weapon so heavy?'

Nesta hesitated as she took in her father's words.

'No, Dada,' she said, 'he wasn't there. I saw no one.'

'You wouldn't have seen him, child, for he does not appear before mortal man, but he was here, in your heart and in your soul, knowing that you needed help to stop the bad man. You didn't do a bad thing, Nesta, you did a good thing and for that you should be as proud as I am thankful.'

'Do you really think so, Dada?' asked Nesta. 'Am I not going to hell?'

'No, child,' said Tewdwr, 'you are not.'

'And you won't hang me?'

'No, sweet child,' whispered Tewdwr, his voice breaking, 'I won't hang you.'

'Promise?'

'I promise,' sobbed Tewdwr and held his arms open.

'Dada!' cried Nesta, and she ran into Tewdwr's embrace, the king hugging his daughter as if his very life depended on it. Eventually the tears subsided and Tewdwr smoothed his daughter's hair as he whispered soothingly into her ear.

'You have done well, Nesta, and I am so very, very proud of you.'

'I couldn't let him kill Tarw, Dada,' she said, 'I just couldn't.'

'Tarw the bull,' said Tewdwr softly, 'it is a good name for a prince.'

The Fishing Port of Solva

August 12th, AD 1081

Five long months had passed since Gruffydd had secured the support of King Olaf to furnish an expedition back to Wales. In that time, Gruffydd had secured further allies as well as finance and now stood ready to embark upon the campaign. Despite his readiness, he had held back, waiting for the right opportunity. Caradog's invasion of Deheubarth was the trigger for Gruffydd and he mustered his forces in Dublin in preparation for the crossing, but seeing an opportunity to strengthen his army, he sent messages to Tewdwr seeking an audience with a view to an alliance.

Tewdwr had answered favourably, but needing to organise the finer details, Gruffydd had secured a skiff to take him across the Irish Sea to attend a secret meeting with the deposed king of Deheubarth and he subsequently found himself sat in the rear of a rowing boat as it approached Solva Harbour in the pre-dawn gloom.

'Ship oars,' said Iestyn, peering into the mist, 'and look to your blades. This may yet be a trap.'

The prow of the boat nudged against the wooden support of the dock and Iestyn's hand gripped the hilt of his sword in readiness for treachery. A face peered down through the darkness, illuminated by the lantern.

'State your name,' whispered the watchman nervously.

'Iestyn of Ynys Mon,' he said, 'we are expected.'

'You are,' confirmed the man. 'I have fellows with horses back amongst the trees. Make haste for the sun will soon be up and we will be visible to those early from their beds.'

Gruffydd joined Iestyn on the dock and glanced towards the boat, now being rowed back out to sea where the Danish skiff awaited its return.

'Follow me,' said the man and within minutes they were on a small footpath leading through a forest. Soon they reached a small bridge crossing a stream and the guide held up his hand, indicating they should stop. 'Quiet,' he hissed and listened intently. Cupping his hands he made the sound of an owl, receiving two in return. 'The way is clear,' he said eventually and continued over the bridge and into a clearing.

Iestyn looked around, always alert for danger. Two men sat upon their mounts, each draped in their heavy woollen cloaks against the morning dampness. Iestyn could see they were men used to conflict and each had a face weathered by time and warfare. Alongside them were a further two horses, saddled and awaiting their riders.

'You are late,' growled one of the men, 'and we were about to return without you.'

'The seas know no master, Marcus,' said the guide. 'Their skiff was delayed upon the crossing.'

'Get mounted and follow us,' said Marcus. He waited as the two newcomers climbed into their respective saddles. Without another word he turned his horse and led the way deeper into the trees closely followed by Iestyn and Gruffydd.

Two hours later and several leagues away, Tewdwr knelt before the table, his head bowed low as he prayed in the simple room of the bishop's palace alongside the cathedral of Saint David. For the past few weeks his movements had been restricted to within the walls of the cathedral grounds, bound as he was by the laws of sanctuary; yet despite his confinement, his influence was still strong across Deheubarth and he had sent messages out to everyone he could think of, seeking information about his missing son, Hywel.

When Dinefwr Castle had fallen, Hywel had been confined to his bed suffering from an ague; despite his worries Tewdwr had soon found out that he was alive and kept as a prisoner by Caradog. At first this was encouraging news, for it would eventually be a simple matter of raising the ransom, but when a messenger told Tewdwr that Hywel had been taken from Dinefwr to be held captive in Caerleon Castle, his heart fell, for now his son was held in Caradog's home kingdom he was far more likely to suffer harm.

Since then there had been hardly any news about Hywel, despite many despatches being sent, and every night both Tewdwr and his wife prayed fervently that their eldest son was still alive.

Outside of the walls, Caradog had posted a small garrison of fifty men tasked with ensuring the king did not leave the confines of the cathedral whilst their master went about his business.

The strict laws of sanctuary meant that no matter how important the plaintiff, or hideous the crime, any man seeking sanctuary in a house of god was protected by his grace for as long as they remained within the boundaries.

Finishing his prayer, he stood up, crossed himself and left the room to seek Gwladus in her chambers, dismissing the two serving girls as he entered. He sat on the side of the bed and held her hand.

'You look tired, my love,' he said gently.

'I'm not sleeping well,' she replied, 'and your new son demands all my attention during waking hours.' She smiled at the sleeping baby held snugly in her arms.

'He is certainly keen to voice an opinion,' said Tewdwr with a smile, 'many is the night he has kept me awake with his bellows.'

'Perchance a natural leader,' said Gwladus. 'But what about you? It seems you have the worries of the world upon your shoulders.'

Tewdwr chose his words carefully.

'I am fine,' he said. 'In fact, I hope to shortly have news that may enable us to return home.'

'What news is this?' she asked, her brow rising with interest. 'You haven't said anything before.'

'I did not want to raise your hopes unduly,' he replied, reaching forward to tickle the baby beneath his chin.

'Then hesitate no longer, dear husband, for good news is in short supply these past few months.'

'Two weeks ago a messenger arrived from Ireland,' replied Tewdwr, 'requesting I meet with King Gruffydd ap Cynan.'

'Why would he seek audience?'

'Because it seems Caradog has formed an alliance with Meilyr and Trahern against the rest of Wales. Gruffydd wants to oppose them and seeks an alliance of our own to stop them.'

'But we have no forces to speak of.'

'Not yet, perhaps but there are many who are still loyal to my banner. All we need to do is send word around the kingdom and we can have an army within weeks.'

'Does Gruffydd know this?'

'He does, and as we speak he is embarked on a journey here from Ireland to discuss terms.'

'Will you have to fight?' asked Gwladus nervously, but before he could answer, a knock came upon the door and the king stood as someone entered the room.

'My lord,' said the servant, 'the bishop Sulien has requested your presence.'

'Tell him I will be along shortly,' answered Tewdwr and waited until the door closed before turning once more to his wife.

'You rest now and I will return this evening. We will discuss it more then.' Without another word he strode across the floor, leaving his wife behind him, her face a picture of stress and worry.

'Lord Tewdwr,' said the bishop, 'please come in.'

'Thank you, your grace,' replied Tewdwr, 'I was told you sought my presence.'

'Indeed, please close the door.'

Tewdwr did as requested and turned back to face the bishop.

'I'll get straight to the point,' continued Bishop Sulien, 'I am disappointed to learn that you have seen fit to abuse our hospitality and indeed, laid waste to the sanctity of the church.'

'I'm sorry, your grace, I don't know what it is you speak of.'

'I talk of God's house being used as a cover for politics and intrigue. You and your family were given sanctuary as your very lives depended on it, yet I have today found out that you have used your time here to plot the downfall of men loyal to King William of Normandy.'

'William is no king of mine,' said Tewdwr, 'and the men you speak of are traitors to the very ground beneath our feet.'

'That is your perspective,' said the bishop, 'and I respect your reasons but you have to understand that the church remains neutral in such matters unless directed by the hand of the pope. As far as I am aware he has not condemned these fellow Welshmen with whom you have a grudge, and though I understand your ire, I will not have death and destruction plotted within these holy walls. Am I making myself clear?'

'I think so, your grace, but can I ask what has brought on this upset?'

'You know what has brought it on, Lord Tewdwr, two men have arrived to see you and if they are who my people say they are then I feel you are on the verge of violating the sanctuary gifted by God.'

'They are here already?'

'They are.'

Tewdwr stepped forward and knelt on one knee, taking the bishop's hand in his.

'Your grace,' he said earnestly, 'if I have offended you or anyone in this holy place then I apologise profusely and will pay suitable reparations in the fullness of time but this is an opportunity I have to pursue. Please grant these men access and I promise I will have them away before the sun sets.'

'One day? What sort of negotiations can take place in such a short timespan?'

'Only the most basic of agreements, your grace. Grant me this audience and I swear there will be no talk of killing within these hallowed walls, only of patriotism and the need to form alliances. If the talks are successful, then I will leave this place by morning and take my burden outside of the city walls to discuss the detail.'

'And your wife?'

'I beg permission for her and my family to stay, at least until these sorry affairs are concluded.'

'And when may that be?'

'Surely before this year is out.'

Bishop Sulien pondered for a few moments before answering.

'My decision is this,' he said, 'you are a good man and hold the word of God in high esteem. I will grant your guests one night within these walls but insist they are gone by dawn. If there is to be any outcome from these talks, then you will ride away alongside them. If they fail, then you are welcome to stay as long as you want.'

'And my family?'

'They should not be involved in the politics of men. Leave them here and I will see they are well taken care of.'

'Thank you, your grace,' said Tewdwr and kissed the holy ring upon the bishop's finger.

'Whatever it is you intend to do, Lord Tewdwr,' said the bishop, 'do not lose sight of the church and ensure magnanimity and mercy are daily words in your vocabulary.'

'That I will, your grace,' said Tewdwr and stood up to leave.

'Your visitors are in the gatehouse,' said Sulien, 'I will have warm food and ale sent as soon as possible.'

'Thank you,' said Tewdwr and left the bishop's palace to climb the hill towards the gatehouse.

———

As he approached the gatehouse, Tewdwr's mind raced. For too long he had felt helpless, unable to do anything about his self-imposed imprisonment. Fleeing to Ireland was always an option but Caradog's men had them securely penned in, and whilst it was possible for messengers to get in and out unseen, to risk his wife and children in such a venture was more than he was willing to chance.

The past few months he had thought of two things only, how to get his family to safety in Ireland and the whereabouts of Hywel, so to host a renowned warrior king intent on killing the very man responsible for their predicament made his heart race with excitement. To date it had never been an option but this opportunity had come unannounced and if it was genuine it gave Tewdwr renewed hope. He paused before the heavy studded door and breathed deeply to regain his composure. Finally, he stepped forward and pushed the door inward.

Gruffydd and Iestyn both turned to face the man coming into the room, their hands resting on the pommels of their swords.

'My lords,' said Tewdwr, looking between them, 'welcome to the cathedral of our saint.'

Gruffydd stared at the older man for a while before answering.

'It is good to return to my homeland,' he said eventually. 'Do I have the honour of addressing Rhys ap Tewdwr?'

'You do, and I assume you are King Gruffydd of the house of Aberffraw.'

'I am. This is Iestyn, my right-hand man.'

'Well met,' said Tewdwr and held out his hand.

Gruffydd took his wrist and held it as an equal.

'Well,' said Tewdwr, 'now the introductions are over, perhaps you can explain why you are here?'

'Did not my messengers tell you the situation?'

'They did but I would hear it from your own lips, for these things have a way of being changed with the telling.'

'It's quite straightforward,' said Gruffydd. 'A few weeks ago I learned that the three traitor kings have forged an alliance to conquer Wales and share it out equally amongst themselves. Obviously this means there will be no place for the likes of you and I, and our ancestral homes will be absorbed into the ownership of lesser men who take the English king's coin.'

'Is it not already the situation that Caradog rules Deheubarth, Trahern rules Gwynedd and Meilyr rules the rest?'

'In reality, yes but politically they are still only minor lords. If we allow this to happen the English king will recognise their claims in return for fealty to the Crown and we would no longer be a nation in our own right.'

'So this is greater than just reclaiming that which was once yours?'

'It is. Of course I want my lands returned but if we lose the rest of Wales at the same time then it is a worthless gesture. No, I think that we have to prevent them achieving their aims and gather what forces we can to confront them once and for all.'

'On the field of battle?'

'If necessary.'

'I don't know,' said Tewdwr, 'Caradog alone is a formidable warrior and his army are vastly experienced. He already holds Gwent, Deheubarth and Morgannwg in a steely grip and I fear his army is too large for equal combat.'

'In full frontal battle perhaps, but if we had surprise on our side then our combined numbers are more than a match for them.'

'How many men do you have?'

'About a thousand men-at-arms and half that again in cavalry.'

'A strong force,' said Tewdwr.

'Ireland is a big place,' said Gruffydd. 'What about you, what number can you raise?'

'A few hundred men-at-arms and fifty or so archers. I may be able to raise more but will need time to send messages across Deheubarth.'

'That may suffice,' said Gruffydd, 'but there is much to discuss. Come, let us light a fire in the hearth and make ourselves comfortable, it looks like this could be a long night.'

For several hours the men talked about many things in the gloom of the gatehouse. At first the talk was of warfare and politics but as the night dragged on, the conversation inevitably turned to matters closer to the heart. Iestyn felt his eyelids struggle to stay open and finally conceded defeat, retiring to a nearby couch. Soon his quiet snores helped fill the gloom and Gruffydd smiled as he poured Tewdwr another drink.

'It has been a hard few days for him,' said Gruffydd, sitting back in his chair.

'As it must have been for you,' replied Tewdwr. 'Please, say the word and I will leave you to rest.'

'I will not sleep,' said Gruffydd, 'for this night is too important to waste on such luxury. Between the two of us, we may hold the key to a united Wales and every moment spent otherwise is a moment wasted.'

'You do realise,' said Tewdwr, 'that if we embark upon this path then many men will die before settlement is reached.'

'An unfortunate outcome of any war,' said Gruffydd, 'but in the longer term, a price worth paying.'

'I'm not so sure,' said Tewdwr. 'Perhaps it is better to accept the way of the world and bow to the might of stronger men?'

'Why would you give up your crown so easily?'

'I have been king for just over a year and have already lost many friends to enemy steel. My son has been taken prisoner and my family are incarcerated in this place, knowing full well that to breach the boundaries of sanctuary means almost certain death. I may not be much of a soldier, Gruffydd, but what I lack in experience I make up for in love for my family.'

'Nobody is disputing your mettle, Tewdwr, and believe me, when first I marched to battle I too doubted my courage, but when right is on your side God grants you the courage needed to deliver justice upon the enemy.'

'But surely the death of even one man is not worth the price of any crown?'

'It's not about the crown, my friend, it is about freedom and fairness the wearer brings to bear.'

'Why would your freedom be any better than that offered by Caradog or one of the others? Surely, men would still pay taxes and be beholden to a landed master.'

'Yes, they would as that is indeed the way of the world but there can be vast differences in how that master treats his people. Caradog is known for his cruel rule and suffers no petition from anyone who questions their own plight. Without recourse to justice, any man subjected to such a rule is no better than a slave and that, my friend, I cannot countenance.'

'So you are saying you will be a good king?'

'I am saying that I will be the best I am able to be but this is not about me, for my path is clear. The question is will you travel it alongside me and send out a signal that every man in Wales can relate to?'

'And what message is that?'

'That while there are men still able to stand unaided, be them king or pauper, then there is no place for tyranny in these lands whether it be wielded by Englishman or Welsh born. Once this message is understood, then and only then do we have a chance to unite our country under one banner and reclaim the nationhood that was once ours under Hywel Dda.'

'Yes, but what use is that message if we fall at the first hurdle, defeated by those who would impose their will?'

'No such message is ever wasted, Tewdwr, but just plants the seed for the growth of the next crop of patriots.'

'You are truly committed to this, aren't you?'

'To the death,' said Gruffydd.

'Even without my aid?'

'Your support will send a signal that no Welshman can ignore but should it be withheld, my task becomes a little harder, that's all.'

Tewdwr sighed deeply before answering. 'Then how could I possibly deny you my support, for though I am more skilled with a quill than a sword, I would rather die a free man than live as a slave.'

'Spoken like a true king.' Gruffydd grinned and lifted his tankard towards Tewdwr.

'To freedom,' he said.

'To freedom,' responded Tewdwr, and both men drank their tankards dry.

Several hours later the two kings took their leave, each motivated about the plan agreed during the night. Gruffydd and Iestyn headed back towards Solva. They had all agreed to meet again in thirty days at a nearby place called Nine Wells Bay, but this time, there would be many more men, each with a grudge needing to be settled.

Dublin

September 10th, AD 1081

Gruffydd ap Cynan paced the deck of the ship anchored in Dublin Harbour, his mind spinning with the preparations he had put in place. Since he had left Tewdwr almost a month earlier, the impetus of his plans had increased and things were coming to a head. Men-at-arms, hearing about the money on offer, turned up on a daily basis and were quickly deployed to his army practising on the fields behind the city. Archers fired volley after volley at distant targets and lancers practised their charges until the grass beneath their horses' hooves was naught but churned mud.

Carts of food, ranging from salted fish to sides of beef, arrived from across the county and were stored in buildings along the wharf until the cogs were ready to be loaded. Sailors watched the skies closely, anticipating the day of their departure.

Day by day the final arrangements came together, until eventually the only thing holding them back was the weather. Finally, Gruffydd woke to a warm morning sun and he ran outside of his cabin to stare up at the sky before turning to speak to the captain who was already up and seeing to his equipment.

'Well, Captain,' he said, 'my inexperienced eye says we have a fine day before us. Should we take the opportunity?'

'My lord,' said the seaman, 'only God knows what the weather has in store, but as a gambling man, I would wager this is as good as you are going to get.'

Gruffydd grinned and his heart raced.

'Thank you, Captain,' he said, 'that's all I needed to know. Pass the word, we sail at noon.' The captain nodded as Gruffydd descended a gangplank to make his own final preparations.

Within hours, supplies were being carted from the stores and carried up gangplanks, ready to cross the Irish Sea in the second wave of the assault. The first twenty vessels, a mixture of cargo ships and cogs, were already anchored offshore, waiting for the order to sail.

'My lord,' said a voice, and Gruffydd turned to see the steward walking towards him with a parchment in his hand. 'The lord Darcy has made good on his promise. I have word that a fleet of six cogs under his banner approach beyond the headland. You have your cavalry.'

Gruffydd's face broke into a thin-lipped smile.

'Thank God,' he said, 'for without his horsemen we would be severely disadvantaged. So, are we now at full strength?'

'As best as we could have hoped, my lord. In addition, the loan from Nial of Limerick will furnish us with enough supplies and weapons to sustain the campaign for two months. The cost was prohibitive yet I am confident we can repay all debts, always assuming of course that you are victorious.'

'Trust me, Master Steward, I will either return victorious or lie dead in some Welsh ditch. There is no other option.'

'Then you are ready to embark, my lord, and I will wish you God's speed.'

'Thank you, Master Steward,' said Gruffydd, 'your diligence in these preparations at such short notice has been recognised and will not go unrewarded.'

'A return to our homeland is all the reward I crave, my lord,' said the steward.

Gruffydd turned and strode away, calling out to the soldiers sat upon the many sacks and barrels of stores still on the dock.

'Sergeants-at-arms,' he called, 'embark the last of the men aboard *The Mallard*. The rest of the merchantmen can be loaded after we leave.'

All around the dock, men jumped to their feet, and carrying their individual equipment they walked up the gangplanks onto the flagship. Some found spaces amongst the stores below deck while others stayed topside, anticipating that fresh air may be a welcome treat during the short but choppy crossing. Within the hour, every-thing was stowed away and Gruffydd stood upon the forecastle.

'Ready when you are, my lord,' said the captain.

'Then order my colours raised,' said Gruffydd, 'and take us out to sea. Before this day is out, I would see the cliffs of my homeland.'

'So be it,' replied the captain and gave the necessary orders. As they sailed away from Ireland, the rest of the ships in the bay weighed anchor and followed them eastward. In the distance, Gruffydd could see Lord Darcy's ships sailing in the same direction and knew that by the time they reached Wales the invading fleet would be as strong as it could be. All he could hope for now was that Tewdwr had managed to raise his own army and was waiting for him in Deheubarth.

Tewdwr sat back against the tree trunk, gazing outward over the Irish Sea, looking for any sign of Gruffydd's fleet. In the last few weeks he had sent messengers across the length and breadth of Deheubarth, seeking those still loyal to him to muster in this valley, fully prepared to take the fight back to Caradog. To date, the take-up had been less than encouraging, but his greatest hope lay in the hands of his loyal comrade, Marcus. He had not yet returned and the success of the quest before them now lay in his hands.

'Sails, my lord,' called a voice, and Tewdwr stood to gaze over the sea. Sure enough, ships began appearing on the horizon and it wasn't long before he counted more than twenty vessels, all heading towards the beach.

'Check with the lookouts,' said Tewdwr over his shoulder, 'ensure there is no risk from inland. If Caradog's men were to arrive now, it would be a disaster.'

A few hours later, Gruffydd's fleet was anchored offshore, the vessels rolling gently in the swell. A multitude of smaller rowing boats ferried the soldiers to the beach and any vessels containing horses lowered ramps into the water, allowing riders to swim alongside their mounts as they braved the cold seas. As they landed, each group organised their equipment and undid the packs containing the weapons. Sergeants called the roll and from his vantage point, Tewdwr watched as Gruffydd's army of liberation took shape.

Finally, the king himself could be seen leaving the flagship and Tewdwr stood to meet him. The rowing boat beached and Gruffydd jumped into the water before wading up to meet the king of Deheubarth.

'Tewdwr, my friend,' said Gruffydd, 'well met.'

'Welcome,' said Tewdwr, 'your army is indeed impressive.'

'We have a large infantry force as well as cavalry,' said Gruffydd.

'Archers?' asked Tewdwr.

'Some, but fear not for I am expecting two hundred from Ynys Mon.' He looked around the beach and up onto the grassy slopes. 'And your army?' he asked, seeing no sign of any large force.

'My men guard the rear,' said Tewdwr, 'for Caradog and his allies are not far from here and we have to take care we are not compromised.'

'A good move,' said Caradog. 'What is your strength?'

'Not good, it has to be said, but we expect our numbers to be swelled imminently.'

'How many do you have, *exactly*?'

'No more than five hundred men-at-arms, a few dozen archers and twenty cavalry.'

Gruffydd visibly flinched at the low numbers. He had imagined twice as many men-at-arms and his army had trained accordingly. The weak numbers meant he might have to reconsider his tactics.

'There are more to come,' continued Tewdwr, 'but you have to understand, we recruit from a kingdom already beneath the heel of another. Give me a little more time and I will provide the numbers you crave.'

'Let's hope you do,' said Gruffydd, 'for even a single man could be the difference between victory and defeat.'

'I understand.'

'I assume you have an encampment nearby.'

'We do.'

'Good. Let us go there and discuss these matters. My officers will organise the men, but in the meantime, you can brief me how lays the land.'

'As you wish,' said Tewdwr, 'come with me.'

As the beach echoed with the commands and shouts of a disembarking army, the two kings headed for Tewdwr's campaign tent.

For the next few hours, Gruffydd and Tewdwr talked tactics and dealt with the constant interruptions from officers from both camps as the armies began to get organised. By nightfall, all those fresh from Ireland were encamped amidst the treeline back from the shore. All of the ships, except for the flagship, had left the bay and now made their way back across the Irish Sea to be restocked, this time with supplies.

Finally, the activity died down and the two kings sat in their respective chairs near the fire at the centre of the tent, drinking warmed wine and eating a cawl made by Walters the cook. The meal ended and Gruffydd stood up to leave.

'Well,' said Gruffydd, 'it has been a long time coming, Tewdwr, and we are as prepared as we can be. All we can do now is hope God is on our side.'

'I pray that he is,' said Tewdwr, 'for the task before us is huge. To fight one king is hard enough but to face three is unheard of.'

'It will depend on who we cross first,' said Gruffydd.

'What do you mean?' asked Tewdwr.

'I have no intention of fighting all three armies at the same time,' said Gruffydd, 'and if possible will seek them out one by one. That way we may have a chance.'

'But that will mean three separate battles. Is that wise?'

'We will soon find out,' said Gruffydd. 'Let us discuss it tomorrow. Please excuse me, it has been a very long day and I need to retire.'

'Of course,' said Tewdwr.

'I have arranged for my guards to join yours at the perimeter,' said Gruffydd. 'It's not that I don't trust your men but we are yet new to each other and have come too far to leave anything to chance.'

'Understood,' said Tewdwr.

Gruffydd turned to leave but Tewdwr stood up and spoke again.

'King Gruffydd,' he said, 'before you go there is a boon I would ask of you. I understand your flagship is to return to Dublin tomorrow?'

'It is.'

'Then I would ask that it conveys a package on my behalf, something more important to me than life itself.'

'And what package may that be?'

'My youngest son,' said Tewdwr.

Gruffydd sat back down and poured himself another tankard of ale from the jug before staring at Tewdwr in silence. Finally, he took a long drink and replaced the tankard upon the table.

'Explain,' he said simply.

'Well,' said Tewdwr. 'As you know, my castle is in the hands of Caradog and what remains of my army is still scattered across the south. My eldest son is still missing, and though we assume he is in the captivity of Caradog, I have received no word from any of my spies as to his whereabouts.'

'Is the rest of your family safe?'

'For now. My wife, daughter and second son take sanctuary in the cathedral of Saint David. I have already once almost lost them all to the hands of Caradog, and his spies keep watch for any chance to deliver them into his hands. While I am away on campaign, I fear he may send men into the cathedral and spirit them away.'

'Not even Caradog would breach the rules of sanctuary.'

'You don't know him like I do,' said Tewdwr. 'I agree he wouldn't do it in his name, but all men have their price, and brigands would have no such qualms. Subsequently, I need to ensure Tarw is safe in case I fall.'

'And if I do this, where would be his destination?'

'Have him sent to King Murcat in the north of Dublin. I understand he is the neighbour of your grandfather.'

'Indeed he is,' said Gruffydd, 'but why send him there?'

'Murcat has been a friend of our family for many years. In his hands I know my son will be safe. If we are victorious in our quest, then I will have him returned to our hearth, but these days are filled with strife and I fear for our family. If we are killed, at least there will be one who can carry on my name.'

'If this is what you wish, then it will be done. But what about your wife and daughter?'

'Gwladus refuses to leave while Hywel is still missing, and since the birth of Tarw Nesta refuses to leave her mother's side. They have been through a lot together and need each other's support. Both will stay and take their chances but Tarw must go, for everyone's sake.'

'So be it,' said Gruffydd, standing once more. 'Have the child brought to the shore before first light. I will ensure he is looked after and reaches King Murcat safely.'

'You have my gratitude,' said Tewdwr and watched the deposed king of Gwynedd leave his tent. When Gruffydd had left, the flap opened and Walters entered to clear away the remains of the meal.

'My lord, is there anything else you require?' he asked.

'No thank you, Walters, unless of course you can conjure me up an army.'

'Soup I can manage, my lord,' replied the cook, picking up the bowls, 'armies are your business.'

'They are,' murmured Tewdwr as he left, 'they are indeed.'

Ten leagues to the north, another meeting of kings was taking place in a farmhouse near Mynydd Carn. Whilst Tewdwr and Gruffydd slept fitfully in their tents, Kings Trahern, Meilyr and Caradog made merry with a cask of ale, anticipating the good times before them. The negotiations had gone well, and though there was still no agreement as to whom would eventually be crowned king of Wales, the problem had been put aside with all three agreeing it was far more important to subdue the minor lords first and leave the details for another day. Secretly, all three harboured the ambition but knew the alliance would fall at the first hurdle should the issue be pressed.

Plans were well advanced for the immediate conquest of Ceredigion further up the coast, before swinging the armies eastward to subdue Builth and finally turning their attention south towards Brycheniog. Once all three had been conquered, they would absorb their lands into their own kingdoms with Ceredigion being annexed to Gwynedd, Builth to Powys and Brycheniog to Gwent. This gave each king an area roughly a third of the size of Wales, and though each knew there was potential for conflict between themselves, the prospect of William sending his armies across the border to impose his will made them focus on the immediate issues, not the outcome that still lay far down the road.

'Right,' said Trahern standing up, 'I will take my leave and return to my command. Once the supplies from Huw D'Avranches have been confirmed, I will send word and we can muster in the hills to the north.'

'Agreed,' said Caradog as he too stood to leave.

'Gentlemen,' said Meilyr, 'the night is yet young. Let us crack a fresh cask of ale and celebrate momentous times.'

'No, I am done,' said Caradog. 'Don't forget I have a ride of several leagues back to my lines while your bed lays a few paces in that direction.'

Meilyr laughed. 'True, but such are the spoils of he who acts first. Perhaps if your army had arrived sooner, you too could be sleeping under a roof instead of canvas.'

'I had important matters to attend to,' said Caradog, 'but enjoy it while you can, my friend. Soon we will share the trail northward and such comfort will be lacking, I can assure you that.'

'Until then,' said Meilyr, lifting his tankard in a toast.

Caradog smiled back and, alongside Trahern, left the farmhouse.

'That man doesn't know when to stop,' Caradog said quietly as they walked towards the horses. 'I hope his love of ale does not become a burden.'

'He will be fine,' said Trahern. 'I have known him a long time and besides, when this is over who knows what accident may befall him.'

Caradog stopped and stared at Trahern.

'What are you saying?'

'Nothing. Just that it is a dangerous world and perhaps he should be careful.'

'As should we all, I would suggest,' replied Caradog.

'Indeed,' said Trahern. 'I bid you a good night, my friend, and will see you shortly on the field of battle, shoulder to shoulder as allies.'

Caradog nodded in reply and without further comment, wheeled his horse to gallop into the darkness.

Nine Wells Bay

September 13th, AD 1081

Three days later a young boy passed through the sentry lines unchallenged and headed towards the cathedral a few leagues away, tasked with passing the message about Tewdwr's son to the lady Gwladus. He rode hard before leaving his horse hidden in a copse and walking the last few hundred paces along the streambed that passed through the grounds of the cathedral. It was a route he had used often when passing messages back and fore and knew it was safe from the prying eyes of Caradog's spies. Or so he thought.

'Hold there,' came a voice and the young boy froze where he was, calf deep in water, his heart beating out of his chest.

'Who are you?' asked the voice. 'And what is your business?'

The messenger thought furiously not knowing whether the hidden man was friend or foe.

'My name is Langdon, sir,' he replied, 'and I am merely looking for fish to feed my family.'

Two men stepped out of the bushes and stood before him, obviously soldiers of Caradog.

'Well, Langdon,' said the first soldier, 'I think you are lying to me and are about the business of the Tewdwr woman.' Langdon swallowed hard. He knew he was in trouble and the thought of dying terrified him.

'No, sir,' he said, his voice shaking, 'I promise my quest is for food only. That is why I am down here.'

'Now we know you speak false,' said the second man, 'for we have seen you come this way before, not two days since. You entered the cathedral and after a while returned whence you came. Waste no more time on such foolishness, for your very life is in the balance. Speak true and we will let you go but if I detect one more falsehood then this stream will run red with your blood. So, what is it to be, boy, your life or the truth?'

Langdon was terrified. Though his loyalty lay with Tewdwr, he feared dying at so young an age. There was no way of knowing if the men were telling the truth regarding sparing his life but he knew he had no choice. Sweat ran down his face and his palms felt clammy as his mind raced, weighing up the options.

One of the soldiers lunged forward and punched him in the stomach, causing the boy to fall back into the stream. Coughing, he stood up, and holding his stomach he looked up at his attacker.

'Make your mind up, boy,' growled the man, 'for the next one will break your jaw.'

'If I say, do you swear to let me go?'

'I swear nothing, but you are in no position to bargain. Live or die, that is the choice before you. Which is it to be?'

'Live,' said the boy, his voice cracking with fear.

'Good decision, now, tell me what business you are about.'

'I travel to give news to the queen that her baby is safe in Ireland.'

'In Ireland? How can that be? They are all hiding like scared rabbits within the cathedral.'

'No, sir, you are mistaken, for though the queen and her daughter are safe within these holy walls, her husband is in Nine Wells Bay and his son was taken across the Irish Sea not three days since.'

Both men looked at each other in shock.

'And you swear this is true?' asked the soldier.

'I do not want to die, sir, so speak the gospel truth, and if I do not, then let God strike me dead upon this very spot.'

'Wait,' said the second man, 'if you speak true, why is Tewdwr at Nine Wells Bay?'

Langdon hesitated, looking between the two men, knowing full well that what he said next could cost a lot of men their lives.

'Spit it out,' hissed the second guard, pressing his blade upon the boy's chest, 'or I swear I will run you through right now.'

'He is organising his army to attack Caradog,' blurted Langdon, 'they train upon the sands as we speak.'

Silence fell for a few moments as the soldiers digested the news.

'What army?' said the first soldier eventually. 'He has no forces around here.'

'Not himself, but he has engaged the help of a king from Ireland and they muster at Nine Wells.'

'How many?'

'I don't know.'

'How many,' hissed the man again, 'you have seen them, have you not? Is there a few dozen, a few hundred, what is your estimate?'

'A lot,' cried the boy as the point of the blade pierced his skin and a trickle of blood ran down his chest, 'perhaps a thousand or more.'

'Oh, sweet Jesus,' said the guard in shock, taking a step back. 'Caradog needs to know about this immediately.'

'Our task was to guard this stream and ensure nobody leaves or enters the cathedral,' said the second guard, 'on pain of punishment. If we leave our post we could end up with a flogging.'

'Are you stupid?' shouted the first man. 'If Caradog doesn't hear about this as soon as possible we could all be slaughtered within days.'

'I have my doubts,' said his comrade, 'that even if Tewdwr has employed mercenaries from Ireland, Caradog has the strength of three armies to call on.'

Langdon looked between the two men as they argued and seeing they were momentarily distracted, seized the opportunity to escape, turning to run as fast as he could back downstream.

'After him!' shouted one of the men.

'No, let him go,' shouted the other, 'there is no time to lose, we have to get to Mynydd Carn.' The two men left the stream and returned to where they had hidden their horses.

Back in the trees, Langdon was astride his own mount, galloping as hard as he could back towards Nine Wells Bay. He knew he should not have talked but his life was at risk and he had to escape alive to warn the others. If he could at least reach Tewdwr in time, then perhaps they could prepare for the storm that was surely coming.

An hour later, Gruffydd ducked into Tewdwr's command tent and looked around the concerned faces of the officers and sergeants within.

'What is wrong?' he demanded. 'Why was I summoned here?'

'Lord Gruffydd,' said a voice and the sea of bodies parted to reveal Tewdwr standing behind a table, 'there have been developments and they are not good.'

'Enlighten me,' said Gruffydd.

'Caradog is aware of our presence,' said Tewdwr, 'or at least he will know before this day is out.'

'How?' shouted Gruffydd. 'Have our ranks been infiltrated by spies already or do we have a traitor amongst us?'

'No,' said Tewdwr, 'my messenger was captured on the way to the cathedral and made to talk. Luckily he escaped to give us fair warning.'

'I hope you had him flogged,' growled Gruffydd, 'for he might have just got us all killed.'

'It was unavoidable,' said Tewdwr, 'and any man would have acted in a similar way.'

'Where is he now?'

Tewdwr looked to one side and the men moved out of the way to reveal a young boy sat upon a chair, his face frozen with fear.

'Be calm, Gruffydd,' said Tewdwr, 'for he is yet a boy and knows not much about the ways of war.'

Gruffydd grunted and walked towards Langdon.

'Stand up,' he said.

The boy got to his feet yet stared at the floor.

'Look at me,' commanded Gruffydd, 'for you are amongst men and how you hold yourself could decide whether you are hanged or not. Now, tell me what you know.'

'My lord,' stuttered Langdon and proceeded to tell him everything that had happened near the cathedral.

'Did they say anything else?' asked Gruffydd.

'I heard them say that Caradog had three armies under his command,' said Langdon, 'and they could mobilise within a few days.'

'A few days?' said Tewdwr, joining Gruffydd. 'That means Meilyr and Trahern must be nearby.'

'Not really,' said Gruffydd, 'a well-trained army can march ten leagues in a day. They could be anywhere.'

'No, my lord,' stuttered Langdon, 'they are nearer than that, for I know where my captors headed after I escaped.'

'Where?' snapped Gruffydd. 'Spit it out, man.'

'A place called Mynydd Carn.'

'Mynydd Carn!' gasped Tewdwr. 'That is no more than five leagues north. His army must be encamped under our very noses.' He turned to one of his officers. 'Gerald, pass the word to the men, we move out before dark.'

'To where, my lord?'

'I know not,' said Tewdwr, 'but we can't stay here, we are trapped against the sea and will be slaughtered.'

'Hold that command!' shouted Gruffydd, and he turned to face Tewdwr as the tent fell silent. 'Now you listen to me. I have not come all this way only to turn and run at the first opportunity. We have sat on this sand for too many days waiting for your reinforcements to arrive. Without question I have taken your word that they will be here, all the time knowing that for every day we delayed we ran the risk of being discovered. Well, that day has now come but if you think I am going to shrink back from it then you are mistaken.' Gruffydd turned to walk away but stopped in his tracks as Tewdwr raised his voice.

'So what are you going to do? Surely you don't think we can fight three armies with what we have. Your numbers may be impressive, Gruffydd, but they are outnumbered threefold.'

'I judge not by the numbers of feet upon the ground,' replied Gruffydd walking over to face the older man, 'but by the size of the heart within a man's chest and from what I have seen these past few days that evens the contest.'

'Do you really think we have a chance against seasoned men such as Caradog's army?'

'If we take them by surprise, then yes, I do. From what I can gather, they will soon learn of our presence and will be aware of our numbers. The last thing they will expect is to be attacked by a smaller army.'

'What are you saying?'

'I think we should take the initiative to them. Attack them with all haste, giving them no chance to get organised. Rip apart their lines with a frenzy such as they have never seen, and before they can muster into defensive lines we can be through them like a sharpened sword.'

'I'm not sure,' said Tewdwr. 'My forces are still under strength.'

'And may remain so. If we don't take this opportunity now, they will organise themselves into a far stronger force and hunt us down like deer. You can do what you want, Tewdwr, but with or without you, my army will march on Mynydd Carn by dawn.'

'I didn't say I would not join you, Gruffydd, but in such situations it is always prudent to have a voice of caution.'

'Granted, but if we are to do this we have to move immediately.'

Tewdwr looked at the expectant faces within the tent before turning to face Gruffydd one last time.

'I have my reservations,' he said finally, 'but will not let you ride alone. My men are yours.'

Gruffydd held out his hand and grabbed the wrist of the Deheubarth king.

'So be it,' he said, and turning to face the rest of the officers, roared out his command: 'Muster the men, for tonight we ride into battle!'

Mynydd Carn

Trahern and his officers walked amongst the tents, talking quietly to his men. The news of Nine Wells Bay had sickened him to his stomach, for just as it seemed the country was opening up before him, Gruffydd had reappeared and seemed intent on once more being an obstacle in his path. Trahern knew that until this boil had been lanced there was no way he could continue alongside the other two kings and had decided to deal with the threat once and for all. His men had been called to arms and prepared to move at first light. Despite Meirion's advice to seek aid from Meilyr or Caradog, he had decided to do this alone. He had defeated Gruffydd once and would do so again.

He looked down at a soldier drawing a whetstone carefully along his sword blade, the repetitive sound somehow comfortable amongst the hubbub of the preparations.

'You seem to be doing a good job,' said Trahern, causing the man to look up from his task.

'My lord,' said the soldier, making to stand up, but Trahern raised his hand, putting the soldier at ease.

'Please continue with your task,' he said, 'it is good to see a man take such pride in his blade.'

'In the heat of battle, it is only my blade between me and my grave,' said the soldier, 'the way I see it, if I look after my sword then my sword will look after me.'

'As good a strategy as any,' said Trahern, 'and one I hope pays off on the morrow. Are you and your comrades ready?'

'Almost. Some queue at the carts for arrows while others collect their allocation of meat for their ration pouches.'

'Good – for who knows when there will next be time to eat?'

Trahern gazed past the soldier and along the lines of tents. Dozens of fires lit the shadows and men-at-arms talked quietly amongst themselves, anticipating the march to confront the enemy. These were the foot soldiers, the men drawn from farms and villages across Gwynedd who did not normally fight for a living but had been forced to join their masters' army on pain of death.

'You do not sit with the rest,' said Trahern, 'why is that?'

'I hold no grudge against them, sire, for we fight beneath the same banner. But they are naught but farmhands who fight with scythes and pitchforks. I hope the Lord will aid them when the fighting starts but fear they will be found wanting. When it comes to war, a man must find like-minded souls and do what he can to survive. He cannot afford to be dragged down by lesser men.'

'An astute point of view,' said Trahern, 'just don't let it cloud the reason you are here.'

'Aye, my lord,' said the soldier, and he watched as Trahern continued down to the tents.

'Get to your feet,' said Meirion Goch as they reached a crowd of soldiers gathered around a fire, 'your king is amongst you.'

'My lord,' said one of the nearby sergeants, standing up quickly, 'my apologies, we were not expecting you.'

'Stay seated,' said Trahern, 'for there may be little chance for such luxuries in the coming days.'

The soldier sat back down, looking around nervously at his fellows. It was rare that the king came amongst the men and none were sure how to react.

'So,' said the king, 'are you all rested?'

'Aye, that we are, my lord,' said the sergeant.

'And are you well fed?'

'We have no complaints.'

'What about your equipment, is it ready for the march?'

'It is,' replied the man, 'though we could do with a few more gambesons.'

'Are there not enough to go around?'

'Most men have their own, my lord, but those new to the ways of war have not the money to have one made.'

Trahern turned to Meirion at his side.

'Are there none upon the carts?'

'All have been issued, my lord, and the cost of new is prohibitive.'

'I thought you said we were well equipped?'

'And so we are but to waste money on those who will fall in the first rush anyway is a pointless folly. We will retrieve more from the fallen when the fighting starts.'

'My lord,' said a voice, 'is it true that there are thousands of Irishmen waiting to cut us down?'

'Even if there were,' replied the king, 'I have every trust in you and all these men. However, let me put your mind at rest. At times such as this, soldiers have a way of building up the enemy in their own minds. At the most there are no more than a few hundred and I expect they are fresh from the fields of Ireland so will be no match for you. I concede there may indeed be a battle, but if Gruffydd is their leader then this may be a good thing, for we can kill two birds with one stone: both he and Tewdwr. Once they are gone then the whole of Wales opens before us and we can set about unifying our country. If God is with us you will be back amongst your kinfolk before the winter sets in.'

'And don't forget,' added Meirion, 'we have allies in Caradog and Meilyr, each of whom bring over five hundred men-at-arms to the field; no matter what the strength of the enemy, we will out-number them at least threefold.'

'Thank you, my lord,' came several voices from around the fires.

Trahern continued his journey, stopping at many more camp-fires as the night dragged on.

———

'My lord,' said Meirion, a few hours later, 'it is time; the men are ready.'

King Trahern opened his eyes and looked around. He had man-aged a few hours' sleep but it seemed he had only just lain down upon his bed.

'Has the sun arisen?' he yawned.

'It lightens the horizon as we speak. By the time we get started the full day will be upon us.'

'Good,' said Trahern, getting to his feet. He was still dressed in his linen trews and woollen shirt from the previous night, and after taking a long drink of honeyed water direct from a jug, he walked over to a chair to get his armour. Leather leggings were strapped around his shins and a long chainmail hauberk pulled over his head to hang down over his waist. A tabard depicting his family crest was worn over the chainmail and a sword belt secured it all tightly around his waist. Meirion placed a chainmail coif over the king's head forming a protective hood that draped down over his shoul-ders before handing him his sword to be placed in the scabbard.

'Ready?' asked Trahern at last.

'Ready,' said Meirion, and he followed the king out of the tent.

As Trahern emerged, a large cheer echoed around the valley at the base of the hill. To one side his cavalry struggled with their mounts, the experienced horses aware that something was afoot. To the centre, over five hundred men-at-arms stood in three ranks facing the command tents, while the crossbow men formed up on the flanks. Beyond them were the carts that would follow later in the day, ready to collect the dead and the wounded.

Trahern nodded in satisfaction. It was an impressive sight and he was confident Gruffydd would be defeated once again, though this time, God willing, his head would be upon a spike.

'Men of Gwynedd,' he announced, 'today we march out to confront the usurper known as Gruffydd. I will make no pretty speeches for you know what is expected; so, waste no more time dreaming of glory; the reality lies before you. Listen to your sergeants and fight like you have never fought before.' He turned to face another man clad completely in chainmail astride a huge charger. 'Marshal, lead us out.'

To an almighty cheer, the marshal and the cavalry turned their horses and led the way down the track. Moments later, the voices of the sergeants filled the air and soon, the whole of Trahern's army were on the move, aiming to put an end to Gruffydd ap Cynan's claim to Gwynedd, once and for all.

Gruffydd lay amongst the wet bracken, peering down into the valley below. Behind him, the majority of his army lay hidden amongst the trees, waiting silently for his command, while on the opposite slopes of the valley, Tewdwr's smaller force also lay hidden amongst the undergrowth. Beside Gruffydd lay one of the scouts who had come galloping back down the valley only minutes earlier with reports of Trahern's approaching army.

For what seemed an age, nobody appeared, but eventually Trahern's scouts came into view, checking the way was clear.

They passed Gruffydd's hidden position without riding up the slopes and as they disappeared into the next valley, Gruffydd let out a quiet sigh of relief. The biggest risk in his plan had been avoided and they could now concentrate on the next part. He settled down to watch, knowing full well that the main army would soon follow, and from his position, he would easily be able to count the enemy's strength, an important weapon in any battle. Sure enough, the vanguard of Trahern's forces soon appeared at the top of the valley, led by his cavalry. The breath from the horses and the following ranks of marching men rose in clouds of steam from the valley floor and many hidden eyes watched in fascination as a complete army passed unhindered below them.

Despite the opportunity for an ambush, Gruffydd had other plans. He and Tewdwr had stayed up through the night planning their strategy. Their spies had reported that the three enemy armies had not yet combined and were encamped a league or so apart from each other, yet using the hill at Mynydd Carn as a central strongpoint, combining their supply lines and administrative centres in an effort to maximise their effectiveness. It also allowed quick communication between the officers of the three kings while keeping apart the main armies, each still wary of the others, traditionally enemies but now allies in a constantly changing political landscape.

Ordinarily it would have made sense to attack the soldiers of Trahern while they were relatively far from reinforcements but Gruffydd had other ideas and had identified a far greater opportunity. It was a risky strategy but he had ordered against any man engaging Trahern's column, planning instead to let them pass unharmed before advancing with all speed to fall on those encamped on Mynydd Carn. If his scouts had reported correctly, the enemy's supply train was also based on the Mynydd and at one fell swoop he could not only defeat one branch of the alliance but destroy their supplies at the same time.

Horses were hidden beyond the hill and every man of Gruff-ydd's army lay motionless amongst the bracken, knowing that one movement or the slightest sound would bring the enemy upon them. Eventually, the last of Trahern's column disappeared southward and Gruffydd rose from his hiding place to signal across to Tewdwr. Both men returned to their command and after mounting up, headed northward, leaving the army of Trahern far behind them.

Across the Irish Sea, Gruffydd's wife, Angharad, sat upon a bench taking in the morning air. Someone approached and she turned to see Adele walking towards her with a tray of pastries and a pitcher of honeyed water.

'Adele,' said Angharad with a smile, 'come sit a while.'

'Thank you, my lady, I thought you may be hungry.'

'A sweet pastry is always welcome, Adele,' said Angharad.

'My lady, you have two visitors at the house wishing to speak to you,' said Angharad, placing the tray upon the wooden table.

'Really? Did they say who they are?'

'No, only one spoke and he would not give his name, only that he was a business associate of your husband and begs a few moments of your time.'

'Strange,' said Angharad, 'I was not expecting anyone. Still, I suppose if they are comrades of my husband, I should receive them. Wait here and I will return shortly.'

Angharad returned to the manor, entering through the kitchen doors before straightening her skirts and walking through to the entrance hall. As she arrived, two men got to their feet and turned to face her.

'Lady Angharad,' said one of the men, 'thank you for seeing us at short notice.'

'You are welcome,' said Angharad, 'but you have me at a disadvantage. I don't believe we have met.'

'We have not,' said the man, 'my name is Nial of Limerick and I am a business partner of your husband.'

'I am surprised, sir, for I do not know your name and my husband usually shares all such things with me.'

'Well, perhaps he had other things upon his mind.'

'Be that as it may,' said Angharad, 'the business of the king remains exactly that and he would not thank me for discussing such matters with people who are strangers to me.'

'Of course,' said Nial, 'and I respect your view, however, this will take just a moment of your time.'

Angharad stared at the two men nervously. The quiet one was obviously some sort of soldier or bodyguard but though his frame and countenance gave her concern, it was the demeanour and attitude of the one called Nial that made her skin crawl.

'I will give you a few moments only,' she said, 'and will then have to ask you to leave. Please come through.' She led the way into a side room and invited the two men to sit at a table. The guard ignored the invitation and stood at the door while Nial walked over to the fire to warm his hands.

'Do you want some refreshments?' asked Angharad.

'No, we are fine,' said Nial, turning around to face her, 'let's just get down to business. Like I said, my name is Nial of Limerick and I am known in these parts as a successful business man, specialising in the field of finance.'

'A moneylender?' said Angharad.

'If you say so,' said Nial. 'A few weeks ago, your husband and I came to an agreement whereby I forwarded him enough money to keep his army in the field for a month.'

'Gruffydd borrowed money from you?' asked Angharad. Her mind was spinning yet she was keen not to show her shock.

'He did,' said Nial, 'and not an unsubstantial amount, it has to be said.'

'Even if he did,' said Angharad, trying to mask her shock, 'what has that to do with me?'

'Nothing,' said Nial, 'at least, not yet.'

'What is all this about?' asked Angharad, disliking the way the conversation was going.

'Allow me to explain. Your husband has borrowed an extremely large amount of money from me and embarked on a quest that could well see him killed before having a chance to repay the loan. Now, that makes me uneasy.'

'But surely you knew of the risks before agreeing the loan?'

'Indeed I did,' said Nial, 'but since then I have heard rumours that he has underestimated the strength of the enemy and is likely to become victim to a far superior force.'

'My husband knows what he is doing, sir, he has fought in many battles.'

'And lost quite a few, it would seem,' retorted Nial sharply. 'Anyway, I am nothing if not a careful man and agreed with Gruffydd that if the day came when he fell, then the debt would be settled against his estate.'

'His estate.' Angharad laughed. 'Anything of value we ever had is on Ynys Mon and if my husband falls then there is no estate.'

Nial walked over to Angharad and without warning pushed her back against the wall, his hand around her throat. Angharad gasped in shock and her eyes bulged as he cut off her airway. Nial leaned forward and sniffed the perfume on her neck.

'Oh, I don't know,' he said menacingly. 'I can think of something that may cover the interest, at least for a week or two, anyway.' He released his grip and Angharad struggled for breath, horrified at the implications.

Nial continued his walk around the room as if nothing had happened, looking at the tapestries and ornaments as he passed.

'This is indeed a nice place you have here,' he said, 'and I would venture is worth a pretty penny.'

'This place does not belong to us,' gasped Angharad, 'so is not part of our so-called estate.'

'Perhaps not directly,' said Nial, 'but under the laws of Dublin, any agreement that remains unpaid upon a man's death is repayable by any surviving family member or their extended kin.' He paused and stared at Angharad. 'And that, dear lady, includes you.'

'No,' said Angharad, 'that can't be true. I played no part in this.'

'On the contrary, it is obvious that as his wife, you have a vested interest.'

'Gruffydd would never expose me to such a risk, there has to be a mistake.'

'There is no mistake, my lady, I have his seal upon a document agreeing to everything I have just said.'

'Then he cannot have read the finer details,' said Angharad. 'I know my husband and he would not do such a thing.'

'Whether he read it or not is irrelevant, I have his signature and his seal. That means that if he falls, which I sincerely hope he does not, then my debt is reclaimable against you.'

Angharad sat down and stared into space.

'Oh don't look so worried,' said Nial, 'it may never come to such a situation. Hopefully he will return victorious and after paying what he owes, whisk you back across the sea to Gwynedd. If that happens then we will all live happily ever after, but if not then I am afraid I will be seeking recompense from you, and though I have seen little of this place, I calculate that this manor and its estate should just about cover it.'

'The manor does not belong to me,' said Angharad, 'it is the property of King Olaf himself.'

'Then he too is implicated in this agreement and if you can't pay, he will be held liable by default.'

'Olaf would never accept the debt of his grandson,' said Angharad quietly, 'he would kill you first.'

'I think not, my lady, for King Olaf is an honourable man and, indeed, I have had opportunity to deal with him in the past. A very prompt payer, if I recall correctly.'

Angharad looked at Nial with astonishment in her eyes.

'Olaf has had need of a moneylender?'

'Oh don't look so surprised, my customers range from paupers to kings and everyone in between. If the harvests are low and the villagers late in paying their taxes, sometimes even kings need a temporary loan to pay the wages of their soldiers. After all, there is nothing more dangerous than an unpaid army within your own castle walls. Fret not, for King Olaf is a fine example of a good customer and always paid on time. However, I suspect even he would struggle to pay your husband's debt, such is its size.'

Slowly Angharad got to her feet.

'What is it you want of me?' she asked quietly.

'Today, nothing. I just thought that as you are in line to inherit this debt should Gruffydd fall, it was only right that you should know.'

'Well, now I do, so if there is nothing else, I would bid you leave.'

'Of course,' said Nial with a sickly smile. 'Hopefully we will never meet again but be warned; if your husband falls, then you will hear from me before his body is cold. I bid you a good day.'

He turned and walked out of the room, closely followed by his bodyguard, slamming the door behind them.

'Oh Gruffydd,' said Angharad, talking quietly to herself, 'what have you done?'

Two Leagues North of Mynydd Carn

September 17th, AD 1081

'My lord,' shouted a voice.

Both men turned to see a man striding up the track towards them.

'Who is it?' asked Caradog, narrowing his eyes to peer past the blazing fire outside his campaign tent.

'It looks like Bowen,' said Peterson.

'Isn't he the scout you tasked to apprehend Tewdwr's bitch back in Dinefwr?'

'The very same.'

'After that embarrassment, I am surprised you have allowed him to live.'

'He is a good soldier,' said Peterson, 'and in the circumstances, most men would have suffered the same outcome that day.'

'See what he wants.'

'Let him through,' shouted Peterson to the guards. The soldier ran up to the tent, gasping to regain his breath.

'Calm yourself, Bowen,' said Peterson, 'what causes you such angst?'

'My lord,' panted Bowen, 'I bring grave news and have ridden here as fast as I could from Mynydd Carn.'

'Then speak your words, man,' said Peterson, standing up.

'My lord, the hill is under attack and men lie fallen in their hundreds. Every tent is ablaze while the horses in the paddock were slaughtered where they stood. All around the Mynydd, men run for their very lives and it was all my command could do to escape the slaughter.'

'What nonsense is this?' roared Caradog. 'The Mynydd was protected by both Meilyr and Trahern. What foe is strong enough to take on two armies?'

'My lord, the rumours are that Rhys ap Tewdwr and Gruffydd of Gwynedd have combined forces and fell upon the Mynydd just before first light.'

'Tewdwr has no army,' spat Caradog, 'and this exile king is a stranger in his own country. How could they field sufficient men to overcome two armies?'

'My lord, only Meilyr's force was present, for Trahern had gone south with his men.'

'Why?' asked Peterson. 'Had he agreed to guard the Mynydd alongside Meilyr?'

'It would seem he had received word about the threat from Gruffydd and was intent on settling a personal score once and for all. He mustered his men and rode south.'

'Without telling me?' said Caradog.

'It would seem so. From what I can tell, Gruffydd lured Trahern towards Nine Wells Bay but played a trick upon him. He let Trahern's men pass unharmed and lay hidden until they had long gone. As soon as they were out of sight, he rode north towards the Mynydd and set upon it with flame and steel. We can only assume he knew of the supplies there and that Meilyr's army was the weaker of the three.'

'Even so, Meilyr is an experienced warlord and should have been a match for any man upon the field.'

'I spoke to some men who had escaped the carnage and they said the sky was filled with flaming arrows before hundreds of men fell amongst them like screaming devils. Cavalry cut the defenders down like corn and in the confusion there was no way to reorganise. It was slaughter.'

'To leave an important position so poorly defended is unforgiveable,' said Caradog, 'and invited defeat. But whoever is responsible for this has not reckoned upon facing my might and is truly an idiot.'

'My lord,' said Peterson, turning to face the king, 'can I suggest quite the opposite? It seems to me that this tactic was a very clever ploy and we should be wary of rushing in.'

'Explain,' said Caradog.

'Think about it, to take on Trahern upon the field of battle was always going to be a dangerous strategy for any man, especially as Trahern had Meilyr at his back and our forces just a few hours ride away. But by doing what he has done, he has put us on the back foot with one fell swoop.'

'How?'

'First of all he has managed to defeat one of the armies by speed of surprise, thus lowering our numerical advantage. Secondly, he has managed to split all three kings and now, instead of having to face us as one, we are spread out across many leagues and a much more manageable threat. In addition, he has decimated our supply lines and forces us into action within days without time to garner any intelligence regarding his strengths or weaknesses.'

'No man forces my hand, Peterson.'

'With respect, this one has, my lord. By destroying our supplies he knows we have to take action immediately. The men have only what is in their food sacks and will hunger within days.'

'We can take what we need from the surrounding farms and villages.'

'We have already drawn heavily upon them and to take their last would turn them against us, adding to Gruffydd's strength. No, he is a clever man and knows he leaves us with only two options. We cannot go north for he will pursue us into lands that may still hold allegiance to his name, while south is out of the question as it seems he has recruited Tewdwr to his cause. That means half of Deheubarth will do everything they can to make our presence difficult whether it be poisoned water or lack of food.'

'West?'

'Powys will not take lightly to seeing a supposedly allied army withdrawing through their lands intact while their own men lay dead upon the field of battle. I suspect the Powys lords will see treachery where there is none.'

'So where does that leave us?'

'It brings us to the second option; to take him on face-to-face and let the victors take the spoils. The problem with this is that it has to be done immediately, else what stores remain will soon run out and the men will take to the field with hunger gnawing at their bellies.'

Caradog stared at the fire for several moments as he considered the options. Finally, he looked up and faced Peterson.

'Once again your counsel is wise,' he said, 'and I have made my decision. He turned to face Bowen. 'Take a unit of cavalry and ride as fast as you can to intercept Trahern. Tell him of what we discussed here and task him with returning to Mynydd Carn with all speed. In the meantime we will muster our forces and ride towards Gruffydd with all haste. If Trahern applies haste, he can be back here the morning after tomorrow when we will fall upon the enemy from two directions, Trahern from the south and us from the east.' Caradog turned back to face Peterson. 'No matter how clever this Gruffydd is, not even he can resist the forces of armies on two flanks. Muster the men, Peterson, there's an itch that needs to be scratched.'

Gruffydd walked between the remains of the camp at Mynydd Carn. All around him hundreds of men lay dead or dying in the midday sun. In the main, they were the soldiers of Meilyr, most of whom were asleep in their tents when the attack came and subsequently had no chance against the manic assault of Gruffydd's men. Some of the attackers had also fallen but compared to the enemy, their numbers were minimal.

Smouldering remains of tents and carts lay everywhere and the acrid smell of smoke still enveloped the hill, undispersed by the stillness of the day. Some of the Irish mercenaries wandered the battle site with bloody spears, dispatching any mortally wounded men with swift stabs to the heart. The day was surprisingly quiet and apart from the moans of the wounded no voices were raised above quiet conversation. Those involved on the assault sat in groups, seeing to their wounds and eating any dried food they had amongst them. It was surprising how many men developed an appetite after surviving a battle.

'My lord,' said a voice quietly and Gruffydd turned to see Iestyn standing behind him. His shirt was torn and his left arm heavily bandaged.

'Iestyn,' said Gruffydd with a smile, 'my heart is gladdened you survived.'

'I am fine, my lord, thank you.'

'And your arm?'

'A cut through the flesh only. It has been cleaned but needs sewing. I will live.'

'Good,' said Gruffydd, looking around the site again.

'Well, the first day goes to us, methinks,' he said eventually. 'God saw fit to keep surprise with us, and though they are the enemy, I can't help but feel sorry for those men who fell for naught more than allegiance to the wrong man.'

'All soldiers make their choices, my lord, and on this occasion, theirs was the wrong one.'

'Perhaps, but death of any man is never a good thing.'

'It is done,' said Iestyn, 'and you should fret not over fallen enemy. The day is won so drink in the victory.'

'The day may be done but the fight has only just started,' said Gruffydd. 'Caradog and Trahern will not let this pass and I expect them to come at us with everything within days. We have to prepare what defences we can ready for their assault.'

'What would you have us do?'

'Split the men into three groups,' said Gruffydd. 'The first to set up a perimeter half a league distant in all directions, not to engage the enemy but to provide us with advance notice of any approach by Caradog or Trahern. The second group will set about cutting stakes from the trees and securing them as obstacles against any advancing army but leave channels between them, filled with pits to slow any cavalry attack. Ensure our archers have clear fields of view to these killing zones.'

'Understood, my lord, but there will not be enough time to build a complete defence.'

'I understand, but where the spaces are open, there we will deploy Darcy's cavalry and the bulk of the men.'

'And the third group?'

'They will remove the dead from Mynydd Carn and pile them at the far end of the valley as a warning to those that come. What we lack in number we will make up for in attitude and the sight of so many fallen will send fear into the strongest of hearts.'

'As you will, my lord, but with your permission, I will have any dead horses butchered to supplement our rations.'

'Good idea and collect what water you can in any remaining barrels. If this battle lasts more than a few days we will need all we can get.'

'Anything else?'

'Yes, what has become of the prisoners?'

'They are secured in the farmhouse near the cairn. But there is something you should know: King Meilyr is amongst their number.'

'He survived?'

'Yes, though he is angry about his treatment and demands an audience.'

'Let him stew in his own juices a while longer. I will see him when I am ready.'

'So be it,' said Iestyn, and he left the king to wander alone amongst the carnage.

Six leagues away, Trahern stood atop the cliff edge looking down into the bay. The signs of occupation were everywhere, from the remains of countless fire pits to discarded clothing and the remnants of butchered animal carcasses. Obviously the area had been busy only days earlier but now there was nothing except an old man picking amongst the debris, hopeful for any discarded item that may be of value.

'Bring him,' said Trahern, and Meirion Goch passed the order on to two of the horsemen. 'I don't understand,' said Trahern quietly, 'why would they go to all this trouble to muster here only to disperse within days?'

'They must have moved inland, my lord.'

'Our spies would have let us know,' said Trahern, 'and there are no tracks leading up this way. The only possible way they could have gone is back out to sea. But to what end?'

'Perhaps they intend sailing to Ynys Mon and will bring pressure upon you from the north?'

'Possibly but why stop here in the first place?'

'Hopefully, he will be able to shed some sense on this,' said Meirion, nodding towards the old man being dragged up the path.

The soldier threw the captive at Trahern's feet and stood back to await his next command.

'Who are you?' asked Merion. 'And why are you in this place?'

'My lord,' gasped the old man without looking up, 'I am known only as Carter. Alas, I can no longer wield the tools needed to earn a crust and I now scavenge for food, no better than a mangy dog.'

'Stand up,' said Trahern, 'and show me your hands.'

The old man struggled to his feet and held out his hands, still avoiding eye contact.

'Are you hungry?' asked Trahern, seeing the crippled fingers knotted amongst themselves.

'Hunger is a constant companion, my lord.'

Trahern nodded towards Meirion who retrieved a hand of bread from his food pouch.

'Here,' said the king, handing over the bread. 'Now tell me, do you know who it was upon the sand?'

'Only that they sailed from Ireland and left yesterday morning.'

'Did you see them leave?'

'Aye, they travelled on foot and horse.'

'You must be mistaken,' said Meirion, 'for there are no tracks leaving this place and I see no other exit from the beach.'

'Nor will you,' said the old man, 'at least not at high tide but should you wait until the waters recede then just beyond that headland is a grassy slope that leads away from this place. If you send your scouts that way, you will no doubt find the tracks of the army you seek.'

'Where does it lead?' snapped Trahern.

'It ends in open country,' said the old man, 'but any man going that way would avoid the main path leading from north to south.'

Trahern spun his head to face Meirion.

'Turn the men around,' he ordered, 'and head back to the road, we move out immediately.'

'To what end?' asked Meirion.

'To catch up with Gruffydd of course!' shouted Trahern. 'He makes for Mynydd Carn.'

Trahern stood up and mounted his horse while in the background, the sergeants set about their weary men, starting them upon the march back.

'You have been a good help, old man,' said Trahern, 'but your news is worrisome.' He turned to one of the soldiers. 'Give him a piece of pork and a water skin,' he ordered, 'and leave him a coin for his trouble.'

'Thank you my lord,' gasped Carter, but Trahern was already riding away, the old man instantly forgotten.

Trahern's column had not travelled a league before their scouts rode back towards them, escorting a man riding from the north.

'Make way,' shouted one of the riders, 'we need to see the king.' They pushed their way through until they finally stood before Trahern.

'My lord,' said the rider, 'this man bears important news from Caradog.'

'Speak,' said Trahern, already concerned about what he was about to hear.

'My lord,' said Bowen, 'Mynydd Carn was attacked last night and most of Meilyr's army wiped out by the alliance led by Gruffydd. As we speak he goes to ground and builds his defences in anticipation of a counter-attack. Caradog is en route and is intent on retaking the Mynydd but anticipates you joining him by dawn.'

'Damnation,' cursed Trahern, his worst fears realised. 'This man is a thorn within my side and I swear I will see his head upon a spike before this matter is done. Marshal,' he called, 'continue the advance but double the pace, we need to get back to the Mynydd as soon as possible.'

'Aye, my lord,' came the reply and once more the tired column was stirred into action.

'What of you?' asked Meirion of Bowen as the king re-joined the column. 'Your horse looks exhausted.'

'I have ridden him hard since leaving Caradog,' said Bowen. 'He needs rest and food before I can once more join you.'

'Then see that he gets it,' said Meirion, 'for it is my belief we will need every man in the field before this thing is done.'

'I will be there as soon as possible,' came the reply.

***

Bowen watched the column leave before climbing back astride his horse. He had no intention of heading northward, at least not yet. This was the closest he had been to the cathedral of Saint David for many weeks, and despite all that had happened since leaving Dinefwr, he hadn't forgotten the humiliation he had suffered at the hands of Tewdwr.

It was common knowledge that Gwladus and her brat were holed up in the cathedral, and though many men valued the sanctity that such protection offered, he was no such man. He spurred his tired horse into action and headed south along the coast road knowing that Gwladus and Nesta were at last within his reach. He had unfinished business to attend to.

Mynydd Carn

September 19th, AD 1081

The hill was surprisingly quiet considering the amount of men upon it. With almost a thousand warriors on the forward slopes, you would think that the noise would be quite loud. But having survived the battle two nights earlier, most were calm and more interested in the tending of wounds and the upkeep of their weapons. Blades of all sorts ranging from meat cleavers and knives to the more savage pike blades and spearheads saw the attention of carefully wielded whetstones. Those few men who could afford, and indeed were capable of using, swords also honed their weapon's edges as they contemplated the main battle they knew was imminent.

Some of the poorer soldiers, the farm hands and labourers who had either been pressganged into service by men loyal to Gruffydd or lost loved ones at the hands of Trahern, sat further back up the hill, drinking ale and playing games of chance with what little they had of value.

Camp followers wandered amongst the fires, trying to sell their wares to the weary, whether that be ointments and poultices claimed to have miraculous healing powers or bowls of lukewarm potage, cooked back amongst the safety of the forest trees. Despite the earliness of the hour there were still women trying to sell their own bodies, fully aware that men close to death did not worry about time of day when it came to such things and good money was always available on the eve of most battles.

Gruffydd stood behind a row of archers firing arrows towards distant markers placed in the ground, watching them adjust their aim as their commander called out the drills.

'Furthest marker,' called the sergeant, 'three shafts, followed by nearest marker six shafts. *Go!*'

'How goes it?' asked Gruffydd, as the archers continued their practice.

'My men are well trained, my lord, these practices are designed to keep the arms loose ready for the fight. If we go a day without such training, the aches can seize in the shoulders which affects the aim.'

'I understand,' said Gruffydd.

'I hear their army is double ours in number,' said the sergeant quietly.

'Possibly,' said Gruffydd, 'especially if you combine the numbers of Caradog and Trahern. However, there is a hunger about us that will match mere numbers and there are some things we can do to even up the tally.'

'What things?' asked the sergeant.

'I will keep them to myself at the moment,' said Gruffydd, 'but rest assured that though the enemy may be cunning, this fox has tricks of his own.'

An hour or so later, Gruffydd walked up the hill towards the remains of the burned out farmhouse, accompanied with two dozen men-at-arms carrying pikes. As he approached, he saw a woman smoothing ointment on the burn of a wounded man. For a second he paused and stared at the woman before looking out over the battlefield deep in thought.

'Wait here,' he said to his guards and walked over to the woman.

'You,' he said, 'what is your name?'

'Bella, my lord.'

'I have seen you before?' said Gruffydd. 'Did you come over from Ireland?'

'No, my lord, I am from Gwynedd and came down with the archers. This is my husband, Derek Loxley.'

'I know you, Derek Loxley,' said Gruffydd crouching down. 'You fought alongside me at Llyn all those years ago.'

'Aye, that I did, my lord,' said Derek, 'along with a detachment of archers from Blackwater.'

'I remember,' said Gruffydd, 'a good group of men, as I recall.'

'The best,' said Derek, 'but alas, all now dead or begging for alms in the streets of Harlech.' For a moment there was silence as all three considered the consequences of war.

'So, do you always take your wife to war?' asked Gruffydd, finally, with a smile.

'Alas, it is how we pay our way in life,' said Derek, 'I hire out my bow while my wife treats the wounded. It's not ideal but it puts food in our bellies.'

'The battlefield is not a good place for a woman; you could be at risk here.'

'My place is behind our lines treating the wounded,' said Bella, 'and if the enemy managed to reach that far, then I would think that Derek was already dead. If that were the case, I would take my own life before they laid a hand on me. We are married before God and live together before God. If it is the Lord's will that we die together, then so be it.'

'An honourable commitment,' said Gruffydd and looked down at the pot of salve in her hand. 'Tell me, what ointment is this?'

The woman offered up the pot and he looked inside, seeing a grey sticky paste at the bottom.

'An ointment made from boiled animal fat and the herbs of the forest,' she replied. 'It soothes the burn and cleans the wound before the rot sets in.'

'Did you make it yourself?' he asked lifting the pot up to his nose.

'Yes, my lord.'

'It has a faint smell,' said Gruffydd, 'but not overpowering.'

'This ointment has healing properties, and needed not the roots to make an odour.'

'Can such a thing be made?'

'In what way?'

'Could you make an ointment such as this, but with a strong smell?'

'Of course,' said the woman, 'but there is no need of a perfume.'

'Perhaps not in this case,' said Gruffydd, 'but I may have another use. Have a pot full of this stuff made as soon as possible and have it brought directly to me. Make it the same consistency but I want a very strong odour, not foul but relatively pleasant. Do you understand?'

'I do, my lord, but I would know its use for different herbs have different properties.'

'The use is not important and I have no use of healing properties, just make it sticky with a strong smell.'

'Of course, my lord,' said the woman. She watched the king return to his men.

'Right,' Gruffydd said with a big sigh, 'let's get this thing done.' He walked towards the empty doorway and as the guards moved aside Gruffydd and his comrades entered the roofless building.

The king stopped and looked around the ruin as his soldiers spread out around the walls. The floor was crammed with prisoners taken on the night of the assault. Many slept the best they could while others stared into nowhere, contemplating their probable death at the hands of a brutal warlord.

Gruffydd walked through the sitting men and over to a pile of rubble, climbing up so he could be easily seen. Gradually the murmurs died down and all the prisoners looked up at the man with their lives in his hands. Gruffydd gazed around the room slowly, trying to make eye contact with as many as possible before speaking.

'Men of Powys,' he said eventually, 'my name is Gruffydd ap Cynan, true king of Gwynedd and the man responsible for your defeat. Heed me when I say I am not responsible for your current situation, for that burden is upon the hands of your foolish king. Two days ago I commanded my army to make every effort to kill you without quarter. Our arrows have cut down your fellows and our blades carved open the bodies of men with whom I had no quarrel. Many died horrible deaths while still abed under canvas, burned to death as they tried to escape. Many more will die of their wounds within days and if I am to be honest, then I have no doubt that some of you will probably dance at the end of a rope before this day is done.'

A murmur rippled around the room as the words sunk in.

'What are you waiting for?' shouted an angry voice. 'Just kill us; get on with it.'

'You are right,' said Gruffydd, 'I should have every man here slaughtered immediately, with no remorse. You came here intent on dealing death to me and my men without cause, yet as I look around I see no man here with whom I have a grudge. Not one face is familiar to me, nor are any of those bodies that are now nothing but meat for the wolves. Yet here we are, sworn enemies upon the field of battle. Yes, I should have you killed, but I'll tell you why I hesitate. I hesitate because you are good men led by traitors.'

'We are no traitors,' said a man standing up. 'We are loyal servants to our monarch, King Meilyr of Powys, and fight here to free Wales in his name.' The soldier was at least a head taller than his comrades and broad in the chest. His arms were bare and hugely muscled from a lifetime of hard work and brutal warfare. His bald head was covered with countless scars and one eye was half closed, the result of a blow from some long-forgotten cudgel.

'Is that what he told you?' asked Gruffydd.

'It is, for it is the truth,' said the man, 'and I will gladly fight any man who says otherwise.'

Gruffydd knew this was a dangerous man and it would be better to hang him before he caused any trouble but there was something about him and he decided to continue his line of questioning.

'What is your name, stranger?'

'They call me Edward Axe-hand,' said the man, 'and I am proud to serve Meilyr.'

'Is this your true name or a title won in battle?'

The prisoner looked over to where a guard stood beside two double-bladed axes, trophies from the battle.

'Return my weapons to me and I will show you why I am named thus,' he growled.

Despite their predicament, a murmur of acknowledgement rippled around the prisoners. Gruffydd stared at the man and the way the captives looked up to him. He was obviously a fearsome warrior and held the respect of his men.

'Well, Edward Axe-hand,' continued Gruffydd, 'what if I was to tell you that your campaign here was not to create a free Wales but quite the opposite.'

'Then I would call you a liar,' said Axe-hand.

Soldiers adjusted their grips on spear hafts around the room as several voices rose to agree with the warrior. Gruffydd held up his hand to calm everyone down.

'Listen to me,' he said, 'hear me out and I will give you your voice.' The noise died down as Gruffydd continued. 'Your king joined an unholy alliance with Caradog of Gwent and the man who has stolen my lands from me in the north, Trahern of Gwynedd. Between them they agreed to sweep away any of the smaller monarchs and nobles who did not swear allegiance to one of them, and to eventually carve up Wales equally, with each king taking a third.'

'You say nothing that is new to us,' said Axe-hand, 'and often such wars are justified to make a greater good.'

'I agree,' said Gruffydd, 'but what if I was to tell you that your kings issued promissory notes in return for the support of the English Crown.'

'Then I would call you a liar,' growled Axe-hand. 'This is about unity, to combine all the warring kingdoms in our country under one banner against the English.'

'That is what they told you,' said Gruffydd, 'but it is untrue. As you would expect, I have spies in many places and they have reported something entirely different. What if I was to tell you that William of Normandy has promised the three kings his full support and indeed that of the lords of the Marches, if they were to unite Wales.'

'Then I would laugh at you, for the last thing the bastard wants is a united Wales.'

'You would think so,' replied Gruffydd, 'but if there was an agreement for suitable recompense, then why would he need to make war on the Welsh? His treasury would already benefit, his men would not risk death along the Marches, and if the document was carefully worded, the country would eventually come under his banner anyway.'

'How?'

'Don't forget, a signed agreement outlives the signatories and once those party to it are dead, their successors bear the responsibility. I believe your king, along with the other two traitors, have signed away our sons' heritage in return for the luxury of undisputed rule now.'

Voices were raised again, this time in anger.

'Wait,' called Axe-hand, raising his hand in the air, 'these are just words, Gruffydd; you make serious accusations yet we see no evidence. For all we know they are just untruths from a bitter man seeking justification for his own ends.'

'I don't expect you to believe me,' said Gruffydd, 'but perhaps you will believe your own king.' He turned to face the doorway as two men escorted a bedraggled man up to the pile of rubble and cast him at Gruffydd's feet.

Many of the prisoners got to their feet in anger and the guards presented their spears in case of trouble. In addition, crossbow men appeared at every window and doorway, each aiming into the crowd. One of Gruffydd's men threw a rope over one of the beams and tied it off before placing a table beneath the dangling noose. Within moments, the guards lifted Meilyr onto the table and placed the noose around his neck.

'Behold your king,' said Gruffydd calling out above the noise. 'This man betrayed you, betrayed Powys and betrayed Wales. Under his command you marched to defeat with William of Normandy as your paymaster. With so many dead, the mighty kingdom of Powys is now an open field for the lords of the Marches. Many children are now without fathers and our country is weaker against the threat of the English.'

He turned to face Meilyr on the table.

'Tell, them, Meilyr, tell them of the unholy deal you made with William.'

'Cut me down from here, Gruffydd,' said Meilyr, 'for I am a king by rightful birth and demand I am treated as such.'

'In what way, Meilyr?' asked Gruffydd as the noise died down. 'Tell me, what is expected of me now? Are you not a defeated enemy? Is not your life forfeit in my hands?'

'You know what I mean, Gruffydd,' whined Meilyr, 'as monarchs we are due leniency and repatriation, even if defeated in battle.'

'And what of these men?' asked Gruffydd. 'Are they not also deserved of leniency?'

Meilyr looked around at the men below him. Each set of eyes stared back, expecting strong leadership from the man they called king. The battle had gone badly for Meilyr, and though he often talked of bravery in adversity, the reality was far different and his insides churned with fear.

'Of course,' spluttered Meilyr, his voice shaking in fear, 'as their king I also request their release.'

'So you would not see them hanged?'

'No, of course not.'

'And you would not abandon them to their fate?'

'Never!' shouted Meilyr.

'Then why don't you tell them where we found you, Meilyr? Tell them where it was my cavalry cut down your guards and took you into captivity.'

The man on the table fell silent.

'No?' continued Gruffydd. 'Nothing to say?'

'I was seeking reinforcements,' said Meilyr quietly.

'Really,' said Gruffydd, 'well, if that's all you have to say, allow me to expand.' He turned to face the captives. 'While you men were fighting and dying in this man's name, your king was caught fleeing the battlefield as fast as his horse could carry him. He and his fellows were found more than two leagues away, heading northward at full gallop.'

'I tell you, I was seeking reinforcements!' shouted Meilyr.

'What reinforcements lay northward?' replied Gruffydd. 'Caradog is east, Trahern is south, yet you went north, the only place that would see no fighting. I put it to you, King Meilyr, the only saving you had on your mind was that of your own skin.'

'No,' shouted Meilyr, 'you are wrong. I could have been back within days with an army big enough to wipe you from this Mynydd.'

'There is no army northward,' shouted Gruffydd. 'My scouts have been ten leagues and more, there are no reinforcements that way. Speak truly, Meilyr, or I swear you will hang this instant as a traitor and a coward.' The men holding the other end of the hangman's noose pulled on the rope, forcing the terrified king up onto his toes.

'This is your *last chance*, Meilyr!' roared Gruffydd. 'Where is this mythical army you speak of?'

'In Chester,' shouted Meilyr, 'under the command of Huw D'Avranches. Now get me down from here!'

Every man present fell silent as the words sunk in. Meilyr looked around, realising he had made a mistake.

'Wait,' he said, as the noose slackened off, 'you don't understand. The earl of Chester is a valuable ally. The agreement between us would make Wales united once more. Yes, there would be a few farms lost but in the main the whole of Wales would have benefitted. Just imagine, no more wars, no more burned farms, no more lost sons. We all would have benefited, especially Powys.'

'How?' said a voice.

'What do you mean?' asked Meilyr.

'Tell me how I, a farm labourer, will benefit from your deal with the English.'

'Well, there would be more work,' spluttered Meilyr, 'and you could raise your family in peace.'

'Under the yoke of the English?'

'Yes, but there would be no more wars. Life would be good.'

'For whom?' said the man. 'For the nobility, perhaps but the likes of me would just work harder to pay more taxes while those lords who take the English coin get fatter and richer. I for one would rather die than serve the English.'

'Aye,' shouted some of the men, 'me too.'

'Yes,' spluttered Meilyr, feeling the mood of his men turn against him, 'but think of your sons, think of the life they could have.'

'My sons lie dead out on that hill,' yelled another. 'They fell in your name so don't preach about how my family will benefit.'

'But I am your king!' shouted Meilyr. 'And there are things you don't understand. Sometimes, some must die so many more will live.'

All the men were on their feet now shouting their opposition to any agreement with the English.

'Wait,' shouted Gruffydd, holding up his hand. 'Your king has a point. Listen to what he has to say.' As the noise fell, Gruffydd turned to Meilyr.

'Say that again,' he said.

'Say what?'

'Your last statement.'

'I said that sometimes a man must die so many will live.'

'And you truly believe that?'

'Yes, it is the way of things. When measured against the benefit of many, then sometimes a man has to lay down his life.'

'It may surprise you to know,' said Gruffydd turning to address the captives, 'that I actually agree with your king on this point. Sometimes, that is how it must be. However, often they are nought but pretty words from those in places of safety. The truth of the feeling is only learned when a man's own life is at risk.' He turned back to face Meilyr. 'You are the king of a proud kingdom, Meilyr, and these men fought bravely in your name. Do they deserve to die now?'

'Of course not.'

'Then I will make you an offer. Someone dies here today and the choice is yours. Whichever you choose, the others will live. Agreed?'

'I don't understand,' said Meilyr.

'It is easy,' said Gruffydd, 'you are the king of these men so you will make the final choice. Once the deed is done, I guarantee the survivors will leave this place alive.'

'And you or your men will not cut us down once outside the confines of this place?'

'You have my word.'

'Then I agree,' said Meilyr in relief, realising he was not going to hang.

'Good, then the choice is this. You or your men, Meilyr, who walks free?'

'*What?*' gasped Meilyr.

'Make your choice who dies here this day, you or all these men before you.'

'That is unfair,' cried Meilyr, 'the choice is not balanced.'

'Why not? These men are yours to do with as you see fit. You expected them to die in your name anyway, what is so different?'

'There is no balance in this!' shouted Meilyr. 'They do not deserve to die.'

'Then choose yourself,' said Gruffydd, 'and let them return to their farms.'

'You expect me to sign my own death warrant?' gasped Meilyr.

'Sometimes one man must fall so many will live,' said Gruffydd, 'is that not what you just said?'

'I did, but . . .'

'But what? Does it not count if it is a king who should sacrifice himself in the service of his people?'

'What would you do?' said Meilyr. 'In my place you would not be so self-righteous.'

'But I am not in your place, Meilyr, I am the victor here. Now, make your choice.'

'You cannot do this!' shouted Meilyr.

'Make your choice!' screamed Gruffydd, drawing his sword. 'Or I swear I will kill every one of them right now and have you boiled alive before this day is out.'

Lances were raised again around the room and crossbows aimed at the prisoners in case the command came.

Meilyr looked around the room and finally made his decision.

'I am a king,' he gasped, 'chosen by God to lead the kingdom of Powys. Therefore, it is only right that I live and my servants sacrifice themselves in my name. I will be the one to walk free.'

The farmhouse fell silent as his words sunk in around the captives.

'So,' said Gruffydd eventually, 'you have chosen to save yourself over the lives of all the men here.'

'Yes,' said Meilyr, 'I am a king and they are bound to lay their lives down in my name.'

'And the prisoners outside?'

'*Yes!*' cried Meilyr, the fear evident on his face. 'Kill them too if you must, kill them all, but let me go free. I am a monarch, I am King Meilyr of Powys and I demand I be treated in a way that befits my station.'

Gruffydd's face scowled in disapproval.

'You disgust me,' he said quietly before turning to one of the guards. 'Release him.'

'*Wait!*' roared a voice and Gruffydd saw Axe-hand pushing his way through the prisoners towards him. Two guards blocked his path but Gruffydd spoke up.

'Let him come.'

Axe-hand approached and after staring at the shamed Meilyr upon the table, turned to face Gruffydd.

'My lord,' he said, 'you were right and I was wrong. We have fought in a false campaign and I know I speak for every man here when I say that had we known the truth, we would never have picked up arms against you.'

'I understand,' said Gruffydd, 'but alas, there is nothing I can do. I have given my word as a king and if I renege on that then I am no better than the coward before us.'

'There is another way,' said Axe-hand.

'Say your piece, Axe-hand.'

'There is no need for my men to die here today. Indeed, given the chance we can swell your numbers against others who fight under false promises. There are over a hundred of us still alive, all hardened in warfare but we have fought on the wrong side. Allow us to live and I pledge my axe to you, to fight against whosoever comes against you in the coming days and months.'

Gruffydd looked around the ruins.

'And these men?'

'They will go where I lead,' said Axe-hand. 'They are honest men who have served a corrupt king. Let them live and we will lead the vanguard into battle to prove our allegiance.'

'Your idea has merit, Axe-hand, but alas, your king chose otherwise.'

'If he was dead, then would you be agreeable?'

'I gave my word not to kill him,' said Gruffydd, 'and my word is my bond.'

'I understand,' said Axe-hand, 'but you spoke on behalf of yourself, you did not speak for me.'

Without warning, Axe-hand pushed Gruffydd aside and grabbed the knife from the falling king's belt. Guards ran forward but before they could do anything, the warrior had jumped up onto the table and stood behind Meilyr, with the knife upon the disgraced king's throat.

Gruffydd called out to his guards.

'Hold your fire,' he shouted and turned to face the two men on the table. 'What do you think you are doing?' he asked.

'Allowing my comrades the luxury of living a few more days,' said Axe-hand, 'by ending the life of a traitor.'

'Traitor or not, if you kill a king, your life will be forfeit,' said Gruffydd, 'according to the laws of Hywel Dda.'

'One life for the benefit of many,' came the reply, 'remember?'

'No,' gasped Meilyr, 'please don't do this.'

'Too late, traitor,' whispered Axe-hand and slowly drew the blade across Meilyr's throat. The doomed king's cries of fear and pain became gurgles as blood poured into his airways and everyone watched in silence as he struggled against the inevitable. Urine soaked his leggings and the smell of faeces filled the air as his bowels emptied in fear. Eventually he fell off the table, the noose tightening into his open throat as his bodyweight extended the rope.

An archer took aim on the chest of Axe-hand, waiting for the command to kill him, but Gruffydd raised his hand to stay any execution. For what seemed an age, he stared at the growing pool of blood as it crept across the floor until finally he looked up at the man responsible for killing a king.

'Edward Axe-hand,' he said quietly, 'in front of all these witnesses you have killed the king of Powys and you know the punishment.'

'I do,' said Axe-hand.

'Then my sentence is this. In the forthcoming battle you will fight the enemy in the name of a free Wales. Should you survive the day, you will forfeit your freedom and fight in any further conflicts directed by me or my officers, until such time as you are killed or suffer such wounds that your life comes to an end. In this way, the laws of Hywel Dda will be fulfilled and honour will be served. Do you understand?'

Axe-hand grinned at the sentence.

'And my men?'

'Will be at your side until this thing is over, then they can return whence they came as free men.'

Axe-hand turned to face the prisoners.

'What say you?' he shouted.

'*Aye!*' roared the men. Axe-hand threw away the knife before jumping from the table and approaching Gruffydd. As he neared the king he stopped and turned his head to look at the guard holding his two axes.

'I believe those belong to me,' he said menacingly.

The soldier took a step backwards and looked towards Gruffydd for guidance.

'Give them to him,' said Gruffydd.

'My lord,' shouted a soldier, 'you place your own life in his hands.'

'Give him his weapons!' yelled Gruffydd. He watched as the giant axe-man snatched them from the guard's hands. Finally, Axe-hand turned and approached the king. Everyone fell silent as they waited to see what happened next. If Axe-hand attacked, there was nothing Gruffydd or anyone else could do to stop him. Both men stared into each other's eyes as if seeking evidence of the inner man.

'To the death?' asked Gruffydd, eventually.

'To the death,' confirmed Axe-hand. He dropped to one knee to pledge allegiance.

The Bishop's Palace

September 19th, AD 1081, early evening

Queen Gwladus walked around the cathedral grounds, arm in arm with her daughter. Ever since the harrowing birth of her brother, Nesta had spent every moment she could with her mother, hardly leaving her side, and now Gwladus had sent the baby over the sea, there was an even greater closeness between them.

'Mother, do you think we are going to be all right?' asked Nesta.

'As long as we stay within the boundaries of the cathedral then no man would dare inflict harm upon us,' replied Gwladus.

'No, I don't mean now,' said Nesta, 'I mean when this is all over, the war between Dada and Caradog.'

'I wish I knew,' said Gwladus with a sigh. 'The politics of men are like ever-changing seasons and I know not from where the next winds blow.'

'Do you think Hywel is alive?'

'I have to believe he is,' said Gwladus, 'and see no reason why Caradog would kill a prince. I think he is worth more as a prisoner and when this is all over, he will be ransomed back to us.'

'I miss him,' said Nesta, 'and desperately want to see him again.'

'As do I,' said Gwladus, 'and pray hard each night that he is being treated kindly wherever he may be.'

'At least Tarw is safe.'

'He is, though I just wish you had gone with him.'

'My place is at your side,' said Nesta.

'A noble gesture,' said Gwladus, 'and in truth you are a daily comfort to me but I would sleep better at night knowing you are safe.'

'Whether safe or not, I will not leave you,' said Nesta.

Gwladus squeezed her daughter's arm affectionately as they continued their walk, silently reassuring her daughter that everything was going to be all right.

'Here we are,' said Gwladus as they reached the cathedral, 'back again and it is almost time for our evening meal.'

'My lady,' came a shout and Gwladus looked up to see Walters the chef running towards them.

'Walters,' said Gwladus in surprise, 'I thought you were with my husband at Nine Wells Bay.'

'Indeed I was,' said Walters, 'but was sent here with urgent information.'

'Then pray tell, for the days stretch unending without news of the war.'

'My lady, your husband has already marched northward alongside king Gruffydd of Gwynedd. They intend to meet the armies of the three kings in battle before the month is out and settle this situation once and for all. I would have come sooner but Caradog's spies swarm like bees around these parts.'

Gwladus's hand flew to her mouth in shock as the news sunk in.

'But surely our forces are not ready?'

'They are as ready as they will ever be,' said Walters, 'and seek the advantage of surprise.'

'Will it be enough?'

'I am no tactician, my lady, just a mere cook and better men than I make the decisions. All I know is that they have marched northward to find the foe and may have already clashed swords.'

'Then I pray God goes with them,' said Gwladus, holding Nesta just a little tighter. 'What of you, will you be returning to his side?'

'No, the king sent me back to ensure your safety.'

'We enjoy sanctuary here in the cathedral, Walters, and our safety is guaranteed.'

'In times of war there is no such thing, my lady,' replied Walters. 'Desperate times breed desperate men, and if Caradog thought your captivity could sway the outcome of the battle then he would not hesitate to breach these walls in search of you and your daughter.'

'I don't agree,' said Gwladus. 'Not even Caradog would risk God's wrath by going against the word of the church.'

'Let's hope that is the case,' said Walters, 'but in the meantime, I will stay by your side.'

'With respect, Walters, you are a cook and as such can offer little protection.'

'The bishop is a kindly man, my lady, but will not allow men-at-arms within the boundary of the cathedral so armed protection was out of the question. However, I have something perhaps more valuable than any ordinary soldier can offer: a certain cowardice that heightens my sense of self-preservation.'

'You are no coward, Walters.' Gwladus smiled. 'As recent events have proved.'

Walter's hand crept to his face, his fingers feeling the lump where his broken nose had healed unevenly.

'I was lucky,' he said, 'and would have died if it wasn't for Nesta. I'm not sure what value I will bring but your husband has placed his faith in me so we need to put things in place that will protect you if they come looking.'

'Like what?'

'I don't know yet,' said Walters, 'but there is no time to waste. The fighting may have already started and we need to have a clear plan of action in case the madness breaches the cathedral walls.'

'Where do we start?' asked Gwladus.

'I think that first of all we should retire to your quarters and talk the options through. I know not this place but you have been here for a while and will have a better idea of what is possible.'

'So be it,' said Gwladus. 'Come this way.' With that she headed towards a small door in the side of the bishop's palace and entered the majestic building as Nesta and Walters followed closely behind.

'So,' said Gwladus, 'tell me about my husband and his endeavours, is he well?'

Walters paced around the room, looking out of the windows as he passed.

'He is well,' he said without turning, 'as far as I am aware.'

'You don't know?'

'The army set out a few days ago and I was sent back as an afterthought. For all I know, they may have already encountered the enemy.'

'So he could already be dead?' said Gwladus quietly, looking over to where Nesta was playing with a wooden doll.

'I would worry not,' said Walters, 'your husband is a resourceful man and Gruffydd is renowned for his ability in battle. Their numbers are adequate though tactics will play the greater part in the days to come.'

'Even so, three armies against one is not a fair fight.'

'War is not fair, my lady.'

For a while there was silence as they both considered the consequences. The stone room was dark but the shadows were lightened by flickering candles. A small fire sent waves of comforting warmth across the cold flagstones and Walters could see a bed had been made up for the queen and Nesta to share. A knock came on the door and Gwladus looked up in alarm.

'It's the servant,' she hissed, 'with the evening meal. Quickly, you can't be found in here.'

Walters ran across to the bed and crawled beneath as the queen composed herself and stood to face the door.

'Nesta,' she said eventually, 'please open the door.'

Nesta turned the handle and stood to one side as two serving girls came in carrying trays, placing them on the table before turning and curtseying to the queen.

'There's pork and cawl, my lady,' said one of the girls, 'and a pitcher of honeyed wine. Will you require anything else?'

'No, thank you,' said Gwladus but as the girls turned to leave, she changed her mind. 'Wait,' she said suddenly, 'would it be possible to have a little extra this evening? I know I ask a lot but I have a great hunger upon me for some reason. Perhaps it is all that fresh air from the walks in the cathedral grounds.'

'Me too,' said Nesta quickly, realising her mother's ploy, 'I could eat a whole cow!'

'A whole cow?' said the servant with a grin. 'Well, I don't know about that, miss, but I'm sure if I speak nicely to the bishop's cook, we can find enough for you to have your very own feast.'

'Really?' said Nesta, clapping her hands. 'That would be wonderful.'

'Of course,' said the servant with a smile, 'you just leave it to me.' She turned to Gwladus. 'I will return as soon as possible, my lady.'

'Thank you,' said Gwladus and closed the door behind them.

'That was very clever of you, Nesta,' said Gwladus. 'You are a very special little girl.'

'We couldn't eat without Master Walters,' said Nesta.

'I'm sure he will be very grateful,' said Gwladus.

'A whole cow,' mumbled Walters from beneath the bed, 'I'm not sure I can manage one of those.'

Gwladus smiled and Nesta had a fit of the giggles, but as they heard the footsteps coming up the stairs again, both mother and daughter composed themselves before the young girl opened the door.

'Here we are,' said the servant, placing the extra tray on the table. 'I found some chicken, another loaf and a pile of ham freshly carved this very morning. That should fill your bellies to bursting.'

'It truly is a feast,' said Nesta, 'a feast of my very own.'

'Thank you,' said Gwladus, 'we are very grateful.'

'Is there anything else, my lady?'

'No, we are fine.'

The servant curtsied again and left the room.

'You can come out now,' said Nesta, 'they've gone.'

Walters emerged and stood up sneezing as the dust from beneath the bed crept into his nostrils. His eyes wandered to the table and the pile of food upon it.

'Come,' said Gwladus, 'join us at the table. There is plenty for all.'

Walters did as he was bid and waited patiently as Gwladus shared out the pork onto two trenchers before putting the bowl of gravy between them for dipping.

'Go on, fill your belly,' she said, 'there is plenty to be had.'

'Indeed,' said Walters, 'I have never seen so much food for just three mouths.'

Without waiting for a reply he dipped the bread into the gravy and pushed it into his mouth, much to the delight of Nesta as the juices ran down his chin.

'Nesta,' hissed Gwladus, 'stop it.'

Walters stopped mid-bite and made a funny face at the young girl. In response she poked out her tongue and was admonished by her mother again.

'Nesta, where are your manners? Master Walters is a guest, and though the circumstances are strange, we will treat him as such. Now, please apologise.'

'I'm sorry,' mumbled Nesta, looking down at her food.

'So am I,' said Walters after swallowing the bread.

'For what?' asked Gwladus, reaching for a piece of chicken. 'You have done nothing to apologise for.'

'I'm sorry they didn't bring a whole cow,' said Walters and winked at Nesta as she looked up in surprise.

For a few seconds there was silence until finally both Nesta and Walters burst into giggles.

'Nesta,' chided Gwladus again but soon all three were laughing heartily. For the rest of the meal, everyone forgot about the predicament they were in and the war being waged outside the walls of the cathedral.

Eventually Nesta yawned and, much to the girl's disappointment, she was ushered to bed by her mother. Gwladus told her a story of when she was a child and as soon as her daughter was asleep the queen pulled up one of the chairs to sit opposite Walters at the fire.

'This is nice,' said Walters as she sat down and handed him a jug of ale. 'A warm room, a full belly and a tankard of ale. Apart from a family, what more could a man want?'

'Do you have a family, Master Walters?'

'No, my lady, I was brought up on a farm not far from here but was orphaned as a boy. Luckily I was taken in by the baker in Dinefwr village, but when he also died I managed to get work in the castle kitchen.'

'So you are the one who made our lovely bread?'

'I did sometimes,' said Walters, poking the logs with a fire iron, 'but mostly I just help out where needed. There's always plenty to do in a kitchen.'

'I suspect it is hard work.'

'It is, and the hours are long but it is warm and I get fed. That is enough for me.' He picked up another log from the pile beside the fire and placed it carefully amongst the flames.

'Tell me, Master Walters, what do you make of all this?'

'I am a mere cook, my lady, and my thoughts are irrelevant.'

'You are a cook who saved my life and the lives of my children. I say that makes your opinion matter.'

'Well, I'm not sure I understand all the politics but I do believe I am stood on the side that is right, and that Caradog and his men will be found wanting when Gruffydd and your husband finally catch up with him.'

'Hmm,' said Gwladus, 'I sincerely hope you are right, Master Walters, for I have my doubts. I love my husband deeply, but I worry about his role in this matter.'

'I have spent a while alongside him these past few weeks,' replied Walters, 'and I have seen nothing to give me similar concern.'

'Yes, but this is only the build-up. His heart is as big as an ox and he holds no fear but we are talking about going up against three warrior kings, each hardened upon battlefields across Wales. How can he even begin to think he can emerge the victor?'

'I'll tell you why, my lady,' said Walters, 'because of the man stood alongside him.'

'You talk of Gruffydd?'

'I do,' replied Walters and took another drink from his tankard before continuing. 'He is no less a warrior than those in the alliance and has spent his life seeking to reclaim what he believes is rightfully his.'

'There are excellent warriors on both sides, Walters, and one man does not an army make.'

'Perhaps not, but Gruffydd boasts an intelligence scarcely seen in most men, and seldom in a king.'

'Am I to take it you know a lot of kings?' asked Gwladus, smiling as she sipped on her wine.

'My lady,' spluttered Walters, 'of course not, I only meant . . . I mean, I didn't mean to offend.'

'I jest with you, Walters,' said Gwladus with a weak smile. 'Please continue.'

'What I should have said,' replied Walters with a nod of his head, 'was I have heard the officers talking in the command tents and they admire the skill of Gruffydd not only as a king but as a warrior and it is they who shout his praises. According to those men, many of whom have served under several masters, Gruffydd ap Cynan is by far the best commander under whom they have served.'

'I see,' said Gwladus, 'and it is your opinion that alongside him, then my husband will enjoy a victory?'

'He has every chance,' said Walters, 'Gruffydd has the wiles of a wildcat and is reputed to often engage methods not expected by his enemies. It is this trait, alongside the quality of his men, that makes me believe victory is possible.'

'I suppose it's all we can hope for,' said Gwladus.

'There is one other thing that gives me hope, my lady, another trait that I have seldom seen in any other man.'

'And that is?'

'A hunger. A desire to reclaim something that he believes is his with all his heart. He has set out upon this task fully committed to either be victorious or die in the trying. There is no other option open to him and when a man carries a quest in his heart as passionately as he does, then it makes him one of two things: mad or dangerous. I suspect the latter.'

'I hope you are correct, Walters,' said Gwladus. 'I truly do.'

For a while silence fell again and both stared into the flames.

'What will you do, my lady?' asked Walters eventually. 'You know, if the worst thing happens and our men are bettered?'

'I don't know,' said Gwladus, 'Tewdwr told me I should try and get to Ireland but my home is here.'

'In my limited experience, my lady, home is wherever you can lay your head in safety. For a while mine was with the baker in Dinefwr, then beneath a shelf in the castle kitchens. Each was as welcome as the other but at this time I can't see it ever getting better than this, even if it is for only one night.'

'Why one night?' asked Gwladus.

'You can't stay here, my lady. Your presence is well known and whether Caradog wins or falls, those loyal to him may well seek retribution. No, we must spirit you away as soon as we can.'

'But to where?'

'I have been thinking upon this and know of a place not far from here where you will be safe. It is small but nobody goes there anymore. If we can get there unchallenged, Caradog's men will never find you.'

'But we can't stay there forever.'

'Perhaps not, but this war will soon be over. If your husband is victorious you can re-join him in Dinefwr.'

'And if he falls?'

'Then we will seek transport to Ireland as soon as it is safe to do so.'

'I don't know, Walters,' said Gwladus, 'it is a great risk to leave this place.'

'I know,' said Walters, 'but it is at the heart of the war and anyone could walk in here at any time with swords drawn. It wouldn't be the first time the cathedral has been sacked.'

'Is this the wish of my husband?'

'He has tasked me with keeping you safe, though the details he has left up to me. I don't know if what I am proposing is the right path but what I do know is that I will die rather than see you or Nesta hurt. This place, despite its grandeur, is far too dangerous, for every man within ten leagues knows you are here. In my opinion we should leave while we have a chance and the place I have in mind is as safe as any.'

'Let me sleep on it,' said Gwladus eventually, and she walked over to remove one of the covers from the bed. 'Here,' she said, handing the blanket to Walters, 'make yourself as comfortable as possible. Tomorrow the sun will shine anew and perhaps give us fresh thoughts. For all we know the war may already be over and we fret for no reason.'

'Aye it could,' said Walters, 'let us hope it is so.'

He lay out the blanket near the fire and turned his back so the queen could get into bed. For the first time in a long while he felt warm, his belly was full and he looked forward to a sound sleep in a place of safety. Little did he know how wrong he was.

Six leagues away, a scout dismounted and ran past the king's bodyguard to give his report.

'My lord,' he shouted, 'Mynydd Carn lies beyond the next ridge.'

'Understood,' said Caradog and looked back along the column of his army. 'Peterson, pass the word for the men to don their armour and drop any burdens here. The reserve will go firm and look after the stores while the rest of us advance.'

'Should we not send scouts to spy out the lay of the land?' asked Peterson.

'I see no reason to wait,' said Caradog. 'They took the Mynydd yesterday morning so have not had much time to create fortifications. Wounds will still ache and tiredness will abound. No, we will not give them a moment's more rest than we have to and strike while they still recover.'

'My lord,' said the scout, 'we saw riders upon the ridge. No doubt, Gruffydd already knows of our approach.'

'All the more reason to make haste,' said Caradog, 'every moment we hesitate is extra time they have to prepare. Peterson, organise the men as instructed. Bring the shield bearers to the fore in case of archers but prepare our own to return the fire.'

'Aye, my lord.'

'Deploy the cavalry on either flank until we see the lie of the land but be prepared to alter formation at my command.'

'Aye, my lord,' said Peterson and rode back down the column issuing his commands. Soon, they were ready to continue the advance though this time each man wearing whatever armour they had accumulated over the previous few months. Behind them a small mountain of stores lay at the roadside, a collection of everything not needed in the heat of battle.

'Men of Gwent,' called Caradog, 'you know why it is we are here. Let us wipe this devil's spawn from the field so we can continue with our aim of uniting Wales. In these past few days we have been let down by lesser men so it falls to your capable hands to put right what has been made wrong. Heed your sergeants in the next few hours and this will be done by noon tomorrow.' He turned to his second in command. 'You know what we have to do, Peterson, lead them out.'

'My lord, they are here,' shouted a rider, reining in his horse.

'Where?' asked Gruffydd.

'Over the first hill to the east. They head for Clearwater Pass with considerable strength.'

'Good,' said Gruffydd and turned to his second in command. 'Iestyn, you will muster our forces at the base of the hill, three ranks deep and across a broad front whilst keeping a hundred in reserve. Do not advance unless I specifically order it, I want as many of the enemy as possible on the battlefield before we commit our men.'

'Understood,' said Iestyn.

'Tewdwr, you position your men to the rear but be ready to fall on any breaches in the line and to defend our flanks. You are to stay fluid and hold back from engaging the enemy unless they break through. If we are to succeed, we need to see their full strength and that can only be done if he commits all his forces to the fray.'

'My men are ready,' said Tewdwr, 'and will not be found wanting.'

'Good, for every blade will be needed in the hours before us.'

'My lord,' said Iestyn, 'how will we know if he holds any in reserve?'

'Leave that to me,' said Gruffydd, 'just wait until you hear the signal.'

'What about me?' asked Lord Darcy.

'Keep your cavalry hidden amongst the trees until you see the counter-attack,' said Gruffydd. 'The signal will be two long blasts of a horn.'

'But surely you will need cavalry before then to counter the threat of their horsemen?'

'I will, but I will use my own troops in the first instance. They will contain them as much as possible and when Caradog thinks he may have us bettered, then you will unleash hell upon his flanks.'

'Understood,' said Lord Darcy, as he stepped back.

'Right,' said Gruffydd, 'we have done everything we possibly can in very little time, now it is down to courage, ability and heart. I doubt he will attack before dawn but we must be prepared. Gentlemen, to your stations.'

All the remaining officers turned and made their way to their prearranged positions knowing that before the day was over many of them would probably be dead. Gruffydd stared over to the far mountain.

'Bring your worst, Caradog,' he said to himself, 'for we are waiting.'

Bishop Sulien sat in the comfortable chair alongside his own fire. His blanket was wrapped tightly around him and he stared into the embers of the night fire. Dawn was only a few hours away yet he could not sleep, nervous about the developing situation and the immense responsibility the care of a queen placed upon his shoulders.

His head started to drop, but he jerked upright as a knock came on the door.

'Who is it?' he asked, sitting up and reaching for the candle.

'My lord bishop,' said a voice, 'you have an important visitor.'

'What is his name?'

'He would not say, only that he comes with great news from Mynydd Carn.'

Sulien hesitated but realised that as he was already awake, he may as well receive the messenger. He walked over to the door and saw his personal servant standing there holding a candle of his own.

'Master Luke, come in for a moment,' said Sulien and as the servant entered, the bishop peered down the corridor before closing the door.

'This messenger,' said Sulien, turning to face the servant, 'is his face known to you?'

'No, your grace.'

'And does he look as if he has ridden far?'

'He does and smells of the horse.'

'Is there anything else you can say about him?'

'He seems of surly character, your grace, not a man I would want to quarrel with. Perhaps you should wait until dawn?'

'No, I will receive him, but first there is something I want you to do.'

The servant listened intently as the bishop gave his instructions. Within minutes he had left the room and scurried away to his task as Bishop Sulien made his way calmly to the lesser hall, the place where all such visitors were received.

Opening the door, he saw a man dressed in the manner of a soldier warming himself at the remnants of the fire.

'Welcome, traveller,' said Sulien, 'I trust you have not been waiting too long.'

'It matters not,' said the stranger, 'for I have been enjoying the benefit of these embers, a luxury most welcome after a long ride in the cold of the night.'

'Indeed,' said the bishop. 'Can I get you a jug of ale or a morsel of food?'

'I neither thirst nor hunger, your grace, and if you don't mind, I would rather pass on my message and be on my way.'

'Of course,' said Sulien as the doors opened again and Luke entered the room. The bishop turned back to the messenger. 'So, pray tell, what is so important that it makes you ride through the dark hours?'

'My lord bishop,' said the man, glancing over at Luke, 'I have brought news from the battle but it is for your ears only.'

'You can say what you will in front of Luke, he has been a faithful manservant to me for many years and is completely trustworthy.'

'Alas, I have my orders,' said the rider, 'and the parchment within my cloak must be seen by you only.'

Sulien was intrigued and turned to his servant.

'Leave us, Luke,' he said, 'I will be fine.'

'But my lord,' said the servant, 'you know not who this man is.'

'Whether he be king or brigand, all travellers are welcome here and my life is in God's hands. Go back to bed and I will see you at morning service.'

The servant nodded and left the room, closing the door behind him. When he had left, Sulien turned back to the stranger.

'Now,' he said, 'I am intrigued. Please share your message.'

The stranger walked towards the bishop, his hand reaching beneath his cloak as if retrieving a scroll. But as he drew near, he pulled out a knife and with a sudden rush pushed Sulien up against the wall, the blade cold upon the bishop's neck.

'You should have listened to your servant, holy man,' he growled. 'He talked a lot of sense.'

'Who are you?' gasped Sulien. 'And what do you want?'

'What I want is the location of the queen,' said the man, his spittle spraying on the bishop's face. 'Tell me where she is and you live; deny me what I want and you get to meet your saviour sooner than you expected.'

'This is a house of God,' said the bishop, 'and your soul will surely rot in hell should you continue upon this path.'

'My soul is already beyond redemption. Now tell me where she is or I will kill you where you stand.'

'I will not,' said the bishop. 'She enjoys the sanctuary of the church and I will not breach that privilege.'

'So be it,' said the man, but as he tensed his body ready to cut the bishop's throat, another figure burst through the outer door and hurled himself on the attacker, knocking him to the floor.

'Bishop, run!' shouted the second man. 'Hide yourself!'

Sulien staggered through a side door and held it shut, listening to the developing fight. Within moments the noise died away and he opened the door slightly to peer through. Much of the furniture was overturned and one man lay motionless on the floor. The outer door to the hall was wide open and the bishop could feel the cool night breeze upon his face.

Sulien walked over nervously and as he approached, the injured man got slowly to his feet before turning around. With profound relief the bishop could see it was the second man, the one who had saved his life.

'Thank the Lord,' said Sulien, 'are you all right?'

'I think so,' said the man, 'but the attacker has escaped.'

'Who was he?' asked Sulien.

'I don't know,' said the injured man, 'I was passing and saw him acting strangely in the cathedral grounds so decided to follow him. From what I heard when he held a knife at your throat it seems he wants to kill the queen.'

'What queen?' asked Sulien.

'Your grace, forgive me but there is not a soul in the west of Wales who does not know of your protection of Queen Gwladus and her children. You are to be blessed for your courage.'

'I only carry out the will of our Lord,' said Sulien.

'Still, these are dangerous times and your safety is at risk, as is that of the queen.'

'As recent events have proved,' said Sulien, looking around the messed up hall. 'Still, the scoundrel has departed and she is safe again.'

'She is not safe yet,' said the man, 'such men rarely act alone and even as we speak, an accomplice could be seeking her out.'

'Surely not?'

'Your grace, Caradog will stop at nothing to secure victory against Tewdwr and there are no lengths to which he will not stretch, even abduction. Luckily, God has seen fit to bring my path this way, for I am a soldier of Tewdwr and ride to join his quest against Caradog. The lady Gwladus is my queen and I would pledge my life to save her. In the circumstances, I cannot leave until I know she is safe.'

'Understood,' said Sulien.' 'I will have her brought down.'

'There's no time,' said the soldier, 'the killer is still at large and presents danger to the queen and anyone else here. You alert the rest of the staff, I will see to her safety. Where is she?'

'Her quarters are at the top of the stairs behind this room,' said Sulien stepping aside. 'Go quickly, before it is too late.'

The man marched across the hall floor, leaving the lesser hall behind him but as soon as he was out of sight he paused and reached for the knife beneath his cloak. The ruse had worked perfectly and the few coins he had paid the brigand to play the part of an assassin was money well spent. Moments later, Bowen of Gwent climbed the stairs knowing that at last his prey was within his reach.

The Valley Below Mynydd Carn

September 20th, AD 1081, dawn

Peterson held up his hand, calling the column to a halt. The valley floor stretched away before him. At the far end, the low hill rose gradually, topped with a small wood of elm and oak. All along the slopes were the remains of the tents and carts that had been decimated by Gruffydd's army. The two farmhouses that had once farmed the valley below now stood like skeletons, their thatched roofs and wooden shutters long gone from the flames that dropped from the sky two nights earlier. The odd wisp of smoke still remained but in the main the Mynydd was quiet, as were the men upon it.

All across the hill, Peterson could see groups of men, lined up in clusters of ten or more. Amongst them he could see those bearing crossbows while others wielded whatever weapons they had managed to collect from the fallen: maces, swords, spears and pikes. Many wore the usual mix of whatever protection they could find, while others stood bare chested their scarred bodies testament to the violent lives they led.

Below the hill, the main army was still deploying across the valley floor, hundreds of men trotting into position before turning and staring across to the approaching enemy. The valley floor was flat, lending itself to full-scale battle and Peterson could see immediately that his own forces outnumbered the defenders but, despite the discrepancy in numbers, it looked like Gruffydd had certainly come here to fight.

——— ———

Gruffydd sat astride his horse halfway up the forward slope, overseeing the field. The sight of Caradog's men was indeed daunting but he knew he had the advantage of the high ground and fixed positions. That, along with the preparations already put in place, meant the odds were just about equal in his eyes, but though he was confident in the abilities of the army under his command there was a situation that he hardly dared to contemplate. Trahern was still at large, and though his army was smaller than Caradog's, if he arrived during the battle, the defenders stood little chance against such overwhelming numbers. To counter this, Gruffydd had deployed as many men as he could spare to the southern approaches, but he knew that if battle was joined there, it was inevitable his men would be overwhelmed by Trahern – and Trahern could be here within hours.

——— ———

Caradog rode up beside Peterson and stared at the sight before him.

'The smell of death is overwhelming,' he said, screwing up his face in disgust.

'They have piled the bodies from their victory over Meilyr at this side of the valley,' said Peterson. 'They lie heaped upon each other and rot in the heat of the day.'

Caradog looked at the piles of corpses spread out along the valley floor, their bodies lying in the grotesque shapes that death often brought.

'What sort of man leaves the dead unburned upon the field of battle?' said Caradog. 'This Gruffydd is truly the spawn of the Devil.'

'I suspect he did it to cast doubt into our minds,' said Peterson, 'but it will be of no use, our men are hardened to such sights.'

'Agreed; still, he has a lot to answer for.'

The two men looked along the defences, seeking points of weakness.

'We outnumber them on the field,' said Peterson, 'and I see no reason to doubt a victory when we come to arms.'

'I see no cavalry,' said Caradog.

'Nor I, but we have to anticipate they are there somewhere.'

'Not necessarily, it is difficult to transport horses on ships. Perhaps he has infantry alone.'

'We will see,' said Peterson. 'In the meantime we should deploy to face the enemy, for if they charge immediately we could be found wanting.'

'Agreed,' said Caradog, 'get them into place.'

'Men of Gwent!' shouted Peterson. 'Line abreast, three deep either side of me. Archers to the fore, prepare for battle!'

Within minutes the attacking army had deployed across the valley facing the Mynydd. Belts were tightened and weapons checked as they anticipated the coming fight. Many took the opportunity to empty their bladders while others drank from skins of ale, knowing there would be little time to stop in the next few hours. Some men knelt and holding whatever items they had of any religious significance, prayed to God they would emerge with their lives intact. Eventually the commotion died down and every man stood still, each alone with his thoughts and waiting for the command that could end their lives.

Caradog checked his forces once more before staring again at the occupied hill. The initial defences were a worry, but after they had breached those, he saw nothing that caused him concern. He turned to Peterson and after a deep breath gave the command.

'Ready?'

'Ready, sire.'

'Then do it!'

Here they come!' roared Iestyn.

'The time is upon us men,' shouted Gruffydd, as the enemy approached, 'steady your hearts and look to your weapons.'

Somewhere along the line, one man started beating his axe on his shield, slowly and purposely. Another joined him and gradually every man along the massed ranks added their own contribution to the beat. Soon the valley echoed with the deafening roars of the defenders.

Despite the intimidating uproar, the enemy continued their advance until the defenders came within range of the archers. The advance stopped and within moments hundreds of arrows filled the air, sending death towards Gruffydd's waiting men. Before the first volley even reached the massed ranks, the second was already airborne and the sky darkened with willow.

'Shields!' roared Iestyn and every soldier dropped to one knee before presenting their shields skyward. Within seconds, arrows fell amongst Gruffydd's defenders like a heavy hailstorm, and though some fell short or overshot the mark, many also found their targets and iron tipped arrows thudded into the makeshift shelter of hide-covered wood.

Screams rippled through the massed ranks as some arrows found gaps and several men fell with arrows embedded deep in their heads or upper torsos.

'Hold firm!' screamed Iestyn. 'Close the gaps.'

Men shuffled closer together, overlapping their shields with those of their comrades as those wounded still capable of crawling dragged themselves back up the hill, desperate not to be trampled underfoot when the battle started.

'Archers,' shouted Gruffydd, 'target the enemy bowmen, volley fire, *release!*'

This time iron-tipped arrows flew in the opposite direction, and though the numbers were fewer, they were enough to make the enemy archers fear for their own safety, easing the threat.

'My lord,' called Iestyn, seeing the enemy deploy into line abreast, 'they brace themselves for the charge. Give the word and we will meet them head on.'

'Not yet,' shouted Gruffydd, 'the ground just before them is boggy. Wait until they wade through the mud before the advance but make sure our men stay on solid ground. The stakes mark the boundary; as soon as they are between those, sound the advance.'

'Aye, my lord,' replied Iestyn and turned to his men. 'Look to your weapons, prepare to move.'

Saint David's Cathedral

September 20th, AD 1081, dawn

Bowen reached the top of the tower stairs unhindered and listened at the door. Nothing could be heard from within so slowly he tried the handle, relieved to feel the latch turn on the other side. He eased the door inward and peered into the darkened room.

A few candles illuminated the bedchamber and in the gloom he could see a bed containing two sleeping forms while another lay curled up under a blanket near the fire. Bowen focused on the one near the fire, for though his target was the queen, to allow any man to live at his back invited trouble. He would despatch him first before turning his attention on the woman and her daughter.

Slowly he walked towards the fire and brandishing his knife, leaned down to pull away the blanket.

For a few seconds he stood there staring at the empty pile of clothes, realising he had been tricked. A noise behind him made him spin around just in time to see the door slam on the chamber. He ran across the floor but just as he grabbed the handle, he heard a sound that made his heart miss a beat, the clicking of the key in the lock.

He roared in frustration and beat upon the door with his fists but there was nothing he could do. Bowen was locked in.

⌣⌣⌣

On the other side of the door, Luke placed the key into an inner pocket of his robe and walked quickly down the stairs. Halfway down he opened the door of a side chamber and looked at the three frightened faces within.

'Come,' he said, 'the bishop is waiting, though I trust there will be questions to be answered.'

'What sort of questions?' asked Gwladus.

'The sort that explains why there was an unknown man in your chambers,' said Luke, glancing at Walters.

'Of course,' said Gwladus stepping out of the doorway, 'but there is a good explanation for that.'

'I hope there is,' said Luke. 'Now come, there is no time to lose.'

Gwladus reached out for Nesta's hand. Holding her tightly they descended the stairs to hurry through the bishop's palace. At the far end of the building they opened a door and found Sulien waiting outside. Alongside him stood two servants, each holding the reins of a horse.

'There you are,' said the bishop, 'I was getting worried.' He turned to look at Walters.

'Who is this?'

'He is a friend,' said Gwladus, 'and was sent by my husband to protect me. Master Walters is the man who saved our lives in Dinefwr all those months ago. I allowed him to take shelter within our rooms for the night.'

'I knew nothing of this.'

'He arrived late last night and was weary from the ride.'

Sulien looked at Luke for confirmation.

'It is true,' said Luke, 'when you first sent me to alert the queen, he was hidden in her chambers.'

'I was going to inform you this morning,' said Gwladus, 'but saw no need to worry you until then.'

'I can't say I am comfortable with the situation, my lady,' replied Sulien, 'but whatever the circumstances, it is clear you can't stay here any longer. I have had these two horses prepared along with food and cooking implements. You have to leave this place while you still have time.'

'I understand,' said Gwladus, 'and you have my gratitude for all you have done.'

'Here,' said Sulien, handing over two heavy woollen robes. 'They may not be garb suitable for a queen but they will keep you warm. I am sorry I can no longer guarantee your safety but such are the times we live in. When the sanctity of the church is abused by mere men I fear for our kind.' He handed over a leather satchel. 'There's enough food there for several days, try to reach a place of safety.'

'Where are we going, Mother?' asked Nesta.

Gwladus looked over at Walters.

'It's best not to say,' he said, looking at the bishop. 'If a cathedral isn't safe then the fewer people who know the better.'

'I agree,' said Sulien, 'and if I know not your hiding place then at least I can respond truthfully if questioned.' He walked over and helped the queen into the saddle.

'Nesta,' said Gwladus, 'climb up behind me.'

'But I want a horse of my own,' said Nesta.

'Alas, I can spare only two, sweet child,' said Sulien with a gentle smile.

'Nesta,' said Gwladus calmly, 'do as I say. There is no time to waste.'

'My own horse is hidden not far from here, Nesta,' said Walters, 'it is only for a short while.'

The bishop helped Nesta up behind her mother as Walters mounted the other horse.

'What about him?' asked Walters nodding his head towards the tower.

'Don't worry about him,' said Sulien, 'I will send for the sheriff later and ask him to bring men-at-arms. No matter what side your allegiances lay, most Christian souls look poorly on any man who threatens the life of a queen, especially one under the protection of sanctuary. Now, go while the day still breaks.'

'Thanks again,' said Walters and as he turned his horse to leave, Gwladus leaned down and kissed the bishop's offered hand.

'Thank you, Lord Bishop,' she said, 'when this is over, I will return to share a service with you.'

'I'll look forward to it,' said Sulien. 'May God go with you.'

'And you,' said Gwladus, and she gently kicked the horse's flanks to follow Walters towards the nearby forest.

Mynydd Carn

September 20th, AD 1081, mid-morning

'*Hold!*' roared Iestyn as the enemy approached. 'Brace!'

Despite the loudness of his commands, few men heard him over the noise of the approaching enemy, each warrior screaming as their pumping legs drove them nearer to the impact. In return the defending army roared their own defiance. In the resulting cacophony, each man struggled to hear his own thoughts, let alone any orders.

With a smash of shield upon shield hundreds of men collided into each other in a furious rage of aggression and hate. Some in the front ranks died immediately, impaled on spears or forced onto blades by the sheer pressure of their own comrades pushing from behind.

For the first few minutes there were no tactics or individual fighting as most men just leaned forward against their shields, each putting pressure on the man in front hoping desperately that no enemy blade would slide through the shield wall or axe blade find its way over the top to cleave their head apart. Men strained with every sinew of their bodies as they pushed forward, supported by those behind. Every step gained was a minor victory and every step backwards a major defeat. Sergeants roared their encouragement from within the ranks, each playing their part in the bloody fighting as the officers stood some way back, overseeing the battle.

Within moments, the manic screams of aggression receded as men needed every breath they could muster to wield their weapons effectively but they were soon replaced with the more soul-wrenching cries of the wounded and dying.

Metal crashed on metal and any man without some sort of armour or gambeson soon fell in agony as flesh and bone were torn apart by blades honed to ultimate sharpness. Men who fell wounded or simply slipped in the mud had no chance to regain their feet and were trampled to death by friend and foe alike.

Even those who were better equipped often found their care-fully prepared protection wanting against the stronger strikes. Hel-mets caved in under the smash of pikes and gambesons were pierced by any pointed blade thrust with enough force. Chainmail was better but even that was no protection against a powerfully swung axe and ribs often collapsed after such an impact, piercing the vital organs beneath.

'We're holding, my lord,' said Iestyn, looking up and down the ferociously fighting lines. 'Our men excel themselves at close quarters.'

'Aye, they do,' said Gruffydd, 'but it is early in the day. I sus-pect Caradog is testing our strength before deploying the rest of his army.' He pointed further back on the battlefield where another three ranks of enemy waited in silence. 'Once he spies a weakness, I suspect he will focus the attack there and breach our lines before attempting to roll up our flanks or even strike straight for the com-mand posts.'

'Agreed,' said Iestyn and looked up as the sound of a horn ripped through the air. 'They sound the retreat, my lord, do you want us to pursue?'

'No not yet,' said Gruffydd. 'Give the order for our men to also fall back and reorganise. Besides, Caradog would just commit his reserves in support and we are not ready for that yet.'

'Yet?'

'I have a trick or two of my own,' said Gruffydd quietly and watched as the two armies disengaged on the battlefield.

Another horn sounded, though this time from the slopes behind the king, and Gruffydd's men also retreated from the conflict to reform at the base of the hill. As the armies separated the toll of the initial skirmishes became apparent, as dozens of men lay dead or dying in the mud. Some tried to crawl desperately back to the safety of their own lines dragging their mutilated limbs behind them while others just lay there, absorbed in their own agony as they waited to die.

'It seems our losses are minor,' said Iestyn.

'I disagree,' said Gruffydd. 'Every man who dies is a major loss. Tighten the ranks, Iestyn and tell them to drink quickly. I expect another attack imminently.'

'Aye, my lord,' said Iestyn and set about reorganising the lines. Those with minor wounds were quickly bandaged and placed in the rear ranks while any unable to walk or wield weapons were carried back up the hill. Similar actions were carried out on the opposite side of the valley but all too soon the sound of the enemy horns echoed off the hills again.

'Here they come!' shouted Iestyn. 'Look to your weapons.'

Gruffydd's army stepped forward in line abreast, bristling with pikes and spears. Once again Caradog's men smashed into them with rabid ferocity and once again the lines held albeit several more men falling to the onslaught. This time the ranks were pressed harder on the flanks and Tewdwr's relief force was called upon for the first time when a gap appeared towards one end of the lines.

Quickly, the attack was repelled by Gruffydd's cavalry, and eventually both armies retreated once more to nurse their wounds.

Over and over the forces of Caradog fell upon the defending positions, each time committing more and more men to the fray, and each time Gruffydd's forces managed to fight them back, but though they were by far the better fighters, the numbers of casualties were growing and Caradog had yet to commit his reserves.

Once again the two armies separated, though this time the break was longer and exhausted men from both sides took the opportunity to ram whatever food they could into their mouths while others took the opportunity to rest or treat their wounds.

Across the field, Caradog stood in conversation with his officers.

'I have seen enough,' he said. 'On the next push we will commit our full strength to the assault.'

'They are to be admired for the ferocity of their defence, my lord,' said one of the officers. 'They fight with no fear.'

'There is nothing before us we need dread,' replied Caradog, 'and I suspect their arms are weary from the fight. They may have the advantage of the high ground but we have fresh troops we can commit to the fray. Deploy our reserves but do not limit the next assault to them only.'

'My lord?'

'The reserve will lead the next assault but those just withdrawn will support them in the rear ranks. I grow bored with the constant sway of the battle and crave a breakthrough. If our men do not share the mettle of the enemy, then we will have to overwhelm them with sheer numbers.'

'Everyone?' asked the officer.

'Every able man-at-arms will join the assault. At the same time I want the archers to send over everything they've got. In addition, commit the cavalry to the centre to punch a hole through their lines. Once we are behind them, the battle will break up and in open warfare there can be only one victor.'

'Is that wise, my lord,' asked Peterson, 'to commit the whole army leaves nothing in reserve. What if the day does not go as you wish?'

'We outnumber them almost two to one,' said Caradog, 'yet our superiority is nullified by their position and tactics. This stalemate could go on for days and I am not willing to suffer a drawn out battle for no reason. Once we have broken through, the victory is just a matter of time.'

'What about you and your staff?'

'I will follow behind the assault,' said Caradog, 'along with fifty men as bodyguards. After their lines have collapsed we will seek out Gruffydd and his officers and deal upon him a fate that befits a traitor.' Caradog looked around his officers. 'So,' he continued, 'that is it. Brief the sergeants and tell them to prepare the men. As soon as they are rested we will resume the assault though this time there is no turning back.'

'Aye, my lord,' chorused the officers and each turned to re-join their commands.

After they left, Caradog turned to Peterson.

'You will stay alongside me,' he said, 'and after the breakthrough will share the honour in capturing an enemy king.'

'My lord,' said Peterson, 'with your permission I would rather lead the men into the assault. I have fought alongside them for many a year and would not take a step backwards now.'

'Understood,' said Caradog, 'though pointless. We have good sergeants in the line so why risk your life?'

'It is difficult enough to stand back and watch men die in the early skirmishes,' said Peterson, 'but if this assault is to break through then my presence may be needed. In battle, men get confused, and they may need a rallying figure. If you are to the rear, I can provide that anchor.'

'So be it,' said Caradog eventually, 'do what you have to do.'

Peterson walked away to brief his men, but before he had gone a few paces Caradog called out again.

'Peterson!'

'My lord?'

'Send word to Gruffydd, I would have parley with him before the conclusion of this matter.'

'Yes, my lord,' said Peterson and turned away again as Caradog stared over the battlefield towards the Mynydd.

'Look to your defences, Gruffydd,' he said quietly. 'It is time for this foolery to end.'

———

Gruffydd walked amongst his troops, offering words of encouragement when Iestyn called out above the noise.

'My lord, look, something's happening.'

The king stared out across the corpse-strewn battlefield to see Caradog's rear ranks marching forward to join those already committed. To the side, riders mounted their horses and archers mustered into ranks.

'Stand to the defences!' roared Gruffydd, and men climbed wearily to their feet, dragging their battered shields from the cloying mud. Slowly they formed into the defensive lines once more but this time, their strength was visibly diminished.

'My lord,' said Iestyn quietly, 'I fear they won't be able to hold on for much more of this.'

'Fear not, Iestyn,' said Gruffydd, 'for if my suspicions are correct, he is deploying his full strength, and that is exactly what I have been waiting for.'

'Who is that?' asked Iestyn seeing a lone rider coming across the valley.

'It looks like a messenger,' said Gruffydd. 'Find out what he wants.'

———————

Peterson stood at the centre of the front rank. Clad in heavy leather leggings and a chainmail hauberk beneath a tabard bearing his family crest, he stood out as a leader of men, and though he knew it made him a target for the enemy archers, it was important for his warriors to see him at the fore.

Behind him, almost a thousand men stood nervously waiting for the advance to begin and to his front, a hundred horses carrying Caradog's lancers snorted heavily, knowing that something was about to happen.

Further to the rear, King Caradog sat astride his own charger surrounded by his bodyguards and he looked around his army in satisfaction. The massed ranks truly looked impressive and compared to the thin lines at the opposite end of the field, were superior in every way.

Gradually the noise fell away and apart from the snorts of the horses, silence reigned across the battlefield. Caradog rode forward alone until he reached the middle of the valley. At the same time a lone rider emerged from the opposite army and rode towards him.

When they were less than twenty paces apart, both men stared at each other for several minutes. Finally, Caradog spoke with a sneer in his voice.

'So, you are the traitor who sends so many Welshmen to their deaths this day.'

'There is only one traitor upon this field,' said Gruffydd, 'and he stands before me as I speak.'

'I command an army of Welsh born,' said Caradog, 'each seeking unity for their country. You command some brigands from the north and an army made from Irish mercenaries. I think God knows who is the true Welshman here.'

'Considering the alliance you have made with William the Bastard,' said Gruffydd, 'it is an insult that you even share the soil beneath our feet.'

Caradog sneered again.

'Sometimes there have to be sacrifices, Gruffydd, and though the short term brings pain, the outcome brings many benefits.'

'Benefits to whom?' asked Gruffydd. 'Apart from your treasury. I see no benefit to any ordinary citizen.'

'Such decisions are the burdens of kings, Gruffydd, but if you had a kingdom you would be aware of such things.'

'I have a kingdom, Caradog, and will soon dwell once more within it.'

'I think Trahern may have something to say about that,' said Caradog.

'He is not here,' said Gruffydd, 'so does not have a say. Already Meilyr's head lays atop a spike at the summit of Mynydd Carn and before this day is out, it will be joined by two others.'

'I admire your confidence, Gruffydd,' said Caradog, 'you lay outnumbered on the field of battle with another army nearby sworn to rip you apart. What possible outcome other than defeat do you envisage?'

'What do you want, Caradog?' countered Gruffydd. 'You requested this parley, so say what it is you have to say.'

'I came to offer you terms,' said Caradog, 'to give you a chance to save the lives of your men and stop this needless slaughter.'

'Ha,' snorted Gruffydd, 'and what terms would they be?'

'I will allow all of your paid men to return home unharmed. I will also pay off any debts incurred by you to raise this army.'

'And why do you suppose I would do that?' asked Gruffydd scornfully.

'Because you will also regain your own kingdom,' said Caradog.

'Is that what you think this is all about?' asked Gruffydd. 'Me regaining my crown? Because if you do you have truly misjudged me. I admit it was the goal that spurred me forward in the beginning, but since the treachery of you and your friends has become apparent, it has become so much more.'

'Do not dismiss me so easily, Gruffydd, we both stand at the head of good Welshmen who may die in the next few hours. There is a way where we can all emerge from this with honour intact and the men can return to their wives before the winter falls. Does not their fate interest you or have they already been abandoned to a pointless death?'

'Anything that stops a Welshman dying interests me, Caradog, so say what it is you came to say.'

'This conflict can be avoided,' said Caradog. 'With the death of Meilyr, Powys has an empty throne. I believe that with my encouragement, Trahern will gladly take ownership leaving the path clear for you and your family to return to the land of your birth. No more men need to die, Gruffydd, you will regain what it is you seek and peace will reign throughout this land.'

Gruffydd stared at Caradog in surprise. He had expected many things from the enemy king but this was not one of them.

'I see you think my offer is a good one,' said Caradog.

'It has its merits,' said Gruffydd slowly, 'but I am waiting to hear the terms.'

'There are no terms apart from a mutual stand down,' said Caradog. 'No surrender, no pledge of allegiance, no loss of honour, just a pact between men to move forward in the interests of their homeland.'

'And you do not expect me to bend my knee to you?'

'No, you will rule Gwynedd as a king in your own right, as it should be.'

'I have to admit,' said Gruffydd, 'I am tempted by the offer but will have to consult my men.'

'Understood,' said Caradog, 'but make haste for my army grows impatient for blood.'

Gruffydd nodded and both men turned their horses to walk in opposite directions but hadn't gone ten paces when Gruffydd's voice called out.

'*Wait!*'

Caradog turned and faced Gruffydd once more.

'If I accept these terms,' shouted Gruffydd, 'what becomes of the alliance?'

'You will take the place of Meilyr and all spoils will be shared equally.'

'Under the auspices of William the Bastard?'

'An unfortunate situation,' said Caradog, 'but necessary if we are to succeed.'

'And is this negotiable?'

'Alas not.'

'Tell me,' said Gruffydd, 'do you bend your knee to William?'

'I have pledged allegiance to his banner but still rule in my name.'

'Do you heed his commands, Caradog? Are you beholden to William of Normandy, King of England?'

'I answer to God alone,' said Caradog.

'But William holds the purse strings.'

'He funds the campaign,' said Caradog, 'but that does not make him my master.'

'Oh, but it does,' said Gruffydd, 'he who pays the piper calls the tune.'

'What are you saying?' asked Caradog.

'What I am saying,' said Gruffydd, 'is despite my desperation to return to Gwynedd, it will never be home while I am beholden to an English king.'

'You are turning me down?'

'I am.'

'Then you are a stupid man,' shouted Caradog, 'for if I return to my men without your agreement, there will be no quarter and you will all die upon this hill today.'

'If we do,' said Gruffydd, turning his horse and preparing to leave, 'it will be as free men, and not slaves to a French bastard.'

———————

'Prepare for battle!' roared Gruffydd as he neared his own lines. 'Officers to me.'

Men ran everywhere as they prepared for the offensive. Commanders of smaller groups gathered around Gruffydd as his squire secured the sword belt around the king's waist.

'Right, listen to me,' said Gruffydd, 'we have little time. Caradog musters his men to attack again. All we have to do is withhold the first assault, and after that, if everything goes to plan there will be an opportunity to get amongst them. Tell the men they will hear the horns sound on three occasions. They are to ignore the first and second soundings, for they are for others to heed but on hearing the third, they are to attack with every weapon at their disposal, strength, heart and steel. Fear not the numbers, for our mettle is greater than theirs, and if we are quick to the fray, we can regain the advantage.'

'Surely the numbers are insurmountable, my lord.'

'Trust me, Iestyn,' said Gruffydd, 'there are things about to unfold that will help the day swing our way.'

'What things?'

'We have no time to explain but you will soon see for your-selves, just be ready to advance.' He tightened his sword belt and placed his sword into the scabbard before donning his helmet.

'Gentlemen, this day is no longer about us or Gwynedd, it is about the future of our country. Do everything in your power to ensure our continued freedom and if you fall, know you died a hero. Now, to the lines, and may God go with you.'

The West Coast of Deheubarth

September 20th, AD 1081

Walters coughed repeatedly as he helped the queen and Nesta down from the horse and joined them beneath the sheltering branches of a nearby oak. The rain was pouring now and they were soaked through.

'How much further?' asked Nesta as her mother wrapped her cape around her daughter.

'Not far,' said Walters, 'we can walk from here.'

'Why can't we ride?' asked Nesta.

'The place we seek is at the bottom of a steep set of steps so the horses are no longer any use to us.'

'We can't just leave them, they will starve.'

'No, but for now they will be safe here. We need to get you somewhere sheltered. Once that is done, I'll return and sell them to a farmer or something.'

'I think the horses can wait a little,' said Gwladus, 'they are hardy creatures but you, Master Walters, look in need of some shelter yourself.'

'Just a little cough,' said the cook, 'nothing to worry about.' He turned to smile at Nesta. 'Not much of a life for a princess is it?'

'As long as Dada and Hywel are safe, then the rain won't hurt us,' replied Nesta.

'Spoken like a true princess,' said Walters and turned to Gwladus. 'My lady, I know you too are tired but we must continue. Don't worry, it's not far.'

He led the fugitives from the protection of the copse and walking through the deep heather led the way along a hedgerow towards the sea a few hundred paces away. Finally, they approached the cliff and looked down through the driving rain towards the turbulent water below.

'Where is it?' shouted the queen above the noise of the gale.

'Down there,' said Walters and beckoned for them to follow. Within minutes they found an overgrown path leading down the cliff face and Nesta held her mother's hand tightly as they carefully negotiated the track.

The path soon led to a set of steep steps carved into the cliff face and the going was tricky due to the moss underfoot. Slowly they descended, buffeted by the wind and the rain, and just as Gwladus was doubtful they would ever see the refuge, they turned a corner, stopping in surprise at the sight before them.

In a cleft of the cliff stood a tiny stone chapel with a single window and a pitched slate roof. The door was hanging off and all sorts of plants crept up the outside of the walls, desperately trying to return the intruding building to nature, but despite this, the structure looked sound. The combination of plants and the natural grey stones meant it blended in perfectly with the surroundings and was almost impossible to see, even close up. Gwladus looked up and could see the overhanging cliff even made the building invisible from above which meant that, overall, the chapel was a perfect place to hide.

Exhausted and sodden from the driving rain they walked up to the building and, after Walters had pushed the ageing door inward, entered to find a single room inside, small but perfectly dry. The shutters still worked though the door hung askew on one iron hinge.

'That can be fixed,' said Walters, examining the doorframe.

'At least it's dry,' said Gwladus looking up at the slate roof.

'It smells,' said Nesta with a frown.

'I think some goats may have used this place as a shelter recently,' said Walters, looking at the droppings on the floor, 'but don't worry, as soon as the rain stops we'll open the shutters and get some fresh air in here.'

Gwladus looked around the room. The floor was covered with the remains of old bulrushes from whoever had last used the chapel as a home while the remains of a broken bed and a table leaned against the wall. At the far end was a simple stone altar and to one side, a trickle of water ran through a hole in the stonework, filling a small trough before overflowing and disappearing through the base of the wall.

'It's clean,' said Walters, seeing her gaze. 'The monk who used to live here diverted a stream so he didn't have to climb the steps every time he needed water.'

'Clever,' said Gwladus simply.

'We need a fire,' said Walters looking around. 'These bulrushes will make good kindling and there is enough wood to make a start but we will need more.'

'Aren't you worried someone may see the smoke?'

'In this weather the smoke will be dispersed,' said Walters. 'Besides, it can't be helped. To stay in these clothes invites illness.'

'Well,' said Gwladus, removing her cape, 'standing here talking is getting us nowhere. Nesta, help me collect anything that may burn from amongst this rubbish.'

For the next half hour or so they cleaned the chapel floor. Anything capable of being burned was piled next to the fireplace while

Walters made a temporary repair on the door. Soon a fire blazed in the hearth, and as Gwladus used some of the bulrushes to form a makeshift broom, Walters left the chapel to find some more firewood. Soon the room was warm and Gwladus looked around in satisfaction.

'That's better,' she said, 'it's almost as good as our room at the castle.'

'I'm hungry,' said Nesta, 'can we eat?'

'Of course,' said Gwladus, 'I'll get a pot on the fire and make a soup. Luckily the bishop has been very generous with the dried meat.' She turned around to see Walters entering the room with an armful of driftwood from the rocks below.

'There's more where this came from,' he said, 'most is wet from the rain but if we place it alongside the fire to dry out we can use it later.' He dropped the wood and started coughing violently.

'Master Walters, are you all right?' asked Gwladus.

'Just a cough,' said Walters, bending to pick up the wood.

Gwladus knelt beside him to help. When they were done, they all sat next to the fire and watched the steam rising from their cloaks as they waited for the soup to cook. Soon they were taking turns to eat the broth direct from the pot, sharing the one ladle the bishop had provided.

'Master Walters,' said Gwladus eventually, 'you are not eating much.'

'I'm not hungry,' said Walters between coughs, 'just very tired. If you don't mind, perhaps I will close my eyes for a while.'

'You should eat, you need to keep your strength.'

'I know,' said Walters, 'and perhaps I will feel better when I awake.'

'I understand, 'said Gwladus, 'the rushes in the corner are dry as are the capes. You get some sleep. Nesta and I will get this place sorted.'

Walters made his way over to the makeshift bed, and though he was exhausted, the frequency of his coughs increased and he tossed and turned in pain.

'He sounds ill, Mother,' said Nesta quietly.

'I know,' said Gwladus, 'but there is little I can do for the moment. Come, let's see if we can make this place a little more comfortable before he wakes.'

Mynydd Carn

September 20th, AD 1081, late afternoon

'Here they come!' roared Gruffydd. 'Every man to their weapons.'

His heart was racing and he knew the odds of success lay with Caradog. Despite this he still had one more ploy to call upon and he knew that if it worked it could swing the battle his way.

'My lord,' shouted Iestyn, 'Caradog's horsemen deploy to the right flank.'

'Send our cavalry to meet them head on,' shouted Gruffydd. 'Do not let them get behind us or we are doomed.'

'Aye, my lord.'

The defending army presented their shields and adjusted the grips on whatever weapons they held. Those in the rear ranks placed their spears on the shoulders of those in front and archers placed arrows in their bows, waiting for the onrushing enemy to come within range.

'Steady,' shouted Gruffydd, 'archers . . . *Release.*'

The air filled with arrows and fell amongst the charging enemy but though many men fell, it made no impression on the speed of the onslaught and the archers only managed to release two more arrows before Caradog's men crashed into the defending lines.

The impetus was overwhelming and, despite many of the onrushing warriors being impaled on the defending spears, the line broke in several places.

'*Plug the gaps!*' roared Gruffydd. He was relieved to see Tewdwr's men rushing to the breaches from the rear. In front of him the men fought ferociously, holding the onslaught, but he knew it was only a matter of time before they would break. In desperation he looked across the battlefield to where Caradog and his staff were watching the battle unfold.

'Come on,' said Gruffydd quietly to himself, 'a few more paces, that's all I need.'

Caradog watched in satisfaction as his lines started to push the defenders back. Soon they would break and the hill would be his.

'Let's get a bit closer,' he called from astride his horse. 'I suspect we will breach their lines within moments.'

As one, the king and his bodyguards urged their horses forward, past the piles of rotting dead from Gruffydd's battle with Meilyr two days earlier.

'The stench makes my stomach turn,' growled Caradog as he passed the grim mounds of dead and rotting bodies. 'As soon as this is over make any prisoners bury these men.'

'Aye, my lord,' said an officer and together they rode forward, leaving the corpses behind them.

'My lord, the line is breaking,' shouted Iestyn.

Gruffydd watched as Caradog got nearer, his progress painfully slow. Finally, he knew he could wait no longer and turned to Iestyn.

'The time is here,' he said. 'Give the first signal.'

Within moments a long blast of a horn echoed around the valley, and though some men looked around wondering what it meant, most fought on, desperate to stay alive in the madness of pain, blood and death.

Down amongst the fighting, nothing changed and men died screaming amongst their comrades but across the other side of the battlefield something stirred, something awful, something terrible.

Compared to the carnage being wreaked before him, the valley behind Caradog was deathly still, with nothing but abandoned equipment and the piles of corpses littering the field, but as he and his bodyguards rode forward, something stirred amongst the cadavers.

Arms that should have been stiff with rigor mortis suddenly broke free of their burdens and frightened crows exploded upward in fear, angered that their easy meals had been interrupted. Legs followed arms and within moments men crawled from beneath their macabre blankets of rotting flesh to gasp at the fresh air they had craved for the past few hours. All four piles of dead soldiers seemed to come alive as those that had been hidden beneath broke free and ran to muster around one man. Silently they formed up into a wedge with their leader at the point and stared at the back of Caradog and his commanders.

The leader of the men who had lain hidden so long amongst the corpses wiped the strong-smelling salve from beneath his nose, the pungent smell of the ointment made by the camp follower having served its purpose against the hellish stink of rotting flesh. Slowly he looked around and saw coldness in the eyes of his men.

They needed no pretty speeches to stir their blood, for they knew they were here for two things only and had suffered the hell of the past few hours to deliver what they had promised: to fight and to die.

Edward Axe-hand raised the two weapons that had given him his name high above his head and with an almighty roar led his men into battle.

———— ————

The shout from behind caused some of Caradog's bodyguards to turn and for a few moments they stared in horror, unable to comprehend what they were seeing. Less than a few hundred paces away, a body of men were charging their rear, and as if that wasn't worrying enough, still more were struggling free from what remained of the piles of rotting corpses. Eyes widened in horror until one voice cried out hysterically.

'My lord, the dead are rising against us!'

Caradog looked at the warrior before stopping his horse and turning to glance at what was unfolding behind him. For several long moments, all fifty men stared in disbelief at the charging warriors about to fall upon them and only the composure of the king saved them from a massacre.

'What are you waiting for?' shouted Caradog, drawing his sword. 'Defend yourselves!'

Scared men groped for weapons, and though some were retrieved, many were too slow as Axe-hand and his men fell amongst them like wolves, hacking at horses' legs to bring down the riders. Men who had lain amongst the dead for so many hours now fought manically, oblivious to pain or danger. Flesh and blood flew everywhere and the cries of horses mingled with the screams of mortally wounded men. Caradog fought furiously but knew the advantage lay with the attackers and there was no way to emerge from this fight victorious.

'Summon the reserve,' he shouted, 'we need more men.'

'My lord, they are deployed at the battle, we have no reserve.'

'Then recall them from the hill.'

'The only way to call them back is if we sound the retreat.'

'*Sound your horn, man!*' screamed Caradog. 'Or we will die where we stand.'

Realising the king was right, the soldier raised the horn to his lips and blew the signal for the army to withdraw. Desperately, those that remained of Caradog's bodyguard fought on, hopelessly outnumbered.

'Again!' screamed Caradog, smashing one of the attackers in the face with his shield. 'Get us some help.'

The retreat sounded again and this time, many of those assaulting the hill turned their heads in confusion, not expecting the recall. Within moments Peterson saw the danger their king was in, but knowing the battle was at a pivotal point, he also knew that to retreat now put them all at greater risk. Realising he had to keep at least half the men in the assault he climbed up on a rock to issue the command but before he could speak, a spear thudded into his back, and he fell gracefully into the bloody mud below.

Peterson lay gasping in the filth, the rusty spear point sticking out of his chest. One of the men knelt down beside him, unsure what to do. Blood poured from around the wound and Peterson started coughing blood from his pierced lung.

'My lord,' cried the soldier, 'lay still, we'll try to get you back to the rear lines. Perhaps the surgeon can get it out.'

'No,' gasped Peterson, 'it's too late. Get the men back to the rear, the king is in danger.'

'But we have the better of them, one more push and their lines will break.'

'Listen to me,' said Peterson through the blood, 'if Caradog dies, then all this will be in vain. You have to get them back before it is too late.'

'I won't leave you here, my lord, they will cut your throat as soon as our backs are turned.'

'I am already a dead man, Joshua. Just do what you can to save our king.'

The soldier paused, knowing his commander was right. There was nothing he could do.

'God go with you,' said the soldier and left Peterson to die as he stood to climb up onto the rock.

'Withdraw!' roared Joshua. 'Back to the rear at all haste.'

All around him men looked at each other in panic, their leader had fallen and the king's signaller was sounding the retreat over and over again. Within seconds, men's voices added to the call and the message to withdraw spread like wildfire.

Confusion broke out amongst the ranks with some refusing to leave, while others ran as fast as they could to the rear; within moments, men were fleeing back across the field in disarray.

Back amongst the wounded, Peterson gasped for breath. He dragged himself into a sitting position against the wheel of a cart. He wasn't afraid to die but feared purgatory as an eternal resting place. Fervently he whispered the prayers he had been taught as a child, begging God for forgiveness as he died. Gradually his gasps for air slowed and he looked up to the heavens, desperately seeking the sign he craved, only to see the emotionless face of a young boy looking back down at him. Both stared at each other for a few moments but as Peterson closed his eyes to meet his God, he heard the familiar sound of a knife being drawn from its sheath and he said his prayer for the last time.

Gruffydd's men couldn't believe their luck and stared around them, gasping for breath. Defeat had been barely moments away but now it seemed there would be a reprieve.

'Reform the ranks,' shouted Gruffydd. 'Give the second signal.'

The sound of the horn echoed across the battlefield and within a few heartbeats, Lord Darcy's cavalry burst from the trees at the far end of the valley to charge at the left flank of the retreating army. As they galloped they spread out across the valley floor, causing men to flee in panic at the sight of the lancers bearing down upon them.

Caradog's own cavalry saw the danger, but as they were already engaged against Gruffydd's own horsemen, there was nothing they could do against the new threat. Within moments the Irish chargers smashed into the attackers, and lancers hacked at those on foot with impunity. The lack of organisation meant there was little response and men fell in their hundreds, either trampled underfoot or as victims of razor-sharp swords.

'My lord, their lines fall apart,' shouted Iestyn, 'the time is right.'

'Agreed,' shouted Gruffydd. 'Give the third signal and let's finish this.'

As the sound of the horn reverberated through the air for the last time, the sergeants amongst the men urged them to one final effort, for there would not be another opportunity like the one before them now.

'Look to your fronts,' screamed Gruffydd. 'The enemy run like startled deer. Men now dead at your side gave their lives so we would have this chance.' He drew his sword and held it high in the air.

'To arms, men of Gwynedd!' he roared. 'Cut them down like the dogs they are. No quarter, *advance!*'

The remnants of Gruffydd's army set out in pursuit of the rapidly fleeing enemy, Caradog himself was fighting for his own life, relying on the skills he had learned since a small boy, smiting anyone within reach of his blade. Over and over again he swung his two-handed sword, cleaving apart the flesh of any man in range. His tabard was sodden with blood and half his men had already fallen to the enemy's manic attack.

A quick glance told him relief was moments away as men raced from the front line, but just as he thought he would emerge alive, an enemy warrior lurched towards him, a great brute of a man, bearing an axe in either hand.

Edward Axe-hand launched into the attack, his immense arms swinging his lethal weapons from side to side. Desperately Caradog staggered backwards, using his sword to deflect the blows, but he was not king for no reason, and roaring his defiance he countered with an attack of his own.

Within seconds he had knocked one of the weapons from Axe-hand's grasp before swinging his sword low to cut deep into his attacker's side. Axe-hand's chainmail absorbed much of the power but the blade still struck deep into his flesh, carrying the rusty armour with it. For a few seconds both men were still and their eyes met coldly as each absorbed the implications. Caradog knew he had the advantage, but before he could withdraw his blade, Axe-hand reached out to grab the king's tabard and with an almighty roar threw his enormous arms around the small of Caradog's back, lifting him off his feet.

Caradog struggled furiously, pummelling Axe-hand with his fists but to no avail. As the pain increased he smashed his forehead into his attacker's face, breaking the warrior's nose, but even as the blood spurted over both men, the grip tightened and Caradog screamed in pain.

Axe-hand grimaced as he used the last of his strength, and as Caradog's screams echoed around the field, the warrior felt the satisfying snap as the king's spine shattered under the pressure and both men fell to the ground in a pool of blood and vomit.

Seeing the king fall caused panic in the remainder of the men, and though they pleaded for quarter, what remained of Axe-hand's men slaughtered them without mercy before turning to face the hundreds of enemy still racing towards them. They closed into a tight group around their fallen leader, determined to sell their lives dearly, but the first of the retreating men to reach them swerved to one side and carried on running towards the safety of the far trees.

'*Where are you going?*' roared one of Caradog's sergeants. 'Come back and fight, you cowards.'

None of the fleeing warriors paused in their flight, and realising the day was lost, many followed suit. Within moments the remainder of Caradog's army were running as fast as they could to the treeline, falling over each other in their desperation to flee the battlefield. Gruffydd's warriors fell upon the stragglers and men fell in their hundreds, struck from behind by those who had been on the defensive for most of the day. Darcy's cavalry wreaked havoc on the flanks and even what was left of Caradog's horsemen took the opportunity to flee the valley, knowing full well that the tide had turned. With Caradog fallen and the army in full retreat, it was obvious there was nothing more they could do – the battle was lost.

Once the last of Caradog's men had disappeared into the forests, Gruffydd's signaller sounded the signal to reorganise and exhausted men picked their way between the hundreds of bodies strewn across the valley floor to muster where Gruffydd had planted his banner. Those few men without wounds helped others to return to their comrades, and back on the hill, camp followers streamed down bearing baskets of bandages and pots of healing salves to ease the soldiers' wounds. Others brought horses carrying skins of water to share out amongst the thirsty victors along with baskets of food to feed the hungry.

Some men just collapsed to the ground, unable to move, such was the exhaustion and mental strain, and though the sergeants went about them with words of encouragement, they were allowed time to recover while the toll was being counted. For over an hour, the scene of the battle was a mess of wounded and exhausted men, each struggling to come to terms with what they had been through. Any battle was hard enough, but to defeat two armies in three days was beyond most men.

Gruffydd went about them offering his thanks and support and eventually, they came together as an army once more, though less than half the size of the one that had set out on the campaign.

Finally, all who were able stood before the king, each thankful they were alive after the hardest battle any of them had ever seen. Gruffydd climbed aboard a cart and addressed the remains of his army.

'My friends,' he said, 'whether you be from Gwynedd, Cork or a place unknown to me, today you have played your part in making history. This day, upon this field at Mynydd Carn, you despatched a second army intent on selling Wales to her enemy. Fret not for those who lay dead, for your comrades died in the name of freedom whilst the enemy died in pursuit of a false promise. Today we have given our country fresh hope, and though we are perhaps many years away from unity, we have taken the first step upon that road.'

'What about Trahern?' shouted a voice. 'He is still at large as is his army!'

'We have not heard from our scouts in two days,' said Gruffydd, 'and can only assume he has gone to ground. I have no doubt that there will have to be a reckoning but it looks like today is not that day. Once we have buried our dead, I suspect we can lick our wounds and get stronger before marching north to Gwynedd.'

'You speak too soon,' said one of Darcy's lancers from upon his horse, 'this day is not yet done.'

All eyes turned to look at the man and then followed his gaze towards the southern end of the valley. For a few moments nobody moved, but as the realisation sunk in, a murmur of fear and exhaustion rippled around the gathered ranks.

In the distance a line of horsemen rode into the valley, each holding a lance in their right hand, on top of each was the head of a decapitated warrior.

'It's Trahern,' said Gruffydd quietly, confirming every man's worst fears, 'and it looks like they have already defeated our rear guard.'

'Surely this day will never end,' said Iestyn.

'We knew the risks when we rode,' said Gruffydd, 'and this was always a possibility.'

'My lord, the men are spent. There is not another fight left in us.'

Gruffydd looked along the ranks of his men, knowing that Iestyn was right. Despite their victories so far, the men were done. Those few who carried no wounds had exhaustion etched into their face and many looked to him in desperation. Gruffydd knew that he could not realistically ask them to fight but to do nothing would mean they would be slaughtered where they stood.

'Listen to me,' he called over the sounds of concern rippling through the ranks, '*listen to me!*'

All the men turned to face their leader still standing upon the cart.

'I know you are exhausted,' he said, his voice ringing out, 'and many of you bleed from wounds untreated but there is one more task to do. The main link in the chain of evil that brought us here stands before us. This day has been a good one for us but the work is not yet done, our quest not yet fulfilled.'

Men slowly walked towards the cart, unable to believe they were being asked to fight yet again.

'We had no right to get where we are,' continued Gruffydd, 'for the enemy were stronger than us, better equipped than us and had the unity that a long campaign brings. Any other time in any other place, this battle would have gone differently and we would all lay dead in the mud, but we do not and do you know why? Because God is on our side. He sees a righteous army fighting in adversity against a foe who would betray his own country. It is God who strengthens your arms and he who guides your arrows. By rights we should all be dead but our Lord has spared us for one more fight, the one that will wipe the Devil's spawn from the field.'

'We cannot better that army,' shouted a voice, 'they are twice our number.'

'As was the army of Caradog,' roared Gruffydd, 'and the army of Meilyr before them. Most of those now lie dead and those who survived our blades run for home like frightened sheep. Those men before you will suffer the same fate if we stay strong and show the same mettle that has made this day fall the way it has.'

'My lord,' said a voice, 'you know I am no coward but even I know this fight is unwinnable. We have done our best and have been found wanting, it is time to go home.'

'You are right,' said Gruffydd, 'we should go home and that is what I intend to do, go back to Gwynedd, the land where I was born. The only thing is there is a man in my way and he sits at the head of that army before us.'

'My lord,' shouted another voice, 'you fight for your homeland but many of these men are from Ireland and fought only for coin. Freedom and a hearth is worth dying for but coins can be earned in other ways. Surely those who have taken payment have earned their pay and can return to their families with their heads held high.'

'Aye, they can,' said Gruffydd, 'and I offer every man here the same privilege. You have done more than I could possibly have asked and I cannot expect more so I say this. If your heart begs you leave, then go now. Walk away knowing you have earned the right and lose no sleep when you are safe amongst your families. Arrangements have been made to pay any monies owed and passage can be gained from Solva if Ireland be your destination. As for me, my home is northward and that man stands in my way. Whether it be at your side or alone, I have one more battle to fight.' He drew his sword and stepped down from the cart. The ranks opened as he passed and he walked out to face Trahern's army alone.

'What is he doing?' asked a voice. 'He can't fight them alone.'

'No, he can't,' said King Tewdwr of Deheubarth and picking up a discarded lance, walked through the massed men to stand alongside Gruffydd.

'Out of my way,' growled another voice and as the men stood aside, Edward Axe-hand limped forward. His chainmail was gone and his chest was heavily bandaged. One hand hung useless at his side while the other held a single axe, its blade still bloody from the day's battle. Slowly he crossed the ground to stand beside Gruffydd and Tewdwr, closely followed by those of his men still able to walk.

'Retire to the hill, my friend,' said Gruffydd, looking across at Axe-hand, 'your work here is done.'

'The deal was to the death,' said Axe-hand, 'and I am a man of my word.'

One by one, men left the ranks and walked over to line up either side of the two kings as Lord Darcy rode his horse out to face those still gathered around the cart.

'Men of Ireland,' he said, 'like you I took a Welshman's money to fight alongside these two kings and like you I also believe our part of the bargain is done. However, this is not just about the plunder, it is about honour and friendship. It is about standing up for right against wrong and showing the oppressors of this world that no matter how strong their hand those with right on their side will struggle until every last drop of blood has been shed. Do what it is you have to do but I for one will not walk away from a promise unfulfilled. My men and I fight with Gruffydd.'

As he and his lancers climbed astride their horses, one of the Irish mercenaries broke ranks and walked over to join the two kings and within moments every other warrior capable of walking added themselves to the defiant show of unity.

Gruffydd looked around at the few hundred men still able to fight. Every one of them bore a wound of some sort and those heavily injured would not survive the first rush, but the looks on their faces said they would sell their lives dearly.

'Your hearts are as big as the hills I call home,' shouted Gruffydd, 'and if we die this day, then even God will acknowledge your greatness.'

'My lord,' said Darcy, 'if we are to die, can I request we do so on the offensive?'

'I agree,' shouted a voice, 'why wait for them to overwhelm us? Let them know fear even if it is for moments only.'

'Aye,' chorused the men, each desperate to be on the offensive, no matter how briefly.

Gruffydd looked around, humbled by the cheering and shouts of support. He looked over at Tewdwr.

'Well,' he asked, 'what do you think?'

'Even a king has got to die sometime,' said Tewdwr, 'so if our day is today then let us do so on the front foot.'

'So be it,' said Gruffydd and turned to look along the remains of the ragtag army.

'Comrades in arms!' he roared. 'Your will is my will. Today we write our names into history.' He held his sword high into the air so every man could see it gleaming in the afternoon sun. 'For Wales, for Ireland and for freedom . . . *Advance!*'

Across the field, Trahern stared in amazement at the sight before him. The body of men starting their advance towards him were less than half the strength he had expected, and though his own men were tired from the fruitless expedition south, they were in a far better state than the enemy approaching him.

'Is that it?' he asked to Meirion Goch at his side. 'Is this the best Gruffydd can send against me?'

'Don't be so quick to stand in judgement, my lord,' said Meirion. 'it seems he has already bested the forces of both Meilyr and Caradog and such a feat demands men of a certain mettle. The dog may be wounded but still has a vicious bite.'

'Perhaps so,' said Trahern, 'but it is obvious the fight has taken a terrible toll and I can surely defeat this rabble with half of my army. Besides, this situation has just taken an unexpected turn, Meirion, one which has distinctive advantages.'

'In what way, my lord?'

'Think about it,' said Trahern, 'with Caradog and Meilyr both dead upon the field, I am the last signatory to the alliance with William. Once I wipe this pathetic army from my path, the last two pretenders will be dead and every man with any claim to the crown of Hywel Dda will be out of my way. Wales will belong to me alone.'

'Then I suggest you leave nothing to chance,' said Meirion, 'and commit your whole army to annihilate what is left. Take no chances, my lord, wipe them out with overwhelming force.'

'I agree,' said Trahern, 'we will meet them on the field and get this done once and for all. After that, we will send messages to William and renegotiate the treaty.'

'Is that wise?'

'Yes, for this time he will be dealing with a single king in charge of a united Wales. That, Meirion, is a wholly different negotiating stance than was on the table before. If we play this right, I can become one of the most powerful kings since Hywel Dda, but first we must deal with the rabble before us.'

'So be it,' said Meirion, 'I will prepare the men for the advance.'

———————

Slowly the remains of Gruffydd's forces marched forward, each man silent as they contemplated their last day alive. Those less able to walk were helped by the able-bodied either side of them. The few archers still alive picked up what weapons they could from the battlefield behind them, knowing that at close quarters, bows were pointless. At the fore, clearly visible to both armies were the two kings, leading the last of their men into one final battle, each fully aware that it would take a miracle if they were to win the day.

They had covered almost half the distance when Gruffydd heard a shout and turned to see Iestyn calling his name from the left flank.

'My lord, look east,' shouted Iestyn, 'we have been tricked. Trahern has deployed his cavalry to roll up our flank.'

With despair in his eyes, Gruffydd stared at the nearby hill and sure enough, hundreds of horses flowed down the slopes towards them. Gruffydd's heart sank and he knew it was finally over; there was no way they could defend against these cavalry as well as the infantry before them. The battle was over before it had begun, and he had lost.

His advancing warriors came to a halt and formed a defensive square, knowing it was a futile gesture but determined to make a last stand.

'That's it,' said Gruffydd to Tewdwr, 'we are done. I will go forward alone and offer terms for us to stand down.'

'Surrender?' asked Tewdwr in surprise. 'After all we have been through?'

'I am the one he wants,' said Gruffydd, 'and will offer my life in return for the lives of our men. It is pointless us all dying.'

'Do you think he would accept such terms?'

'I don't know but I will not see our men slaughtered for no reason. We tried, Tewdwr, God knows we tried, but we fell short. The battle is over.'

Together the men stared at the advancing cavalry and Gruffydd's head fell forward onto his chest, the feeling of helplessness as painful as any sword.

Tewdwr looked at him before turning back to stare at the new threat. His eyes squinted against the afternoon sun and he took a step forward to peer intensely at the advancing horsemen

'Gruffydd,' he said slowly, but received no answer. 'Gruffydd. Look.'

'What now?' Gruffydd sighed, his voice burdened with the pain of helplessness.

'Don't be in such a rush to die, my friend,' said Tewdwr, over his shoulder. 'The time for such things is when your hair is white with age.'

'You speak in riddles, Tewdwr,' said Gruffydd, 'I fear neither you nor I will see this day out.'

'Oh, yes we will,' shouted Tewdwr suddenly, and turned to face his ally with excitement in his eyes. 'Those horsemen are allied to Trahern, Gruffydd: they carry the flag of Deheubarth.'

'That's impossible,' said Gruffydd, standing up straight, 'all your men are dead or alongside us.'

'No, they're not,' shouted Tewdwr, 'don't you see, Gruffydd? It's Marcus Freeman and by the look of it he has half the men of Deheubarth in support.'

Gruffydd stared in amazement as the riders bore down on them. Within moments a rider reined in his horse before Tewdwr, removing his helmet in salute.

'My lord,' he said with a grin, 'I hear you are in need of reinforcements.'

'Never a truer word spoken, Marcus my friend,' said Tewdwr, looking at the cavalry organising into attack lines. 'Where did you get all these men from?'

'When word of your plight got out, my lord, it seemed every man capable of riding heeded the call. It took longer than anticipated but we are here now and yearn to bloody our blades.'

'Then who am I to deny such patriotism, Marcus?' said Tewdwr. 'Lead them into the fray and take the enemy apart like the traitors they are.'

———

Gruffydd rallied the last of his infantry to follow Tewdwr's cavalry into the attack. Seeing the threat, Trahern immediately committed all his men to the fray and men of both sides were spread around the battlefield like chaff in the wind, each frantically committed to the life or death struggle.

Man and beast alike were struck down with bloody wounds, their cries indistinguishable from each in the carnage. Metal crashed on metal and screams of agony filled the air, combined with the shouts of the sergeants on both sides as they tried to make sense of the mayhem. Even the three kings fought amongst the carnage, each carrying their own wounds as they fought furiously for victory.

Gruffydd swung his sword, cutting straight through the arm of an attacker. A kick sent the man sprawling and the king stamped on the man's face, crushing the skull beneath his heel before stepping forward to engage the next opponent.

An enemy warrior wearing chainmail ran towards him, obviously familiar in the way of the sword, and for several moments the two men fought desperately, each weakening the longer the fight wore on. Finally, they stepped apart, gasping for breath but staring intently at each other, each wary that the other may spring a surprise move.

Gruffydd wiped the sweat and blood from his eyes, drawing in the desperately needed air.

'You fight well, stranger,' gasped his opponent, 'and have the movement of a noble in your ways.'

'I take no compliments from one who serves the traitor,' replied Gruffydd. 'Look to your sword, this is yet unfinished.'

'Wait,' said the man, 'I know your voice, who are you?'

'My name is irrelevant,' said Gruffydd. 'Just know that soon I will sit once more in my place in Aberffraw.'

The man straightened a little and his sword lowered before he answered.

'You lie,' he said. 'The true king of that hall lies dead in an Irish grave.'

'What tales are these?' snorted Gruffydd. 'For if he is truly dead then a corpse stands before you. I am Gruffydd ap Cynan, lord of Aberffraw and true king of Gwynedd. Now defend yourself and die like a man.'

'Wait,' said the man again, 'if you speak true, reveal your face, for I fought alongside my king at Llyn. If the death of Gruffydd is a lie, then I serve the wrong monarch.'

Gruffydd paused. To remove his helmet invited danger but if this man's words were true, it changed the situation immensely.

'What is your name?' he barked. 'I have no time for discourse.'

'I am Henry of Flint,' said the man, 'and led the king's forces at Llyn.' As he spoke he removed his own helmet and wiped away the blood from his face.

Gruffydd straightened up and lowered his sword. Before him was a man who had once served him loyally when he ruled in Gwynedd.

'*Henry,*' he gasped, 'is it true? Am I waging warfare on one I once called comrade?'

Henry watched as Gruffydd removed his helmet to reveal his true identity.

'Sweet Jesus,' he gasped, 'my lord, I truly thought you were dead.'

'I have been exiled for many years,' said Gruffydd, 'but return to claim my crown. Surely you were aware of this?'

'No, my lord. Any survivors from Llyn are formed into a separate unit and told very little. We fight for Trahern only because we thought you were dead and feared for the lives of our families.'

'Well, I can assure you I am no spectre, Henry, and fight to the death to reclaim what is mine by right.'

'My lord,' said Henry, dropping suddenly to one knee, 'forgive me, I never knew.'

Gruffydd breathed heavily as he slowly realised the importance of the situation, for despite the addition of Tewdwr's cavalry, his own ranks had been decimated and the battle could still be lost. However, the appearance of Henry meant there was a possibility all that could soon change. His heart raced; this was surely a sign from God himself, gifting him the strength he needed to secure victory.

'It is not your fault, Henry,' he gasped. 'Regain your feet and if you truly believe in your own words then help me finish this thing.'

'Of course, my lord, what would you have me do?'

'How many men do you command?'

'There are about a hundred true to your colours.'

'Do you think they will change sides and fight alongside me?'

'In an instant, my lord.'

'Then there lies your path. Pull your men to one side and brief them accordingly. Tell them to smear a bloody cross upon their shields or chest so they will be recognised as friend not foe, I will pass on the arrangement to my men. Once done, turn your effort against the rear of Trahern's forces with everything you can bring to the fray. With God's help, it may just be enough.'

'Aye my lord,' said Henry and held out his arm, 'welcome home.'

'We are not home yet, Henry,' replied Gruffydd, taking his old friend's arm, 'but the green vales of Ynys Mon are almost in sight.'

Without another word, Henry ran to one side, calling men to him as he went.

'My lord,' shouted Iestyn as he ran over, 'I saw what just happened, is everything all right?'

'Aye, Iestyn,' said Gruffydd, wiping the sticky blood from his blade on the gambeson of a dead man at his feet, 'it is now.'

For the rest of the day the battle swung back and fore until every man was exhausted. Breaks in the fighting were often but neither side would capitulate, such was the balance. Eventually darkness fell and both armies withdrew to spend the night amongst their original lines. Gruffydd and Tewdwr took shelter inside one of the few tents left at the rear, and as they discussed the tactics for the following day, two guards dragged a man under the tent flap, throwing him on the floor at their feet.

'My lord,' said one of the guards, 'this man has something to say to you.'

'I am busy,' said Gruffydd. 'Tie him up with the rest.'

'My lord, I think you should hear what he has to say.'

Gruffydd looked at the red-haired man at his feet.

'Get up,' he said, 'and for your sake I hope this is important. Who are you and what do you want?'

'My lord, my name is Meirion Goch and I am the right-hand man of your sworn enemy, Trahern of Gwynedd.'

Gruffydd stared at the prisoner. He had heard of this man and knew he possessed considerable power.

'Well,' said Gruffydd eventually, 'what a prize we have before us. Find the man who captured him and mark him down for a night amongst the whores in my name.'

'I was not captured,' said Meirion, 'I walked here of my own free will.'

'Then you are more stupid than I thought,' said Gruffydd, 'and will hang by dawn.'

'Kill me and you will lose the chance to end this war.'

'The fight will be over by this time tomorrow.'

'The battle may be won but the war will continue. Is that what you want?'

'What I want is for you and that traitorous king of yours to hang,' snarled Gruffydd and turned to the guards. 'Take him away.'

'Wait,' said Tewdwr, 'we should at least hear him out. He may have important information.'

The guards looked at Gruffydd for confirmation who after a few moments, nodded his acceptance. Tewdwr turned to Meirion.

'Your life hangs by a thread, stranger, so say what it is you came to say.'

'Thank you,' said Meirion, 'the facts are these. I am in a position of influencing King Trahern and believe I can persuade him to seek terms.'

'And why would he do that?'

'Trahern is no fool,' said Meirion, 'and sees that the battle swings your way. It is far better to seek terms now while he still has some bargaining power than wait until he suffers a defeat. Yes, you could kill me and take the victory anyway but it is not guaranteed and how many more men must die to satisfy the egos of kings?'

'Does he know you are here?'

'No, it is entirely of my doing.'

'Then you betray your master.'

'Call it what you will but my way everyone achieves what they came here for.'

'If you can do this,' said Tewdwr, 'what do you want in return?'

'Trahern has a healthy treasury which I can give you access to. Give me a fifth and I will disappear from your lives forever.'

'A steep price,' said Tewdwr.

'Yet one well within your means,' replied Meirion. 'Trahern's treasury is vast and a tenth will make me a wealthy man. The rest is yours to do with as befits a king.'

'What say you?' asked Tewdwr turning to Gruffydd.

Gruffydd walked across to the table at the far side of the tent and retrieved a flask of ale, drinking deeply before wiping his bearded mouth with the back of his hand. What he wanted more than anything was to kill Trahern with his own hands yet he knew his men were exhausted and would not last another day. The addition of Henry's men may make the difference, but even then, outright victory was unlikely and terms would eventually be agreed. In the meantime, many more men would die and Gruffydd was sick to the stomach at the endless slaughter. Eventually he placed the flask back on the table and drawing his knife he strode across the tent and placed the edge of the blade against Meirion's throat.

'The fact that you betray your master repulses me,' he growled, 'and I should kill you right here, but the life of even one of my men is worth a hundred of you so I will take you at your treacherous word. You go back and arrange the terms and our army will be on the field at dawn to receive the surrender but know this. If there is the slightest hint of treachery, I will hold you personally accountable and there is no place in this world where you can hide.'

'Understood,' said Meirion. 'Are we done?'

'We are done,' said Gruffydd and turned to the guards. 'Take this dog from my sight and return him whence he came.'

After they had left, Tewdwr walked over to Gruffydd with the flask in one hand and a tankard in the other.

'Do you think he can deliver what he boasts?' asked Tewdwr, pouring himself a drink.

'We will soon find out,' said Gruffydd, 'for the night is already half done. Get some rest; if God is with us, our blades will taste no more blood on this campaign.'

The guards escorted Meirion back the way he had come and left him walking into the darkness that was no man's land. No fires lightened the night sky for to do so invited the arrows of enemy archers. Slowly he walked forward, painfully aware that he could be struck down by an alert bowman at any time.

'Hold, stranger,' said the voice, 'state your name and business.'

'Meirion Goch,' replied Meirion, 'returned from the enemy camp on the king's business; get me to Trahern as quickly as you can.'

Ten minutes later Meirion ducked into the king's tent to find him pacing back and fore, a look of concern upon his face.

'Meirion,' he said spinning around, 'you have returned. How went your quest, did they fall for the ruse?'

'Aye, they did, my lord,' said Meirion, 'and their army will be formed up facing ours by dawn.'

'Excellent,' said Trahern, 'now all I have to do is send our cavalry around the hill to form up at their rear, and as the sun rises, we will fall upon them from both directions. In the confusion there is no way they will be able to reorganise into any formation of strength. This day will be ours before the sun has crested the horizon.' He turned to a squire, fast asleep against the centre pole of the tent and kicked him heavily in his back. 'Boy, bring me a skin from the supply carts.'

'Aye, my lord,' said the squire and ran from the tent into the darkness.

'Sit,' said Trahern, offering Meirion a chair, 'and drink with me for within hours I will be the king of all Wales while you, my friend, will be granted the title of first lord in return for your loyalty.'

Minutes later the boy returned with a fresh skin of wine and filled the king's tankard.

'Meirion,' said the king holding up his drink, 'to the unification of Wales under one king.'

'To the one king,' said Meirion and both men drained their tankards.

Mynydd Carn

September 21th, AD 1081, the early hours

The sergeants and officers of Trahern's army walked quietly amongst the exhausted men, urging them to rise from their cold rest and look to their weapons. The sun still hadn't crested the horizon but the darkness of the night was gradually replaced with the grey coldness of a wet morning.

'Come on, boy,' said one of the sergeants to a shivering youth, 'there is hot soup back at the tents. Get yourself over there and return as quickly as you can so your comrade can also eat.'

The boy got to his feet and pulled his cape closer around his shoulders.

'Do you think we will better the enemy today, sergeant?'

'Aye, boy, I do,' he said but before he could say any more, a roar of anger ripped through the dim morning light and all eyes turned towards the king's tent set on the high ground to the rear.

'What's going on?' asked the boy but the sergeant ignored him and drew his sword before running towards the tent. Other soldiers had the same thought but as they neared the command post, the tent flaps flew open and a red-haired man came out with a bloody sword in his hand.

'*Murder*,' he roared to the approaching soldiers. 'An assassin has crept amongst us and killed the king.'

The sergeant was the first to reach him and paused momentarily before pushing him aside and entering the tent. The dark interior was lit by the central fire and within moments the sergeant's eyes could see two bodies on the floor. One was the king, while the other was his squire.

The sergeant knelt beside Trahern and checked if he was alive but his eyes were open and the glaze of death stared coldly back up at the soldier. He checked the king's body but found no sign of wounds so turned his attention to the squire. This time the cause of death was clear, a sword wound to the boy's chest that still leaked redundant warm blood. Two more men entered the tent accompanied by Meirion.

'What happened here?' demanded the sergeant. 'Where is the man who killed the king and his squire?'

'I killed the squire,' said Meirion coldly, 'but I did so in an effort to save the king.'

'Explain yourself,' said the sergeant.

'I stayed here last night,' said Meirion, 'and spent the dark hours with our king planning the strategy for this morning. He was drinking heavily and sent the squire for wine but halfway through the night, Trahern said he felt ill and retired to his bed while I slept in this chair. When I awoke I found the squire kneeling at his side, checking to see he was dead.'

'You make no sense,' said the sergeant, 'why would he do that?'

'Because he poisoned the wine,' said Meirion. 'He must have done it when he went to the carts hoping that we would both die. Unfortunately for him I was drinking ale and was unaffected. When I caught him checking his awful deed was done, I regret I lost my calm and flew into a rage. Alas, I cut him down before we had chance to find out the name of his true master.'

'I suspect there are no mysteries there,' said an officer. 'He must have been in the pay of Gruffydd.'

'I know this boy,' said another, 'and he has ridden with us for many months. He would not do such a thing.'

'Really?' said Meirion turning to stare at the officer. 'Is he not from Gwynedd?'

'He is.'

'Well, just yesterday we saw over a hundred men defect to the enemy based on nothing more than the place of their birth. This boy may also have thought he saw a better future under Gruffydd than under Trahern. He may have been paid, he may have been threatened or he may even have been mad but that's not important, the thing is the king is dead so where does that leave us?'

All the men in the tent stared at each other in silence.

'My lord,' came a shout, 'the enemy are forming up into attack lines across the valley.'

'Stand to the men!' shouted one of the sergeants. 'Defensive lines!'

'Wait,' called an officer, 'let us think about this. With Trahern dead, why do we fight on?'

Again the men looked at each other, not knowing the answer.

'You know I am no coward,' said the officer, 'and have fought alongside Trahern for many years. My heart aches that he now lies dead before us but that is the reality. This fight has been about the kingship of Wales, and even if we win that battle out there, we have no king to claim the prize. Don't you see? Yes, we can fight on, but what's the use? Men will die, and for what?'

All the men in the tent looked around in silence, each knowing there was no future in continuing the fight.

'What would you have us do?' asked the sergeant eventually.

The officer looked at Meirion.

'You,' he said, 'Meirion Goch. You had the ear of the king. Someone such as you may be listened to by the enemy. You will ride out under a flag of truce and seek terms for our surrender.'

'*What?*' gasped the men in the tent.

'What other choice do we have?' roared the officer. 'The king is dead, the battle hangs in the balance and even outright victory will bring no benefit except to the crows. I say we end it now and let our men go home to their farms.'

For a moment there was silence until eventually Meirion Goch spoke up.

'He speaks wisely,' he said, 'this crusade, noble as it was, is over. It is time to extract what we can from a useless situation and rebuild. I will do as asked and seek terms for our surrender, unless of course there are any objections.' He looked around the tent at each man in turn. 'Then it is settled,' said Meirion and turned to one of the sergeants. 'I need a horse and a flag of truce.'

The sergeant nodded and left the tent.

'Well,' said Meirion looking around at those who remained, 'it seems our work here is done. I will arrange for the king's body to be prepared as befits his station. In the meantime, I suggest you muster the men.'

'What about him?' asked a voice, pointing at the dead squire.

'He was a traitor,' said Meirion, 'hang him up for the crows.'

Ten minutes later, Meirion made his way over to the horses to set out upon his task. As he went, he felt the small leather flask of hemlock in the pocket of his cape and suppressed a smile. The death of the innocent squire was unfortunate but a necessary part of his plan. His ruse was coming together nicely; better than he ever could have hoped.

An hour later, the remains of the two armies faced each other across the battlefield. The air was silent except for the cawing of the circling crows as they descended in their hundreds to feast upon the dead across the valley.

Between the armies, two small groups of men rode slowly towards each other, one showing the colours of Gwynedd and the other the colours of Deheubarth. When they were a few paces apart, the riders stopped and for a few moments there was silence between them as they all stared their enemies in the face.

'Who speaks for you?' asked Gruffydd, deliberately showing no sign of recognition.

'I do,' said Meirion.

'And who are you?'

'I am Meirion Goch of Gwynedd, and speak on behalf of the king.'

'Where is your king?'

'He lies ill in his tent but has requested I speak in his name.'

'And what says your master?'

'My king graciously accepts that men die for nothing and only death will be the victor here. Therefore he offers to withdraw his forces and return to Gwynedd immediately on condition his army is not harassed on their retreat.'

'You are surrendering?' suggested Tewdwr.

'No,' said Meirion, glancing at Tewdwr with cold eyes, 'for it is not in our nature. If you want the army of Trahern to bend their knee there will be slaughter before this day is out. My king suggests we mutually agree to withdraw and seek our different paths.'

'If we do this,' said Gruffydd, 'who is to say our blades won't be crossing again in a few months or years?'

'Good king,' said Meirion, 'there are no guarantees regarding that matter for who knows what path the Lord places before any man, but I would say this. Look around you. The young and the strong already rot upon this field and even if Trahern should want to seek revenge, which he doesn't, then it would surely be generations from now. We request you show the true compassion of kingship and allow all our surviving young men, yours and ours, to return home to their families.'

'And who will wear the crown of Gwynedd?'

Meirion glanced at the officer on either side before answering.

'You, my lord,' he said eventually with a small bow, 'and I am empowered to negotiate detailed terms on Trahern's behalf.'

Gruffydd glanced at Tewdwr, making eye contact before returning his attention to Meirion.

'And what about Deheubarth?' he asked.

'We recognise Rhys ap Tewdwr as true heir of that kingdom,' said Meirion, 'and will send despatches to all of Caradog's men who remain there to withdraw to Gwent.'

'What say you?' asked Gruffydd turning again to Tewdwr.

'Me?' said Tewdwr, looking around the devastating scenes on the battlefield.

'Well?' asked Gruffydd.

Tewdwr turned to face Gruffydd before removing his helmet and scratching at an open wound upon his face.

'I have a kingdom to rebuild,' he said with a sigh, 'a missing son to find and a scared family to embrace. To be your ally was an honour, Gruffydd ap Cynan, but me and my men are done with all the killing. I say aye.'

Mynydd Carn

September 21th, AD 1081, early afternoon

Black clouds of acrid smoke rolled mournfully across the battle-field and the stench of burning flesh filled the air. Men from both sides had spent the day building pyres and throwing the bodies of their comrades into the fires. Soon the fat from the corpses fed the flames and the funeral pyres became self-fuelling from the flesh of the fallen, needing no wood to sustain them. When they were done, each army retired to their positions and took care of their wounded.

Hungry crows called out amongst the smoke, angry their feast had been snatched from them but still searching for the odd morsel the rotting dead had left behind.

Gruffydd stood outside the farm building atop Mynydd Carn surveying the devastation. Someone approached and he turned to see Tewdwr leading a horse towards him.

'Tewdwr,' said Gruffydd, 'it would seem you are going on a journey?'

'Indeed I am,' said Tewdwr. 'I have to return and see to my interests back in Dinefwr. My wife and daughter are in hiding, though I know not where. I have one son in exile in Ireland and another taken prisoner by the forces of Caradog. I am needed there, Gruffydd, so have come to say goodbye.'

'I understand,' said Gruffydd, 'for I too will soon be making the trek northward to my home on Ynys Mon. There is much rebuilding to do and I am not just talking about masonry.'

Tewdwr nodded. 'I will leave most of my men here to help with the clean-up,' he said, 'and take just a dozen as bodyguards.'

'Thank you,' said Gruffydd and looked out over the battlefield. 'It is a terrible thing we gaze upon, Tewdwr, but what we have done here will go down in history and hopefully be the beginning of a process that will see a free Wales.'

'If that is so, then all these men, on both sides will not have died in vain.'

'Agreed,' said Gruffydd and turned to face the southern king.

'I am in your debt, Tewdwr, and if ever you are in need of support against any enemy, then don't hesitate to call upon my name. If I can, I will do all I can to repay the debt.'

'If there is a debt to be paid then it is owed by me,' said Tewdwr, 'for my lands have been returned to me and that is down to you and your men.'

'Then we are indebted to each other,' said Gruffydd, 'so let us agree to maintain this alliance whenever there is a need.'

'Agreed,' said Tewdwr and held out his arm. 'Until the next time, dear friend.'

'Live free, Tewdwr,' said Gruffydd, taking the other king's arm, 'and rule well.'

Tewdwr smiled and turned away. At the bottom of the slope he mounted his horse and rode southward back towards Dinefwr.

———

Within moments Meirion Goch joined Gruffydd and watched the southern king ride away with his men. Finally, Gruffydd spoke.

'So, what really happened to Trahern?'

'He was poisoned by a squire.'

'And is that the truth in the matter?'

'It is what the men believe and that is enough.'

'And where does that leave us?'

'I will honour the agreement but need to ride north to meet an Englishman called Huw the Fat, he holds the treasury of Trahern in his name.'

'An Englishman?'

'Yes, but there are papers drawn up ensuring that if Trahern falls, I am named as executor of his estate. All I have to do is go there and explain the situation and the monies will be released.'

'How do I know there is not treachery in your heart?'

'You don't, but I have lands on Ynys Mon, and if I should break my word, they are yours to do with as you see fit. Give me a month and you will be back at Aberffraw with a ready-made fortune.'

Gruffydd stared into the man's eyes and was met with Meirion's own steady gaze.

'So be it,' said Gruffydd eventually, 'but know this. Betray me and I will hunt you down even if it takes the rest of my life.'

'I understand your concern,' said Meirion, 'but there is no need for such angst. I will see you at Aberffraw within the month with treasures untold. Until then, fare ye well, good king.'

The Chapel of Saint Govan

September 23rd, AD 1081, mid-morning

Twenty leagues away, Gwladus sat next to Walters, wiping his fever-ish brow with a damp rag. For three days the cook had lain uncon-scious, a victim to the terrible weather they had endured on the trek from the cathedral, and Gwladus knew that if he didn't improve soon, she would have to go for help.

'Is that broth ready?' asked Gwladus.

'Just done,' said Nesta from the fireplace and filled the ladle before carrying it carefully across the flagstone floor.

Gwladus dipped a clean rag into the warm liquid and squeezed it between the lips of the semi-conscious cook.

'Come on, Master Walters,' she pleaded, 'just a little.'

But despite her best efforts, he was unable to eat and soon fell back into unconsciousness. Gwladus discarded the rag and sat back with a sigh of exasperation.

'How is he, Mother?' asked Nesta, a look of fear in her eyes.

'Not good, Nesta,' replied Gwladus, 'the fever doesn't seem to be breaking and the treatment he needs is beyond anything I can do. He needs a place of constant warmth and the attention of an apothecary if he is to pull through.'

'But how can we do that?' asked Nesta. 'Even if we could go back to Dinefwr, he is too heavy to carry up the steps.'

'I don't know, Nesta,' said Gwladus, 'but this man saved our lives on two occasions and now that it is our turn to help him we fall short.'

She stood up and walked around the room before sitting on the bench and turning to face her daughter.

'Nesta, we can't go on like this, I have to do something but can't do it alone.'

'What do you want me to do, Mother?'

'I want you to stay here and care for him the best you can. Try to make him drink half a cup of water whenever he stirs, and if he should regain consciousness, make him a little soup.'

'Where are you going?'

'I have to go for help before this poor man dies, we cannot do this alone.'

'What if Caradog is still out there?'

'It is a chance I have to take. Besides, Master Walters must have got these supplies from somewhere. If I can find the same place, I will explain everything and seek help in the king's name. Do you think you can do this for me?'

Nesta nodded.

'Good. If I am not back by dawn tomorrow, you will have to leave him and seek help wherever you can find it. Understood?'

'Yes, Mother.'

'When I have gone, bar the door. Don't open it unless you hear my voice or your life is in danger.'

'Yes, Mother,' replied Nesta. She watched as Gwladus wrapped up in her warm cape.

'I won't be long, child,' said Gwladus, 'be brave.' She leaned down to kiss Nesta before walking through the doorway and out of the chapel.

Nesta locked the door behind her and sat down beside the unconscious cook.

'Hang on, Master Walters,' she said quietly, 'Mother is bringing help.'

⎯⎯⎯ ⎯⎯⎯

Gwladus climbed the rocky steps to the cliff top before gazing inland, hopeful of seeing a building or at least some smoke from a distant chimney. When she saw there was neither, she pulled the cape about her and started walking, knowing it would only be a matter of time before she came across a pathway.

Within the hour she found herself upon a track and headed south, knowing that the further she went the more likely it would be that anyone she found would have allegiance to Tewdwr. For an age she walked, and though there were no apparent buildings, her heart leapt when she saw a group of four horsemen in the distance riding towards her. For a few moments she thought her prayers had been answered but the hope was soon tempered by common sense. They may not be friendly and a woman on her own, in the middle of nowhere, no matter what her station, was asking for trouble.

Quickly she ran to a nearby copse of trees and waited until the horsemen got near. As soon as she saw their colours she knew she had been wise to be cautious for their tabards bore the emblem of Caradog.

Nervously she watched them ride by, and once they had disappeared into the distance, she turned to regain the path but jumped in fright as she saw a man standing right behind her.

'Well, well,' said the man, 'if it isn't the long lost queen herself.'

'Who are you?' gasped Gwladus. 'Your face is not known to me.'

'Perhaps not,' leered the man, 'but yours is known to me. Your husband once banished me from Dinefwr and branded me a brigand.'

'I know nothing of such things,' said Gwladus, 'and I am certainly no queen.'

'Oh, but you are,' said the man, 'and I know this for I followed you from the cathedral of Saint David. I lost you for a few days but knew you would emerge eventually.'

'Who are you?' asked Gwladus again. 'And what do you want of me?'

'My name is not important,' said the man, 'and let's just say we have a mutual friend, one who is now secured in a tower of the cathedral awaiting the judgement of the local sheriff.'

'You are a comrade of Bowen?'

'Oh, not a comrade, just an acquaintance. You see, he paid me to play the part of an assassin at the cathedral and then to fight him so his ruse would fool the bishop, but when I was done I got to wondering what all this was about and hid in the shadows to find out. I heard everything,' he continued, 'and followed you through the night until I lost you in the storm.'

'What do you want?' asked Gwladus again. 'For I have no money.'

'A queen without riches?' said the brigand sarcastically. 'That is a shame, which leaves us in a bit of a tricky situation.'

'I don't understand.'

'Well, if you have no value to me, what am I to do with you?'

'You could take me to a place of safety,' said Gwladus, seeing a chance, 'and I will see you are handsomely rewarded.'

The brigand thought for a minute before answering.

'Nah,' he said eventually, 'I like my life as it is. I guess I'll just take what I want and then be on my way.'

'I told you,' said the queen, 'I have nothing of value.'

'Oh, but you do,' said the man, 'something better than all the riches in the land.' He drew his knife and walked towards her, forcing her back against one of the trees.

'Now you listen to me, sweet lady,' he said, 'if you are nice to me, you'll live to see another day, but if you struggle or cry out, I'll stick you like a pig, understood?'

'Please,' gasped Gwladus, realising what he intended to do, 'not that, I beg of you.'

'Shut your whining, bitch,' snarled the brigand. 'Your husband owes me, see? Now if you ever expect to see any of your family again I suggest you lie down right there and raise your skirts.'

'Wait,' said Gwladus, 'I have this.' She reached to her neck and revealed a jewelled necklace. 'Leave me alone and it is yours to keep.'

The brigand's eyes widened at the piece of jewellery and waited as Gwladus undid the clasp. She handed it over and he examined it closely before putting it in a pocket within his jerkin.

'A pretty bauble indeed,' said the man. 'Now, where were we?'

'You were going to let me go,' said Gwladus.

'I don't recall agreeing to your terms, lady,' he replied and pushed her back against the tree, his fetid breath heavy on her face.

'*No,*' begged Gwladus, 'please, let me go and I will make you a rich man.'

'Too late for that,' said the brigand, pushing the blade against her throat, 'now what is it going to be, me or the knife?'

Slowly Gwladus lowered herself to the ground, the tears of fright rolling down her face. If it wasn't for Nesta needing her back at the chapel she would have fought this man even unto her own death but dying wasn't an option, too many people were relying on her.

'That's better,' said the man looking around to check there was nobody else in the area. 'Now, you be nice to me, queenie, or I swear this ground will drink your blood before this day is done.'

For the next ten minutes, Gwladus tried to blank out the grunts and groans of her rapist. Her mind was numb to any sensation apart from the pain of his brutality, and when it was over, she lay there in shock, staring up at the sky as the man adjusted his clothing.

'There,' he said, fastening his belt, 'that wasn't so bad was it?'

The queen pushed her dress downward but said nothing. She blocked out everything; her only thought was that he would let her go now and she could find help for Nesta.

The man finished dressing as she sat up and leaned against the tree, staring at him with eyes as cold as ice.

'So,' he said eventually, 'what are we to do with you now?'

'You said you would let me go,' said Gwladus quietly.

'I did,' said the brigand, 'but you see, there is a problem with that. If I let you live, no doubt your husband would scour this land high and low until he found me and I don't fancy dancing at the end of a rope.' His face changed from false joviality to deadly seriousness as he again drew his knife. 'I'm sorry, lady, it was all very nice but this ends here.'

'No,' shouted Gwladus, getting to her feet, 'you *promised.*'

'I know,' said the man, 'but such is the way of people such as me. We have to lie sometimes to get what we want.'

'You son of a pig,' cursed Gwladus, 'you will rot in hell for this.'

'Perhaps so,' said the brigand, 'but there will not be many there who can say they bedded a queen.'

'*Bastard!*' screamed Gwladus, and she lunged forward, reaching for his eyes. The brigand ducked to one side but not before Gwladus had gouged her nails deep into his flesh, tearing open his face from eye to jaw. For a few moments they struggled but Gwladus was no match for the man and he knocked her backwards with a single punch. Gwladus fell sprawling into the mud and the man stood over her, his face contorted with rage.

'Nice try, bitch,' he said, 'but enough of this nonsense.' He knelt down with the knife poised to strike but before he could plunge it into her back, a voice echoed through the trees.

'Hunter, seize him!' it yelled and a dog launched itself from nowhere to pounce on the attacker, the vicious fangs stretching for the rapist's throat.

The man screamed and got to his feet before staggering away from the scene, closely pursued by the dog.

Gwladus looked up as a bearded man walked over to stand above her. His sheepskin cloak hung down to his knees and his bedraggled hair grew down past his shoulders.

'Who are you?' asked Gwladus eventually, her voice breaking between shuddering breaths.

'My name is Dylan,' said the man. 'I have a farm not far from here. I found some horses a few days ago and figured there may be someone in trouble hereabouts. It seems I was right.'

'You saved my life, Dylan,' said the queen quietly, 'and for that you will be suitably rewarded.'

'Who exactly are you?' asked Dylan.

Gwladus stared at the man, trying desperately not to break down in tears.

'My name is Gwladus ferch Rhiwallon, Queen of Deheubarth,' she replied, 'and I desperately need your help.'

For a second, Dylan stared open mouthed at the queen before dropping to one knee and facing the floor.

'My lady,' he said, 'please forgive me, I did not know.'

'There was no way of you knowing,' said Gwladus. 'I find myself in a terrible situation, Dylan, but before we proceed, there is an oath I require from you, a promise that you must keep until your dying day.'

'Anything,' said the farmer.

'What happened here today, what that man did to me, must forever remain between us and no other, do you understand?'

'But surely your husband will want to hunt him down?'

'He cannot learn of this, for if the king was to find out his lady had been violated by a brigand, he would surely die of a broken heart. You have to swear that you will never allow any words of . . .' she hesitated for a moment, looking for the right words, 'of what just happened to ever pass your lips and take the secret to the grave.'

'What about him?' asked Dylan nodding the way the injured man had fled.

'Forget him,' replied Gwladus, 'all I need you to do is swear an oath of silence.'

'I understand,' said Dylan. Silence fell, broken only when Dylan knelt to retrieve something from the floor. 'It looks like he dropped this,' he said, holding up the queen's necklace. He offered it back to Gwladus but she shook her head.

'No,' she said, 'keep it. In gratitude for saving my life.'

'But . . .'

'It is yours, Dylan, the choice is made. Now we must hurry for there are other lives at risk. A man lies close to death's door nearby. We have to get him some help.'

'Where is he?' asked Dylan.

'In a chapel on a cliff, not far from here. My daughter looks after him but I fear for his life.'

'You talk of the chapel of Saint Govan,' said Dylan, 'I know it well.'

'Good, then we will need horses and a cart to bring them to your home. Once there perhaps you can give us shelter until the time is right.'

'Of course, my home is your home,' said Dylan, 'but may I ask, why do you not return to the castle at Dinefwr?'

'I have no means of knowing if it still lies in the control of Caradog,' said Gwladus, 'and I can't take the risk.'

'My lady,' said Dylan in astonishment, 'have you not heard? Your husband and King Gruffydd of Gwynedd vanquished the three-king alliance at Mynydd Carn not three days since.'

Gwladus's face lit up in hope. 'What about Caradog?'

'Slain upon the battlefield. His men return to Gwent as we speak and I believe all have left Dinefwr.'

'And my husband?'

'He is alive and well, my lady, the war is over. You and your children are safe.'

Dinefwr

September 30th, AD 1081, early afternoon

Seven days later, Rhys ap Tewdwr stood on the plain below his castle, looking up at the damage Caradog and his men had wreaked upon his home. The slopes were alive with people from the village, each one happy to help clean up the mess. Messages had been sent out to villages far and wide, seeking carpenters, blacksmiths and stonemasons, each to muster at the castle in the spring to engage upon the repairs but in the meantime, there were other things upon the king's mind. No word had been received from Gwladus and the only information he could find out was that she and Nesta had ridden south with Walters a few weeks earlier. Since then there had been no report of her whereabouts. Men rode in every direction, seeking any news but there was nothing; it was as if she had disappeared into thin air.

'My lord,' said Marcus, appearing at his side, 'we are ready.'

Tewdwr nodded and walked over to where a crowd had gathered next to a large tree. From its branches dangled a hangman's noose and sitting chained in a nearby cart a frightened man pushed himself back as far as he could, away from the fate that awaited him.

'Bring him over,' said Tewdwr coldly.

The prisoner was dragged from the cart and the noose placed around his neck. Men pulled upon the rope until he was standing on tiptoe to ease the pressure around his throat.

'Mercy,' he croaked, 'please, in the name of God, show mercy.'

The crowd silenced as Tewdwr walked up to him and stared into the condemned man's eyes.

'You want mercy?' he asked. 'Well, let me tell you, Bowen of Gwent, this is indeed a merciful end for a man such as you. Within minutes you will be a dead man even though my heart yearns to see you tortured for months on end. If I was a harder man I would have you skinned alive as slowly as possible so you could endure a small part of the pain I now feel.'

'I swear, my lord, I know not the whereabouts of your wife or indeed your daughter.'

'Perhaps not,' said Tewdwr, 'but that does not mean you were not responsible for the terror they experienced while my wife was with child.'

'My lord, you forget it was I who told you where they were. Surely that deserves mercy.'

'In normal circumstances perhaps, but after that you sought them out, intent on revenge for your humiliation, and if it wasn't for the actions of Bishop Sulien back in the cathedral, I suspect they would now be dead by your hand. The day the sheriff told me of your captivity, my heart leapt with excitement. Alas, yours will soon lie idle, nothing but a foul tasting morsel for the wolves.'

'Wait,' cried Bowen, 'they may still be alive and if so you hang an innocent man.'

'Even if you be innocent of their deaths, Bowen, I'm happy you are guilty of many more sins though they may be unbeknownst to me.'

'If you do this, you will be judged as a murderer before God.'

'I will take my chances,' said Tewdwr and turned to give the order to the men holding the rope.

'Wait,' called a voice and all heads turned to stare down the track towards the village. A few hundred paces away a cart rolled along the path, pulled by two horses. A man held their bridle and beside him walked a woman and a young girl.

The cart stopped at the edge of the crowd and Tewdwr's heart leapt as he realised it was his wife and daughter. Quickly he ran forward but Gwladus raised her hand.

'Stop,' she said, 'don't touch me.'

Tewdwr pulled up short, shocked at the response. He had wanted to take her in his arms but there was a coldness about her and a pain reflected deep in her eyes. Nesta ran forward and threw her arms around her father's waist, sobbing quietly as the king and queen stared at each other.

'My love,' said Tewdwr quietly, addressing his wife, 'your manner worries me. Are you hurt?'

Gwladus swallowed hard, wanting to tell him everything and ask him to take away the hurt inside but she knew her burden was hers alone. She glanced over at Dylan before answering.

'I am well,' she said eventually, 'just tired and hungry. Forgive my demeanour but it has been a long journey and we seek only the comfort of our home.'

'I understand,' said Tewdwr, 'and your chambers have already been prepared in anticipation of your return.'

'Is there any news of Hywel?'

'Alas no, but I have men riding to Caradog's estate as we speak, seeking audience with his successor.'

Tewdwr looked at his queen. Her clothes were filthy and her face drawn from exhaustion. An awkward silence fell between them.

For a few moments, nobody spoke until taking a deep breath she turned to face Marcus.

'Marcus,' she said, her voice shaking with emotion, 'there is a dead man in the cart. Ensure he is given a Christian burial.'

'Yes, my lady,' said Marcus, 'what is his name?'

'Mark his gravestone as Walters of Deheubarth,' said Gwladus, as tears started to flow down her face, 'a name to be proud of.'

'The cook?'

Gwladus nodded, unable to speak such was her upset.

'Walters is dead?' asked Tewdwr. 'What happened to him?'

'I will tell you our tale later,' said Gwladus, 'but for now, see he is given every honour.'

'Of course, my lady,' said Marcus and nodded to two nearby soldiers who ran off to make the arrangements.

'When you are done,' continued Gwladus, 'give this farmer a purse of silver the size of your fist and have him escorted safely back to his home.'

'Yes, my lady,' said Marcus.

'One last thing, Marcus, when the masons have finished restoring the castle, there is a small chapel on the coast that needs their attention. I want it restored and a candle kept alight on the shrine therein until the day I die.'

Marcus glanced at Tewdwr and received a silent nod in return.

'Consider it done,' said Marcus.

Gwladus finally turned to face her husband.

'What goes on here?' she asked, looking around the gathered crowd.

'We have an old adversary of yours,' said Tewdwr, 'Bowen of Gwent. I understand he tried to kill you in the cathedral of Saint David.'

'He did,' said Gwladus and walked through the crowd to stand in front of her would be assassin.

'My lady,' gasped Bowen, 'you are alive. Thank God.'

'God?' asked Gwladus. 'Or a humble cook who now awaits the coldness of a grave?'

'I'm sorry, I don't understand,' said Bowen, his voice coarse as the rope around his throat tightened. 'I would never have killed you. I swear.'

Gwladus turned to walk away but stopped as he cried out again.

'My lady, you are a good Christian soul, if there is the slightest amount of kindness in your heart, please ask the king to cut me down. I will serve you as your loyal servant the rest of my days.'

Gwladus looked towards Tewdwr for a few seconds, contemplating Bowen's pleas for mercy.

'Well?' asked Tewdwr.

'Is this the man responsible for the death of Annie Apples?'

'She died by his own hand,' said Tewdwr.

For a few moments there was silence as Gwladus turned to stare at Bowen.

'My lady,' pleaded Bowen, 'spare me I beg of you. In the name of God show mercy!'

Gwladus looked at her husband.

'The choice is yours, my love,' said Tewdwr. 'Say the word and we will cut him down.'

Gwladus paused a few moments longer before taking a deep breath.

'No,' she said, 'he does not deserve to live. Hang him as the rat he is.'

Chester Castle

October 1st, AD 1081

Huw the Fat sat in his seat beating out the time with his hand on the table. The drumming was building into a frenzy and the dancing girls whirled around the floor like spinning tops, their skirts flying wide as they spun. With a flourish, the music ended and all six girls dropped to the floor, their heads bowed low into the colourful frills of their skirts, their hands extended in an exaggerated parody of a curtsey.

For a few seconds, the silence in the hall was absolute but within a second the watching guests erupted into cheering, every one complimentary about the excellent routine and even better execution.

As the applause continued the girls quickly stood, and after a more customary curtsey, ran from the hall and back to their temporary quarters within the castle walls.

'My lord,' called a voice, and Huw turned his attention to the gaudily clad jester, the master of ceremonies for this travelling group of minstrels. Slowly the room fell silent again, each of the fifty guests keen to hear what treat was due next for their entertainment.

'My lord,' said the jester again, 'please allow me to introduce John of Kent, storyteller extraordinaire who will regale us with the tales of King Arthur and his wondrous knights.' He bowed low and walked backwards from the floor as another man walked in to sit on the edge of the king's table.

The audience applauded, always willing to hear the tales of the legend that was Arthur, but Huw was not so enamoured, he had grown up hearing the stories and as far as he was concerned there were only so many versions that could be heard before the stories got stale. He leaned across and talked quietly to his guest, Robert of Rhuddlan.

'Are you enjoying yourself, Robert?'

'Aye, you throw a grand feast, Huw, it has to be said.'

'The times are difficult, Robert, yet to feast lifts us higher than the perilous circumstances that beset our daily lives.' He leaned forward and ripped a chicken leg off the carcass before him, the juices running down into his beard as he bit into the succulent deep flesh of the bird.

'Any circumstances in particular?' asked Robert as he waited for the earl to finish chewing.

Huw swallowed the mouthful of chicken and swilled it down with several mouthfuls of ale before letting out a deep belch and returning his attention to the remainder of the chicken.

'Not really,' he replied as he pondered the next piece to select, 'the matters of court are a constant annoyance, of course, but alas, they are a burden set upon men such as us.'

'Rather those than the life of a peasant, my lord.'

'Ha,' exclaimed Huw, the half-chewed meat visible as he turned towards his friend. 'Can you imagine the life?'

'I would rather not,' said Robert. 'God has seen fit to deliver me into the life of a noble and I see no reason to doubt his reasons by contemplating the alternative. Heaven knows we enjoy troubles enough without imagining more where they do not exist.'

'And what troubles are your burden?'

'Well,' said Robert leaning towards the earl and lowering his voice, 'see that comely wench at the side of the Earl of Worcester.'

'I do indeed, that is his betrothed, the widow Bethan of Underhill Forest, and a fine-looking woman she is.'

'I agree, but it is not a month since she warmed my bed when I was a guest at his manor.'

'Really? I thought he was enamoured of her and has talked of marriage.'

'I believe he has but let's just say his prowess in the joust is not matched by his prowess beneath the covers.'

Huw guffawed at the image, causing heads to turn in his direction.

'So,' he said between gasps of breath, 'you saw fit to relieve him of said duties and dragged her to your bed.'

'Trust me, Huw, she needed no dragging and it has to be said that if carnal knowledge was a tournament event, she would be champion of champions.'

Again the earl laughed out loud and wiped the tears of mirth from his eyes.

'Robert,' he said eventually, 'you amaze me with your boldness. Not only do you court friendship with one of the best swordsmen in the Marches, but then go on to steal his lover from beneath his very eyes. Surely this is a path that can only end in tears.'

'It is, and therein lies the problem.'

'What problem? Just enjoy the memory and count yourself lucky your head is not alongside the stags that adorn his trophy room.'

'You don't understand,' said Robert miserably, 'I did not know they were invited this evening and were staying within these same walls. If I had known I would have graciously declined the invitation.'

'Why?'

'To avoid what has now come to pass.'

'Which is?'

'She wants a repeat performance and has sent a message via her handmaiden that I am to meet her in the depths of the night.'

For a second Huw stared at him and then broke out into laughter once more, hardly able to breathe.

'What's so funny?' asked Robert miserably when the earl's breathing had at last returned to normal.

'Oh your face,' said Huw. 'Never have I seen a man so forlorn at the thought of bedding a beautiful woman.'

'She is a woman with demanding needs, Huw, and though I am usually accommodating in such matters, it is not good to stay around one source very long, especially one who is nurtured by such an excellent swordsman. I have already expressed my reluctance but have been warned that unless I meet with her demands and she experiences complete satisfaction then she may let slip about our previous encounter.'

'If she was to do that, Robert, then she too would suffer ill consequences.'

'Apparently not, for she is well known for such indiscretions, but such is the earl's love for her, he always gives forgiveness, which is more than he gave some others who have been discovered as her lovers.'

Huw smiled again but this time kept his mirth to a snigger.

'Then it seems you are in a quandary, Robert, though it has to be said, one which is easily escaped.'

'How?'

'Simple. Just bed her as she demands and then retreat to Rhuddlan on the fastest horse you can find. Keep your head low for a few months and she will surely turn her attentions to some other lucky soul. Who knows, I might even risk becoming a trophy myself!'

Huw looked towards the storyteller who was nearing the end of the tale, his story interrupted with jeers or cheers depending on the protagonist at the time. A door opened at the far end of the hall and

Huw watched as a gate guard talked to a servant in hushed tones. Both men glanced in the earl's direction before the guard left and the servant made his way through the hall towards his master.

'What is it?' asked Huw as the servant reached his chair.

'My lord, you have a visitor.'

'Is it someone I know?'

'Apparently so.'

'What is his name?'

'He won't say but assures the guards he has urgent news for your ears only.'

Huw nodded and looked around the room. The feast was going well and he still had designs on one of the dancing girls but he was also aware that information was often the difference between life and death.

'Take him to the kitchens and give him food,' he said eventually, 'I will come as soon as possible.'

'Yes, my lord,' said the servant and crossed the hall to leave the room.

'Trouble?' asked Robert, seeing his face.

'Nothing that won't wait,' said Huw, 'but come, you must tell me of these desires of the lady Bethan.'

A few hours later, Huw walked quietly down the stone corridor built deep within the keep walls, a heavy woollen cape wrapped about him to keep out the cold. Candles flickered in the recesses and he pushed open the heavy oak door to the gloomy but warm kitchen. The large fire in the far wall was still lit as always, its constant hunger fed by the never-ending supply of firewood from the small boy curled up on the rugs alongside, and the flickering flames sent dancing shadows around the kitchen, revealing the mess from the previous night's feast. One man was busy about his work despite the early hour and, for a few seconds, Huw watched with interest as the baker placed balls of dough into the ovens, the first of the many loaves needed to feed the castle garrison.

The baker turned and was about to challenge the visitor when his eyes widened with recognition and he fell to his knees.

'My lord,' he said, 'forgive me, you was not expected.'

'So I can see,' said Huw, glancing around the messy kitchen. 'Is this place always left thus after a feast?'

'The rest of the servants are grabbing some rest, my lord, and I am tasked with waking them up in plenty of time to clean the room and prepare the morning meal. I could wake them now, if you so desire.'

'No,' said Huw, 'that won't be necessary.' He walked around the kitchen, picking at the remnants of the cooked meat from earlier. 'Tell me,' he said eventually, 'I sent a traveller here earlier to be fed and watered. Do you know where he is?'

'I do, my lord, he is sleeping in the dry stores. The cook offered to find him a place in the upper quarters but he asked to remain down here.'

'Show me,' said Huw and was led to the side storeroom. The baker pushed the door open and looked down at the man asleep upon the carpet, snoring heavily under the heavy blanket.

'Leave us,' said Huw and after closing the door, stepped forward and kicked the sleeping man's legs. 'Wake up, stranger, and tell me why this subterfuge is necessary, for you keep me from a willing wench.'

The man jumped to his feet and after rubbing the sleep from his eyes, bowed deeply.

'My lord,' he said, 'thank you for seeing me.'

Huw's eyes narrowed as he recognised the man's red face and beard.

'I know you,' said Huw, 'you are the right hand of King Trahern.'

'I am,' said the man, 'Meirion Goch, we met when the king was last here.'

'I remember,' said Huw, 'are you here on the business of Trahern?'

'Alas, the king is dead,' said Meirion.

'Trahern has fallen?' gasped Huw. 'How can that be? He shared an alliance with two other kingdoms. Surely that exile Gruffydd could not have raised an army strong enough to defeat all three?'

'He was not alone, my lord, he had alliances of his own, but it was not a blade that cut him down, it was poison, administered by the hand of his own squire.'

Huw took a deep breath and looked around the candle lit room.

'I would hear more,' he said, 'but this is not the place. Come to my quarters and you will tell me everything.'

'Of course,' said Meirion, picking up his cloak.

'The way is dry,' said Huw, 'there is no need for cloaks.'

'With respect, my lord, I am a Welshman in an English stronghold. I am also aware that my features are distinctive, so as I fully intend to return to Gwynedd, I would rather not be seen frequenting the halls of an English earl.'

'Understood,' said Huw, and he waited as Meirion got dressed before leading him back through the kitchen.

'You,' he said as he passed the baker, 'bring hot wine to my rooms immediately.'

'Yes, my lord,' said the baker.

'And get this place cleaned up,' snapped Huw, 'before I have you all whipped for laziness.'

'Yes, my lord,' gasped the baker, shocked at how the earl's mood had changed so quickly.

Gwynedd

May, AD 1082

'My lord, riders are approaching,' shouted the guard and several men ran to the defences to stare down the road. Gruffydd had returned to Gwynedd but the situation was far from calm. English nobles had been given property by Trahern all over the north and until they either left of their own accord or were physically driven from the land Gruffydd and his men had to be on their guard. Subsequently they had made a farmhouse their base at the foot of Mount Snowdon and bided their time there as they tended their wounds and drew men to their cause.

'Who is it?' asked Gruffydd, walking out of the low stone building. 'Can you see their colours?'

'Not yet, my lord,' said Iestyn, 'but the defences are prepared.' Gruffydd climbed up on top of one of the temporary palisades they had erected around the farm and stared at the approaching riders. Slowly a grin appeared on his face and he turned to shout down to the courtyard below.

'Stand the men down and open the gates, it's Meirion Goch returned from Chester.'

The gates creaked open and Goch led the column in to the courtyard. At the centre of the riders came three carts, each pulled by a team of two horses.

'Meirion,' said Gruffydd, walking across the courtyard, 'if truth be told, I have to say I am surprised you have returned.'

'I gave my word,' said Meirion, 'and in the carts you will find that which I promised.'

Gruffydd walked over to the first cart while one of the men cut the binding on the heavy linen covers. Meirion joined the king and, after a pause, pulled back the sheet to reveal a pile of ornate treasures. Beautifully engraved goblets and platters were scattered haphazardly across the bottom of the cart and a sack had burst open revealing a hoard of copper coins, glistening in the sun. Ornamental swords with handles inlaid with intricate designs of pure gold lay alongside superbly decorated shields while in the centre of the cart lay two ornately carved chairs inlaid with silver and gold.

Gruffydd stared in awe, for even when he had ruled Gwynedd all those years ago, never had he seen so much wealth.

'What's in the chests?' he asked, pointing to several caskets secured with chains.

'Silver coins,' said Meirion. 'The other three carts carry similar loads but there is something else, something special.'

'Show me,' said Gruffydd.

Meirion reached under the cart seat and withdrew a flat chest secured with a padlock. He removed a key hanging on a chain around his neck and after unlocking the chest, handed the chest over to Gruffydd.

The king placed the chest on the seat of the cart and lifted the lid. Inside he found one of the most beautiful things he had ever seen in his life.

'A crown fit for a true king,' said Meirion, 'compliments of Huw D'Avranches, Earl of Chester.'

'This is from Huw the Fat?' asked Gruffydd.

'It is,' said Meirion, 'he had it made especially and it is forged of pure gold.'

'Why would he do that for me?'

'Huw sees you as a valuable ally,' said Meirion. 'He told me say that too many men have died over petty land squabbles and sees no reason for any more deaths. He proposes that each man respects the other's right to rule and proposes a treaty outlining the extent of each other's borders. He sends the crown in recognition of your kingship and requests you agree to meet him at his home to discuss the finer details of such a treaty.'

'And what would William the Bastard have to say about such an agreement?'

'William has gifted the lords of the Marches freedom to run their lands as they see fit with no interference from him. Huw the Fat acts well within his powers to offer such a treaty. Of course, it will have to be ratified by William but in the circumstances that is just a formality.'

'There is much to think about,' said Gruffydd. 'Come, let us retire to somewhere warmer and you can tell me more.'

'My lord, what would you have me do with all this?' asked Iestyn.

'Have it brought inside and place a guard upon it,' said Gruffydd. 'I will decide its destination on the morrow.'

***

Five days later, Gruffydd sat at the head of a column heading eastward. The value of the treasures were beyond his wildest dreams and, after consulting with his officers, decided that the chance of a truce between the English and the beleaguered people of Wales was too good to miss, especially as the throne and all law-making powers would stay within the Welsh borders. The thought of crossing into enemy territory was a concern, but as he took over a hundred of his best men with him, he feared no ambush that may fall upon him. Subsequently, he had travelled the twenty-five leagues over four days and now sat astride his horse, staring down into the valley containing Chester Castle.

'Impressive,' he said.

'It is,' said Iestyn. 'I had heard that some nobles now use stone to build their fortifications but this is the first I have seen.'

'It will be interesting to have a closer look,' said Gruffydd, 'and we will use this visit wisely. Have the men stay alert but show no threat. This is a mission of peace and, from what I know, the man genuinely seeks a path to that end.'

'Let us hope so,' said Iestyn, 'or the road back may be a little more difficult.'

'My lord,' shouted the servant running into the hall, 'they are here.'

'Excellent,' said Huw the Fat, 'is the food ready?'

'It is,' said the servant.

'Then let's give them a warm welcome; this is an opportunity that comes around very rarely.'

Servants ran everywhere, ensuring the banqueting hall was fit for the visiting king and his entourage. Minstrels played in the far end of the hall and the aromas of roasted boar wafted through the keep while Huw the Fat and his officers walked out into the bailey wearing their colours proudly over gleaming chainmail.

Gruffydd rode slowly up to the gate of the fortress, watching carefully for any sign of trickery. As his column approached, the gates swung open and heralds sounded horns upon the palisades.

Two lines of foot soldiers ran from the gate and for a second Gruffydd paused, thinking it was some sort of attack, but his nervousness was soon eased when he saw each carried a flag bearing the flag of Gwynedd in his honour.

'A compliment indeed,' said Iestyn, 'Englishmen bearing Welsh colours.'

'I am beginning to like this Huw the Fat more and more,' said Gruffydd as they neared the walls.

Within moments he entered through the gates and saw a welcoming committee waiting for them at the far end of the bailey. At the bottom of the motte stood a dozen officers in all their finery while at the top of the steps he could see a hugely fat man flanked by two squires.

'That must be him,' said Iestyn quietly.

'It would seem so,' said the king and both dismounted to approach the officers.

'Gruffydd ap Cynan,' announced one of the officers stepping forward. 'My name is Alan Beauchamp. On behalf of Huw D'Avranches, Earl of Chester, I offer you a warm welcome on such a momentous occasion.'

'It has been a long ride,' said Gruffydd, 'but I trust our meeting will prove fruitful. This is my second, Lord Iestyn of Ynys Mon, and these men are my personal guard.'

'They are all welcome,' said Beauchamp. 'The earl invites you and your personal guard to a feast in your name to be enjoyed this night before you talk business on the morrow.'

'What about the rest of my men?' asked Gruffydd.

'They will be well taken care of,' said Beauchamp, 'and I believe entertainment has been laid on to satisfy their needs, in every aspect.'

Gruffydd smiled at the implication. Like many warriors as long as there was ale and food they would be happy but if there were also whores available then they would be ecstatic.

'Your hospitality does you justice,' said Gruffydd, 'and I am happy to accept your master's invitation.'

'Good,' said Beauchamp, 'if you and your guard follow me up to the keep, my seconds will take care of your men.'

Gruffydd nodded and, along with his officers, walked up the steps to the stone keep. As he reached the top, Huw the Fat stepped forward and bowed his head in deference to Gruffydd's higher status before offering his arm in friendship.

'My lord,' he said with a smile, 'Gruffydd ap Cynan, lord of the house of Aberffraw and true king of Gwynedd, welcome to my home.'

That evening, Gruffydd ap Cynan and his officers enjoyed the best hospitality they had ever seen. The king and his men were treated to the choicest meats and the most succulent vegetables they had ever tasted and each man was sat alongside one of the earl's men in an attempt to break down barriers.

On the top table, Gruffydd sat alongside the king, while Iestyn sat alongside Alan Beauchamp. Throughout the evening, course after course of mouth-watering food made the tables groan and as soon as the visitors' tankards emptied they were immediately refilled by scantily clad wenches.

Minstrels played songs dedicated to the famous Welsh king Hywel Dda and storytellers regaled guests and hosts alike with tales of famous battles from times long past. Before the night was done, men from both countries roared their appreciation for warriors of old, irrespective of nationality, and every man made new comrades from those they once called enemy.

'I have to say,' said Gruffydd over the noise of the banquet, 'you keep a fine table, Earl D'Avranches, never have I seen such generous hospitality. I only hope that when you come to Ynys Mon, as you must, that I can provide even half of the generosity you have shown us here today.'

'It is a small price to pay,' said Huw leaning towards him. 'The cost of this is nothing compared to the cost of fielding an army for even a day.'

'A truer thing was never said,' said Gruffydd, 'and surely there is no better way to spend your hard-earned coins.'

'Agreed,' said Huw, 'but the best is yet to come.'

'There is more?'

'Indeed there is,' said Huw, 'a surprise especially for a man of your stature.' He stood up and clapped his hands together, sending a signal to the minstrels. Immediately the tune changed to an intoxicating rhythm of drums and pipes and as the drunken men banged the tables in time, a door opened and a line of dancing girls streamed into the hall.

The cheers of the men echoed around the walls as the women danced their way around the tables, eventually ending up behind each of the guests. Their hands sensually massaged the shoulders of Gruffydd's men and as they wandered lower over the officers' chests, the roars of delight doubled in anticipation of what might come next. Prolonging the pleasure, the girls' hands came back up to their subjects' heads, running their fingers through their hair before sensually kissing the sides of their necks.

Gruffydd laughed out loud, highly amused by the faces of his men and turned to face Huw.

'I have to say,' said Gruffydd between laughs, 'you certainly know how to manipulate my men-at-arms.'

'I certainly do,' said Huw coldly and raised his hand to stop the music. Gruffydd's tankard stopped halfway to his mouth, but as he turned in confusion, the hall burst into activity of another kind.

Within seconds each woman grasped the hair of the man in front of them, yanking his head back to expose his neck as Englishmen who were drinking partners only moments earlier, drew daggers and pounced upon their unsuspecting victims. Throats were sliced open and blood squirted everywhere, soaking man and woman alike in the carnage. Some of Gruffydd's men escaped the first assault but were soon struck down by sheer force of numbers. The sounds of laughter and jollity were replaced with cries of pain and slaughter and within moments all of Gruffydd's men lay dead or dying around the table.

Gruffydd tried to stand but the feel of cold steel on his own throat kept him sat firmly in his seat as he witnessed the slaughter of his guards. Beside him, Iestyn had been beaten to the ground and was lying unconscious on the floor, bleeding from his nose and mouth.

'Treachery!' growled Gruffydd. 'I should have known. God will judge you for this.'

'Leave God's judgement to me,' said Huw coldly as he stood up from his chair and turned to face the traumatised king. 'Did you really expect me to make an alliance with such a pathetic excuse of a man such as you?'

'I should have known never to trust an Englishman,' said Gruffydd through gritted teeth, 'you are all rotten to the core and have not an ounce of honour between you.'

'Empty words from a vanquished king,' said Huw. 'Your lands are mine by default and you will disappear from history as the nobody that you are.'

'Stop your gloating, fat man,' spat Gruffydd, 'and tell your man to drag his blade. The air around me stinks and I welcome death.'

'Oh, I have no intention of killing you, Gruffydd,' said Huw, 'at least not yet.'

'Spare no thought of trying to ransom me,' said Gruffydd, 'for the treasures you sent have already been despatched across the Irish Sea.'

'I have no need of those few pathetic baubles,' said Huw, 'and it amuses me you think them generous. I have lost more on wagers than I sent back on those carts. You Welsh are really easily impressed.'

'Our wealth is in heritage and history,' said Gruffydd, 'not silver and gold.'

'I know which I would prefer,' said Huw. 'Anyway, you begin to bore me. Take a look around you, Gruffydd, for before you lay the best of your officers, victims of English superiority.'

'What about the rest of my men?'

'Rest assured they also enjoy the same hospitality and their heads will soon adorn the palisade, naught but meat for the crows. Your reign is over, Welshman, your time is done.'

***

Down in the bailey, men screamed as blades were plunged into their backs, and though many died, over fifty were taken prisoner by Huw's soldiers. Those who still lived were bound together and placed at the centre of the bailey, guarded by a unit of sober, well-armed men.

'Why do you wait?' roared Edward Axe-hand, looking up from the floor. 'Kill us now or I swear I will slaughter every last one of you.'

An English soldier walked over and after a few moments pause, smashed the sole of his hobnailed boot into Axe-hand's face, breaking the prisoner's jaw.

'Shut your stinking Welsh mouth,' snarled the warrior, 'your time will come soon enough.'

***

The following morning, Gruffydd was released from the bare stone room where he had been held overnight and tied to a chair. Two men dragged him to a window so he could see the activity in the bailey below before the door opened and Huw the Fat entered behind him.

'A very good morning to you, ex-king,' he sneered, 'I thought that before we introduce you to your new home I would allow you some last entertainment.'

He nodded to a guard who ran from the room and down the stone stairs to give the signal.

Gruffydd looked out of the window in despair as the fate of his men was decided before him.

'I want these men split into two groups,' shouted Beauchamp as soon as he had the message to proceed. 'Welsh and Irish.'

Soldiers went amongst the prisoners with spears, finding out the men's nationality until eventually there were two distinctive groups, one containing twenty Irishmen and the other a dozen of Welsh birth.

'Take the Welsh to the keep,' said Beauchamp, 'while the others can be brought to the block.'

As the first group were forced up the steps of the motte, a wooden executioner's block was dragged to the centre of the bailey and an axe-man stepped forward.

'Bring the officers,' said Beauchamp and watched as the first of three men were thrown in the mud at his feet.

'You men are guilty of waging war against the allies of William of Normandy,' announced Beauchamp, 'a crime punishable by death. What say you?'

'Get on with it,' spat Lord Darcy, 'for I tire of your stink.'

Beauchamp nodded towards the guards who dragged Darcy forward and leaned him across the block. Without further ado, the axe-man swung his weapon down with all his might, watching with satisfaction as Darcy's head rolled across the bailey floor.

'Next,' roared Beauchamp and over the next minute or so, the bailey echoed with the cheers of English soldiers as two more heads followed the first. Beauchamp turned to face the rest of the prisoners, seeing the fear in many of their faces.

'You have seen what happens to those who take Welsh coin to fight against William and his lords,' said Beauchamp. 'Let it be known that from this day forward, any who follow in their footsteps will be dealt with in a similar fashion. However, we are aware that you were led here by men who should have known better. We may issue swift justice, but we are not animals. You men before me are pawns in a greater game and will not be held responsible, so, thanks to the mercy of Huw D'Avranches, you will be allowed to return to Ireland as free men.'

The remaining prisoners looked at each other with surprise, none had expected such leniency.

'However,' shouted Beauchamp above the rising chatter, 'there is a price to be paid. In order to ensure you will not return as an enemy to be fought again in the future, each man will pay a tally.'

'We have no money,' spat one of the men, 'as well you know.'

'We seek no money,' said Beauchamp, 'only the part of your body that bears your weapons.'

The prisoners fell silent as the implications sunk in.

'Fear not,' continued Beauchamp with a sickly smile, 'we have a physician at hand to ensure your wounds are treated.' He turned and looked over at a blacksmith pumping bellows into the bottom of a brazier.

'You bastard,' spat the man again but gasped in agony as one of the guards drove a blade through his back and up into his heart.

'Listen to me,' shouted Beauchamp, 'the choice is simple. Men-at-arms will lose their sword hand while cavalry will lose one foot. Archers will lose both thumbs so they can no longer draw their bowstring. Accept and step forward of your own free will or suffer the same fate as your brave but foolish comrade.' He glanced down at the dead man at his feet before looking up again at the prisoners.

'Make your choice but be quick about it, for I have not yet broken my fast and a hearty meal of pork and eggs awaits me in the kitchens.'

For a few moments nobody moved.

'Well,' shouted Beauchamp, 'are there no takers?'

Again nobody moved but as the guards all drew their swords to carry out the slaughter, one man stepped forward.

'I will take the choice,' he said, his voice shaking with fear.

'And who are you?' asked Beauchamp.

'Arron of Limerick,' said the man, 'archer.'

'Strip him,' said Beauchamp and waited as the guards tore the jerkin from his back, revealing the overly developed right shoulder, a sure sign of a bowman.

'He speaks true,' said Beauchamp, 'remove his thumbs.'

The scared man was dragged to the block and within a minute, his cries of pain echoed around the bailey as his thumbs were hacked off with a small wood axe. Two men dragged him to the brazier and the waiting blacksmith withdrew a red-hot iron before applying it to the open wounds. The archer screamed again, and passed out as the smell of his charred flesh wafted across the bailey. The guards dragged his unconscious body to a waiting cart and Beauchamp turned to the remaining prisoners.

'Well,' he said with an evil grin, 'who's next?'

Up in the keep, Gruffydd looked on in horror as his Irish mercenaries were mutilated before being thrown on a cart. Two men chose death rather than mutilation and they were quickly despatched by knives before also being thrown amongst the wounded men. Finally, the gates opened and the horse-drawn cart was led away to begin its journey westward, but just as Gruffydd thought it was all over, another man was led out from a tent, his hands tied behind him.

'Iestyn,' said Gruffydd quietly.

'Indeed it is,' said Huw from behind him, 'your right-hand man.'

'Set him free, D'Avranches,' said Gruffydd, 'he is only guilty of following my commands.'

'Alas, I can't do that,' said Huw, 'and have reserved a special treat for him.'

Both men watched as Iestyn was stripped to the waist and tied to a pole in the centre of the bailey. The watching soldiers all fell quiet as a man led two snarling dogs from one of the huts and stood before the prisoner.

'What are they doing?' asked Gruffydd. 'In the name of God at least give the man an honourable death.'

'Watch and learn, Gruffydd,' said Huw, 'for such is the fate of traitorous men.'

As Gruffydd watched in horror, Alan Beauchamp stepped forward to stand before the prisoner and, with a quick cut of a skinning knife, sliced open Iestyn's lower belly. As he cried out in agony, Iestyn's intestines poured out and hung down to the ground, lying there in a stinking pile of bloody flesh. Despite this, Iestyn was still alive, and as he realised what was about to happen, his screams of fear echoed far beyond the boundaries of the castle walls.

With a nod of his head, Beauchamp gave the dog handler a signal and the man released the hounds to leap hungrily forward.

Gruffydd stared in horror. He had seen many men die throughout his life, but the sight of Iestyn's innards being devoured by starving dogs brought his hardened heart to the verge of breaking and tears ran down his battle weary face in a river of hopelessness.

An hour later, Gruffydd was once more marched from his place of confinement before being taken to the ground floor of the keep. In a darkened room, lit only by a single candle, Huw the Fat and several other men stood in a half-circle. Before them was a hole in the ground that dropped away into darkness.

'Behold your new home, Welshman,' said Huw. 'This well once sustained the garrison within this castle but dried up long ago. You will be imprisoned here, until I decide otherwise, and will be fed scraps from the kitchen, if it so pleases me. A rope hangs down the inside for you to clamber down.'

'I will not,' growled Gruffydd.

'Climb or be thrown,' said a voice, and Huw turned to see Meirion Goch enter the room.

'*You?*' gasped Gruffydd. 'I should have known.'

'Yes, you should have,' said Meirion, 'for I made it absolutely clear back at Mynydd Carn: my path lies wherever best lay my interests. In this case it was obviously with the strongest warlord within a hundred leagues. Even you, pathetic as you are, should have worked that much out, but no, your eyes were clouded with greed.'

'Your soul is truly fated for the fires of Hell, traitor,' growled Gruffydd, 'and I swear that should I ever escape this place, I will personally witness the last gasp of God's air that you ever breath.'

'I don't think I shall worry too much,' said Meirion, 'for there is no escaping this place for you. As for the fires of Hell, I shall worry about those when I arrive. I'm sure the Devil will cut a deal.'

'Enough talking,' said Huw the Fat, 'throw him in.'

'You can't do this,' shouted Gruffydd. 'I am a king and demand to be treated as such.'

Three men grabbed Gruffydd and dragged him to the edge of the well.

'I demand you release me,' shouted Gruffydd as he struggled. 'And where are the rest of my men?'

'Oh those,' said Huw coldly, 'don't worry, you will see them soon enough.'

Before Gruffydd could respond, the guards forced him over the lip of the well and he fell into the darkness, anticipating death at any moment. When he landed, the breath was knocked out of him but he realised he was relatively unhurt as the landing was soft. He looked up at the circle of light above, seeing a ring of faces peering down.

'Goodbye, Welshman,' said Huw, 'for I doubt we will ever meet again.'

'I am not dead yet, fat man,' growled Gruffydd. 'So don't sleep too deep when you are abed at night.'

'I will sleep well enough,' said Huw, 'though I suspect your dreams will not be so sweet, despite the soft mattress I have given you.'

As his face disappeared from view, a flaming torch was dropped down the shaft and a wooden cover pulled over the opening to the well. For a few moments Gruffydd peered up before finally turning and picking up the rapidly fading torch. He looked around the base of the well and as the flames of the torch died down, his eyes widened in horror as a primeval cry ripped from his throat.

Beneath his feet were the still warm bodies of the rest of his men, each with their throats slit open from ear to ear, and amongst them all, having finally fulfilled his oath, was the cold stare of Edward Axe-hand.

Epilogue: Dinefwr Castle

November, AD 1082

Deep in her quarters at Dinefwr Castle, Gwladus ferch Rhiwallon sat in a chair by the fire, watching her year-old son toddle around the room chased by the laughing Nesta. Tarw had been returned to her after many months in Ireland and as soon as the repairs to their castle had been completed the family had returned home. She smiled gently at the antics of the children but looked up suddenly as the door burst open and her husband entered, making his way over to the fire to warm his frozen hands.

'My love,' she said, getting to her feet as the children ran over to greet him, 'I did not know you had returned. Do you have any news of Hywel?'

'It was another false alarm,' said Tewdwr with a sigh, 'but at least we know he is alive.'

Gwladus's shoulders slumped at the dreaded news and she stared at the floor for a few moments before lifting her head and staring at her husband with tears in her eyes.

'How long can this go on?' she said quietly. 'He is just a boy and surely there is nothing to be gained from his continued imprisonment?'

'On the contrary,' said Tewdwr, picking up his youngest son, 'the child of a king is always of value to an enemy. Without an army of note, all we can do is keep petitioning the English king until he releases him back into our care.'

'Do you think he is in London?'

'He has to be,' said Tewdwr, 'for I have petitioned every castle and manor house from here to Ynys Mon and nobody knows Hywel's whereabouts.'

'Then perhaps he is truly dead,' whispered Gwladus.

'No, he is alive,' said Tewdwr, 'I'm sure of it. But if he is in London, then there is little more I can do.'

'I know,' said Gwladus, 'and your continued efforts make me proud to be your wife.'

'I will never give up on him, Gwladus,' said Tewdwr. 'If I have to storm the walls of London itself, I swear that one day he will be returned to us.'

Gwladus embraced her husband and they both stared hopefully into the flames, thinking about their missing child.

———⌣———

Twenty-five leagues away, deep in a dungeon of Montgomery Castle in mid-Wales, a frightened boy also looked hopeful as the door of his cell opened. Yet again his hopes for the arrival of his father were dashed, and though he was now used to the disappointment, the man who entered was new to him.

'Who are you?' asked Hywel.

The man did not respond as another two men entered carrying a trestle table.

'What's that for?' asked Hywel standing up. 'What are you going to do?'

'Hywel,' said the second man, 'I need you to be brave. What we are about to do is at the orders of William himself.'

'What are you doing?' cried Hywel as the men dragged him up onto the table. 'Where is my father? I want to go home.'

'Be brave, Hywel,' said the man, 'this won't take long.'

A few moments later the boy's screams echoed around the dungeons and as a surgeon and an apothecary entered with salves and sutures, the torturer made his way back up the steps, casting the castration wire to one side as he went.

Across the Irish Sea, another queen sat staring into the comforting flames of a fire, contemplating the events of the past twelve months. Angharad's initial joy at the news of Gruffydd's victory had turned to devastation when she heard of his subsequent capture by Huw the Fat. Despite many letters to nobles across Wales over the following year, nobody could tell her where he was imprisoned or even whether he lived or died. Even letters sent to Huw the Fat himself went unanswered and she found herself in a terrible place, not knowing whether her husband was alive or dead.

The treasures Gruffydd had sent her twelve months earlier had long gone, for once the moneylender had been paid back, the mercenaries' wages settled and the death money issued to the widows of those who had died in her husband's name, there had been little left to spare. Subsequently, she found herself with little money and a child to support. She looked around in sadness, realising this was the last time she would sit alongside the fire of her own hearth, having accepted an offer from King Olaf to lodge within his own castle.

A gentle knock came upon the door and Adele came in to kneel beside the queen.

'My lady, it is time,' she said quietly.

'The carriage is here?'

'It is, we should go.'

'It is with a heavy heart I give up on this place,' said Angharad, 'but I swear this before you and before God. While there is a chance my husband is alive, I will never, ever give up on him. If it takes a lifetime, I swear I will wait for him, chaste from all other men until the day he returns.'

'And if he does not return?'

'Then I will die not knowing the touch of any other man.'

Adele squeezed the queen's hand and smiled in the gloom.

'I may not be able to help much, my lady, but I will be here at your side and above all things I know this. If any man can survive captivity, it is your husband. Worry not, he will return.'

Angharad stood and walked with Adele to the door. Deep in her heart she knew the struggle was over and that she would never again walk the green fields of Ynys Mon.

Little did she know that, one day, she would give birth to a child that would change the future of Wales.

Author's Note

Though the story is based around real events at the time, certain minor things had to be changed in order for the book to flow. For example, the very strong tradition at the time of naming sons after their fathers throughout the generations meant there were relatively few names in existence compared to the following centuries, especially amongst the incumbent nobility in Wales. The term 'ap' seen between many of the names means simply 'son of', and similarly 'ferch' means 'daughter of'. Subsequently, Rhys ap Tewdwr means Rhys son of Tewdwr and Gwladus ferch Rhiwallon would mean Gwladus daughter of Rhiwallon.

With this in mind, some names had to be changed slightly or we would have had a series that had men called Rhys talking to others called Rhys and Gruffydds talking to Gruffydds. If I had stuck religiously to these facts then the reading experience would perhaps have been somewhat diminished. Subsequently, some names may have been altered slightly to make the storyline work but only where absolutely unavoidable. These have been explained below.

In addition, dates have been tweaked to allow the timeline to flow more naturally and if the historians out there are annoyed at the artistic license, I can only apologise. The liberty was taken with the strength of the story in mind.

GRUFFYDD AP CYNAN

Gruffydd ap Cynan was a senior member of the royal house of Aberffraw based on Ynys Mon (modern-day Anglesey). His mother was the daughter of King Olaf of Dublin and he married a woman called Angharad ferch Owain.

Gruffydd first tried to gain the throne of Gwynedd in 1075 but was defeated by Trahern on the Llyn peninsula, forcing him to retreat to Ireland. In 1081 Gruffydd forged an alliance with Rhys ap Tewdwr, getting his revenge on Trahern by defeating him and the other two armies at the battle of Mynydd Carn the same year.

RHYS AP TEWDWR

Rhys ap Tewdwr (called simply Tewdwr in this tale) was the king of Deheubarth from 1078 to approximately 1093. He was married to a noblewoman called Gwladus ferch Rhiwallon and fathered several children. In those times, children outside of wedlock were common and the exact number of Tewdwr's sons and daughters are unknown. However, three of the characters mentioned in the story above were certainly his, Nest ferch Rhys (called Nesta in our tale), Gruffydd ap Rhys, (the baby called Tarw in our tale) and Hywel ap Rhys, the older son who was castrated sometime in his early life, probably by Roger of Montgomery. Rhys ap Tewdwr is reputed to have had more children via affairs with others, and though two of his other sons died at the Battle of Brecon where he eventually met his end, they have been omitted from this tale for the sake of continuity and enjoyment.

DINEFWR CASTLE

The Tewdwr family was based in and around Dinefwr Castle in Deheubarth (South Wales) but were temporarily ousted in 1081 by Caradog ap Gruffydd, king of Gwent. The castle in 1081 would probably have been of a motte-and-bailey construction. It was rebuilt in stone in the later part of the 12th century by the Lord Rhys and still stands today.

THE THREE KING ALLIANCE

In 1081, Trahern ap Caradog (who had already defeated Gruffydd ap Cynan at the battle of Bron yr Erw on the Llyn peninsular in 1075) made alliances with Caradog ap Gruffydd of Gwent (South East Wales) and Meilyr ap Rhiwallon of Powys, (Mid Wales) agreeing to meet them at Mynydd Carn on the west coast. Caradog had already ousted Rhys ap Tewdwr from his ancestral home at Dinefwr, forcing him to seek sanctuary in the cathedral of Saint David, but he was unaware that Tewdwr had been in contact with Gruffydd in Ireland and arranged an alliance of his own. Subsequently, in 1081, the armies of Rhys ap Tewdwr and Gruffydd ap Cynan combined to defeat the three-king alliance at the battle of Mynydd Carn. All three rebel kings died in the battle and Gruffydd once more returned to Gwynedd as ruler while Rhys returned to rule Deheubarth in the south.

HUW THE FAT

Huw D'Avranches was the Earl of Chester in 1081 and had gained a reputation for ferocity against the Welsh. Over the years, he became so obese he became known as Huw the Fat. After the battle of Mynydd Carn, he invited Gruffydd ap Cynan to his castle under the guise of friendship, but the Welsh king had been betrayed and Huw the Fat had Gruffydd imprisoned for many years.

ST GOVAN'S CHAPEL

This chapel is a real place on the coast of Pembroke and is reputed to have been the last resting place of Sir Gawain of the Round Table. It is said to be built over a natural cave in the rocks and during the Dark Ages would have been made from timber. Later on it was rebuilt in stone.

About the Author

Kevin Ashman is the author of fifteen novels. He started writing in 2011 and immediately enjoyed significant success with his historical fiction, including the bestselling *Roman Chronicles* and highly ranked *Medieval Sagas*. Always pushing the boundaries, he found further success with the *India Sommers Mysteries*, as well as three other standalone projects, *Vampire*, *Savage Eden* and the dystopian horror story *The Last Citadel*. Kevin was born and raised in Wales and now writes full-time. He is married with four grown children and enjoys cycling, swimming and watching rugby. Forthcoming works include the highly anticipated *Blood of Kings* series, of which *A Land Divided* is the first instalment. Links to all Kevin's books can be found at www.kmashman.co.uk